WICKED
Little
SINS

A.R. BRECK

No part of this book may be reproduced in any form or by any electronic or mechanical means, including information storage and retrieval systems, without permission in writing from the publisher, except by reviewers, who may quote brief passages in a review. The characters and events in this book are fictitious. Any similarity to real persons, living or dead, is coincidental and not intended by the author.

Copyright © 2021 by A.R. Breck. All rights reserved.

Cover design by Hailey Rehmann

Formatting by Cat at TRC Designs

Editing by Black Lotus Editing

Proofreading by Rumi Khan

WICKED Little SINS

A.R. BRECK

PLAYLIST

The Bird and the Worm by The Used
Until the Day I Die by Story of the Year
Bloody Romance by Senses Fail
A Favor House Atlantic by Coheed and Cambria
Calling All Skeletons by Alkaline Trio
My Darkest Hour by Scary Kids Scaring Kids
Knee Deep by Job for a Cowboy
Wage Slaves by All Shall Perish
Disarm by The Smashing Pumpkins
Everything Went Black by The Black Dahlia Murder
All About Us by t.A.T.u
Going Under by Evanescence
Buried Myself Alive by The Used
Emily by From First to Last
Burn It Down by Linkin Park
Make War from First to Last
Die Romantic by Aiden
Zombie by The Cranberries
Bring Me to Life by Evanescence
The Taste of Ink by The Used
What I've Done by Linkin Park
When a Demon Defiles a Witch by The Black Dahlia Murder
All the Things She Said by t.A.T.u
I'm So Sick by Flyleaf
115 by Treyarch Sound
The Suffering by Coheed and Cambria
Sweet But Psycho by Ava Max
Breaking the Habit by Linkin Park
Note to Self from First to Last
All That I've Got by The Used
Crawling by Linkin Park

What a Horrible Night to Have a Curse by The Black Dahlia Murder
My Immortal by Evanescence
Given Up by Linkin Park
A Box Full of Sharp Objects by The Used
Where is My Mind? by Pixies
Not Gonna Get Us by t.A.T.u
Secrets Don't Make Friends by From First to Last
Hold Me Down by Halsey
Bleed It Out by Linkin Park
1979 by The Smashing Pumpkins
In The End by Linkin Park

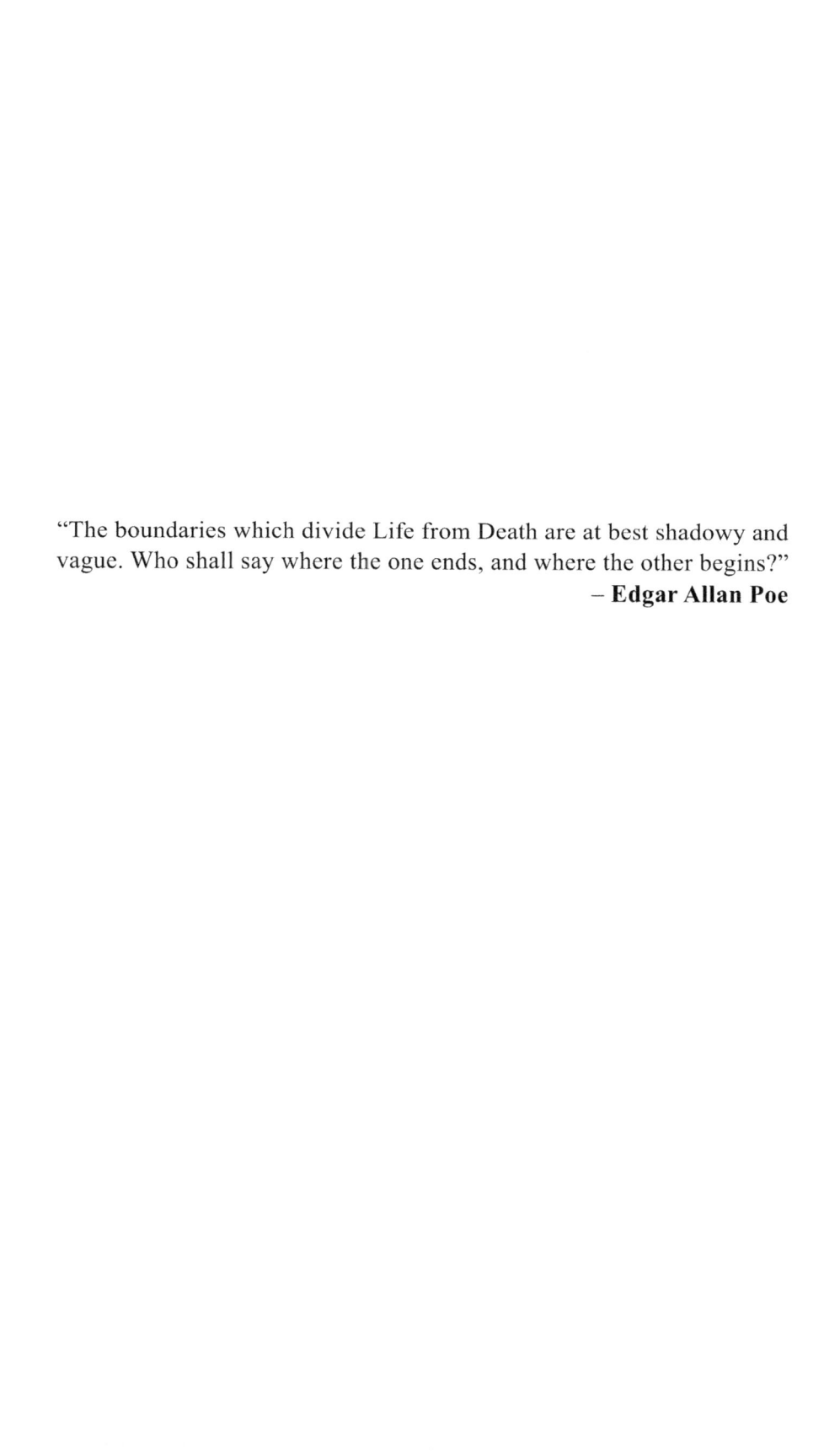

"The boundaries which divide Life from Death are at best shadowy and vague. Who shall say where the one ends, and where the other begins?"
– **Edgar Allan Poe**

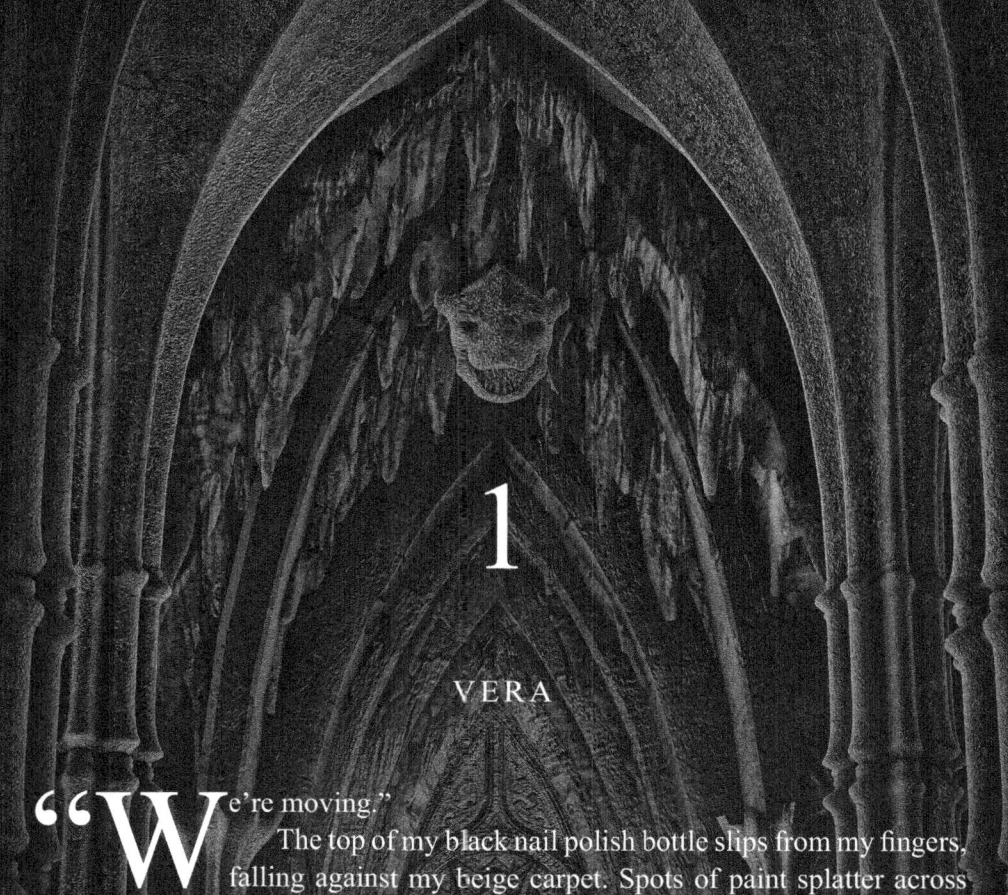

1

VERA

"We're moving."

The top of my black nail polish bottle slips from my fingers, falling against my beige carpet. Spots of paint splatter across the soft fibers, but I barely notice the mess as my head cranks backward and I stare up at my mom's stoic expression.

"What?" I ask, my tone sharp. I reach down and curl my fingers around my phone, ready to bolt. To where, I don't know. To Sacha's, maybe. Or Leena's. I don't really care at this point. My best friends would save me from whatever hell my mom is pouring down on me.

I can hear the rubbing of my mom's tights as she walks around me before sitting on the corner of my bed, the springs creaking obnoxiously. I glance down at my fingers, the glossy black paint is perfectly painted, except my blank pinkie finger that stares back at me, asking me what the fuck I'm waiting for.

I sigh, grabbing the top of my nail polish and screwing it back on the bottle. No use in trying to finish it now. Whatever she's about to say has my hands shaking like mad.

"Vera."

I keep my head tipped toward the floor but lift my eyes up to meet hers. She watches me sympathetically, an eager look creeping onto her face, though her eyes stay lowered with a hesitancy, like she's so damn excited to tell me her news, but she knows I'm not going to like it.

I know it, too.

"We're moving," she repeats.

Her lips move. I even hear the words she says, but none of it registers. I don't think I really understand much of anything at this point. It's all static in my brain. I refuse. I absolutely refuse.

I unlock my phone with shaky fingers, pulling up our *Bitches Aren't Snitches* group chat and start typing out a text. The words don't even come out correctly, each one being autocorrected as they turn into a non-sentence.

My phone slips from my hands, and my nostrils flare when I look up, seeing my mom standing above me with my phone pinched between her slim fingers.

"Listen to me, Vera. This is important."

I push my black bangs from my eyes, my jaw clenching as I stare at her. "I don't want to know what you have to say. I'm not leaving this house. I'm not leaving my friends. You might as well save your breath, Mother."

Her eyes narrow into small slits and all I can see is too much makeup as she stares down at me. My room grows cold from our standoff, and it feels like the creamy walls turn black, encasing her in darkness. "Listen to me, please. Would you just drop the attitude for one damn second?"

She props her hand on her black skirt, ironed with not one crease on it. Her navy blouse is made from a fine silk and tucked beneath the hem of her skirt. She looks every bit of the marketing coordinator that she's meant to. Too bad I'm not in the mood for her today.

Although lately, it seems I'm never in the mood for her.

"What do you want?" I sigh, lifting my hand and snapping my phone from her grasp, the tips of my fingers arched out to not ruin my freshly coated nails.

She squats down, her toes becoming more visible through her tights. Her nails are red. Dark, deep, blood red. She always gets her nails done at a fancy salon.

I paint mine with Walgreens polish.

See how different we are?

"Vera." She snaps her fingers in my face. I glance up at her again, although now she's closer to my eye level. "I met someone, baby."

My nose burns, my eyebrows lowering until they're nearly covering my eyes. I can feel the muscles tense in nearly every part of my body. Pure, raw anger begins boiling in my veins.

I say nothing. I do *nothing*.

I anticipate as many things as I can in life. Any bad thing that may happen, I always attempt to predict it. I don't like to be blindsided. But this—*this* is something I never fucking expected.

She reaches out, settling her warm palm over my sweatpants-covered knee. I slap her hand away, my knuckles knocking against hers. She looks hurt as she pulls her hand back to her side. "You would like him, Vera. His name is—"

"I don't fucking care what his name is, and I'm not leaving! You go ahead. Move on with your life. Start over. Forget everything else." I stand up, my nails accidentally swiping across the carpet. Streaks of black are bold against the beige. I swallow down a scream as she stands up and takes a step toward me.

I take a step backward, anger and so much damn hurt building in my chest, I feel like I'm going to explode.

"If you would just give him—"

I swipe my hand through the air, cutting off her ridiculous nonsense that I don't care to listen to.

"How could you do this to me? To him?" I shake my head. "I fucking hate you."

With that, I clutch my phone and grab my bag, running out of there in my sweats. No destination in mind, nothing to do on a Sunday night. But I'm not staying here. No way.

I hate her.

I sit on the hill, aimlessly gazing down at the lights and noises of downtown Fargo in the distance. A burnt-out cigarette sits pinched between my fingers. I shouldn't smoke. I want to, but I shouldn't. I know what it could do to me, but it doesn't stop me from buying a pack, taking a hit out of one here and there. It calms me. When I'm most flustered, just one drag settles every nerve in my body.

I've already taken a drag. I can't afford to take another, but my blood still simmers beneath my skin. I'm torn between feeling numb and feeling everything. I can't feel the night breeze as it brushes across my cheek, but every blade of grass feels like shards against my bare feet.

I don't want to move.

At first, I went to my best friend Sacha's house, but in the end, I was too furious to be around anyone. No one really understands what I'm going through, even though they've known me my entire life. They know the struggles I've been through. They know me.

Except they don't.

I walked here, to the random hill that's in between the city and nothing. Crickets and mosquitos fly behind me and only noise and lights are in front of me. It feels like my life right now. Stuck in between two different lives. Two different worlds. Which way should I go?

I pocket my cigarette butt and shove my bare feet into my Doc Martens, pushing them into the soles as I stand up. My palms go to my butt, swiping across my sweats to brush away any lingering dirt and twigs.

My hand slides through the loop of my backpack, swinging it over my shoulder before I start making my way down the hill. The sun is long gone, the only light coming from the businesses up ahead. Every few steps, I trip over a larger rock, making me stumble forward and almost fall to my knees.

"Fucking stupid." My voice bounces as I walk down the hill. By stupid, I mean the rocks and my situation.

I don't know where my mom wants to move to. I don't know what her plan is. But after talking with Sacha and Leena, I don't have anywhere else to go.

No one wants to take in the misfit.

I've been friends with Sacha and Leena since I was young, or else their parents wouldn't let them hang out with me. They blame me whenever we get in trouble, perpetually saying I'm the problem child.

Well, fuck everyone.

My friends fuck up just as much as I do. Sometimes more. But it doesn't matter, because the girl with the black-and-white dyed hair, septum piercing, and permanent black clothing is always the first to take the blame. Talk about profiling.

My friends look and dress similar to me, but I guess when you look at your child you always try to see the best in them. My friends' parents... well, they're blind whenever we steal cute bras and panties from Kohl's. Or come home halfway into the night tipsy and smelling like weed. Or when the police show up, carting us to our parents' doorsteps at three in the morning, the finger is pointed in my direction. Every single time.

It doesn't stop my friends from hanging out with me, but it definitely puts a sour fucking taste in my mouth.

So, it shouldn't have shocked me when I asked both of them if I could move in. One look in their parents' eyes and I swear—*I fucking swear*–I could see them holding back laughter. What came out of their mouths was, "I don't think that's such a good idea." But what they were thinking was, "*Hell to the fucking no.*"

My hand lifts, my middle finger pointing to the sky.

Fuck everyone.

Life for me hasn't always been so... jaded, I guess. But shit happens. Me and my mom used to have a great relationship. Like best friends. Now she spends most of her time working, and I'm left alone. Left alone to do whatever the hell I want to do.

What I want to do is stay here, but for some reason my mom wants to be a parent now, thinking she knows what's best for me.

Hilarious.

I sigh as I make my way through town and into the nicer neighborhoods. Turning onto my street, I see my house up ahead, illuminated by our outside light. My mom sits on her bench, rocking back and forth on our large wraparound porch. Our modern two-story home is pristine, the white siding against the dark roof and windows something that makes our house a little different from all the other creams and browns. We live in a quiet neighborhood, even though we're surrounded by the university and the airport. Somehow our small pocket seems tucked away from the noise. It's beautiful here, and it makes an even bigger pit fall into my belly.

I sigh as I keep walking. I can't see her eyes from here, but I can feel them. Boring into me.

I guess it's now or never.

Unlocking my phone, I open up our group chat and type out a quick message.

Me: If I'm not at school tomorrow, I'm either dead or I've committed murder. Don't come looking for me.

I slip my phone into my side pocket and make my way toward our front steps. The wooden steps barely squeak or groan as I walk up them. I watch as my mom's feet press into the porch, stopping her rocking. She pats the spot next to her, and I slip my backpack off my shoulder, dropping it to the ground with a thud. I tuck my hands into the front pocket of my sweatshirt and sit down. She pushes off, letting us rock a little while we both stare off into the distance.

I can feel her hand hovering before her fingers curl around mine. The pads of her fingers brush my nails, half blackened, and half swiped away in my hurry to flee earlier. "I know this isn't what you want, and I'm sorry if you feel ambushed by it."

"Where are we going?" I ask, keeping my face forward.

"Castle Pointe."

I look over at her, confusion lining my face. I've never heard of Castle Pointe before, and that only means one thing. It's far away from here.

She can read my face, and she tries to cover her wince, but it's clearly readable in her worried eyes. "A small town, just north of Duluth."

My eyes widen. "Duluth? Duluth—as in, all the way on the other side of Minnesota?"

She nods, nibbling on the corner of her lip.

I slouch, my spine slamming against the back of the bench. It shakes and rocks us back and forth for a second. Anger, so much anger, fills me. Defeat does as well, because I feel like I have no options.

"Can't I stay here?"

She shakes her head. "No, Vera. Shara is putting the house on the market tomorrow." Shara is her longtime realtor and one of her greatest friends.

Tears cloud my vision. I feel like she is betraying everything I've ever known. Our life here, she's throwing it away like it's never meant anything to her.

"How could you?" I whisper, pain crippling my voice. I want to curl over, the tightness in my stomach agonizing. It's like she's backstabbing me. Like she's backstabbing *him*.

Her eyes water, and she brings her perfectly manicured finger up to her cheek. She wipes the tear before it can fall, catching it on her knuckle, then settles her hand in her lap, her tear still clinging to her skin. "Vera, it's hard to understand. I know it must be painful for you… but… it's time we all started to live again. We can't be stuck in this bubble forever. It was very hard, but I had to learn how to breathe again. And I found someone who helped me do that."

It feels like my entire world tips on its axis.

"How long has this been going on?"

She stares at me, her lips scrunching up as she decides whether to be truthful or not. "We've been seeing each other for about six months."

Her eyes search mine, the pale blue the same shade as my own. Like a perfect quartz crystal. Our features are fairly similar as well. We both have large eyes and slender noses with pouty lips. My mom's hair is a sandy brown, but mine is a dark chocolate, just like my father's.

Though, through the years I've dyed it so many times, I'm not quite sure what the natural color is anymore. I keep it nearly black, and the other week Sacha helped me dye the side of my hair an icy blonde.

"Why are you just telling me about this now? It's obviously serious."

Her face turns to the distance, the yellow streetlamp glowing in her eyes. There's a guilt darkening the blue, so much that she can't look at me directly. "I didn't think it was necessary to say anything until it was serious."

"Well, clearly it's fucking serious."

Her head whips toward me, her eyes irritated. "Seriously? Language."

My head tilts back, my jaw cracking open and an evil laugh barking out. "Right now? You're going to reprimand me right now? Come on, Mother, you know me better than that."

She takes a deep breath, her blouse-covered chest lifting with irritation before shaking to a settle.

"His name is Samuel Myers."

The name rolls around in my brain, ping-ponging within my memory to see if I recall hearing of him anywhere.

"Where'd you meet him?"

A soft smile lifts her lips. "We met at one of the real estate conventions."

I scowl. "So, while I'm alone at home and you're off working, are you even off working? Or are you off sleeping with Samuel Myers?"

She rolls her eyes. "No, I do actually work, you know."

I think back on all the times she's been gone lately, and lately she's been gone more frequently. She's in real estate marketing, so she travels and goes to different conventions and meetings all the time, but most recently... it's like she's always gone. "Those times when you say you have to travel for work, are you even traveling for work? Or are you meeting with him?"

She's silent for a moment, crossing her arms over her chest. Defensive. Uncomfortable. It's written in the way she sits and in her eyes. "I've visited with him on an occasion or two."

"On an occasion or two," I mock, standing up. I run my fingers through my hair, walking back and forth along the deck. I hit a weak board or two, causing an obnoxious groan to fill the silence. My fingers go up, and I pull on my septum ring. My hands and fingers can't stop moving, irritation licking at my ankles and heating my entire body.

How could she do this?

"I'm not going," I say with finality. Sweat sticks the baby hairs to my temples. My fingers lift and I peel them off, even though they just slap back against my face. It's not even warm outside, the cool Fargo fall air makes it chilly this far north. But I'm engulfed in fire on the inside.

"Yes, you are." She stands up, blocking my path and stopping my pacing. "We're leaving in two weeks. The house goes on the market tomorrow. I expect you to keep your room clean, and I don't want any more complaints about it. It's a done deal."

I shake my head. "I'm not leaving. Emancipate me or something."

She rolls her eyes. "You're not getting emancipated. That's enough of this. I've already contacted your school and started the transfer."

My eyes widen, literal rage burning up every muscle and nerve ending. I look down at my fingers, expecting to see smoke coming off them.

I don't. Just horrible tremors racking my body.

With a deep breath, I walk to my backpack. Lifting it into my arms, I unzip the big pocket.

"What are you doing?" she asks, a lilt of hesitation in her voice.

My hands dig into the depths of my black bag, until my fingers curl around the smooth square. I pull out my Marlboros, slipping my lighter and a fresh cigarette from the pack. She scowls at me, hating that I smoke, but she can't fight me on it because she knows I won't stop. She pretends I don't see her slip a secret cigarette on the occasion as well.

I light it up and tuck the lighter into my bra. Taking a deep inhale, I slip the strap of my backpack over my shoulder and exhale, blowing the smoke into her face.

Her eyes only narrow further.

"You shouldn't smoke, Vera. You know the risk you're taking. Why are you doing this to yourself?"

"Why are you doing this to me?" I snap back. She says nothing, staring at me with disgust and fear and regret. "I'm going to pack, Mother." I open up the front door, walking straight inside with my lit cigarette.

I hear the creaky boards only moments before her fingers wrap around my wrist, tight and steady. "What the hell are you doing? You aren't smoking in the house!"

I rip my wrist from her hold, glaring at her as I take another drag. "Try and fucking stop me." Her arm grabs onto my backpack this time, ripping me backward and straight out of the front door. Her other hand plucks the cigarette from between my lips, and she tosses it onto the front yard. I watch as the cherry gets buried within the blades of grass, the barely noticeable glow disappearing in the distance.

My nostrils flare as I take a deep breath, then I turn around, pressing my hands against her shoulders and shoving her. *Hard.* She stumbles, the heel of her shoe getting stuck between the floorboards. It falls off, making her one-heeled foot falter even further. Her hands go to the railing, and she looks over her shoulder at me. Anger and surprise in her gaze. She walks over to me, hobbling up and down with one heel on until she stands right in front of me.

Crack.

My face whips to the side, my mouth falling open due to shock. Tears instantly fill my eyes. Hurt and pain shoots straight to my chest. My hand goes up, pressing against my warm cheek. The stubborn tears fall over the rim this time, wetting my cheeks. It does nothing to cool the burn. A teardrop hits my hand, seeping beneath my palm and suctioning against my skin.

My mom points her finger in my face. "This attitude you've had these last couple years is over. I'm through with it. You'll pack your bags. You'll quit the smoking. You'll quit acting out. Wherever the real Vera has gone, make sure she comes back for the move."

My palm drops, smearing tears and makeup against my cheek as I watch her. She turns around, dismissing me as she bends down to pick up her heel to slip it back on her foot.

"You would know where the real Vera has gone if you would have stopped working for a second and quit fucking Samuel Myers long enough to pay attention to your only daughter."

Her entire body freezes, but I don't wait for a response. I'm already stomping up to my room and slamming the door behind me.

I'm done with her. I'll move because I have no other choice, but I'm done with her.

Fuck everyone.

2

MALIK

The bass rumbles through my chest as Levi passes me the joint. I pinch it between my fingers, bringing it to my lips and taking a pull until my lips burn. The burn travels to my chest, a cough roaring out of me so sharply that I sit up, leaning forward as my head turns hazy.

"Shit," I mumble, handing off the joint to Felix. My voice is raspy, my throat raw from the vicious cough tearing through my lungs.

"Told you. My cousin got this shit from Colorado," Levi screams over the music.

I lean back on my leather couch, staring at the smoke-filled room. The Smashing Pumpkins rip through the speakers, my foot tapping to the beat and my fingers fluttering against my jeans as I play the song in my head.

"Thea wants to meet down at the pier. She's there with the girls," Atticus says. I look over at him, watching his fingers fly over the keyboard on his phone.

Ah, Thea and the bitch crew. The girls at school that will slide their pleated skirts up and reveal their racy black panties if we so much as blink in their direction.

But fuck it, I guess. Why not? Nothing else to do on this Sunday night.

The screaming voices in the room come to a halt, my ears ringing from the dramatic change in volume. We all turn toward the stereo system on the wall, seeing my dad's tall form standing there, his dark suit pressed and shiny, even in the dark room. The scowl on his face is heavy, severe lines creasing his forehead, his nostrils flared in distaste.

"Malik, what did I tell you about smoking in here? It's going to stain the ceiling," he lashes out at me.

I shrug. "Paint over it."

I watch as his neck grows red, the color traveling up his cheeks and all the way to his hairline. "Malik," he warns.

I sit up, my hands pressing against the cool leather as I stare at him. I'm rarely in the mood for his shit. Most of the time, I'm able to avoid him, but for whatever reason he decided to come down to the basement this evening. Which means he wants to talk about something.

He looks around at my friends. "We have something to discuss."

I stare at him, waiting.

"Alone," he emphasizes.

I crack a smile, my teeth razor-sharp. The guys even let out a little chuckle, and I watch my dad's frown turn into a scowl.

"We're leaving, so get on with whatever the fuck you need to say." I stand up, bending over to grab my phone off the black coffee table. Much like everything else in this house. Black couches, black tables, black wall art, black rugs on top of black floors. The only thing that isn't black are the walls, and those are gray.

People who've never been to Castle Pointe might question why our house looks the way it does. They might question us as people. But those people don't know Castle Pointe like we do. It's a small town on the corner of Lake Superior. People want to stop here on their way up to Canada or on their way down to the city, but one step in here and they leave before their second foot can step over the border. It's always dreary, always a little cold, and the entire place stays cloaked in a layer of darkness.

That's how we live here in Castle Pointe. Constantly shrouded in a cold, eerie shadow. Like we're all haunted with the past and history of our town. Sometimes it seems like this small town is in a world of its own, completely separated from the rest of the world. We don't live like they do in other cities. I travel to Duluth on occasion, and it's as if the world is living normally. The sun shines, the water of Superior looks brighter, the cliffs and rocks not as dark, sharp, and demanding.

Then you travel through the tall, green trees, along Superior, heading north along the edge of Minnesota. The trees grow denser, the sunlight dimming as the thickness of the woods grows, until the branches turn nearly black. The moment you pass the sign that says *Welcome to Castle Pointe*, one that's engraved into a brick stone, weathered with age and the cool winds from the water, the world changes. It turns into a blackness, an almost unnatural world where you're taken back in time to abandoned cemeteries, and tall, old brick buildings that look like castles, half decayed, while also half magical.

There's something about this place, like it hangs on the thread of death, teetering on the ledge. One swift breeze from the coast of Superior, and you'll plummet into a pitch blackness. So thick and heavy that you'll never find your way out.

"I met someone, and I've invited her to come stay with us."

I look over at Felix, his black hair swept so low over his forehead I can barely see his eyes. But the darkness peers through, staring at me in shock.

I swing my eyes back to my father. "Now, why would you do that to her? Do you want her to hate you?"

Atticus laughs deep in his throat, and a smile cracks on my face.

My dad scowls at me once more, his eyes darkening to the color of his black suit. "Malik." I'm guessing by his tone this will be his final warning. It's almost comical, though, because I could damage him tenfold—inside and out—and he could never lay a finger on me.

My dad is the largest real estate mogul in the upper Minnesota region. From the border of Canada down to Minneapolis, his name is everywhere. My father, Samuel Myers, Felix's father, Oliver Port, Atticus's father, Michael Berlin, and Levi's father, Jack Sloan. They own their own real estate company—Pointe Real Estate Group. He might have the brains to earn millions, but he'll never, ever be able to gain the upper hand over me. No matter how hard he tries.

"Okay, you're having a woman come stay with you? Thanks for letting me know." I nod toward the guys, and they all stand, ready to get out of there.

"She has a daughter, Malik. She'll be staying with us too. She's seventeen, a year younger than you, so I expect you to behave yourself. She'll be going to your school." He clears his throat. "I expect that you'll be on your best behavior, so it'll be in your best interest to be respectful to her and her daughter. It is serious, Malik."

So many fucking things lie within that statement. My mind spins, and I can feel the guys' eyes on me, questioning, waiting. Wanting to be smartasses like I want to be right now, if I wasn't so damn speechless.

My eyes narrow, and I stare at my dad, curling my lips back as I bare my teeth, sharp and fucking angry when I snap at him. "Don't worry, as soon as she realizes the fucking bastard you are, she'll be out before I can do any damage."

I head up the stairs, my shoes echoing on the marbled black floors. I can hear the guys' shoes shuffling behind me.

I don't even make it to the top of the stairs before I hear the crash of a vase hitting the wall.

Fucking bastard.

The wind whips the hair from my forehead, the cool air at the pier slashing against my cheeks. I clench my jaw, staring down at the filter of my cigarette as I squish it between my thumb and forefinger.

My fucking father.

The nerve of him. To bring a family into my house and act like I'm going to be an upstanding citizen. I chuckle under my breath.

"Baby, want to come over to my house tonight? I've missed you these last few days." Thea presses against me, a hint of vodka blowing from between her lips, swirling into the cool air and slapping me in the face. She presses a kiss against my jaw, her plump lips slightly sticky as they hit my chin. I close my eyes, bringing the cigarette to my mouth and taking a drag. The edge of the cherry brushes her dark hair, and I listen to the strands sizzle, the smell of her burning locks sliding into my nose.

"Not tonight." I lift my head away from hers, not in the mood for her clingy attitude. I don't usually mind. She suctioned the label of girlfriend/boyfriend on me last year before I could fucking blink, but I never refuted it. Don't ask me why. Maybe I just like the fact that someone is there to warm my bed whenever I want, and Thea seems to warm it well.

But when she gets extra clingy like this, all I want to do is fling her scrawny ass over the side of the pier.

The dark sky clashes against the dark water, everything mixing into a black abyss that feels just as ominous as this town behind me.

"But why?" she whines. I take another drag of my cigarette and drop it, crushing it beneath my black boot. I look around, looking for the boys so I can get away from Thea. I see Atticus standing by the railing talking to Felix. Thea is still complaining to me, but I grab her by the arms and push her aside.

"I'll talk to you later, Thea."

"But, babe," she sighs.

The wind carries her voice away, and I don't turn back. I walk up to my friends, stopping beside Atticus. The three of us stand in a row, all encased in dark clothing with dark features and dark hair. Levi must be somewhere behind me. He's casually dating Thea's friend, Fiona. But he cares about Fiona just as much as I care about Thea.

So, barely at all.

"What's up?" Felix looks me over, his eyes red, baked.

I shrug. "Another day."

"So, you're getting a sister?" Atticus smiles at me, a look shining in his eyes like he wants to have fun. He wants to play a game.

We play a lot of games here. We do what we want with who we want. There are no limits with us, and most people think we're dangerous because of it.

I think it's the air of Castle Pointe. The toxic air poisoning us. That and our parents. Overly arrogant, a little crooked. The highest profile families in Castle Pointe that live in the biggest castles on the most jagged cliffs. Even if we lived in a normal world, in a normal city, people would look the other way, just because of our last names.

Malik Myers.

Felix Port.

Atticus Berlin.

Levi Sloan.

Myers. Port. Berlin. Sloan.

People walk the other way when there's one of us around. It's just instinct. If you want to be around us, you'll most likely regret it in the end. None of us have mothers. We're the men raised by men. We're brutal and gritty, and people fear us. They *should* fear us.

"She's not going to be my sister. I give them a week before they crumble and attempt to flee."

"But what if they don't?" He brushes his locks from his face, nearly untamable in the whipping wind. It's always windy here. There's constantly a howl reverberating beyond the thick trees. It's like the ghosts are screaming, is what people say. The ghosts of our pasts, screeching in anguish.

Because in Castle Pointe, the ghosts never really move on.

"Then it looks like I'll have to make them leave."

Levi walks over, adjusting his black joggers from wherever he just came from. "What're we talking about?"

"Mal is saying how he plans to run his new family out of town." Felix smiles, a darkness entering his gaze.

Levi runs his hands together. "Count me in. Are we playing a game?"

I shrug. "We'll see. This town might be enough to make them run all on their own."

We all look over our shoulders, our small group of people with our black cars all parked in the middle of the pier. Behind us sits a wall of rock that lines the main road. The tallest of trees sits on top of the hill, thick and dark and so full of mystery.

"It's been a while since we played," Atticus grumbles, always the eager one to get into trouble.

"No one stays here long enough anymore," Levi says, leaning his arms along the black railing. He presses his feet on the bricks below him, leaning over the side so he can watch the dark waters below. "Maybe we need to hit up another town. Shit is getting boring here."

The harsh wind whips my cheeks, and I can feel my skin chilling. It's only the fall, but this far up north it never grows too warm, and nights are always cold. Summer or winter. There's always a chill, more so here than any other town in Northern Minnesota.

This town is like home to me, but it doesn't make living here any more enjoyable. My dad is a piece of shit. He always has been. He thinks he's a good father because he makes enough money to keep my great grandchildren comfortable, but he doesn't have any father-like capabilities in his body. He's an emotionless douchebag, and unfortunately, I know those tendencies roll in my blood, too.

My own mother was gone the moment she realized how fucked up this place really is. How deep the evil really runs through my father. Years ago, so young I only remember small glimpses here and there, I remember she packed up her bags and was ready to leave without a backward glance. She didn't even want me to go with her. She knew whatever lay in my father's eyes also lies in mine. The poison of Castle Pointe has seeped so far into my veins, I thrive in it. It's part of me at this point, and I know nothing else besides the demons of my family name and the demons of this dark town.

She never really loved me. She never loved any of us. And because of that, tragedy struck her as she tried to leave, and only death was her saving grace. Her body lay in a pile of bones in my backyard. It was never discovered what happened to her, but with the evil that lie in this town, those questions were never even uncovered.

I don't care enough to dig. My dad has never been a good man. She always knew what she was getting into before she spread her legs for him. Her deciding to flee and leave me behind in this evil place is enough for me to wash my hands of her and regret ever loving her in the first place.

A gust of wind snaps me out of my past and brings me back to the present. I chew on my lip, contemplating what I'm about to say. "I have a feeling that once my new family moves in, we won't have to worry about being bored." There is a truth to my words. The moment my dad told me about this lady and her child, my blood ran cold, and something came alive in me. Like it's anticipating something's about to happen. Something that I'm unaware of, but my blood rushes for it, and that gets me excited. "I don't think we'll be bored at all."

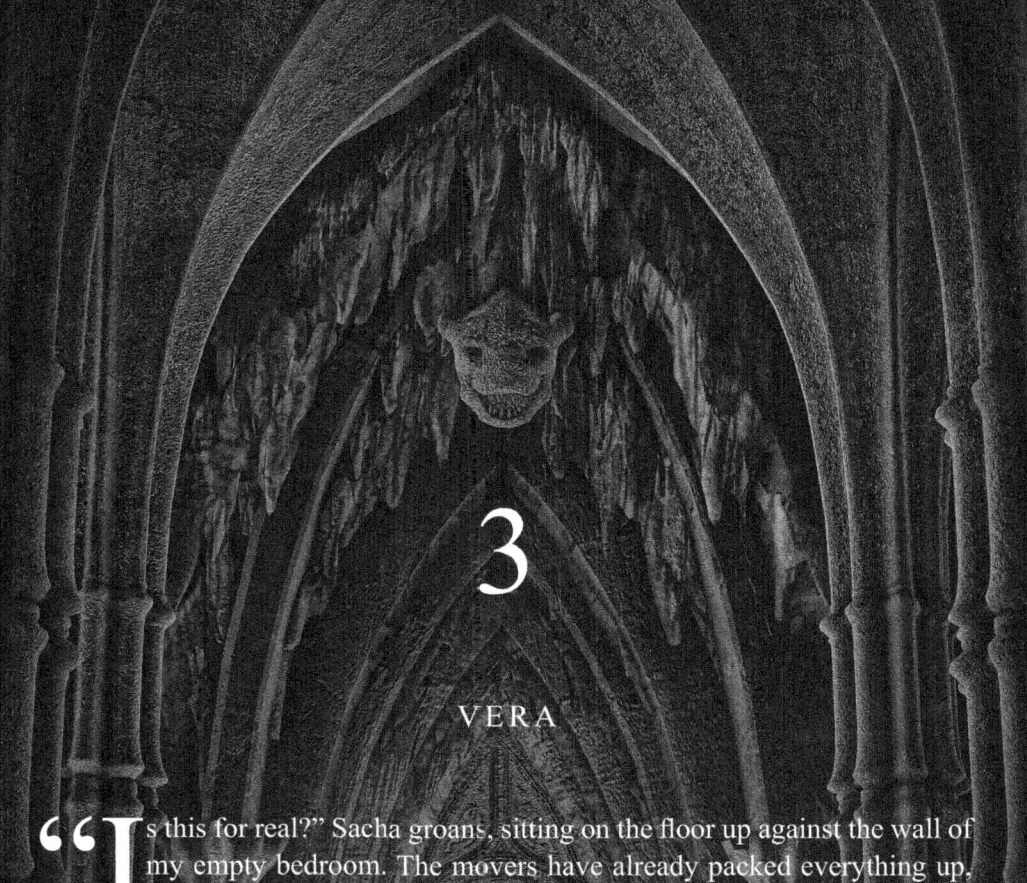

3

VERA

"Is this for real?" Sacha groans, sitting on the floor up against the wall of my empty bedroom. The movers have already packed everything up, the house that I've grown up in now an empty shell of the place I used to love.

I look around my creamy-colored room, the lines near the door showing each height I was at different ages. The million holes from pictures and tape residue on the walls from all my shitty posters of my favorite bands.

"This is for real." I sit up against the opposite wall, my bag at my feet and nothing else. I think about smoking a cigarette in here and stubbing it out on the carpet just in spite of my mom. I glance at the spot where the smudge of black nail polish recently was. The cleaners were able to get it out with ease. It only makes me want to stub my cigarette out on the carpet even more.

But on the off chance she chooses to leave me here for being an ass, I'd be sleeping in the fields since no one seems to want to take me in.

"This is bullshit. I say we make a run for it." Leena walks in, her combat boots shoving into the freshly cleaned carpet. She walks up to my bedroom window, sliding onto the wooden edge and cracking it open. Her hand digs into her purse, and she pulls out her blue glass bowl and lighter. She lifts it to me, eyebrows raised.

I shrug my shoulders, rolling over to stand up. As long as the window is open, I guess.

Leena is beautiful. With her long, dark hair that nearly catches her waist. Her leather jacket covers her arms and her small, washed-out jean shorts form to her tiny thighs.

Sacha worries less about her looks with her joggers and the hoodie that's pulled over her head, her wavy, blonde locks flowing out around her face.

I'm somewhere in between the two. With my fishnet tights and black shorts, combined with my black hoodie, I'm in the *I don't give a fuck* department of life. If you don't like how I dress or what I look like, you can fuck right off to the next lane. I don't have time for you.

Period.

"Where would we go?" My thumb presses on the metal, sparking the flame over the freshly grinded green. A tickle burns in my chest, and I bend over, sticking my head out the window as I blow the smoke out and cough until my eyes water.

"We can go to Mexico," Leena says, grabbing the bowl from my hand to take her own hit.

Sacha laughs. "You know that'll never work. Our parents will catch us before we hit Iowa."

"That is true." Smoke trails out of Leena's mouth with her words.

My shoulders drop. There's nothing I can do about my situation. Best-case scenario, I finish the last two years of school and come back here to be with my friends. I can work at Starbucks or some other job that doesn't require a college degree. I could probably bartend at one of the college bars. That's *best-case* scenario.

Worst-case? Shit, I don't even want to think about that.

"Is this the last time I'm going to see you guys?" I clutch my throat, feeling like it's swelling, filling with emotions or something. I fucking hate emotions.

They both shake their heads.

"Fuck that," Sacha says. "We'll come visit. Or you can come visit here."

"That's, like, a five-hour drive."

Sacha shrugs. "Wouldn't be too bad."

I press my hand on my windowsill, staring out the window. "Just watch, you guys will forget about me." My mom's Audi pulls into the driveway, and I wince. "Shit, my mom's pulling up. Put the bowl away."

Leena smushes the burnt green with the lighter before sticking it into her pocket. It smells heavily of skunk in here, and I'd normally love it, but my mom's been on edge these last two weeks, and once she figures out we're baking up in here, she'll pop a fucking gasket.

"Vera?" my mom calls from downstairs. Her voice echoes in our empty house. Leena sighs beside me, and I nod. Conversations with my mom never go well anymore. She's not a friendly person like she used to be.

Unfortunately, neither am I.

I listen as her heels clap on the wooden steps as she makes her way upstairs. The moment her face clears the doorway, she's got a fierce scowl on her face. "Are you smoking pot in here?"

We all vehemently shake our heads.

Her eyebrows lower, an ugly frown pulling her cherry red lips down at the corners. She steps into the room, her black pencil skirt pressed against her tanned legs. Her hair is done up, too. Big, wavy dark curls lay gently on her shoulders. I should have guessed something was up once she changed from being depressed and constantly in sweats, to dressing like she's a hot, single woman with no children. I should have known then that she was seeing someone, but I guess I felt like ignoring the signs.

Which also doesn't surprise me, because I've been nothing but in my own world these last few years.

My mom looks like a model at only thirty-five years old. She and my dad had me right out of high school, and she probably could have been a model back then, except she became strapped with a baby on her hip. Her long, dark hair, long limbs, and tanned skin looks so much different from my short form, white-and-black hair, and pale skin. My mom also dresses like she lives in Beverly Hills, and I, well, I dress like the girl whose parents want to forbid them from hanging out with you.

Yep, I'm the kid who looks like she's from the wrong side of the tracks.

Too bad I'm at a point in my life where I don't give a shit. I'll take my black clothes, my ripped jeans, my fishnets, and combat boots to the fucking grave if I have to. It also gives me a little bit of happiness when my mom frowns at my appearance, like she's ashamed of me. She always stares at the small hoop of my septum ring with a look of disgust.

It only makes me want to get more piercings.

I snap out of my thoughts when my mom walks through the room, her nose turned up as she searches from the blank carpet and up the empty walls. Like there will be a fucking joint taped to the ceiling or something.

She brushes by Leena and steps up to the window. She looks outside, then glances over her shoulder, giving each of us a seething glare.

Her eyes swing to mine, lethal and so bitchy. "Are you kidding me, Vera? Smoking when showings start tomorrow? The cleaners *just* left. And why are you smoking, anyway? You can't be doing this shit, Vera. *Cut it out.*"

I shrug. "Whatever."

Her nostrils flare, the muscles in her jaw tensing in aggravation. "You are such a little—" She pauses as she takes a deep breath and glances at Leena and Sacha. Taking a step back, she growls, "Grab your bag, Vera, it's time to go. Say goodbye to your friends." With that, she turns around and stomps out of the room.

I wait until she's at the bottom of the stairs before I turn to my friends. "Well, I guess this is it then."

Their scowling faces turn sad. Our tense bodies slouch, and the feeling of tension in the room melts into one of sorrow.

"I don't want you to leave," Sacha whispers.

I smile, though it never fully makes its way to my lips. "I wish I didn't have to."

"Will you text us when you get there?" Leena walks over to me, curling her arms around my waist. I bury my head into her neck, inhaling the scent I've grown up with. My second home. Her and Sacha. Since a few years ago, I've been with at least one of them more than I've been with my own mom. More than I've been at my own house. I'm being pulled away from the only thing I know, shoved into a place I don't want to be.

"The moment I get there. No, scratch that. I'll text you the entire way."

Sacha walks up behind me, and they both sandwich me in between them, squeezing me tight and holding me close.

"I'll miss you guys." My eyes burn, but I dare not cry. My mom is a witch and doesn't deserve my tears over this.

"We'll miss you, too," Sacha says.

"Vera, we have to leave! Now!" my mom shouts from downstairs.

We all sigh together, our bodies inhaling and exhaling in the same breath. Separating from them, we all walk toward the door. I bend down, curling my fingers around the strap of my bag and sling it across my shoulder. Our steps are somber as we walk downstairs, and I want to do nothing except fight and resist every step of the way.

My friends walk ahead of me and step outside. I linger in the doorway, glancing over my shoulder and staring into my room. The empty walls, the empty floor. It's all gone now, shoved into a trailer already on its way across the state.

With one last glance, I slap the light off and turn around, walking away from my life, and stepping directly into the unknown.

My ass hurts.

Like, literally, it's throbbing in pain. I didn't realize that sitting for this long would make my butt ache as bad as it is, but I want to jump from the car that's flying seventy miles per hour just to relieve myself of this torture.

"Are we almost there?" I groan, shifting onto my side. We just passed Duluth. Not much to see. Big city crammed into a small area. The water of Lake Superior glistened in the distance. It looked almost like an ocean, it's that big. Except there's no beach, at least from what I could see as we drove by. It just looked like a whole lot of water and a rocky shoreline.

It only took minutes for us to pass Duluth, and it seems like the world continues growing darker and colder the farther we travel north.

"Not too much longer." Her hands grip the steering wheel, her blood red nails freshly done only the day before. I watch as they clench, unclench, clench, unclench, over and over again.

"What's got you so nervous?" I ask, barely turning my head her way. Not that I care, because I really don't. She could have bubble guts, or period cramps. I'd probably laugh, to be honest. She's dragging me here, maybe she deserves just a twinge of suffering.

She sighs, her breath a little shaky. The trees are growing denser, the sky a little more ominous with every minute that passes. "There's something I wanted to speak with you about."

"Do I even want to know?"

She looks at me, and I can tell from her heavy glare on the back of my head. "Samuel has a son, who also lives at our new house."

I roll my eyes. "Great, so I'm going to have a snot-nosed kid breathing down my neck every second of the day? Just what I fucking wanted." I can at least thank my mom for making me an only child. A sibling is not something I've ever been interested in.

She pauses, not saying anything for too many seconds.

"What aren't you telling me?" I finally glance her way, and her tanned skin is a little pale from whatever she's holding in. "Never mind, I don't want to know." I don't, I really don't. If she's this nervous about it, it's definitely going to piss me off.

She takes a deep breath. "He's eighteen."

My black fingernails press into my bare thighs. They're smeared and a complete mess compared to my mom's, but I love them.

I love my imperfections.

My head tilts back, and I bark out a laugh. "This is so fucked." I bring my fingers down to the leather seat below me, scratching my nails along them in irritation.

"Stop scratching my leather!"

I whip my head toward hers. "Screw off. You lied to me."

She scoffs. "I did not lie."

I squeeze the leather. It's cool from the air conditioner my mom has been blasting for the last hour. I wish my nails would puncture the thick fabric.

My mom's hand comes down, peeling my fingers away from the seat. "Vera, I'm sorry for not telling you about Samuel's son. I knew you wouldn't be too happy about it—"

I snort. "You've got that right."

"But, I really think this will be a good thing. For the both of us."

I bend down, reaching for my black bag below me. "And how is that?" I unzip the front pocket, pulling out a pack of cigarettes and my lighter. I shouldn't smoke. These last two weeks I've been smoking way more than I usually do. Which is still barely anything, but each hit is terrible for me.

"You're not smoking in here."

I flick my white lighter, sparking the end of my Marlboro. Blowing smoke from my nose, I turn around and stare at her. "Except I am. You've pulled me from my home, and you aren't telling me about all the details of the place I'm supposed to be calling my new *home*. Forgive me for feeling a little uneasy. I think I'm going to smoke if I fucking feel like it."

She turns on her blinker. "I'll just pull over," she bites out.

I sigh. "Whatever."

She pulls onto one of those scenic lookouts on the side of the road. It overlooks Lake Superior, and luckily, there's only one other car in the lot. I hop out before she even shifts into park, walking away from her SUV and over to the edge of the brick. I sit down, letting the cigarette burn between my fingers as I stare out across the water. It's dark blue, and the chilly air hits my cheeks.

I reach behind me, sliding my hood over my head as I glance down at my cigarette. The ash sits an inch long, and I tap the filter, watching the white flecks flow away in the cool breeze.

"You know, I really don't want this to be how it's going to be for us," my mom starts, walking over to me. Her arms are crossed over her chest, the hair on her arms raised from the crisp air. "How we've been these last few years, that's not how I want us to be. Think of this as a chance for us to start over. For us to be a family again. I love you, Vera, and I only want what's best for you. I might not have been the best mother these last few years, but I'm here now."

I can hear the sincerity in her voice. I can see the pain and sadness on her face. She means what she says. She says what she feels.

Too bad it's all bullshit.

Everything she says has a motive. She says these things because they benefit her. She says them because we're going someplace new, and she doesn't want an asshole kid in tow. If it was her choice, maybe she would have left me on the street back in Fargo, but she couldn't, so she wants to salvage the little bit of our relationship that she can. If we weren't here, she would never have said these things. We would still be at arm's length with each other. She would be gone, and I would be all alone in our house, with my lonely thoughts and my wounded heart.

I needed her two years ago. I needed her when I was at my lowest. But she wasn't there. She hasn't been there. And now she expects I'll be there for her?

Fuck. That.

"You're too late." I brush the cherry along the bottom of my boot and slip the short into my pocket. Her face drops, a combination of sorrow and irritation crossing her face. I slip past her, folding my arms across my chest as I walk back to the car.

She stays outside a moment, her brown hair blowing in the wind as she watches the small waves. A young family with a baby take a picture nearby, the baby smiling brightly as she points to the waves as they crash against the shore. Life used to be simple like that. Seamless. Easy. Happy.

It's none of those things any longer.

The door cracks open, and my mom slides into the driver's seat. Her cheeks are tinged pink, and she runs her hands together before starting her car. "If you don't want to forgive me, fine. But I expect you to behave while we're there."

"Yup," I mumble, popping the *p*.

With a sigh, she reverses out of the lookout and continues our drive.

Welcome to Castle Pointe.

The sign looks like it's wrapped in evil, the square brick crumbling on the edges, with a vine wrapping around the top. The moment we pass the sign, any lingering sunlight left in the sky becomes shrouded by clouds. Lake Superior disappears as we continue driving, tall pine trees that are so green they look black crowd the road on both sides. A light fog lingers in the area, making goosebumps break out along my arms even though my mom turned off the air con a long time ago.

I look up the hill, seeing fallen rock littering the edge of the pavement. In between the trees is filled with darkness, shadows, and growing gray fog, making it impossible to see into the forest. Every once in a while, I'll see a house. A tall brick monstrosity that looks abandoned. Maybe haunted.

"This isn't it, right? I hope this isn't it." I laugh, feeling like this is some sort of a prank. A fucking joke, right? Because I'm not living here. Like, at all.

"This is it. But, Vera, don't be so quick to judge. Samuel says Castle Pointe has a lot of history and can be very beautiful."

"Beautiful is the last thing I'd call this."

Before we hit the sign, the car thermostat said it was forty-two degrees, and the moment we passed the sign, I've been watching it drop, degree by degree. Now it's thirty-five. How can one town be degrees colder, and why would it happen the moment we got into said town?

"It's not so bad. Look at that house up there." Her red nail points up the hill, at a large, gray mansion. The tops are pointed, like a castle. The circular driveway is littered with pine needles, as if it hasn't been driven on in a while, except there's a midnight black Mercedes-Benz sitting in front of the house.

A massive gate sits at the entrance of the driveway, like a celebrity lives behind the iron rods. Why anyone would want to break into a house like this, I have no idea.

Half of me hates this place, but some weird, warped part of me is intrigued by the mystery.

"Your destination is on your left," says the monotone GPS.

My eyes widen.

The house before me is like every house we've seen so far, combined into one. The house is tall and wide, very castle-esque with its pointed tops and second-level balconies. The bricks are gray, with black vines curling up the left-hand side, like the earth is slowly making its way around the deathly building. There's an archway curving from the house to the garage. A fountain sits in the middle of the circular driveway, unused, unkept. In the center of the fountain is an angel, one wing completely broken off.

And just like the house before, a massive gate, with sharp, bladed points sitting on top of the rods, expands around the front of the house.

This one looks abandoned like the others we've passed; except, I know it's not. There's a black Range Rover sitting underneath the archway, in perfect condition, shiny and new.

"This isn't it." I lean forward, my head hanging over the airbag with my jaw slack. "This can't be it. Who the hell are you dating? Mr. fucking Addams from the Addams Family?"

A small chuckle leaves my mom as she slaps the back of her hand on my thigh. "Cut it out. Samuel is a real estate agent. Nothing more."

"Unbelievable," I mumble, leaning back in my seat as my mom parks next to the Rover.

I see the moving company truck up ahead toward the back of the house. The top is opened, and most of the back is already empty.

"Well, let's go check things out." Mom turns off the car, grabbing her purse and opening her door.

A moment later, the front door opens, and a tall man in a pressed suit steps outside. His dark hair is swept to the side as he stands there stiffly with his hands in his pockets. He looks to be in his mid-forties. He's slender, with dark eyes and a strong jaw. Handsome, even if he does look quite a bit older than my mom.

There's something about him, though. A little creepy. Like the darkness of Castle Pointe made its way inside of him.

His face softens, any type of seriousness about him dropping when his eyes land on my mom. "You made it! How was the drive?" His hands slide from his pockets, and he opens them as he walks down his gray steps, heading straight for my mom.

"It was long, but we're here." My mom wraps her arms around him, and he presses his lips to her cheek in a familiar gesture. The entire way they hold each other is familiar, like they've done this many times before. They're comfortable with each other.

It makes me sick.

I turn away, just as his eyes land on mine.

"And you must be Vera. Your mom has told me so much about you." He steps away from my mom, walking toward me with a smile gracing his lips. His face is clean-cut, very sharp and a little intimidating.

"I can't say the same for you," I say as I stand there, my bag slung over my shoulder.

"Vera," my mom chastises.

Samuel lifts an eyebrow, his lips tensing slightly at my words.

"I'm sorry," I apologize.

He smiles again, this time his lips slightly stiff. "Don't be sorry. I understand this is hard for you. But don't worry, I think you'll really enjoy it here."

Um, one, what is that supposed to mean?

Two, I really fucking won't.

"Thanks," I say with a smile. Fake. *So fake.*

He slips his hands back into his pockets. "Well, the movers are almost done unloading your things. How about I show you around before you get settled in? I'm sure you're both tired from the drive."

"We are." My mom walks up to Samuel, lacing her fingers with his. I look away, sliding another cigarette from my bag.

My mom's eyes widen, giving me a warning look. I glance away from her as I shove the cigarette back into my bag, not able to handle their intimacy. It feels wrong. It looks wrong.

This is all so, so wrong.

"Well, come on." Samuel gestures for us to follow him. He walks up the front steps, long and wide. A grand entrance up to a large, double door. The wood is dark, nearly black, with a door knocker in the shape of a gold lion. The gold is worn and chipped away, though, and the eyes are black.

The lion looks like death.

Samuel presses on the door handle, opening it into a large entryway with tall ceilings with gray walls. The floor is nearly black, either stone or an expensive tile. A chandelier hangs above us, the yellow light creating a dim glow above us. It's old, historic, and Gothic with its sharp iron rods, spiky and deadly-looking.

The staircase is off to the left, the steps made of another blackened stone, long and wide as they curl around the side of the wall up to the second level. Movers walk through the house, and we step aside as they take my dresser upstairs.

The railing is a dark silver. It looks cold.

This entire house looks cold. Nothing like my last home, which was filled with warm memories and happy feelings. Even if it was all fake, at least there was something comforting about it.

This feels so off.

We pass a set of dark doors on the right. "This is my office. Nothing to see in there."

I frown, looking up at Samuel, but his face is blank, and he's already walking off down the hall. The walls are decorated with old, ancient-looking pieces of what looks to be possible ancestors. Black-and-white photos. Creepy portraits and paintings of scenery that look similar to Castle Pointe. Every frame is detailed and textured with fine carvings that look about one million years old. Everything is so… Gothic.

This entire place gives me the creepy vibes. Goosebumps pop up along my arms, and I rub my hands over them. It's so fucking cold in here.

"Why is it so cold here?" I ask him.

He glances over his shoulder at me, a cross between laughter and menace lingering in his eyes. "Castle Pointe has its quirks."

Oh, is that what we're calling it?

"It feels like this entire town is haunted," I grumble.

Samuel lets out a chuckle, a low grumble from deep in his chest. "I wouldn't be surprised."

My eyes widen.

My mom laughs. "Well, that's just silly. I'm sure it's just an old place. Like you said, there's a lot of history here."

We walk into the kitchen, the only modern-looking room in the house that I've seen so far. Black appliances mix with dark granite countertops and cabinets. A massive island, larger than a kitchen table, sits in the center of the room.

"Through the hall there is a mudroom which leads to the garage." He points to the right. "And the formal dining room is through there. I haven't eaten in there much, but maybe now we'll have the opportunity to take advantage of it more." He smiles, and I glance away from him, looking at the oversized wooden table with high wingback chairs sitting around it in the next room. A large chandelier hangs over the center of the table, and that room definitely seems antique, with a black-and-white wallpaper littering the walls.

"Here is the informal dining area and the living room." He points to the left, where large pillars separate the two rooms. The black, wooden kitchen table is long, with two candles sitting in the center.

The living room is carpeted, with two black leather sofas sitting around a coffee table. A built-in entertainment center sits against the wall with a large TV in the center.

For some reason, I'm thinking in this house, this area doesn't get used much.

We walk through the living room to a set of double doors. "And this here," he pauses as he turns the knob, and the door creaks as it's pushed open, "is the library."

The smell of old paper slaps me in the face and my eyes widen, taking in the three walls of floor-to-ceiling bookshelves. The ceilings are high, and the rolling ladder that sits up against one of the walls goes all the way to the top shelf. A black chandelier hangs from the center of the ceiling. The dark, rich wood of the shelves extend from bottom to top, all of which have moldings along the trim. The only color in here is provided by the spines of the books.

So many books.

They all look old, too. No modern novels sit on these shelves. They all look historical, maybe no fiction books at all. A large desk sits off to the side, cleared of any debris. Only a small L-shaped lamp sits off to the side. A therapist-looking chair sits against the window, and a few other chairs are placed around the room. This place is huge, like a miniature library has been placed in this home.

Samuel smiles when he sees my face. "Feel free to come in here whenever you'd like. You can take any book. They're yours."

"Thank you," I say genuinely, my first honest comment I've made since I met him.

This is a fucking dream.

"Sir, we're finished." We all look behind us to see one of the movers with a clipboard in hand.

Samuel grabs the clipboard and pen from the mover before glancing back at us. "Why don't you guys go ahead and explore the rest of the house? The basement is right down the hall if you want to look around, otherwise you can head upstairs if you want to check out your room."

My mom reaches her hand up, her red nails clinging to Samuel's black suit jacket. "That sounds lovely. We'll go wander around and find you in a bit."

He bends down, pressing his lips to my mom's cheek.

I heft my bag up farther over my shoulder as I avert my eyes, stepping around the mover and out of the library.

"I think I'm going to check out my room."

"Do you want to go check out the basement with me?" My mom has an excitement in her eyes as she looks around the house. I get it, it's a big house, beautiful, but it's also a little cold. It makes me feel like I'm in the house on a haunted hill or something.

I shake my head. "I'm tired from the drive. I think I'm going to lay down for a bit. I'll check out the basement later tonight."

She gives me a small smile, her eyes already focused on Samuel as she wraps her arm around his bicep, happiness that I haven't seen in so long lighting up her entire face. Samuel smiles back at her, a tenderness he doesn't seem capable of having softening his harsh features.

I take the nausea in my stomach as my cue, slipping out of the library and walking back toward the living room. I feel like I haven't even checked out half of the main level, but this place kind of gives me the creeps. It's dark in here, and it's not just because everything around me is dark and gray. The trees outside cover every bit of sunlight that would ever make its way inside the house. I walk up to the window near one of the sofas, peeking outside and into the backyard.

Trees that tower as tall as the house fill the entire backyard. Barely any grass is present, the only green being the amount of pine needles that litter the ground. My fingers press into the wood of the windowsill, the trim old and worn, scratches and dents here and there, yet it still looks pristine and expensive as it lines the window.

There aren't any plants around the house either, I realize. But I don't imagine any plants would be able to flourish in this environment, mostly with no sunlight. This feels like a place where you go to die, not to live.

I shove off the window, turning around and seeing the vast, empty room. It smells like pine in here, like the trees outside have snuck their way through the cracks of the doors and windows and made themselves a permanent fixture in the air.

With my worn, black backpack in hand, I walk toward the staircase. My boots thump against the floor as I walk through the empty house, echoing with each step. I pass the double door office, and I step up to it, my hand poised above the knob. Maybe I can uncover something about Samuel, get my mom to hate him, and we can go back to Fargo where we belong.

My hand presses against the handle, the silver cool against my palm. I grip it, and a blast of cold air hits the back of my neck. I whip my head around, glancing over my shoulder, expecting Samuel to be there with his fierce gaze, looking at me with disdain, and yelling at me for encroaching on his private area.

Except no one is there.

My hand reaches up and I press my fingers against the raised hairs on the back of my neck as I step back from the door. Shivers rack my body as I make my way to the staircase. Each stair is long, about four feet in length. The stone steps are shiny, and I grip the cool railing as I make my way upstairs. It curves around, and I feel like I'm in a dream as I make my way to the second level.

This place really is creepy. There's no other word for it.

The railing extends over the second level, and once I make it to the top, I glance over the edge, my face the same height as the chandelier. I look down the hallway to the left and see only darkness. Looking right, I again only see more darkness.

Which way do I go?

I decide to head right, leading me down the hallway that's nearly pitch-black the farther I go. There's more artwork up here, eerie paintings of Castle Pointe, dark castles, the forest with fog. I stop when I get to some portraits. Old, black-and-white photos of people that don't smile. Heavy lines crease their faces as they stare at the camera angrily.

Weird.

Are these their ancestors? Who else would they be? What a weird fucking family.

I step away from the photos and walk up to a door, pressing my hand around the knob and turning it, only to find it locked.

I look around for a light switch, not liking standing in an almost completely blacked-out hallway, but I can't find one.

There's one other door down this way, and that one is also locked. The hall goes even farther, but for some reason, I don't think my bedroom will be down there.

"Well, shit." I walk back the way I came, heading toward the other side of the house. The first room I hit has its door opened, and glancing inside, I see my bed and dresser placed against the wall.

I drop my backpack in the doorway. "Well, I guess this is it." It feels weird seeing my stuff here. Like this is my room, except this isn't my room at all.

I glance farther down the hallway, seeing it extend for what seems like forever. I walk across the hall, opening up the door and seeing a bathroom. Gray and black. That seems to be the theme. Dark wood trim and crown moldings have made their way around the entirety of the house. The place is old, although bits and pieces seem to be modernized, as industrial as they may seem. There is no color here, no feel of warmth. Only darkness and coldness.

The shower is a walk in, no curtain and no door, just a dark, gray stone shower, and peeking around the corner, I see an oversized showerhead that puts a smile on my face.

That looks nice.

The bathroom itself is large, with a double sink, linen closet, and a jetted tub. None of it really looks used at all, actually. There is no toothbrush sitting in its stand. No towel that was hung to dry. Nothing in the small waste basket. It's like this place is one of the model homes my mom has brought me to.

Staged.

Where is the stepbrother?

My head pops out of the bathroom, and I look down the hall I have yet to explore. Pressing on my tiptoes, I walk as quietly as I can to the next door. It's closed, and I press my ear against the wood, listening for any sounds.

Nothing.

I think about opening it, even just trying, but the feeling of being watched burns into the back of my head. I twist, my head glancing over my shoulder as I look for some creep lingering behind me.

No one.

The hallway keeps going, everything dark and quiet. I stand there, in the middle of the hallway on the black marbled floors, when a low groan echoes down the hall, like someone is leaning back in a rocking chair. Or someone stepped on a creaky floorboard. Except the floors aren't wood.

My back twitches with a shiver, and I turn around, rushing back into my room, kicking my bag out of the doorway and swiftly shutting the door. I lean my back against it, scared of nothing and everything.

This is an old house, of course there're going to be weird as fuck noises.

After my heart settles, I press off the door, walking over to my window and looking into the backyard. The sun is going down, and the forest is looking even more doomy than it was earlier. I watch between the trees, and my skin grows cold.

I swear I see shadows in there.

My eyes raise to the sky, seeing dark gray clouds rolling in, clashing with the next one as they grow bigger, darker, sinking lower into the sky. Like I can reach my hand up and my fingers will swirl into them.

I see a flash of lightning, followed by a clap of thunder.

Stepping away from the window, I walk to my bed, already made with my comforter from back home. I slip between my sheets, pressing my face against my pillow that smells so familiar my eyes burn. But instead, I close them, curling my arms around the softness. Just as the rain starts pelting my window,

I fall asleep.

4

MALIK

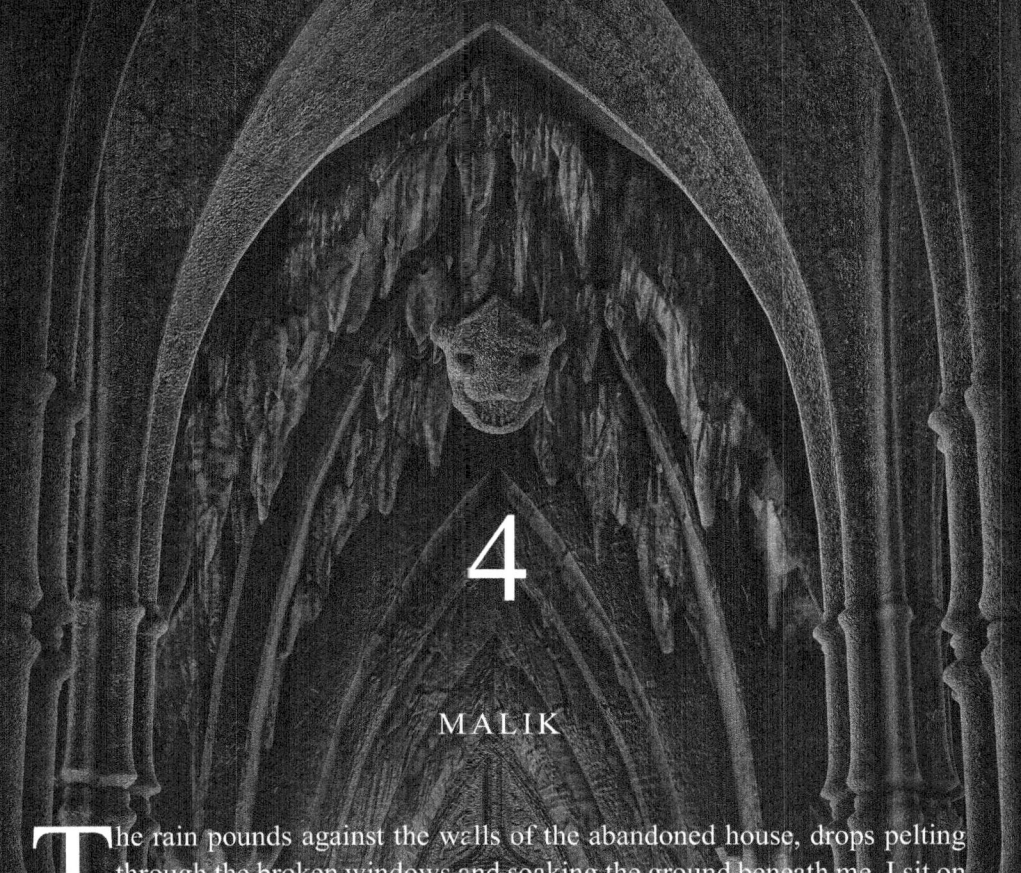

The rain pounds against the walls of the abandoned house, drops pelting through the broken windows and soaking the ground beneath me. I sit on a broken couch, the old thing stained and ripped from years of wear and neglect. One of the sides is completely broken off, laying on the ground beside me. The entire thing sits slanted, so I have to tilt as I sit so I don't fall over.

"Shit, we're going to get drenched walking back to the car," Felix says as he walks down the stairs. His hair is damp, and he shakes the droplets off. Half of the upstairs is missing a roof. There's no spot in this place that isn't exposed to the outside. But it's still our secret place in the middle of the woods. The place where we go to fuck around when we don't want to be around our parents, or anyone else for that matter.

I shrug, taking a drag of my cigarette. "Doesn't matter to me."

He lifts his eyebrows. "You know, your new roommate should be at your house by now."

I know. I fucking know. Hence the reason I'm sitting here, in an abandoned house at night, in the rain, instead of at my house.

We left school halfway through the day, because I do whatever the fuck I want, and we came here to chill. We've been drinking, smoking, doing whatever we please, but we don't usually hang out this long, and I know the guys are ready to go. We haven't eaten all day, and it's getting cold outside. This abandoned shithole doesn't block the wind or the rain, and we're vulnerable to all the damn elements.

But the last thing I feel like doing is going back home to be with my dad, his whore, and the whore's child. Sorry, but I'd rather hang out in this piece of shit and have my balls freeze until they're numb.

"What do you think she looks like?" Felix plops down on the seat next to me, the couch so uneven he slopes toward the floor.

"I don't really care." I flick my cigarette into an empty can at my feet.

Footsteps pound down the stairs, and soon Levi and Atticus are in front of us, dripping wet.

"It's a bad fucking storm." Atticus stares out the window at the trees blowing in the wind. The branches scrape up against the side of the house, making scratching noises that make me seriously uneasy. The hair on the back of my neck stands on end.

"All the storms are bad here," Levi says, taking a pull of his beer. "But I'm fucking hungry, and I'm ready to head home."

Felix looks at me. "Malik doesn't want to go home."

Atticus smiles. "We could fuck with her."

I show my teeth, a vicious smile covering my face. "I've already thought about it."

Levi lifts a dark eyebrow. "What do you have in mind?"

"I haven't gotten that far yet." I run my palm along my jaw, thinking of all the ways I can run the little bitch out of town. What is she like? Is she sweet or sassy? Is she tall or short? Thick or thin? Does she kneel beside her bed at night and pray to God? Or does she slide between her sheets as she worships the devil?

"We could drug her, shave her head. That'll have her running." Atticus rubs his hands together, the thought of pranking again making his heart race. I know it. I can hear it.

He loves the pranks. No, we all love the fucking pranks.

I shrug, feeling like that's something we would've done three years ago. We're more extreme now.

"We could bury her alive in the old cemetery like we did to that one guy the other year," Felix mumbles beside me.

Levi laughs darkly. "Or if he's still there, we could bury her with the guy."

I chuckle, always curious if he ever made it out or if we committed a murder.

"I'll have to see what kind of girl we're playing with before we decide our game." I press against the cushion of the couch, hearing it crunch as I shove myself up to stand. The floral-patterned sofa has seen better days.

Fifty years ago.

Walking to the window, I watch as the rain finally lets up. "Either she'll bow down at the first sign of weakness, or she'll put up a fight and we'll have a real game to play."

We're all silent, listening to the rain hit the crumbling roof. Droplets of water start seeping from the ceiling, making their way around us. The strong smell of rain mixed with wet wood invades my senses, and I take a deep inhale, the cool air slapping against my skin.

I know each one of them has the same thoughts as I do.

I hope she plays the game, and I hope she plays it well.

5

VERA

"Vera?" I shoot up in bed, momentarily disoriented as I look around. *Where the hell am I?*

"Vera? I brought you some food." I blink up at my mom, seeing her standing there, changed into leggings and a tank top that accentuates her chest. I frown at her, wondering why she's trying to look so fucking attractive. Doesn't the guy already like her? Why is she trying so hard?

She points to my bedside table, and I look over, seeing a matte black plate with a cover on top. My bottles of medicine sit beside it, and I sigh, wishing she'd just leave me alone. Quit acting like she actually cares.

"I'm not hungry."

She frowns, her hand reaching out to clutch my bare knee. I glance at her red nails, anger and animosity building in me for no legit reason. I'm just angry, and her staring at me and trying to be a parent is only making it worse.

"You should really try and eat something, and you need to take your medicine. It's been a long day."

"I've been timing my own medicine for two years. Don't try to pretend like I'm incompetent now."

She's silent for a moment. "I just worry about you."

I keep my eyes averted because her concern feels fake. Maybe I'm wrong and am being a complete bitch, but if I were to be honest with myself right now, her absence these last two years has only shown me how little she cares.

So, it feels false, like she's putting on a show for her new man. It makes my stomach turn.

My hands press against my worn sheets, and I slide into a sitting position, slinking away from her hand. "I think I'm going to take a shower. I feel kind of gross."

"You need to take your meds, Vera."

I roll my eyes, falling onto my side and popping the pills out of the bottle, then toss them onto my tongue. Lifting the top on the plate, I grab the warm roll and shove half of it into my mouth. "Happy?" I say around a mouthful of bread. Sighing, I chew my way through the dryness as I slide off the edge of my bed.

Her hand reaches out, curling around my fingers. "Hold on a second. Can you sit down? I wanted to talk to you about something quick."

I narrow my eyes at her, instantly on guard. I almost don't want to know what other kind of details about this move she's kept from me, and from the hesitant look on her face, she already knows I'm not going to be happy about it.

I sit back down on the bed, though only on the edge. I don't care if it's raining, or if we're in the middle of nowhere in some weird alternate universe, I'll run my ass all the way back to Fargo. It's too much.

"It's about school," she starts.

I groan, looking for my bag. Talk of school makes me need a cigarette.

I find it on the floor near my nightstand. Bending over, I curl my fingers around the worn strap and lift it onto my lap. Unzipping the front pocket, I pull out my pack and lighter.

"You aren't smoking in here. You aren't smoking at all for that matter. Give me the cigarettes."

My nostrils flare, and I press them against my lap, tired and fucking irritable. "What is it you needed to tell me?" No way in hell is she taking away the cigarettes.

"There's only one school in Castle Pointe." She winces.

I nod my head. This town doesn't look like it would have five different schools. "I kind of figured that. So, great. I get to go to school with kindergarteners. I don't really care."

She takes a deep breath. "It's a Catholic school."

I blink at her.

"It's a private Catholic school. Very old-school. You'll be expected to wear a uniform, attend Mass. According to Samuel, there're priests, nuns, the whole nine yards. It'll be much different than what you're used to." She nods her head toward my closet.

I follow her gaze, looking into my opened walk-in closet and see it empty, except for one long row of dark gray and black uniforms. Skirts, jackets, and white, short-sleeved button-ups.

Huh, I never noticed them earlier.

I bite my lip, turning my gaze back to my mom.

A laugh bursts out of me. I laugh so damn hard that tears stream down my face and I can barely catch my breath.

"What's so funny?" Her voice is no longer gentle, but a little put out. Slightly offended.

I wipe my cheeks with the heels of my palms, looking up at her. "I think it's absolutely hilarious that you expect me to go to school there. There is no chance in fucking hell I'm doing that."

She straightens, popping her hands on her hips as she stares down at me. That's her intent, to stand taller than me. To gain the upper hand. Because it's the only way she knows how. I think she knows, deep down, that given the chance, I'd lay her on her ass so quick, she wouldn't know what to do with herself. "You don't have a choice in the matter, Vera."

I nod. "Yes, I do. You can homeschool me, or I can get my GED for all I care. I'm not going to some stuck-up, weird-ass Catholic school. There's no chance— *no damn chance*—that I'll go there. I give you props for trying, though." I reach up, patting her hand with mine.

Her eyebrows lower, and she scowls down at me, tearing her hand from beneath mine. "This is exactly the reason you're going, Vera. Your attitude sucks. You think you're in charge. You think you have a say in any of this. Well, let me tell you something, *you don't*. Not even slightly. I'm your mother, and if I tell you you're going to a Catholic school, well, then you're putting on the damn uniform and you're going to go there with a smile on your face and manners in your back pocket. You need this school, Vera. They need to whip you into shape a little bit. Lord knows I've tried."

I laugh again, this one evil. Sinister. "You've done nothing but open your legs for a man who lives in a creepy house and looks like he could be your fucking father."

She grabs me by the ear, pulling me off the bed and onto the floor. "I am tired of you talking to me like this. I am your mother, goddammit. You better change your attitude real quick, Vera, or you'll be in for a rude awakening."

She drops me, and I fall to my knees on the ground. They pound against the floor, and my hand goes up to my burning ear, rubbing away the ache. I glare up at her. "You're such a bitch." I turn away from her, crawling toward my cigarette pack and lighter that's on the bed. Before I can grab them, though, my mom is there, snatching them from my hands and walking toward the door.

"*First rule,* no more smoking. Goodnight, Vera. Eat your food while it's hot. And get some rest, school starts tomorrow."

She shuts the door, leaving me alone on the floor in my room.

I raise my middle finger, wanting to shove my black nail straight into her eye socket. I'd love to paint my own nails red, only this time with her blood. She's betrayed me many times, and this time was the last.

I push myself up, rubbing my ear once more that still has a lingering thump. I'm sure if I looked in the mirror, it'd be bright red.

I ignore the plate of food on my bedside table. I'm not eating. Not tonight, anyway. I've lost my appetite. I ate enough to not get nauseous from my pills, and that's all I care about.

Walking to my door, I open it up slowly and peek around the corner. Both directions are empty, dark, and silent. No noise. No echoes from downstairs. Wherever my mom and Samuel are, it isn't anywhere near here.

I slip into the hall, closing my door behind me, then walk into the bathroom. I slowly glide the door closed, keeping the knob turned to keep it as silent as possible. I don't want another run-in with my mom tonight. Not for my safety, but for hers.

She took my cigarettes? *She took my fucking cigarettes!*

Holy shit, I am going to kill her.

I pull my shirt over my head, my heavy breathing the only sound in the bathroom. I turn toward the mirror, pulling my black hair aside and glancing at my ear.

Just as I expected, the tip is flaming red. I scowl at it, like my ear is the one to blame for this. It's not.

It's my mom.

I reach behind my back, unsnapping my black bra and dropping it to the floor. I stare at my small chest, hating the deep, dark scar that sits from just below my collar bone all the way down my torso, directly between my breasts. My fingers trail along the puckered skin, hating the reminder. Hating the memories.

With a shake of my head, I drop my arm, hooking my thumbs beneath my shorts and underwear and sliding them down my legs. I step out of them, walking into the stone shower. Turning the knob, I finally let my shoulders drop and the tension drains from my body as the steaming water pelts my skin.

I tip my head back, letting the water wash over my face and hair. It's hot, and I let each drop of water beat into my muscles until they ache. It feels so good I press my hands against the stones and lean forward, letting the water dig into the knots in my neck.

Fuck, that feels good.

Opening my eyes, I lift an eyebrow when I see my shampoos and soaps sitting on the ledges. I don't know exactly what is in the movers' job description, but I have a feeling putting away my personal belongings goes a little above and beyond.

A little weird.

I grab my bottle of shampoo, tipping a generous dollop onto my palm and massaging it into my scalp. My black-and-white hair falls to the middle of my back. I should have bought some dye before I left because my roots are already starting to peek through. I'm going to have to find a store near here that I can pick some up. I'm thinking of dying half of my hair purple next time. Or a dark blue. Dark like Castle Pointe. My hair should match my mood, and I don't think anyone that lives in this town could ever be bubbly.

The thought makes me laugh.

I rinse the shampoo from my hair, repeating the same step with my conditioner, then lather my body with soap. I'm a little rough as I scrub at my skin, my nails digging in as aggravation hits me.

I mean, seriously, my mom wants me to go to a Catholic school? Does she know who her daughter is? Because I seriously think I'd rather go live on the streets than attend any kind of school that requires a uniform. *Are the people there weird as hell? Like as weird as this town?*

That thought makes me think about the MIA stepbrother. I imagined someone older, maybe a little rugged and moody. If he goes to a Catholic school, is he going to walk in with glasses and a tie? Tell me that he'll help me study or lend me his Bible?

I mean, come the fuck on.

I laugh, my voice echoing in the bathroom as I rinse my body.

My mind is so preoccupied that I don't notice the dark figure step into the bathroom until suddenly, arms wrap around my waist, lifting me into the air. I let out a scream, but a large hand slaps over my mouth. I attempt to grapple against the hands as my eyes fly open, coming face to face with a tall, shadowed man.

An *angry* man.

He sets me down by the sink, my feet digging into the rug beneath me.

My hands curl over my chest, covering the scar, my eyes wide, annoyed, shocked, slightly nervous. "What are you doing?"

He stares at me, the running shower making the air thick and foggy with steam. The man's face quickly becomes damp with perspiration. "I shower at night."

My mouth drops open, my lips curling up and showing my teeth. "Not tonight, asshole. Obviously, I'm taking a shower." I go to walk past him, but he steps in my way.

"No," he growls, staring down at me. The way he bares his teeth is menacing. They are sharp, razor-like as they shine down on me. Like a fucking ravenous wolf.

The air starts to cool my skin, and goosebumps break out along my wet body. "I'm getting in the fucking shower. I'm not even done rinsing. Get out of my way." I point at my sudsy hair.

His hand reaches down, and he pulls his shirt over his head, revealing a toned stomach, ripped all the way from his pecs down to his hip bones. There isn't an inch of his body that isn't rock-hard.

He looks lethal.

"You must be the son," I mumble, staring at the dip near his hips that lead below the belt.

His eyes swing to the space between my legs, his tongue poking out to run across his lower lip. "And you must be the little bitch coming to sleep in my house." I step around him, and his hand goes to my bicep, his fingers digging into my skin.

I stare at his muscular hand, the tendons cording up his wrist and forearm.

He releases me quickly, shaking his hand out and scowling down at his fingers. He looks like he just touched a pile of shit instead of my wet arm. "Get the fuck out of here."

My nostrils flare, done with this back and forth. If the fucker just let me hop in the shower and rinse off, I'd let him get on with his jacking off, or whatever the hell he does in the shower at night.

I go to move past him again. "Move out of my way."

He picks me up this time, his arms circling my waist, his hands firm against my slippery body. I slap and scratch at his naked back. I can feel his skin shred beneath my nails. "Fuck you, let me go!"

He opens the door with one hand, and *literally* tosses me into the hallway. My wet limbs crash to the dark tiles, the hardness slamming against my knees and ankles.

He doesn't say another word, slamming the door in my face.

I can feel my face turn red, and I stand up, my hand going straight for the knob to open it again, only to find resistance.

Locked.

Dread and hate drip into my stomach. I couldn't hate a human more than I do right now. If I can even call him that.

I stand in the hallway, the darkness surrounding me, freezing my flesh all the way to my bones. Shivering, I rush back into my room, slamming the door shut as hard as I can behind me. It shakes the wooden trim, and I wish for a second my slamming would have broken the entire house.

This place is a damn nightmare.

6

MALIK

I sit over my kitchen table, my phone laying in front of me as I scroll through another endless number of messages.

You're so hot.
Let's meet tonight.
Want to hang out after school?

No. No, I fucking do not.
Swipe left. Swipe left. Swipe motherfucking left.
Are any of these girls at Castle Pointe Academy worth meeting? Do I ever feel like sliding between any of these girls' legs?
No, I really don't.
"You got home late last night," my father calls as he walks into the kitchen. He adjusts his black tie, a smirk on his face like he's living his best life.
I guess at least one of us is.
A moment later, the sound of heels starts clacking down the hallway. I grind my teeth together, watching as my dad takes out two cups from the cupboard instead of one.
"You didn't get to meet Daphne, or her daughter."

Oh, Pops, that's where you're wrong…

"Good morning!" A tall woman with dark hair walks in, her large curls bouncing with every step. She's dressed to the nines, like she's headed for a cocktail party instead of wherever the hell she actually works. Castle Pointe doesn't have many businesses around, so I don't know where she plans to go with that dress. It's short and in a midnight blue that molds to every curve.

How old is she? She looks like she's in her twenties, but I know that can't be true, because she has a daughter in high school.

"You must be Malik. I'm Daphne." She smiles brightly, a look in her eyes that screams she's happy to be my new mother.

Fuck no.

I lift my spoon from my cereal bowl in a wave, barely sparing a glance from my phone.

Delete, delete, delete.

"Don't be rude, Malik," my dad barks.

I drop my spoon, and it clanks against the black bowl. Staring up at her, I spear her with dead eyes and a blank face. "I'm sorry, where are my manners? I'm Malik." I give her a smile, showing her my canines.

She blinks at me, a lick of unease dripping into her gaze.

I can hear my dad sigh from the other side of the kitchen.

She doesn't say anything else, turning around and walking up to my dad. He hands her a cup of coffee, and she takes it contentedly, stepping straight into his arms.

My face drops back to my phone.

That only last seconds, though, when I hear the sound of heavy boots pounding down the hallway. Pissy, angry, rude as hell boots doing their best to scuff the dark floors.

Daphne clears her throat, and I can feel the tension seeping from her pores. It fills up the room, and it suddenly feels stuffy in here, when it's usually the temperature of a freezer.

I see a shadow from the corner of my eye, and lift my head slightly, grinding my teeth together when I see the stupid brat from last night.

She wears a pair of combat boots, laced up to her shins. They're black, worn but shiny, like she wears them often but does her best to keep them clean.

It's the fishnets that have my teeth turning into dust.

They stretch across her long legs, holes and tears in them as they lead up her thighs, disappearing beneath her uniform skirt. It's rolled up a few times, and I know that easily. The skirts the girls are given at school brush their knees. Ugly, thick fabric that gives away nothing and turns their figures into boxes. This girl's skirt brushes her upper thighs. The white button-up shirt she has on forms nicely to her curves. She had to have tightened it somehow, because the shirts do not fit like that either.

Wait, what?

I hate her. I really fucking hate her.

Her hair is dried, laying against her shoulders in a flat sheet. It's black, dark as the town we live in, but there's parts of it that are white. She's got one of those ridiculous piercings in her nose, the bull piercing or whatever it is. It's dainty, barely noticeable unless you look at her straight in the face. Her eyes are dark as well, and there's too much makeup shading her features. On her back sits a miniature backpack. One of those things that can't hold much more than a wallet and a paperback book. A white cord is trailing out of it, draping from in between the zipper and up to her ears.

The bitch is listening to music.

She looks jaded. A kid who pouts and screams when she doesn't get her way. It makes me realize, whatever game I decide to play with her, she's going to fight back. She's going to fight back real hard.

A smirk pops up onto my lips. *Good.*

"Good morning, Vera. How did you sleep?" her mom asks, setting her coffee cup down on the island.

Vera says nothing, bobbing her head to the music as she sits on one of the stools. She scrolls through her phone and looks to be typing something, a small smile on her lips as her fingers fly across the keyboard.

What the hell is she doing?

"Vera," her mom says. "Vera!" She leans over the counter, pulling on the cord. The small buds pop out of Vera's ears, and I secretly watch as her eyes darken, pure hatred in them as she stares at her mom.

"What the hell are you doing?"

Daphne's eyes narrow slightly, and I can tell she has a nasty remark on the tip of her tongue, but she holds it in, standing straighter and smiling. "I'm just wondering how you slept?"

"Horribly, actually."

Daphne's mouth tightens, her lips bunching together until they turn white. "Well, while you are both here, there is some news we both wanted to speak with you about."

Daphne's face lightens two shades, creating a glow on her cheeks. She looks up at my dad, and I watch his features soften. It makes me want to punch him in the jaw.

"Do you want to do the honors?" she asks my dad.

He turns to me, clearing his throat as he settles his coffee cup on the counter. He takes a step toward me, then second-guesses, staying behind the island.

Good idea, Pops.

"I just want to start out by saying none of this was planned, and while we're extremely happy, we never meant to hurt anyone or to leave anyone out."

"Mom..." the little witch sitting on her stool growls at her mom.

Daphne doesn't look at her, keeping her glistening eyes on my father. *What the hell does she see in him?*

"While Daphne and I were out at our conference a few weeks ago in Las Vegas, one thing led to another, and, well, we eloped."

I push my cereal bowl away from me, the spoon rattling as it slides across the table.

It's pure silence in the room, no noises heard. It's so quiet I can hear my eyelashes slap against my cheekbones.

One.

Two.

Three.

Four.

Vera forces her stool back, and it groans against the floor.

"Where are you going?" her mom asks, a hint of panic in her tone.

"Where are my cigarettes?" Vera asks with no emotion. No happiness, or sadness, or irritation. Just a pure blank face as she asks her question.

I lick my lips, my eyes trailing down her legs.

Fuck, I hate her so much.

"I threw them away. Honey, listen—"

Vera puts her hand up in the air, and all the noise in the room ceases. Her face is a void. There is nothing there. It's eerie. A part of me wants to slap her across the face to see if I can gain a reaction from her. The other part of me wants to bend her over and fuck her in those tights and that skirt to see if her pussy is as cold as her personality.

I hate her. I hate the look of her.

I hate her so much, I might have to kill her.

"I don't care. Anything you have to say, I don't care." Vera's voice is calm as she speaks to her mom.

Daphne's eyes start to water. "Baby." She steps around the island, walking toward Vera. "I'm sorry. Can we go talk?"

Vera takes a step back. "I have to go to school."

"Malik can take you," my dad pipes up out of nowhere, constantly oblivious to the silent meltdown happening in the room.

"No," both Vera and I say at the same time.

She looks over at me, a look of hatred simmers in her eyes. They're blue. Much bluer than the sky and the lake put together. But right now, they're dripping with venom.

Good.

My nostrils flare, and I curl my teeth around my lip. "She can walk."

"Malik," my dad cautions.

My gaze goes to him, and I want to flip this table over in outrage. He knows he has no control over me, so attempting to gain some in the presence of others makes me want to prove him otherwise.

"You will take her to school." His eyes widen, a warning in his irises.

I glance at Vera, hating watching her stand there, in my kitchen, with her tiny outfit on, her arms folded across her chest and a heavy frown on her face.

"Fine." I push my chair back and glare at Vera. "Let's go."

Shoving past her, I stomp outside as I fish the keys from my pocket. Walking down the steps and underneath the archway, I hop into my Range Rover. Stupidly, my father has an identical one. It hums to life, purring beneath me, and I swear it makes me fucking hard.

I shift into drive, turning on one of my playlists and tapping my finger on the steering wheel.

And wait.

Really, bitch?

Then the door swings open, and I listen as the doorknob pounds against the wall inside the house. She grabs the handle, slamming the door shut as hard as she can.

Stomping over to me, her dark-rimmed eyes narrow at the slight smirk on my face.

Just as she's about to place her hand on the handle, my foot releases from the brake, and I press on the gas, the car rolling forward and away from her.

She throws her hand in the air. "What the fuck are you doing?"

I roll the passenger-side window down, leaning across the center console and showing her as much of my razor-sharp teeth as I can. Not in a smile, no, in a damn snarl. My eyes drop down to her bare legs, her skirt lightly fluttering in the wind. The thick fabric brushes the tops of her thighs, and I can't stop my eyes as they take in her fishnet tights. They are ridiculously sexy, and the small rips make my fingers twitch.

Did she tear them herself, or did some other hungry fuck rip them with his greedy fingers?

"I don't know where you've been, and from the looks of it, nowhere decent." My tongue dashes out, wetting my lower lip. Vera's eyes narrow in disdain, even while they drop to my lips. Her jaw loosens, going slightly slack as she watches my tongue. "I don't let just anyone settle their ass on my leather seats. A walk might brush the filthy from you. It's about five miles. That way." I point into the woods, knowing she'll never be able to find her way.

Pressing on the gas again, the smoke from the exhaust momentarily clouds her image in my rearview mirror. Once the smoke clears, I see Vera with both hands up in the air, her dirty middle fingers raised directly at me.

I roll my window down, lazily sticking my middle finger in the air back at her.

Fuck her. Fuck her mother.

She's not just a new roommate. She's my damn stepsister.

The thought makes me shiver.

I hate that I want to tear between her legs. I hate that she catches my eye at all. More than anything, I hate that I hate these feelings. I don't want to feel anything toward her.

I want to hate her, and I do.

I shake my head, clearing my unnecessary thoughts. All I need to focus on is getting her out of here. Any girl who isn't from around here would flee in a fucking second.

For some reason, I don't think Vera will. I don't think she will at all.

7

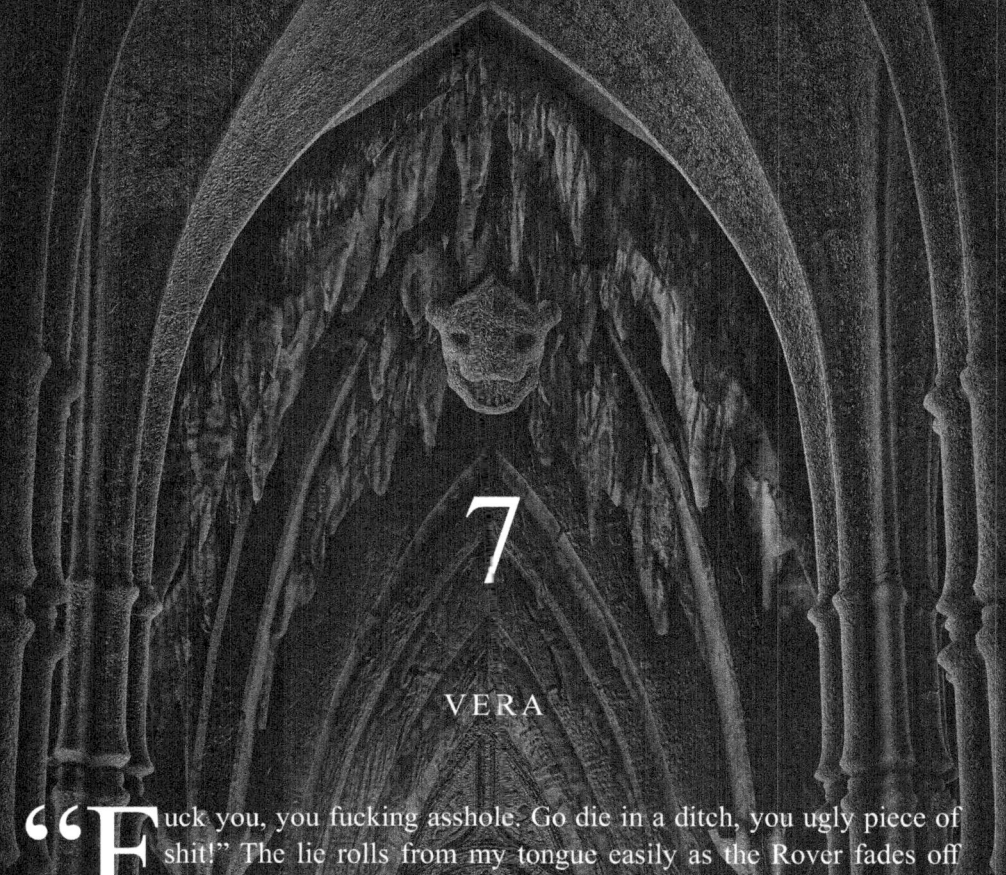

VERA

"Fuck you, you fucking asshole. Go die in a ditch, you ugly piece of shit!" The lie rolls from my tongue easily as the Rover fades off around the trees.

I can literally feel the steam rolling out of my ears. I spin around, my teeth grinding as I walk toward the door. I see the garbage bins tucked around the corner of the house, and I cut right, heading straight toward them.

I lift the brown lid, seeing my white and red pack of Marlboros and my white lighter sitting directly on top of a black garbage bag.

I chuckle. "Idiot."

I grab them, pulling a cigarette from the pack and instantly lighting it up. Stomping toward the house, I open the door, walking inside with my cigarette in hand.

Glancing up, I see my mom pressed against the island with Samuel's hand snaked beneath her skirt, gripping one of her ass cheeks in his large palm.

The sole of my boot goes up, and I shove the door closed with a bang. He flings back from my mom, not looking the least bit concerned. He should be.

My mom looks embarrassed and a little sad as she stands up straight, righting her skirt back into place.

"Vera? What're you… What's going on?" She takes a step toward me, her eyes dropping to my hand as she notices the burning cigarette pinched between my fingers. "Are you smoking in here?" she shrieks.

I bring the cigarette up, taking a heavy drag and blowing the smoke out through my nose. "Yes."

She looks at Samuel. "I'm so, so sorry, Sam. Vera, put that out right now. Where did you get those?"

Samuel starts walking toward me, and I stand up straighter. My mom rushes behind him, her heels clapping against the ground. I bring the cigarette up for another drag when Samuel reaches up, plucking the cigarette from between my fingers. His arm snakes behind me, opening up the door and tossing my cigarette outside. "We do not smoke in here," he mumbles in my ear. His tone makes shivers run down my spine. It's threatening. No-nonsense.

He is the boss of this fucking castle; that's what his tone says.

"Samuel, this is so embarrassing." She buries her face in her hands before looking up at me, a heavy glare on her face. "Whatever you think you're doing, just stop, right now. Why aren't you on your way to school? Malik was supposed to drive you." She takes a huge breath, her chest shaking from irritation. "More than that, why the hell do you think it's okay to smoke in the house?"

My hand lifts, and drops back down, slapping against my thigh. "He left."

She narrows her eyes. "And you didn't want to get in the car with him?"

My blood starts humming, and if Samuel wasn't standing right there looking ominous, and honestly, slightly scary, I might lash out at her.

I glare at him. "I tried. He left me in the driveway."

Samuel's eyes narrow. I watch as his jaw grinds and his entire body stiffens to stone.

My mom looks up at him. "Well, there has got to be some sort of mistake. Maybe he didn't see you or something. Don't worry, I'll take you."

Samuel raises his hand. "Don't worry about it. You have to get to work. I'll take her."

My mom's eyes widen, and my blood runs cold.

Well, this day keeps taking a turn for the worse.

He walks over to the end table against the wall in the front entryway, grabbing his keys from a small bowl sitting in the center. "Let's get going, then. Don't want to be late on your first day."

I look at my mom, pleading for her to take me instead. I don't want to ride in the car alone with him. His son seems like the devil, I can't imagine the type of evil this guy is.

"I think that sounds great. Thank you, Samuel. Have a good day at school, Vera." She leans in, pressing a kiss against my hair. "Behave." Her fingers grip my bicep, giving me a tight squeeze.

What I wouldn't give to light her hair on fire.

My mom steps back, and Samuel's already standing behind me, holding the front door open as he waits for me. I give my mom a menacing glare. What kind of a terrible person does she have to be to constantly put the blame on me?

I walk out, lowering my head to the ground as I follow Samuel to his black Rover. He unlocks the door, and it makes an expensive click as the locks disengage. I open the door, a whiff of clean leather invading my senses as I slide into the seat, sitting as close to the door as I can. I press my elbow against the window, my chin settling into my palm as I stare outside. I don't want the small talk. I don't want to talk to him at all, actually.

He settles into his seat, letting out a breath that makes its way to me. Mint and coffee. He says nothing as he starts the car and pulls out of the driveway.

Once we hit the main road, a fog covers the area. It's thicker than it was yesterday. So dense I can barely see mere feet in front of me. I watch the thickness cover the car, trapping us in a dim cloud.

"You shouldn't be so hard on your mother."

I press my chin into my hand even harder. He has no right. *No fucking right.*

"You don't know her," I mumble.

He lets out a puff of air. Like he's laughing or something. *What the hell is funny?*

"On the contrary. I've known her for about a year now. I think I know her pretty well, despite what you might believe."

This time my arm drops, and I swing my eyes to his. "You *don't* know her."

His smile drops, and he lifts his eyebrows as he glances at me. "I know that your disrespect toward her is uncalled for. I know that you have no sense of authority. I know that while you're living under my roof, you're going to treat me, your mother, my son, and my house with respect. No more smoking in my house. No more being rude to your mother. She's been through enough."

My hand goes to the door handle. Just as I'm about to open the door of the moving car, Samuel slaps on the lock button. "You do not want to get lost in these woods, Vera. That's the very last place you want to wander off to."

"Anywhere would be better than here," I whisper. Because it's true. *She's been through enough?* Fuck him and his opinions. He doesn't know anything about our past. He doesn't know anything about anything. He found a young woman he can take advantage of, and that's exactly what he's chosen to do. He doesn't know me.

He doesn't know me.

The fog remains thick as we travel through town. Samuel drives down the roads with ease, no sense of hesitation in his twists and turns as the roads curve and curl around trees. I can't see into the forest, only the tops of the pine trees peeking through the fog.

Soon enough, the fog clears slightly as a brick building comes into view. Samuel turns left into the parking lot, and my lips slouch into a frown at the sight in front of me. The Catholic school is large, tall and wide with old, gray bricks expanding the entire perimeter. The top peaks of the building are pointed. All of them small with one of the main points being larger, with a huge, oxidized metal cross sitting on top. To the left sits an oversized bronzed bell, weathered from however many years this atrocity has been standing.

"You've got to be fucking kidding me," I mumble.

"The school does not tolerate cursing of any kind. I suggest you swallow down your words before you enter."

My nostrils flare as I glare at him. "Maybe it'll get me expelled, and I can go back home. Thank you for that insight."

He smirks. "They don't expel here, Vera. They punish. Maybe it'll be good for you."

Punish?

Punish how?

"Would you like me to walk you into school? Help you find your way to the office?" he asks as he parks in front of the entrance.

I wrap my fingers around the straps of my bag, wishing I could run out of this town. But Samuel's words stuck to me, which I know is what he hoped for.

That's the very last place you want to wander off to.

I open the door, stepping out without looking at him. "I think I can manage on my own."

I can feel his smile on my back. "See you at dinner, Vera. Have a good day at school."

I slam the door shut. No kids lingering outside. No one smoking at the end of the parking lot. No groups of friends hanging out in their cars.

What kind of a weird-ass school is this?

I walk up the steps, the brick worn and cracked. There's a railing in the middle, the metal paint chipped. I know if I glided my hands across it, the chips of paint would shred across my palms.

I keep my hands on the straps of my backpack as I head toward the entrance. Opening the front door, I grunt once I realize how heavy the wood is. Once I step into the hallway, I notice it's completely silent. No kids, no hall monitors. Nothing.

Shit.

This place.

This place is unlike anything. A literal castle sits in front of me. Large brick stairs, twelve feet in length, lead to a second level. The railing is made of stone, a solid gray that's sculptured with the sharpest edges. The *entire* building is stone. Not the painted white bricks at my old school, with school mascots and posters littering each wall. No, there is no *school* anything on these walls.

It's all religion.

Crosses and paintings of Jesus Christ sit elegantly on the walls, but there are only a few, the rest is bare. The ancient, Gothic structure so tall and ominous I wonder how this could be a school at all. It feels like I stepped into another time, another world. It doesn't feel real.

How could a place like this be up to code for schooling kids? It's not even bright enough in the building. It's dim, the dark gray walls feel like they swallow me as the door shuts and clicks behind me.

What the hell did my mom get me into?

I glance left, seeing a small window that looks somewhat like a main office. I step toward it with a stomach full of lead, opening the door.

Holy shit.

Emphasis on holy.

She's decked out in the nun dress. Her black dress covers every inch of her body. The white fabric around her neck is stark white, with a heavy crucifix placed in the center.

"May I help you?" she asks. She doesn't seem friendly. But no one in this town seems to be.

"Uh. It's my first day here."

She looks me up and down, a heavy frown taking over her features. "You must be Vera Lowell." She doesn't seem pleased by this fact.

"I am."

She grabs a piece of paper, placing it on the counter in front of me. "Here's your schedule. You're already late to your first period. I'll give you a pass because it's your first day, but we do not allow tardiness, Ms. Lowell."

"My ride left without me," I deadpan.

She stares at me, her face stiff with thick lines around her eyes and mouth. "Like I said, I'll give you a pass because it's your first day. Tomorrow we will expect you on time."

I grab the piece of paper from the counter, sliding it off and letting it crumple beneath my palm. "I heard you."

I start walking toward the door when she calls my name.

My body stiffens with my hand against the handle of the door. I barely glance over my shoulder, but just enough for her to address me. "We have strict guidelines with dress code here. I think you're violating just about every policy we have. I also expect you to come to school tomorrow without those tights on your legs and some suitable shoes, and please, lower your skirt to its appropriate length."

I walk out, letting the door slam behind me.

No. No, I will not.

She doesn't call my name again, so I walk off, heading down the hall. I glance at the paper in my hand, searching for my locker number. The hallway is dark, like there aren't enough lights in this place. It smells like a church, like the air is covered in a mixture of holy water and Bible pages.

I find my locker, the metal dinged and dented along the door. The paint is chipped on the corners.

I open it after two tries, shivers racking my body from the cool air. A puff of dust slaps me in the face when the hinges creak open. I close it, not sure why I went there anyway. It's not like I have anything to get out of it. Maybe it's just habit. I slam it closed, glancing down at the sheet of paper to find my first class.

History.

I walk down the hall, my shoes squeaking on the black-and-white checkered tiles. My heart rate speeds up once I reach my classroom. I hate this. I've been going to the same school forever, with the same kids and the same teachers. Going here, now, to some weird-ass place with some creepy people, my entire body screams with unease.

I don't know whether to walk in or knock, but I decide to walk in at the last second, interrupting the class as every single eye in the room turns to stare at me.

A nun stands at the front of the class, her outfit the exact same as the woman in the office. She looks me up and down, a look of displeasure taking over her face as she observes my state of dress.

My eyes swing to the students, a mixture of guys and girls sitting in the small desks. The guys wear gray collared shirts with a black tie and black pants. The girls wear the same as I do, skirts, white shirts. But their shoes are nice. Either flats or shorter heels cover their feet.

They are so, so fucking ugly.

I grunt under my breath, wondering how I'll ever gain any allies here if they all dress like they're five steps away from being a nun themselves.

The teacher lifts her hand, wiggling her fingers for the piece of paper in my grasp. I take a step toward her, handing it to her. She glances at it briefly, looking back at my legs, my short skirt, and my shoes.

I think I'm going to dress like this every day, only because they seem so damn enthralled.

"Class, this is Vera Lowell." She turns her gaze toward mine. "You may take a seat in the back."

Thank you.

I grab the paper back from her, sliding in between the aisle of desks as I make my way toward the only empty one in the back of the room. I can feel the eyes of everyone as they stare at me. I can feel their curiosity, their wonder of why I'm here.

I slide into my desk, the silence in the room lingering on too long. I feel itchy, like the eyes of every single person are crawling over my body.

The silence stretches on a few more seconds, until the teacher starts her lesson again. I drown her out. My entire mind goes blank as I stare out the window and into the foggy trees. It feels like I'm in another dimension as I sit here.

Some place people go and never have the chance the leave again. A black hole that I've slipped into with no exit in sight.

I feel like I'll never find my way out.

8

MALIK

The bell rings, and I'm out of my seat, ignoring the girls that want to cop a feel and the guys that want to ask where the next party's at as I head to my locker. Felix already slouches against it, his finger scrolling through his phone.

I can feel Levi and Atticus walking behind me, and together we make our way into our small circle.

"How was it?" Atticus asks, leaning his shoulder against the locker next to mine. One of the guys in a grade lower than us walks toward the locker, and when he notices us, he stops, turns around, and walks the other way.

I glance away from him, opening up my locker and shoving my shit inside. I know he's talking about the new unwanted additions in my home. "Interesting."

Silence.

"Okay? Interesting? Interesting how? Are they weird? Ugly? Rich? Poor?" Felix pockets his phone, glancing up at me with anticipation.

"It was interesting. She's a bitch, and I'm going to enjoy every minute of getting her out of town."

"Who. The fuck. Is that?" Levi asks, not paying attention to a word I'm saying. I follow his eyes, landing directly on my new stepsister.

I snarl, "That's her."

"That's who?" Levi's voice is coated in lust, and for the life of me, I don't understand why I want to jab my pen into his eyes.

"My new roommate. No, my new fucking stepsister."

"What?" All three of them burst out at the same time.

I sigh. "My dad, and her mom," I seethe as I nod toward her with a scowl, "got married last month. Already a done deal."

"I cannot fucking believe I'm saying this, but I have the hots for your sister," Atticus grunts.

I slam my locker closed. "She's not my fucking sister."

"Look at how short her skirt is," Levi groans.

Felix leans in close. "She looks like trouble."

My eyes land on his. "She is, but not for long. She's not staying."

"Does that mean it's game on?" Levi asks.

I take a step away from them. "It was never off. She can dress like a slut all she wants. She can even beg to suck my cock. She's not fucking welcome here."

They look at me in relief. They love our games. I love our games. Toying with people is a part of our lives. Causing people pain is just a part of the game.

I walk up to Vera, the crowd splitting down the middle as they always do for me. She doesn't notice me until the last second, and by then I already have her history book in my hand. Her eyes go wide for a moment before she notices it's me. Her face morphs into an expression filled with rage, her hands reaching out to grab for her book. "Give it back."

I turn away from her, heading toward the bathroom.

"Malik, I'm serious. I'm not playing this game anymore. Give it back."

Oh, baby, the games have only just begun.

I kick open the boys' bathroom door, not even sparing a glance at my confused peers as they watch in horror as Vera follows me on my heels.

"Enough, Malik. Fucking enough!"

I open the stall door—who fucking uses a stall, anyway? Just use the fucking urinal—and see a guy taking a piss, his dick the size of my pinkie.

I stare at him as he takes a leak in the toilet, his pee stopping midstream when I barge into the stall.

"Sucks to suck," I say, dropping Vera's book directly into the piss-filled toilet.

The guy quickly tucks his junk into his slacks when Vera walks into the stall behind me. She sees her book sinking halfway into the toilet and lets out an obnoxious screech. "I fucking hate you!"

I chuckle, shoving past small dick and Vera, leaving the bathroom, and heading back to my locker.

The guys are where I left them, smiles of approval on their faces once they realize what I've done.

"You're going heavy quick, Mal." Atticus laughs.

I grunt. I need to. She needs to be gone. She should've never been here in the first place.

I grab my books for calculus and shut my locker. We start making our way down the hall, most of the hallway already cleared out, except for a few stragglers.

Suddenly, small hands press on my back, trying to shove me in the most pathetic attempt I've ever felt.

"You bastard," Vera growls behind me.

I can hear the guys stop breathing beside me, their bodies frozen at her audacity.

Her fucking audacity.

I slowly spin around, looking down at her red face, her stupid nose piercing, her ridiculous black-and-white hair, and those fucking fishnets that I want to shred with my teeth.

My hand goes up, wrapping around her neck. I shove her backward, until her back slams against the lockers. Leaning in close, I let my body press against hers so she can't even think about going anywhere. My body towers over hers, her shallow breaths hitting the part of my shirt over my pec. Her head inches upward, and I squeeze my fingers until I know she's barely getting any air. Just barely.

My head bends down, until my lips brush against the shell of her ear. She shivers, and it makes me both angry and fucking pleased as hell. "Watch your mouth and watch your hands, baby. I make the rules. I make the game." My other hand wraps around her waist, squeezing her hip bone. "Next time you so much as lay a finger on my body without me telling you to, I might just cut you open, from here," I continue, with my fingers trailing between her legs, pressing against her sex, which is on fucking fire beneath her skirt, up her stomach, between her breasts, until my pointer presses against her plump lower lip. I pinch the thickness, and her jaw slackens. My finger goes over her tongue as I whisper, "To here."

Fire lights in her blue eyes, and she bites down on my finger. Not enough to draw blood, but enough to draw pain, if I felt that type of thing.

"Keep biting, baby. Bite the entire thing off, if you want. I'll make you clean up every last drop of blood."

She spits my finger out. "You're disgusting." Her lips scrunch up, and she spits at me, the warm glob hitting my neck and dripping down beneath my shirt. She smiles at me, a venom in her eyes. A warning. A dare.

I press my fingers further into her neck, cutting off her circulation completely. I want to squeeze until her vocal cords disintegrate in my palm. I want to end her life, and I barely even know her.

I shove off the lockers, leaving her slouched against them, chest heaving, cheeks reddened. "And you're a slut begging for some cock with that short skirt of yours. Your best shot at survival is to go back to wherever you came from."

"I hate you," she growls.

I ignore her, walking back to the guys. They watch me, not used to seeing me so aggressive so early on.

They don't realize that she's pressed my buttons. Every single one. They don't know that she's digging underneath my skin.

I need to get rid of her.

Fast.

9

VERA

My fingers press against my neck, where my skin is hot but my blood runs cold. I'm sure there are red fingerprints.

That asshole. What I wouldn't give to drown him in the toilet, right next to my history book and the bowl full of urine. He's big, though—strong. I can put my fist in his face, maybe even knock out a tooth if I hit him at the right moment.

I left the book in the toilet, right beside the kid with the small dick. He can finish peeing on it, or whatever he wants to do. All I know is that this school sucks, the people suck, my new stepfather and stepbrother, fucking suck.

My hand drops from my neck, and I pull my backpack from my shoulder. Yanking the crumpled-up schedule from my bag, I glance down to figure out my next class.

Great. Science.

I crumple it back up and shove it in my bag, once again walking through the empty hallway as I search for the science room.

This time the door is open, and the teacher is busy doing something at the front of the classroom, so I'm able to sneak in the back and slide into one of the desks. Eyes are still on me, though, watching my every move. I don't pay attention to any of them, keeping my eyes averted to my desk as I pull out my phone.

I don't have service here. I haven't had service since we got into this stupid town.

What's wrong with this place?

The teacher stands up, and luckily, I'm sitting behind some tall guy, so she doesn't notice me as she starts the class.

"Hey," comes a voice from beside me.

I don't look. Don't even act like I can hear where it's coming from as I clutch my phone in a tight grip. I don't want to deal with anyone right now. Not when my blood hums with a murderous rage.

The fucking balls of Malik. He puts his hands on me, thinking he has a power over me. He thinks he's the one in charge? He doesn't know me. He doesn't know what I'm capable of.

Not only that, but he chose to embarrass me in front of his friends. I saw them, the three guys standing behind him who looked like carbon copies of Malik. Their dark hair, their tall forms, the evil emanating off each of them.

Malik is more, though. He's a little taller, a little darker, more ferocious in the way he holds himself. There's a darkness that surrounds the town, but there's this separate… entity that clings to Malik and every single thing he does.

Part of me is drawn to him. To the darkness. My curiosity is boundless, and when it comes to Malik, it's even more so. But the other part of me wants to see him suffer. The boy who is cruel to the core. I can see it in the way he looks at me. He likes to torture. He plays games, and he likes to win.

Unfortunately, I like to win, too. And I don't go down easily without a fight.

I snap out of my thoughts when I hear the same whisper again. "New girl," comes from beside me.

My head lolls to the side. The sole of my boot presses against the metal foot on the desk, and I tap my foot in irritation, making the entire desk shake. It's a rickety old thing, pencil carvings along the edges. Something that should've been burned fifty years ago, but for some reason, they still allow kids to sit on it.

A girl sits at her desk, a bright smile on her face while she stares at me. She has dark hair, with thick bangs cut directly at her eyebrow. She's wearing the same outfit as me, although hers is how it's supposed to be, with the buttons on her shirt done up all the way to her neck, and the skirt underneath her desk brushing her knees.

I'm about to turn away from her, when she adjusts her arm, and I see the tiniest tattoo scrawled on the inside of her wrist.

My eyes widen, and I lean in further. Finally, someone normal.

"What's your name?" she asks, pressing her chin into her palm, a smile still gracing her lips.

"Vera. Yours?"

"Hazel. Where are you from?"

"Fargo," I whisper. "What's up with this place? It's weird."

She nods. "I'd say you'll get used to it, but you never really do. I, uh, I saw you fighting with Malik in the hall. How do you know him?"

I chew on the corner of my lip, hesitating on whether I should tell her my whole story yet. I mean, she could secretly be screwing Malik behind closed doors. She might walk out of here and walk straight to him and tell him everything I say to her.

But something about her makes me know I can trust her. "He's my stepbrother."

Her eyes widen, and she leans back in her seat, her back pressing against the black metal of the chair that digs uncomfortably into your spine.

Her wide eyes lower, and her mouth screws up into a wince. "That seriously sucks."

I nod. "What's his deal?"

She shakes her head. "Don't ask."

I lower my head, tilting closer to her. My fingers curl around the edges of the desk, the wood worn and jagged against my skin.

"I live in his house. *My mom* lives in his house. I have a right to know if there's something wrong with him. If he's... dangerous or something."

She doesn't even blink. "He *is* dangerous. The friends he hangs out with, they're dangerous. His father, their parents, dangerous. But Malik, himself? I don't think there is a good side to him."

A throat clears, and we both look up, seeing the teacher standing beside my desk, staring at the both of us with a heavy frown. "I'm sorry, we haven't met. I'm Sister Marjorie. You are?"

"Vera," I grumble, folding my arms across my chest.

Just like everyone else in this school, she looks at my outfit with a lick of disgust in her gaze. Her mouth opens, like she's about to reprimand me.

"You don't have to say it. Everyone has already bitched about my outfit today."

A ruler comes down, and I can hear the whistling in the air as the wood flies toward my skin. It slaps my knuckles of the fingers that are curled around the edge of the desk.

My mouth flies open, a yelp squeaking out as my fingers uncurl from the desk. I shake them out, rubbing at the red marks along my fingers with my other hand. "What the fuck?"

Her hand snaps out, her long, cold fingers wrapping around my wrist. My eyes widen as I look up at her. Her skin feels so cold, like she's dead. I glance at her face, double-checking to make sure she's really alive.

She presses her hand on my wrist, pinning it to the desk. Her other hand grips the ruler, and brings it down, slapping my already throbbing skin a second time.

"Foul language is not acceptable here. I suggest you don't use it a third time, unless you want your skin to break."

My body starts to shake, and I rip my hand from hers. "You can't do this."

"I just did," she says. Her words are ominous, like a promise of what else is to come. The black veil of her dress cloaks around her face, darkening her pale skin behind the shadows of her clothing.

I grab my bag, ready to book it out of here, when she presses her hand on my shoulder. "What is your name?"

A lashing remark rolls around on my tongue, but I appease her, only because the bones in my fingers feel broken. "Vera."

She nods. "Vera. I'm not sure where you've come from, or what it was like where you lived. But here at Castle Pointe Academy, the students behave and follow the rules. If you feel like straying from your thin line, well, there will be severe consequences."

"So, you abuse children? That's what gets you off in this place? Bruising and beating kids?"

She smiles, her fingers digging into my collar bone. It feels like she's pressing an evil sentiment into me, and it makes me nauseous with pain.

"Call it what you like. You will not speak to me in that tone again." I stare up at her, seeing her pale gums, dried with her thin teeth glaring down at me.

I look away, not sure what she's capable of. But for the first time, I don't really want to find out.

I swallow, lowering my head and nodding into my desk.

She releases me after one last squeeze, walking toward the front of the class to continue her lecture.

"When class is over, follow me," Hazel whispers, and I give her a barely noticeable nod, keeping my head tilted down until the end of class.

The bell rings, but it's not from one of the electronic alarms that rings over the speakers. It's the old-school bell that thrums against the cast iron material, loud and slow as it bangs once, twice, three times.

Sister Marjorie stares at me as I stand up from my desk. I avert my eyes, walking behind Hazel as we leave the room.

I don't head to my locker. I want nothing to do with the kids, or the teachers, or even Malik right now. Sister Marjorie's warning put me off, made me feel incredibly creeped out. I want nothing but to leave. Even going back to the creepy mansion in the woods and curling in my own bed would suffice. But being here right now…

I shiver, chills breaking out along my body.

"It's lunch time. Let's go outside," Hazel says from in front of me. I follow her through the halls and out the back door. We don't even grab food from the cafeteria, just bypass everyone and everything and walk right outside.

My eyes widen when I see the school is on the edge of Superior. Up on a hill, near rocks and not much else. The sight makes me dizzy, how far suspended we are into the sky when I didn't even realize it. The rocks are sharp below us, one trip over the edge and you'd split into a hundred pieces. There is no surviving the leap.

The fact that students linger near the edge, without a care or worry in the world, only makes my stomach shake further.

"You can stick with us from now on. This place will eat you alive if you only stick to yourself," Hazel says, walking toward two girls off to the side, sitting on a large rock.

"What do you mean, *this place*?"

She looks over her shoulder, her dark hair blowing in her face. It's windy, the breeze whistling against the heavy trees. The cool air raises goosebumps along my chilled skin. "I meant exactly what I said, Vera. This place has its own rules. You have to follow them."

"And if I don't?" My heart starts beating fast, and glancing down, I can see the flutter against my shirt.

"Then goodbye."

We reach the rock, and Hazel sits down on the edge. I stand in front of it, staring at the two girls that are watching me with curiosity.

"You're the new girl? Vera?" a girl with long, bright red hair asks. She's pretty, with a speckling of freckles along the bridge of her nose.

"Obviously. We never have new people." Hazel rolls her eyes.

"I'm Blaire," says the redhead.

I nod. "Vera." Looking over my shoulder, I expect Sister Marjorie or any of the other nuns to be lingering behind me, ready to hit me again. There isn't anyone there, though. Only other students, but I'm still uneasy. Glancing down at my knuckles, I see a purple bruise already forming. "Can I smoke here?"

Blaire shrugs. "Why not?"

I flash my hand. "I'd rather not get beaten to death by a group of nuns."

"See these rocks?" Blaire points to the huge stones in front of us, some as tall as my knees, others go up to my waist. All are different sizes and shapes. Some look smoothed over, nearly shiny. Others look full of dirt and sand.

"What about them?" I ask.

"Where the grass cuts off from the rocks is the end of the boundary for the school. They can't touch us over here, no matter how badly they want to."

I rub my fingers along the bruises on my knuckles. Blaire notices and winces. "Sister Marjorie?" I nod. "She loves her ruler. Just make sure you don't get on Sister Mary's bad side. She likes to put you in The Room of Atonement."

My eyes widen. "What the fuck is *The Room of Atonement*?" I think back, feeling like her name sounds familiar. "I think I had her first period."

"History?" Hazel asks.

I nod.

She shakes her head. "Seriously, don't get on her bad side. I swear she enjoys putting people in The Room of Atonement. They come out pretty fucked up."

"What is The Room of Atonement?" I repeat. I feel like screeching the words. Maybe jumping off the ledge isn't such a bad idea, after all.

They all shake their heads. "I don't know what The Room of Atonement is. But you go there, and it fucks you up real good," Hazel mumbles.

I drop my bag to the rocks with shaky fingers. Unzipping the top, I pull out my pack of cigarettes and lighter. "I need to get the hell out of here."

A dark-haired girl stands up from the rock and walks over to me. She lifts her hand, palm out and asks, "Can I bum a cigarette?" I lift an eyebrow, placing one in her hand. I light mine up and pass her the lighter.

"Even though it's never been confirmed, people die in that room. People say the old sisters come back from the dead and tear you apart," she whispers.

"That's just a fucking rumor, Piper. No one knows if those people *actually* died in there." Blaire rolls her eyes.

Piper lights up her cigarette, glancing down at the white lighter with a smile before passing it back to me. "Did you ever see those kids again, Blaire? No, you didn't. Because they fucking died. It's not a rumor. This place, this entire town and everyone in it, is haunted. Whether or not you want to believe it."

It feels like I'm being cloaked with something sinister as she says these words. Like an invisible blanket of noxious venom is spreading over my skin in a sticky substance that I can't shake off.

Piper watches me as she takes a drag of her cigarette. "I'm Piper. I moved here about five years ago. You seem like me, like you want to leave this shit place the first chance you get?"

I nod, eyes narrowed as I take a drag.

She shakes her head. "That was my hope at first, too. Until I came to realize that the people who come here only leave to be buried. Unless you want to jump." She points over the side of the cliff. "There's no other way that you'll leave. I didn't want to believe it, but once you're in this place long enough, you'll figure it out. The sun doesn't shine the same. The rain doesn't fall the same. The wind doesn't blow the same. This place, it shouldn't exist, but it does. And now you're living in it."

"Can't you just walk out? Like, literally, walk out of here?" I ask, turning around and looking at the school. I stub my cigarette out as I watch the kids sit on the front steps, their trays of food propped on their laps as they eat and converse with each other. It's like they're puppets, or robots, playing their games, following the rules.

It's not how I live. I live by my own guidelines.

I notice Malik's Range Rover, with him and his friends sitting on the hood. As if he notices I'm staring, he turns his head, glaring at me from across the yard. His friends look after a moment, too. All of them sending me the same look, like they're hoping I catch on fire at any moment, combust into flames. Maybe plummet over the side of the rocks.

"Holy shit," Blaire whispers. "What the hell did you do to get on his bad side?"

"That's her new stepbrother," Hazel says.

Blaire and Piper scoff. "Well, this is an interesting turn of events," Piper says.

"Trust me, I hate it. He's a piece of shit, and I want nothing to do with him." I glare at him, watching as he glares straight back. We're in this void, where only the two of us exist. He sees me, and I see him. There's no school, there're no students. It's just us, in a space full of hate and misery.

"I don't think I can say the same for him. It looks like he wants to swallow you whole," Piper breathes.

"Or chop your body into pieces," Blaire chimes in.

"And scatter you across Superior." Hazel chuckles.

I smile. "He can try, but I'll be the one to tear him apart. I'll enjoy watching him fall to pieces at my feet."

Hazel makes a noise in her throat. "I like you. You'll fit in good here, with us."

I look back at them, the three girls who are the only ones who seem somewhat normal. The only ones who talk to me in this strange town. I like them, and I want to befriend them. But I also don't want to get too close, because I don't plan to stay here long.

10

MALIK

Her skirt flutters in the breeze, going so high up her fishnet-covered thighs, I swear an inch higher, and I'd be able to see her panties. What does she wear? Granny panties? No, I know for a fact she doesn't. She's the type of girl that'll wear something scandalous. Something that shouldn't be worn by a seventeen-year-old girl. She'll be a bit risky with what she wears underneath her clothes, and I know it, because from the way she stands, and what she has on as she walks past the nuns and the crosses plastered to every wall of this morbid place, she has no fucking innocence in her.

Not one drop.

She sneers at me, and Felix chuckles. "She wants your cock."

I sigh. "I'd rather fuck Sister Mary."

"I'd fuck your sister, Mal. Maybe we could be real brothers someday." Atticus cackles.

A fire ignites in my stomach, and I want nothing more than to run him over with my car right now. Not because I like the bitch, no, but because the thought of her sliming her way into any of my friends makes me want to tear her apart with my bare hands.

"You fuck her and I'm not taking your ass to the doctor when your dick is about to fall off." I don't spare him a glance, keeping my eyes on the witch in front of me. She breaks eye contact, turning around and talking to the three girls in this place that will only cause Vera more trouble.

Those girls are trouble, though they seem to keep their heads down in the school. I know for a fucking fact Vera is trouble. Together, they'll just corrupt each other completely. Maybe burn the fucking town down.

Whatever.

I slide off the hood of my car, running my hands through my dark hair as I glance up at my friends. "Doesn't matter, anyway. She's not going to be here long enough for any of us to put our dicks in her."

I can still feel her dried-up spit against my chest.

I clench my fists, feeling like the only thing I've been thinking about all day are ways I can get back at her. Ways to punish her. I hate myself for wanting one of them to be bending her over and turning her ass purple.

My dick twitches in my pants, and I sneer at the ground, wishing she would've never shown up in the first place. Why couldn't she have been some innocent girl that prays for good fortune and bathes in holy water? I would've scared that girl away the first night.

This girl. Vera. It's like she wants to play my games. The vibe around her is toxic, and I'm worried I've already become tainted.

My pen digs into my lined paper, and I scribble down a mindless chemistry formula. I'm so tired of school, and at the end of the day, I don't even need to be here. I'm going into business with my father, and you don't need a high school education to become a real estate agent or become a millionaire. But he nails into me time and time again that I need my diploma.

So, here the fuck I sit.

But then, why do I listen to him, anyway? He's a piece of shit in his own way, and I can't wait until he gets too old to run his business. I'll swipe it out from beneath his feet and watch him wither away in a corner as he grows frail and incompetent.

I tap the end of my pen into the paper, my body too big for these small, square desks that have been in this building since before Castle Pointe even existed.

I think before this town was established there were a ton of pilgrims living on the land. Rumors of black magic and witchcraft have been spread for years. I don't care about a word of it, to be honest. The town is fucked and whether or not there was some evil shit going on hundreds of years ago, it doesn't change what the town is now.

And now, today? We live among the dead. Except the dead never sleep.

I glance down at my paper, every tap of the pen creating a black dot, smudging the work I've only half worked on. I sigh, growing restless as the end of the day grows near. I should've bowed out at lunch like Levi suggested, but after a day or two of not showing up, Father Norris usually calls my father, and then my father feels like being extra fatherly for a few days.

That is until he grows bored and goes back to being disinterested in everything except his company. And I guess now Daphne can be added to the list as well.

My eyes glance up when something catches my attention. Through the glass window I see Vera, with the wooden rectangle dangling in her hand that says 'bathroom'. That looks like the last thing she needs, though. The overwhelmed look on her face makes me think she's using it as an excuse to take a breather. Like this day has been the day from hell.

I nearly laugh.

I stand up, ignoring Sister Maxine as I head to the door. She knows not to mess with me. Everyone knows not to mess with me. Any issue and they take it straight up with my dad.

I open the door, feeling everyone's silent eyes on me as I walk into the hall. I pull on the handle, slamming the door shut behind me enough to rattle the glass on the windows.

That'll earn a phone call to my father.

Vera is already gone from the hallway, and I walk quietly, looking down every corner and in every empty room.

She's nowhere.

I stop in front of the girls' bathroom. It's like my body starts thrumming, a mixture of rage and something else I don't want to examine start pounding beneath my skin.

Here she is.

My hand goes to the metal handle, and I slowly pull it open. It barely squeaks, only slightly. I slip inside quietly and let the heavy door knock against my foot to silence it as it closes. I stand as quietly as I can as the smell of cigarettes instantly invades my nose.

My lip curls, a smile crosses my face.

I take a step forward, my shoes pressing against the floor so softly, so silently.

"Uh, hello?" Her voice rings out, unease and hesitation in her tone.

I take another step, not sure what my motives are, but the anger in my blood screams to be set free.

"Who's there?" she asks again. Her feet slam on the ground, and I imagine she was propped up against the back of the toilet. The tiny window on the top of the wall is cracked open, like that's going to lessen the heavy smell of cigarette in the slightest.

Idiot.

I take one more step, and I can smell her fear behind the stall. The metal is a faded gray, banged up and old as dirt. I know the small hinge on the other side barely hangs on. One heavy breath and the door will blow open.

"Quit fucking around. I'm taking a shit!" she shouts.

My foot lifts, and I kick the bottom of the door. The hinge cracks as the door swings open, slamming against the wall. Vera screams, her hands raising in the air. The cigarette poised between her fingers sits there, a trail of smoke swirling from the cherry.

"I imagine your shits smell more like death and less like a Marlboro Red."

She stands up straight when she notices it's me. Taking another drag, she blows it directly in my face. It makes my eyes dry up, and I inhale the smoke through my nose.

"What do you want?" she growls.

"You. Out of my town." I take a step into the stall, getting directly in her face. "You, out of my life." I snatch her wrist, her free hand without the cigarette. I pull it up to my neck, where she spit on my chest earlier. It's still there, dried, barely noticeable unless you put your finger on it. I smash the tips of her fingers against my neck, trailing it down the dried spit below my shirt. "Your spit has been lingering on my skin for hours. Do you know what it feels like, to have someone spit on you that you absolutely despise?" I press on the tip of her finger, until the nail scrapes my skin, just enough to incite pain. "You should be getting on your knees and praying to God that I let you live to see another day."

She leans into me, her fingers curling around the neck of my shirt. She pulls down, yanking me toward her. "I think it's you that needs to bend your knees, big brother, and hope you make it to the end of this game in one piece."

An intense burning hits the side of my neck, and my eyes widen in outrage when I see she's pressed the cherry of her cigarette against my skin. I bat her hand away, the cigarette flying from her fingers and landing on the ground.

"You bitch," I growl, grabbing her silky hair in my fingers and pulling her neck back as far as her body allows. Then I pull a little further. "You really have no idea who you're dealing with, do you?"

Spinning her around, I pin my front to her back. She stiffens when she feels my hard cock, but that only makes me push harder. "Don't worry, baby, this isn't for you. Pain turns me on."

My hand goes to her waist, and I bend her over, my hand curling into her stomach until her head suspends over the toilet. I should drown her in here, let her atone for her sins. Suspend her in the water of the Catholic school and hope it's holy enough to cleanse her.

"Stop," she barks at me. Her feet kick back in an attempt to shove me out of the way.

I laugh. "You'll never gain the upper hand, Vera."

She kicks me again, this time connecting with my shin. I swallow down a grunt, the heel of her boot hitting the bone. She brings her foot up to the toilet, pushing off as hard as she can. I shuffle back a few steps, off balance and caught off guard.

She spins around, her hair still in my hand. Her fingers raise to my cheek, and she claws at my face. "You son of a bitch. Let go of me!" she screams.

My hand falls to my pocket, and I pull out my switchblade, opening it and pressing the black metal against her jugular. The tip presses against her skin, and she freezes, her entire body coiled tight with tension and fear.

"I have to say, I'm surprised. I knew you liked to fight, but I didn't know you liked to play dirty," I rasp, my heart beating heavy and fast and my dick hard as a rock. I could bend her over the toilet and stain her skirt in my cum. Let her walk around and show everyone the type of girl I know she is.

Her hands raise in the air, ever so slowly. "Please, let me go. I don't want to play your games. I just want you to leave me alone."

"How can I leave you alone, when everywhere I turn, there you fucking are?" I press the tip in deeper, wanting so badly to draw blood.

Suddenly, the door swings open, and there stands Sister Mary and Sister Maxine, heavy lines of disapproval lining their eyes.

"What in the world is going on here?" Sister Mary asks, her eyes widening when she sees the state we're in.

I drop my knife, folding it and slipping it back in my pocket. I release Vera, stepping back from her and righting my clothes. "Sister Mary, Sister Maxine." I go to walk out, when Sister Mary raises her hand.

"Where do you think you're going?"

I level her a look. "I'm going back to class, unless you want to explain to my dad that you kept me from my education? You know how important he believes it is."

She drops her hand, knowing the power my dad has over this town. Over this school. No one messes with him.

No one dares to mess with me.

"Is that… is that smoke I smell in here?" Sister Maxine asks, taking a step farther into the bathroom. She steps in front of the stall, seeing the squished, burnt-out cigarette laying on the floor. "My goodness, who on earth is smoking in here?"

I walk out, leaving Vera to pick up her own pile of shit. I bring a hand up, running it over the burn on the side of my neck. It feels puckered, raw. Like there will be a liquid-filled blister there, at the very least.

I crack my neck, heading back to the classroom, ready for this day to be over with.

Fuck her.

11

VERA

"Is this your cigarette?" Sister Maxine asks me.

I glare at the door behind me, literally boiling on the inside that Malik left me to deal with this on my own. If he never would've came in here, I could've finished my cigarette and left before anyone would even notice me gone.

But no.

He decided to dip out and make me fend for myself.

What a psychopath.

Would he have literally plunged the knife beneath my skin? Would he have let me bleed out on the tiled floor of the girls' bathroom? I bet he would have. I bet he would've smeared my blood across the floor, smooshed the blood between his fingers, maybe even gotten a contact high off the metallic smell in the air.

"Vera, I asked you a question," Sister Maxine says, placing her hands on her hips. The black fabric bunches at her waist.

"It is." I realize I can't lie. I mean, I could blame it on Malik. Say that he was the one who was smoking. They may even believe it, but I don't think anything would ever come of it. The way he walked out of here without even a slap on the wrist. For being in the girls' bathroom, for pressing a knife against a girl's throat. There are no boundaries when it comes to Malik, I realize. None at all.

Sister Mary steps up to me, a thick line pitched between her eyes. "I didn't think it would come to this on the first day, Vera, but I do have to say, I'm not surprised."

I fold my arms across my chest, now irritated as hell that she's not surprised. I'm not like the other kids around here, I fucking get that, but to outright point out that she thinks I'm a rotten seed? *Screw her.*

"Screw you," I sneer at her. "How you guys do shit here is crazy. You realize that, right? I could file charges on you for child abuse. I could shut this shithole down. This isn't how the world runs. This isn't how school is. This shit, it's not right!" I scream.

Sister Mary and Sister Maxine look at each other, a silent conversation running between them. Sister Mary nods and takes a step toward me. "Come with me, Vera."

I take a step backward, my back hitting the cement wall. "No." I shake my head. I glance over my shoulder, at the tiny window I'd never be able to squeeze through. They shift, blocking the door.

Shit.

There's no other way out.

She lifts her hand, her pale white palm outstretched. Her skin is wrinkled, weathered. All their skin has a gray tinge to it, like the toxins running through the air of this town is embedded beneath their flesh.

Like everyone here is… is dead.

I shiver just thinking about it.

"You can come willingly, or you can come unwillingly," Sister Maxine says.

"Where am I going?" Fear sinks in, and for a second, I wish Malik was here. Would he protect me? I want to laugh at the thought. Of course, he wouldn't. He'd never protect me. He'd probably lift me in his arms and help carry me to whatever torture chamber they want to bring me to.

"You'll see." Sister Mary retracts her hand, squeezing them together. Her skin turns a sickly white, and I frown at it.

"I'm not going anywhere. I want to talk to my mom." Surely, she wouldn't let me go anywhere I didn't want to, right? She wouldn't be okay with this shit.

Sister Mary shakes her head. "No, dear. Now come, follow me."

In a split-second decision, I bend down, grabbing the strap of my backpack and make a run for it. My boots squeak along the bathroom tile as my toes punch the ground. Arms, stronger than they should be, wrap around my elbows and haul me back.

"I'm not fucking going!" I scream.

What feels like a ruler lashes against my back, thick and heavy and so fucking strong as it whacks my skin.

My back arches, sharp stinging spreading from my waist to my shoulder blades. I whimper, the pain so bad my fight gives out. They lift me, pulling me from the bathroom and dragging me down the hall. I attempt to get out of their hold, but they walk too fast, and I can't catch my footing. My toes catch the ground every few seconds until I stumble, the tops of my boots trailing along the tile floor.

They pull me upright, and a door is opened. They toss me in, their arms swinging back and letting go of me on the swing forward. I tumble to the ground, my hand instantly going to my lower back. It feels like the lashing ripped through skin. My shirt feels dry, so I don't think so, but it hurts. Really bad.

I scramble to my knees, seeing both the sisters standing in the doorway, the only bit of light I can see from in here.

"Please. I'm sorry." I'm not, not really. But I don't want to be here. Wherever here is.

"You should learn quickly how things are done here. We aren't like other schools, no. But here you are, and our rules, you will listen to. If not, well, you'll be getting acquainted with The Room of Atonement rather quickly," Sister Mary says. The smallest smirk is on her face, a lick of maliciousness rimmed around her eyes. The darkness in the room casts her mouth in shadows, and it looks like her teeth are rotting away.

She looks positively frightening.

With that, they shut the door, encasing me in pitch darkness.

My blood turns cold, along with my skin and my bones. I let out a shaky breath, leaping to my feet, running to the door. My hand searches for the handle. I can't see anything, not even my own body.

"Hello?" I scream.

My hands search the door from top to bottom. It's cold, smooth. It feels thick and heavy against my palm. No window, and searching every inch of the door, no knob either.

My fingers skate around the trim, my nails digging in the crack, but it's no use. This door is sealed and sealed tightly.

"Hello!?" I cry out, my fists pounding as hard as they can. They ache, but I keep going, hoping for someone, even an enemy, to help me.

Even Malik.

"Please! I'm trapped in here! Someone help me!" Tears spring to my eyes, and I'm not someone who cries often. Not out of sadness, and not out of frustration.

But this feeling in my stomach, it's one of hopelessness and utter fear.

I feel a brushing along the back of my neck, like someone lifted my hair and grazed their fingers along my goosebumps-ridden skin.

I fly back around, seeing only darkness. "Who's there?"

Not a noise. Nothing.

But I feel something. I feel so much of something.

I breathe out, feeling like the air in the room drops twenty degrees.

"Hello?" I mumble, barely audible.

Nothing.

I walk along the wall, feeling for something, anything to help get me out of this hell. The moment I get out of here, I'm telling my mom. She's going to get me the fuck out of here, and I'm never coming back.

Not ever.

The wall is cement, old, and slightly damp. It smells like old carpet in here, which doesn't really make sense, since the floor is tile, and the walls are cement.

I hear a breath, almost like a growl, only inches away from me. Directly behind my ear.

My back slaps against the cement, and I bring my hands in front of me, expecting to connect with a body, but all I get is cold air.

"Who's there?" I cry. I can feel the tears streaming down my face, and I don't even have the desire to wipe them away at this point.

After a moment of not hearing anything, I continue walking, my fingers running along the rough, bumpy surface of the cement.

"Ouch," I whisper, shaking my fingers out. I can feel the sliver that's now embedded in my skin, and I blindly reach for the pad of my finger, until I feel the tiny wooden shard and pull it out. "Fucker."

My hand goes to the wall, and it connects with the wooden object. With both hands, I try to pull it off the wall, but it feels like it's cemented there or something.

"What are you?" My fingers run along the outline, and it doesn't take long for me to realize what it is.

A cross.

It's long, about the size of my forearm. The wood is thick, barely smoothed out. No wonder I got a sliver so easily. I try to pull it off again. No luck.

"Wait…" My eyes widen as my fingers hover over the wood. My body snaps back and tremors rack my muscles. "Is this shit upside down?" An upside down cross? In a Catholic church? Are you fucking kidding me?

Panic floods my body, and my breaths comes out in heavy pants as a panic attack takes over.

A burning pain suddenly sears my skin, and a scream tears from my lips. "Ouch! Ohhh, holy shit." I whip around, the back of my head slamming against the wooden cross. I bring my hand to my back, feeling what I know was real.

My shirt is shredded, like a sharp nail sliced straight through the thick fabric. My fingers dance along my skin, against the burning scrape, and this time, they come off wet.

Someone scratched me.

I know it in my bones.

I know what it feels like to scratch at my own skin. An itch? I've had one a million times before. It felt exactly like that, only ten times worse. Someone wasn't scratching me.

Someone was coming after me to make me bleed.

My hand shoots out, thinking this time I'll connect with someone.

I don't.

"Please go away," I cry.

I walk backward, until my back hits the corner of the room. My legs give out, and I fall to my butt, curling my legs up until they hit my chest. I wrap my arms around my legs, curling up into a ball and burying my head into my thighs.

"Go away," I cry.

I hear a laugh, like a raspy chuckle of an old woman who has smoked for too many years. I bury my head in my legs further, knowing even if I look up, I won't see anyone. I won't feel anyone.

There's no one there.

Except there is. I can sense it. I can hear it. This room feels filled with people, and I think it is.

I just don't think any of them are alive.

I hear a latch, and light filters in. I lift my head, shading my eyes with my forearm as I see two black shadows in the doorway.

I rock back and forth with no sense of time or reality.

I've slept, or maybe I haven't. Maybe I've been awake. I have no idea how much time has passed, but it feels like days, maybe a week.

I've felt fingers along my skin, I've felt the brushing of hair slide across my arms. I've heard voices, whispers.

So many whispers.

The two figures walk up to me, grabbing me by the arms and pulling me out of the room. At this point, my body is depleted. No fight is left as they drag me from the hellish room and down the hall, toward the front office.

They open the door, and the nun that sits behind the front desk stands up, my bag in hand. "Here are your things."

"We expect you back here tomorrow and not tardy this time," Sister Mary says, no smile, no apology. Nothing.

I don't plan to come back here tomorrow. But I don't want to tell them this in case they throw me back in hell.

I nod, grabbing my bag from her hands just as the final bell rings. I keep my eyes averted to the ground as I walk outside, down the steps. My legs give out on the last step, and I grab onto the railing, sitting down.

And wait.

Within seconds, the front doors slam open, and a flood of kids start pounding down the stairs around me. Most of them stare at me, turning around once they hit the parking lot to see what happened to the new girl.

I'm sure I look like hell.

How long was I in there for? Has my mom been wondering where I've been?

My body seems to have a permanent chill on it, and I wish for a second that I had one of my oversized hoodies to keep me warm. I unzip my bag, pulling out my pack of cigarettes and lighter. I tap them on my knee, watching the parking lot empty out.

Then he appears.

Malik.

I see him sitting in his car, his friends sitting in the passenger seats. I stand up, walking into the parking lot. They watch me, their faces blank and emotionless.

Please give me a ride home.

I hope to convey my pleading, my temporary truce just long enough to get me home. He turns on his car, and I breathe out a sigh of relief, hoping, praying, that he's waiting for me.

The moment I'm within a few feet of his car, he presses on the gas. His car flies forward, and all I can see are his eyes in the rearview mirror.

"Hey! Stop!" I beg, having no idea where we are in town. No idea where his house is located. Not having the energy or strength to figure it out myself. For once, I want my mom. I just really want my mom.

He doesn't slow down, cutting his car left and flying down the road, leaving me in the dust.

My hands fly into the air and slap down against my thighs. "Now what the fuck am I going to do?"

"He really is a piece of shit, isn't he?" I startle, my entire body shaking as I turn around.

"Holy shit, you scared me." I press my hand to my chest, seeing Hazel, Piper, and Blaire standing there with their backpacks in hand.

"Looks like your ride home bailed. Need a lift?"

I look off into the distance, seeing the lingering dust settling back to the ground.

I grunt, not in the mood for friends right now. Not in the mood to talk to anyone, really. I feel out of it, discombobulated, and a little bitchy, to be honest. The last thing I want to do is snap at these girls who have been nothing but nice to me.

"I'll just call my mom." I pull my phone out of my backpack, unlocking the screen and scrolling down to her name. I press the call button, only for it to beep at me. "Fuck, out of service." I shake my phone in frustration. "Why is there no signal, like, anywhere here?"

Hazel raises her eyebrow. "If you haven't figured that out by now, I might have to reconsider our friendship."

I try one more time, only to get the same results. "It just... doesn't make sense."

"And it never will. Come on, you look like shit. Let us take you home," Blaire says, pulling on my backpack. I follow her, feeling useless and exhausted.

She pulls me to a black Dodge Charger, and I slip into the back seat. I don't talk as Hazel turns on her car and pulls out of the lot. It seems like I don't need to give her directions, like she knows exactly where she's going.

"Can I ask you a question?" Piper asks.

Silence. I turn around, seeing all of them staring at me.

"Oh, what, me? Sure, I guess," I mumble.

"What was it like?" There's an eagerness in her voice, and it confuses me.

"What was what like?"

"The Room of Atonement."

My insides tense, not really wanting to discuss it. Any of it. "Bad. It was bad." I turn back toward the window. "How many days was I in there for?"

"What? Days? You were in there for three hours." Blaire laughs. "Wait, why do you think you were in there for days?"

I turn toward her, my face bunched up in confusion. "That's… that's impossible. It felt like I was in there for nearly a week. There's no way… there can't be…" My voice trails off, confusion making me feel sick to my stomach.

Was it possible I was only in there for a few hours? It can't be true. I could feel the hours ticking by, my internal clock telling me when to sleep and wake up.

It's just… it's impossible.

I shake my head, not sure what's real and what's fake anymore.

"I knew there was something fucked up about that room," Piper growls.

"What happened in there? Anything weird?"

I shiver. "I don't really want to talk about it."

"I hear it's because you were doing drugs in the bathroom," Blaire says.

"Someone said you were having sex in the stall," Piper sighs.

I shake my head. I guess some things are the same in this school. Drama and rumors are bound to happen, I just didn't want them to happen to me. I stay in the cut, low-key. I keep to myself, besides my closest friends.

I hate being the center of attention.

I don't answer their questions or confirm or deny any claims. I just go back to staring out the window, waiting for this nightmare to be over.

Soon enough, Hazel pulls into the long driveway. Malik's car isn't there, and neither are my mom's or Samuel's.

I grab my bag from my lap, putting my hand on the handle before the car even stops.

I smile, not looking at any of them. "Thanks for the ride."

"Hey, Vera," Hazel starts before I can shut the door. I bend down, looking into the car. She looks apologetic, like somehow, she feels at fault for whatever happened to me. "Whatever happened, it's over now. You don't have to worry about it anymore. We won't let anything happen to you again."

I smile, but it feels fake.

"Thanks."

12

MALIK

I fly down the street, heading toward the pier. The smell of marijuana fills the car, and I look away from the rearview mirror. Away from the girl who looked so fucking torn. So wrecked.

Why? How?

She wanted me to die only hours ago. The look in her eyes the last time I spoke to her was full of malice. She looked almost… *beaten*, standing there in the empty parking lot.

"Heard she went to The Room of Atonement." Felix coughs, passing the joint off to Atticus.

My entire body freezes, and my foot lifts from the gas. "What?" I growl at him from the front seat. Felix is as serious as me when it comes to shit. He doesn't play around often, unless we're doing one of our pranks.

That, and he knows how fucked up people get in The Room of Atonement. He loosely dated a chick that went in there last year. She thrashed around and fought every step while he was helpless, standing there in the hallway.

He never saw her again.

"Where'd you hear that?" It was a piece of shit thing for me to do, making her fend for herself in the bathroom against the biggest bitches at Castle Pointe Academy, but one more second around her, and I might have really plunged the knife beneath her skin. It felt so good, the sharp blade, the point against her thin, creamy skin. The flutter of her racing heart was erratic, I could see her vein literally pounding from her neck. How easy it would've been to apply only a little bit of pressure, watch the tip sink beneath the softness of her flesh.

"Fiona saw them dragging her down the hall. Said she wasn't even fighting it."

Levi nudges my shoulder, and I lift my hand, grabbing for the joint.

I pinch the joint too hard as I take a hit. I can barely feel the smoke in my lungs. There's something unfamiliar pounding against my chest. Something that shouldn't be there.

Part of me wants to turn around and fucking demand answers from her about what happened. Shout in her face until she tells me every detail she encountered in The Room of Atonement. No one ever knows what exactly happens in there, but we all know it's fucked up. And no one, I mean no one, comes out the same person.

No one.

Instead, my foot presses on the gas, and I continue on my way to the pier. I don't care, and I can't, at the end of the day. Whatever inkling of feelings I have for Vera is fake, like a phantom pain. It's not real, and the hate I have for her supersedes that feeling.

She's just another problem in my life, and I'm ready for her to get out.

"She already looked like she's cracking. Might be an easier game than we thought." Atticus laughs, and I shake my head, passing the joint back off to Felix.

"We should go get her, play some games with her tonight." Levi chuckles.

Atticus leans forward, his hands going to my headrest. He pulls back, and it shakes my entire seat. "Dude, we could dangle her over the edge of the pier. In the middle of the night? She'd piss herself for sure."

I laugh, the thought of watching her scream until her voice is hoarse. Hearing her beg to me, plead for her life. The thought heats my blood, but then her face flashes in my eyes, the pitiful, broken, horrific look painted in her blue eyes.

Something happened.

"I don't know if she'd survive it after tonight. Probably have a heart attack or something hanging from the edge." I shake my head. "Another night."

Silence.

Levi turns his head, and it feels like slow motion until his eyes land on mine. "Another night?" He barks out a laugh, a sharp, evil sound ripping from his throat. "What the fuck is that?"

I clench my fingers on the steering wheel, hearing my knuckles pop from the force. "I'm drawing it out a bit. I want her to suffer." I bend my neck to the side, showing him the small circular burn on the side of my neck. "She'll fucking get it. But it's going to be on my time. Not anyone else's. Got that?"

His eyes widen. "She did that?"

I nod, turning right onto the pier. "Yeah. But right now, I'm done talking about my bitch of a sister." I see Thea standing there, her legs crossed as she sits on top of her black Grand Cherokee. The side of her thigh is on display, her skirt pushed so high I can see the side of her ass. A couple of the other guys take note of it too, staring too long, double-glancing her way.

I shake my head, disgusted.

I press on the brakes, the hood of my car only inches from Thea's knees. She gives me a sly smirk, not thinking I'd hit her on purpose.

She knows nothing about me.

The guys hop out, and Felix gives me a look over his shoulder. "You coming?"

I shake my head. "I'll come back for you."

He smiles and shakes his head. "If you change your mind about your baby sis, you know where to find us," he says before shutting the door.

I nod my head, and Thea slides off the hood of the Jeep. Her skirt rides up, showing off a hint of her fire red panties. I watch her, my eyes hooded, and my blood humming through my veins. I feel on edge, slightly chaotic, and I hate it. I don't like not feeling in control, and right now, I feel like even the slightest thing will make me snap.

Thea opens the door. "Hey, baby. Where are we going?"

The moment the door shuts, I press on the gas, cutting onto the highway and going directly into the woods. It's gravel, although there isn't much back here. No one ever drives the back roads, usually sticking to the main ones. Driving into the forest means the potential of getting lost.

And things that get lost here never get found.

But I like the mystery. I like the darkness of the trees, so green they seem black in the shadows. I like the constant cover of looming clouds that look so heavy and thick, they'd drown out the entire town if it started to rain.

A lot of the homes in town are abandoned. People who fled many years ago when they realized how toxic this place was. Families who were able to escape before the entire town became cursed. But as time went on, this place only got darker. The air only grew heavier.

"Mal? Where are you taking me?" Thea asks, her fingers reaching out and grabbing onto my thigh. I fly down the road, past abandoned home after abandoned home. There's only one that interests me, and I cut right, driving down the gravel path until we end up in front of my deserted hideout. "What is this place?" She looks at it in disgust, and I swallow down a sigh.

I don't take her here. Only the guys and I know about this place, but for some reason, the chaos inside of me made this the destination for the evening. Unfortunately, she's the one sitting beside me tonight.

"It's just a place," I say, grabbing my keys from the ignition and slipping them into my pocket. I open the door, sliding out without looking back at her. "You can stay in there if you want."

I walk in the already propped open door, noticing the floor is still wet from the last time it rained. I walk to the couch, to the side that's more elevated than the other, and plop down. It smells like mildew, and the cushions are slightly damp as my arms run across the worn fabric. I reach down to the ground, lifting the bottle of whiskey. We always leave a bottle and a bag of green stashed here. On the off chance we come here unplanned, there'll be something if we need it.

Unscrewing the top, I bring it to my lips, swallowing down a few mouthfuls.

"What the hell are we doing here?" Thea walks in, her arms hugging her body as she takes wary steps inside. Her face is scrunched up, her eyes darting to every corner of the room. Her skinny knees knock together as she shivers. "Let's go to my house. My parents are working late."

I shake my head. "Come over here."

Her eyes widen, and she glances at the ground, then the couch. "I don't want to do it here. It's gross."

I sigh, disappointed in her. She flashes her ass to everyone in school but can't even get a little dust and dirt on her knees? Whatever.

I stand up. "I'll take you home, then."

"No, wait." She puts her hand up, shifting from foot to foot. Her eyes dart from me to the couch, to the ground, and back to the couch as she worries her lip. After too many minutes, she comes to some resolution, dropping her arms to her sides and shaking her hands out a bit. "Okay, I'm fine."

I sit back down, kicking my legs out and spreading them.

She slowly walks toward me, swaying her hips as she pulls out her high ponytail. "Fiona said there's a new girl. Have you met her?"

"I live with her."

She stops, her ponytail only halfway freed. It lobs to the side, a frown taking over her face as she stares at me. "What do you mean, she lives with you?" Her voice takes on a possessive tone, and I don't like it.

I lift an eyebrow. "I mean, she sleeps right down the hall from me."

She narrows her eyes.

"She takes showers in the same bathroom I do."

She curls her lip up, taking another step toward me.

It turns me on, her anger. It fuels me, and all I want to do is make her grow so furious she breaks.

Breaking people is my most favorite game of all.

My hand snaps out, and I grab her messy hair, pulling her the rest of the way until she falls into my lap. "Just last night, I grabbed her naked body in the shower, all full of soap. Her ass was round, fucking perky as hell. Maybe not as big as yours, but I'd still sink my teeth into it." I smirk.

She growls low in her throat, her fingers going to the back of my neck and scraping downward. "Why is she in your house? Does she know you're seeing someone?"

"I'm seeing no one," I whisper.

She shifts her legs, until she's straddling my waist. Leaning back, she looks me in the eye. "You're seeing me. You've been seeing me for a long time."

"Whatever you say." I don't really care either way. Whatever she wants to say, she can say it. I know she fucked some senior last year after we fucked the night before. She knows I sleep with anyone I want, whenever I want. She's never seemed bothered by another girl. Until now.

"I don't like this. When you go home tonight, tell her you have a girlfriend, and she needs to stay the hell away from you." She leans down, pressing her lips to my neck, her hands skating down to the bottom of my shirt in an attempt to pull it over my head.

"I think you need to shut up and take this dick before I give it to someone else." I grab her by the hips, turning her around. No more talking. Her whining is killing any type of fucking mood I'm feeling.

She glances over her shoulder, lifting her skirt over her ass so I can see the tiny scrap of lace threaded between her cheeks. "I'm serious, you know. If I see her in school, I'll tell her myself."

"You do whatever you need to do, Thea." Truth is, I think Vera would lay her flat on her ass. Something I'd maybe be interested in seeing it if I were in a good enough mood.

Her hand reaches back, and she grapples for the button on my slacks. I backhand her hand away, pulling my pants down low enough for me to pull out my cock. It's only half hard, because tonight Thea can't shut the fuck up.

"I'm going to look for her tomorrow. Tell her you're mine." She looks over her shoulder. "You're mine, Malik."

I grab her hair, yanking so hard she lets out a yelp. I spin her around, pressing her face over my erection. She takes it greedily, humming as she deep-throats, all the way to the base. "Just shut the fuck up, Thea."

She does, but it's like I can still hear her thoughts. Her irritation, her jealousy, her possessiveness.

I press on the back of her head until she gags, spit drooling all over my cock and dripping to the couch beneath me. I hold her there, the twitching of her throat enough to finally get me hard.

I stand up, sliding my cock from her mouth and spinning her around. I grab a condom from my wallet, sliding it on with quick motions before plunging into her. She falls forward, her hand grabbing the back of the couch. Her fingers squeeze the fabric, and I know she's disgusted by the dampness.

It only makes me fuck her harder.

Every thrust makes the couch hit the wall, and I pound into her, my hands on her shoulders as I rock her body aggressively.

"Holy shit!" Her hair swishes along her back, and for a moment, I imagine it's black-and-white hair, not blonde.

"Fuck off," I growl, pounding harder, until her screams turn pained.

I fuck her until the rain starts, dripping heavy drops on my shoulders and into her hair. Until the lightning strikes, lighting up the dark, depilated house. I pound into her until the thunder rattles the walls, and Thea turns limp beneath me, too worn out, too damn satisfied.

And when I'm finished, I pull out, feeling more unsatisfied than when I started. There's always been something missing when it comes to Thea, but my thoughts strayed extra hard tonight.

I refuse to think of the reason. I refuse to contemplate what's got my thoughts so screwed around. I don't really care, at the end of the day.

I hate Vera.

I just can't get her off my mind. And I know, without a doubt, that the prank I've been wanting to hold off on for another night has to—needs to—be played out tonight.

13

VERA

"Vera?"

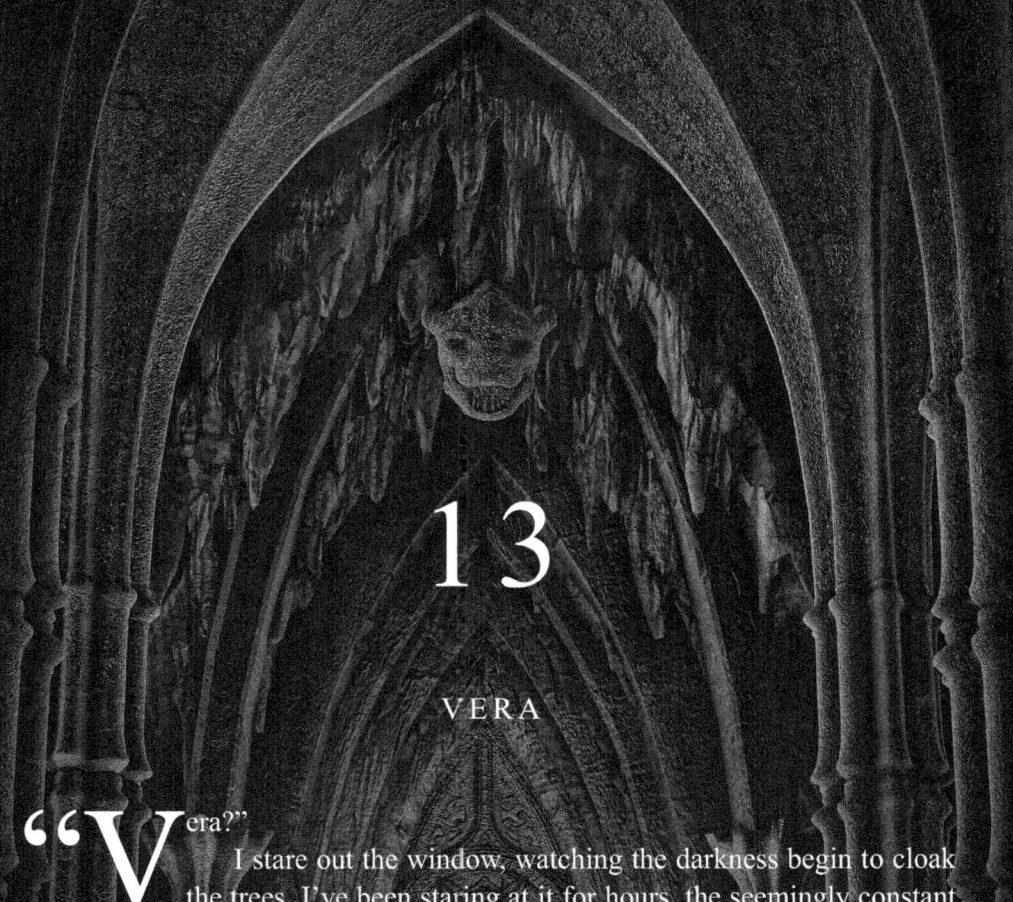

I stare out the window, watching the darkness begin to cloak the trees. I've been staring at it for hours, the seemingly constant fog filling up the air and making the visibility almost impossible. A tree hangs near the window, the naked branch scratching the side of the house with every little breeze.

"Vera, it's Mom."

I squeeze my eyes closed, visions of today flashing before my eyes.

I walked into my room the moment Hazel dropped me off, slipping straight into bed. I haven't left. Haven't slept. My soft sheets suction me to the bed and it's the only comfort I'm able to find right now.

I was able to find some crackers left over in my bag and ate enough to swallow down my meds, but I haven't eaten anything else.

The door creaks open, and the heels of my mom's shoes clack along the floor as she walks around the bed. I roll onto my back, staring at her in fear. The first emotion I've shown her besides anger in… I don't know how long.

She stalls a moment, her eyebrows furrowing. "What's wrong?"

"Please don't make me go back there," I whisper.

She sighs, walking to the edge of the bed and sitting down. The springs of the mattress creak, and she reaches out, placing her hand on my ankle that's hidden beneath the covers. "I received a call from the school today." Clear disappointment is written across her face, and it instantly raises my guard.

I sit up. "Mom, do you know what they did to me?"

She cocks her head to the side. "Is there going to be any reason smoking inside the bathroom of a school would ever be okay?"

I slide my hand from beneath the covers, showing her my dark red-and-purple bruises. "One of the teachers hit me. Look!"

She looks down, her eyes widening for a second before glancing back up at me. "You were smoking in the bathroom, Vera. And swearing constantly, from what they say. This isn't Fargo. This is a Catholic school. The same rules don't apply."

My jaw unhinges, my eyes burning with rage and frustration. "Did they also tell you that they threw me in *The Room of Atonement*?"

Her eyebrows raise. "Well, they put you on a timeout? Maybe you needed it."

"Mom! You don't understand! There were... Something happened in there!" I squeeze my sheets between my fingers, caught between wanting to strangle the nuns and wanting to strangle my mom. "Something isn't right with that place!"

"What happened in the room?" She stands up, straightening her skirt as she looks down at me. "Was there someone in there with you?"

I shake my head. "No. I heard... voices. I felt something. These people, they don't care if I live or die! That place is fucking evil!"

She chuckles, like I'm playing a joke on her, and she's fallen for it. "Come on, Vera. Think about what you're saying right now! You do realize you were in a school, right? There are voices. The walls are thin! You probably heard other students walking in the halls or something." A genuine smile lights up her face, and it only enrages me further.

"Mom! The walls are solid-ass cement! Why aren't you fucking listening to me!?" I scream at the top of my lungs. I spin around, lifting my shirt to show her the scrapes on my back. "Someone scratched me in there!"

Her face widens in bewilderment for a moment before blanking out. "I really hope you didn't do those to yourself, Vera. Hurting yourself isn't going to get you out of the school. And if you are hurting yourself, maybe this is a bigger conversation that we need to be having."

I want to blow up. Literally fucking explode and take her out with me. "You aren't fucking listening to me!" I shriek.

Her eyes narrow, and she scowls at me. "This, this is exactly what I'm talking about." She points her fingers at me, only inches from my face. I want to grab her pointy red nail, snap it straight from her cuticle. "I think this school will be good for you, Vera. Teach you some damn manners and respect for authority," she growls, stepping back as she walks toward the door. "I'm done with your bad behavior. I don't want another call from the school again, or your punishment will go beyond what your teachers do to you."

"I'm not going tomorrow." I'm not. No way in hell am I stepping foot back in that school. I lower my shirt, shrugging back under my covers.

She chuckles. "Yes, you are. You're going there tomorrow, and the next day. You better get used to it now, because it isn't going to get any easier if you don't start following the damn rules."

I let out a shaky breath, betrayal ripping through me. "I hate you," I mumble.

She smiles in the doorway, her hand pressing against the frame. She looks evil, just as evil as the nuns who abused me today. "I'm not too fond of you right now either, Vera. If you don't help yourself, no one else will be able to help you either."

She walks out, leaving me by myself.

My hands fist, shaking at my sides. "*Ahhhh!*" I scream, walking to my dresser and lifting a picture frame from the top. I chuck it at the door, hearing the glass shatter against the wood and falling to the ground.

Walking back to my bed, I grab my bag from the floor, pulling my phone from the front pocket. I attempt to send a text to Sacha.

Me: GET ME OUT!

The red exclamation mark immediately pops up, telling me it's undeliverable. Glancing to the top of the screen, I see there's no service.

How can there be no service everywhere?

I pull up my thread to Leena.

Me: Can you see my texts? This place is BULLSHIT.

Another small exclamation mark pops up. I chuck my phone against the wall, grabbing my bag again and pulling my cigarettes and lighter from inside. I head to my window, pushing on the wooden frame until it cracks open. Placing my cigarette between my lips, I cup my hand around the front and light the tip, watching as the tobacco glows a bright red.

Everyone can fuck right off.

The breeze washes over my skin, and I watch the darkness and listen to the cracks and crunches off in the distance. I imagine the spirits of this eerie town, wandering around aimlessly in the night. Nowhere to go. No one to talk to. A constant feeling of loneliness filling you.

I shiver.

A glow lights up ahead, and I watch as a pair of headlights turn onto the driveway, the car making its way up to the house.

Malik.

I flick my cigarette into the distance and close the window. I do not want to deal with him tonight. After abandoning me not once, but twice, he can go to hell for all I care.

I rush over to the door, closing it and flicking off the light. Leaping into bed, I curl the covers over my face and pretend I'm sleeping.

Please. Please, after today, just leave me the hell alone.

It doesn't take long for me to hear the sound of footsteps pounding up the stairs. Not just one set, but four.

Shit.

Soon enough, I hear the door creak open, and heavy breathing fills the room.

Dammit, why didn't I grab my pocketknife?

I hold my breath as they walk around my bed. They're quiet, too quiet. I know whatever is about to happen isn't going to be good.

Are they going to kill me? Is this the end? Maybe I won't have to go back to that damn school, after all. Maybe these guys will take me away from my misery. Take away my choice altogether.

Riiiiiip.

The sound of duct tape makes my eyes fling wide. A heavy hand slaps against my shoulder, and I'm wrenched onto my back. The scratches from earlier scream in agony.

I open my mouth to let out a wicked scream when a sock is shoved into my mouth, and the stickiest tape I've ever felt gets slapped across my lips.

A scream rips from my throat, muffled from the thick fabric of the sock. I gag around it, using my tongue to push it as far to the front of my mouth as I possibly can. Tears of rage spring to my eyes, and I swing my hands out, looking to punch any of the menacing-looking dark figures in front of me.

I know it's Malik and his friends. I can smell him. His manly, intoxicating scent that has a mixture of evil meshed in.

Then he's there, pinning my arms against my sides as he hovers over me, his teeth snapping at me as he snarls, "Consider this payback for the little cigarette burn you decided to inflict on me earlier."

"Fuck you!" I roar around the sock. No one can make out a word, I'm sure, but the venom spitting from my eyes should give them enough of an indication of what I'm trying to say.

He smirks. "I must not have shoved the sock deep enough in your throat if you can still talk shit. Can you deep-throat, baby sister? Doubt you'd be able to speak if I shoved my dick down your throat instead."

Fuck. Gag me. What a disgusting fucking human.

He glances to the other side of the bed. "Grab her feet. I'll grab her arms. We need to get out of here, fast, before her mom or my dad see us."

Mom.

My neck arches back and I let out the most tortured howl I've ever made. If the sock and tape weren't across my mouth, I bet I'd wake the entire town. And the dead.

Malik's fingers go to the skin right below my eyes, his nails digging in deep. "I don't know what kind of torture you went through today at school, but I can guarantee, if you make another scream like that, what we do to you will be much, much worse."

I swallow around the sock, my eyes wide as silence fills the room.

In an unspoken agreement, they all move at once, lifting me and carrying me across the room like a dead body in a body bag.

I want to scream so badly, but fear of the consequences leaves the words trapped in my throat. They carry me down the stairs silently, out the front door, and into the cold night. Drops hit my face, making me flinch. I look up, seeing ominous, fast-moving clouds clashing together.

Great. Another storm.

They throw me in the trunk like a bag of potatoes, then shut the door behind me. A moment later, the car doors open and the four of them jump into Malik's Range Rover. The rough fabric of the trunk itches against my bared arms. It smells like fresh, new car back here, mixed with a hint of marijuana.

The Rover rumbles to life, the quiet vibration heavy beneath my body. They talk quietly among themselves, and I bring a hand up slowly, peeling the tape from my lips. I wince as each baby hair is ripped from my skin. After a few moments, my lips are free, and I gag the soggy sock from my mouth.

Where are they taking me?

I keep my back to them, so they can't see my uncovered mouth. I breathe heavily as I think on what to do.

How the hell can I get out of this?

I feel like my only option is to literally fight them to the death. I can scratch at their skin and kick them in the nuts, and hope—fucking pray—that I can escape some way or another.

We roll down a gravel road, my body rocking side to side until he punches the brakes. My body rolls to the door of the trunk, my face slamming against the expensive plastic.

Son of a bitch.

"It's been a while," one of them murmurs. There's an excitement in his voice, and my face scrunches in confusion. *Why the hell is he so excited?*

More than that, what is he excited for?

"She seems so damn docile. I figured she'd put up more of a fight than that." A guy with a deep, raspy voice seems disappointed. I wish I knew which one he was, because I'd punch him in the nuts first.

The car doors open, casting me in a low light before quickly going into darkness once again.

Okay. It's now or never. If I want to live another day, I'll have to act fast and fight hard.

I can feel them stepping around the door of the trunk. Their shadows glow behind the back window. Four tall, menacing-looking figures stand before me.

I take a deep breath, my body tensing as I wait.

Click.

The back door pops open, and I swing my feet out, knocking with the thighs of someone, I'm not quite sure who. I hear an *oomph*, and kick again, connecting with another body. Hands grasp at my ankles, and I pull myself forward, my fist swinging and connecting with someone's cheek.

"She's feisty!" Someone laughs, but I don't find it funny at all as I swing again. Someone makes a grab for me, and this time I think it's Malik with how strong and possessive his hands are. I scratch at his skin, digging in deep until I break the flesh.

I won't let them get me. Not today.

I swing my feet up until my knees hit my chest, then punch them forward as hard as I can, knocking them out of the way.

And I make my escape.

Curling my fingers around the expensive material, I shove myself out of Malik's car, sprinting as quickly as I can into the woods. Branches and twigs break around me, and it doesn't take long for me to hear heavy footsteps pounding into the darkness behind me. My bare feet are poked bloody with each twig and pine needle in the woods. But I can't think about that as I search for any kind of safety.

They're coming.

I zip left and right, turning different ways, getting myself lost and hopefully making me disappear from their sight.

An oversized trunk comes into sight, and I sprint to it, squatting down and hiding behind it. I gasp, holding my hand over my mouth to quiet my pants as footsteps make their way closer.

"Oh, little sister. Come out, come out, wherever you are." Malik's voice is a mixture of playful and deadly. He wants to play a game, but at what cost?

"You have to let me have a little fun, Mal. She got me fucking good," someone grunts, and I smirk, knowing he must have been the one I kicked straight in the balls.

"I think we all need a piece of her after how spicy she just got," another one growls, and I clench my fingers into my palms, feeling them dig deep into my skin.

The footsteps grow closer, and I shift my feet, ready to bolt, when everything stops.

Everything.

I feel a cool brush of air on my arm and close my eyes, so worried I'll look behind me and see someone. Or maybe I'll see nothing at all. I don't know which would be worse.

A crack of a branch sounds as they ascend upon me, and I know they've spotted me.

I have to go. *Now.*

"Get her!" one of them shouts.

My arms pump at my sides as I run through the forest. My eyes grow wide when I see a white shadow deep in the trees. A face with dark features. Black eyes.

Suspended in the air.

I scream as I run, pointing into the trees. "There's someone in the trees! Someone's out there!"

They don't listen as they silently run after me.

"Listen to me, you pieces of shit! Someone. Is in. The woods!" I holler, panting with each breath. But they don't care, they don't listen. Their only goal is to get me and do wicked things to me.

No.

I see a bridge in front of me, and I curve, making my way to the old wooden structure. A small wooden, rotted railing holds it up. Something that doesn't look like it'll hold me, but I have to try. *I have to.*

Pieces of the boards are missing, but I leap over it, rushing onto the long bridge that suspends over Superior. We're high up, but not too high. It would be a scary drop, but hopefully—as long as there aren't rocks underneath the water—I'd maybe survive the fall.

"Oh, shit," one of them says, and it stops me in my tracks. I stand in the middle of the bridge as I glance over my shoulder, all four of them stand on the edge, staring at me with apprehension.

"What, now y'all are fucking scared? Of a rickety old bridge?" I laugh, grabbing onto the railings as I shove side to side. It rocks easily, swaying in the night air.

"No, baby sister. We're waiting to see what you do. You can keep running, straight into the dark woods. We won't follow you on that side. It sits untouched and has for years. I don't know what stays over there. No one knows what lingers between the trees at night. Otherwise, you can jump over and hope you survive. If you don't, maybe you're just saving me the trouble."

I swallow, looking over my shoulder into the pitch-black woods. They are so dense I can barely see between the trunks. Glancing below me, the water crashes angrily against the shore. Yes, I might survive.

But I might not.

"Or you can come back to us. Pay for your misgivings and how you've treated us this evening and fucking pray to God that we let you see the light of day tomorrow."

I grip the rotted wood. It's squishy beneath my palm, and I realize how weak it is. I shouldn't be standing here. It isn't safe, and I'm surprised I haven't fallen through yet.

The question is, though, which path do I take?

They all stare at me, expectant and impatiently waiting.

"Fuck all of you," I whisper into the wind, turning my back to them and making my way into the dark forest. I might not know what waits for me on this side of the woods, but I know what waits for me if I go back to them, and it's not a risk I want to take.

I step on an overly warped board. It feels like my bare foot steps on a sponge. *And it snaps.*

My hands reach out, my fingers digging into the soft wood. It gives underneath me, but I keep hanging on as a scream breaks from my chest. "Someone, help! Please, help me!"

I glance over, my hands searching for more and more stability as I glare at the four men on the other side of the bridge.

They stare at me, shock and maybe a little boredom in their eyes. Malik stands at the forefront, his hand gripping the wood as his jaw clenches to stone.

"Help me, please," I whisper.

A flicker of something passes his gaze. What is that… hesitancy? Fear? Worry?

I almost laugh, suspended in the air. He couldn't be worried about me, right? But I am.

His mouth opens, and his soft words float through the night and slide around me light as a silk scarf.

"Warned you."

And I fall.

The wind swallows my cries as my arms and legs flail around me for only seconds before I crash into the frigid water. The current is light, but the water is colder than ice as it chills my body down to my bones.

I break through the surface, gasping as the cold water freezes my lungs. I can barely catch a full breath as I doggy paddle toward the shore.

Once my feet hit the sand, I fall to my knees, flopping to my stomach as my fingers dig into the wet, thick sand and I pull myself the rest of the way to the shore.

My face sinks to the sand, and I catch my breath as constant shivers rack my body. My sopping wet clothes stick to my skin and do nothing to protect me from the frigid wind whipping through the air.

I roll over so my legs are out of the water and stare up at the night sky.

How will I ever find my way home?

Surely, I'll catch hypothermia before the night is over if I stay out here.

I can see the glow of headlights before I hear the hum of the car. I think about getting to my feet and making a run for it. But where at this point? The cliff on either side of me makes it impossible to scale either side. I could run into the water or run toward the oncoming car. I have no other option.

But most of all, my fight is spent. Whatever they want to do to me at this point is inevitable. I'll never win.

I keep my head toward the sky, even as the heavy, slow footsteps of feet step up to me.

"I hope you realize, if you don't play by my rules, this will only be the beginning of a long, long fucking road of torture." Malik's voice rings into my chest, and I want to cry as he gently lifts me up.

I want to curl away from him. I want to fight him. I do neither of those things. I stay limp in his arms as he walks me back to his truck, settling me much nicer into the trunk this time. I feel like a wet dog as I curl into the corner, keeping my eyes averted from his as he stares at me a moment.

I feel like a wreck. Burrowing my face in my arms, I can feel his hatred burn into me, warming my frosty skin before the trunk slams closed.

I know his friends are still in the car. I can feel them watching me, but I'm depleted of energy. Hunkering into the corner, I close my eyes.

Tonight, I'm done. After The Room of Atonement and the guys' sick games, I'm spent.

I'm done.

14

MALIK

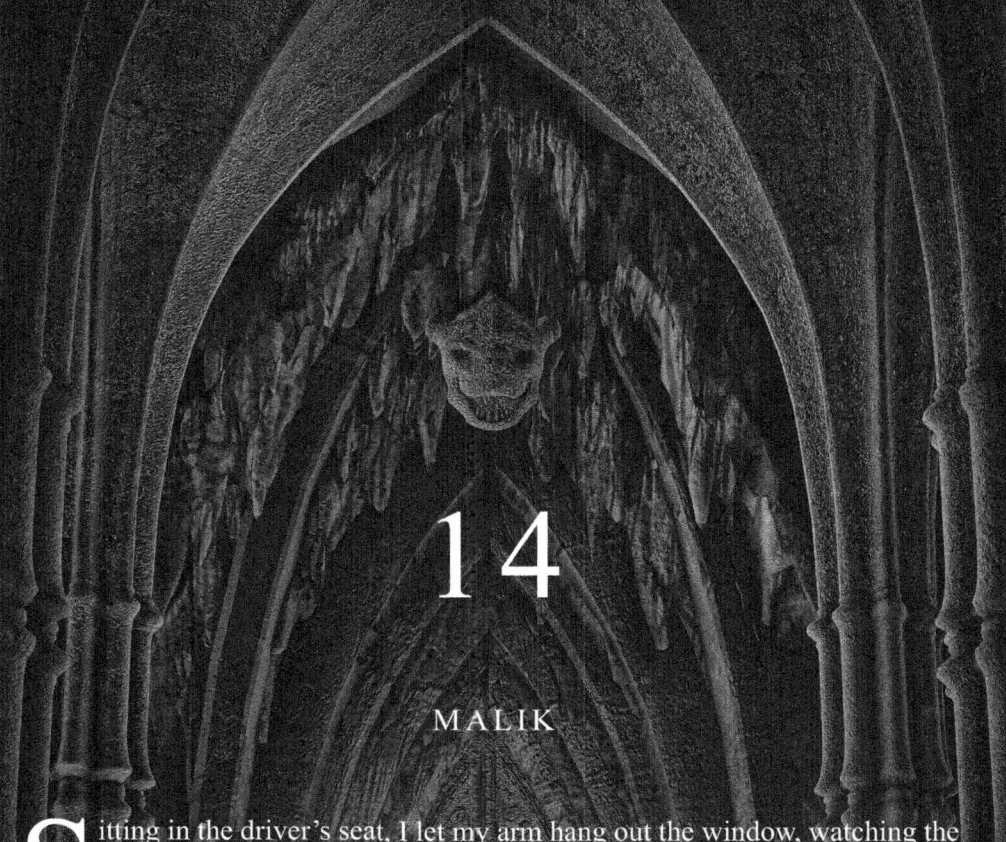

Sitting in the driver's seat, I let my arm hang out the window, watching the trail of smoke float from the cherry. I flick the filter, letting the inch-long ash tumble to the ground.

My eyes can't leave the window upstairs. The yellow glow from inside the room. Don't tell me how I know this, but I can just feel her fucking rage from here. Her defeat. Like she's moments from walking back to that bridge and drowning herself this time.

I brought her home, her barely conscious body lying limp in my trunk. I carried her upstairs myself, the guys knowing she'd hit her breaking point for the night. After tossing her on the bed, I walked straight back outside, ready to go cause some more havoc around town. Light this shitty place on fire and watch it burn from the ground up to the tops of the trees. I'd relish in it. I'd feast on the fear of the townsfolk, and I'd laugh at the screams of the dead burning beneath the dirt.

I want to leave, but the fear in her eyes as she dangled from that bridge chills my entire body to the bone.

With an irritated growl, I take my keys out of the ignition, tossing my cigarette onto the ground and walking inside. It's empty, all the lower lights turned off. Glancing to the right, I see my dad's office door closed. A low glow comes from below the door, and I sneer at it, heading for the stairs.

Wherever step-monster is, she must also know to leave my dad to whatever the hell he does behind closed doors at night. Probably plotting ways to continue corrupting the world to further his wealth.

I shake my head, ridding thoughts of my dad. That's for another day. Tonight, my mind is stuck on one thing, and I really need some damn answers.

I take two steps at a time, making my way up the curved staircase and to the second level. The sound of water running through the old pipes hits me, and I cut left, heading straight to the bathroom. My dick twitches in my jeans, and I ignore it as I barge in.

I can barely see her around the corner of the shower, but her shoulder twitches.

She knows I'm here.

I walk up to her, staring into her eyes. Her dark makeup runs down her face, making her look like a raccoon.

"What happened today?" I ask her.

She gives me her back. I look over her thin frame, noticing three deep gashes in the middle of her back. Her ass is plump, on display and so fucking close I could reach out and grab a handful. But the wound grabs my attention.

It looks gnarly, and I can see the pain in the way her skin separates from the scrapes, the raw inside of her flesh is exposed and bright red.

I reach out, brushing my fingers along the open wound. "What happened?" I ask again.

She flinches away from me, stepping farther into the shower. "Why do you care?" She doesn't even look over her shoulder at me, just continues rinsing the shampoo from her hair.

I do grab her ass this time, squeezing tight and pulling her against me. Her soaking wet back dampens my uniform shirt and the front of my pants. I don't care.

I snake my hand around her waist, hovering right over her soapy sex. Knowing I could dip a finger in, and she wouldn't even protest. "Tell me. What the fuck happened?"

She elbows me in the side, and I step away with a growl.

"You mean, besides how you fucking tortured me in the woods?" she snaps, her exhaustion long gone as her anger roars to the surface. "When you guys fucked with me like some prey. Do you have any idea what it felt like to run through the woods, like a tracked deer? I felt like the hunted." She looks up at me, and there is such an overwhelming rush of venom in her gaze it nearly makes me stumble back. "And you guys were the hunters."

I squeeze her ass, and she scowls at me. "What I did was nothing. *Nothing*. Do you not realize what I'm capable of? Do you not realize the danger you're in from just standing in my house?"

She keeps her back to me, and the hideous scrapes on her stay at the forefront of my mind. "You want me to be scared of you. Like you're a big, bad wolf. You think I should tremble at your feet? Bend to my knees and worship you like a god? You like games. I could see the eagerness in your eyes as you lifted me from my bed and tossed me in your car. It makes you hard to play with me like I'm some weak, mindless toy. You want me to be pliant, folding and listening to your every word." She steps out of my hold, farther into the spray and deeper into the darkness of the shower. "I don't fold for anyone, Malik. Least of all you. At the end of the day, you'll find your head bowed in front of me. You'll realize it's me you worship with your fingers steepled in front of your chest, not the devil I know you love."

Anger pounds against my chest, and I step into the shower, my shirt soaking through as I grip her neck, squeezing the skin. "I'm done with your filthy words. Tell me what happened to you in the room now, or else I'll make sure you spend the rest of your life between those four walls."

She rips herself out of my hold, a snarl on her face as she glances at me over my shoulder. "I was sent to The Room of Atonement, okay? The room I only heard about today, where people *never survive*. I was there. Now, if you don't fucking mind, I want to take my shower and forget about this entire horrible day."

I snap a hand out, wrapping my fingers in her wet locks. Her head bows back, her eyes meeting mine upside down. "Tell me about it," I mumble.

Surprisingly, her eyes glaze. Only slightly, and she looks pissed off that it happens. "It's horrible." Her hand reaches up, squeezing my fingers until I release her hair. "Not something I would wish on my worst enemy. Even you." She looks me in the eyes at this, wringing her hair out. She turns around, her arms folded and pressed against her breasts. They squish together, covering every bit of her tits. Are they ugly? Why does she hide them? It's not like she's self-conscious. Her cunt and ass sit on display and her hands don't even flinch to cover herself.

Her body is fucking sinful, even though I want to break her into dust.

I lied to Thea earlier. Vera's ass is way nicer than hers.

My eyes trail down, watching the water as it trails down her stomach, rolling into her belly button before tumbling out, rushing between her sex. She's bare, not an inch of hair covering her cunt. I didn't look the last time, too pissed off about her being in my house to notice her banging body.

But it is. It's the sexiest thing I've ever seen. Too bad I hate her with everything in me. I'd rather hear her scream my name in fear than in pleasure.

My hand wraps around her body, and I press into her cut, one that isn't from scraping against something. No, it almost looks like…

Someone scratched her.

"Where'd you get this?" I ask, leaning forward until my cheek presses against hers. Water drips from her hair onto her ear, rolling down until it slips off, landing on my lips. I lick it clean, feeling the gash on her skin. Pressing into it until she whimpers. "Who gave this to you?"

Her hands go up, and she presses her palms against my chest, pushing me away from her. "Go. Get the fuck out of here. It's not like you care. You're evil, Malik. This morning you left me, this afternoon you left me. This evening you fucking tortured me. You wouldn't care if I rotted away in that room, with all the other dark spirits. You probably wish I did. Fucking bastard." She brings her hand up, flicking water in my face. "Fuck off, big brother. I don't want to talk to you."

Her arm covers her chest, like that's going to lend her any amount of decency.

My hand lands on her waist, my fingers digging into her back while my thumb presses into her belly button. It's an uncomfortable feeling, and I press until I know her discomfort borders on pain. "Be careful what you wish for, little sister. You don't want to somehow end up back in that room. Or worse, end up in my hands. You don't want to know what I'd do with you."

Her eyes land on the burn on my neck. The burn that's turned into an itch and an ache, and it makes me wish I would've plunged the knife into her neck. Even just a little.

"I'd rather be at the mercy of one thousand deadly spirits than spend a second with you." She smirks, and it borders on psychotic.

My dick twitches again.

"And, you never know, another second with me, and maybe you'll end up with another burn on your neck."

"You fucking bitch," I growl, my fingers flexing with a need to choke her out. To end her for good.

She slips out of my hold, stepping farther into the shower. "Come on in,

Malik. Step in and see what I'm capable of."

I crack my knuckles, wanting so badly to break her. To be done with this horrible stepsister that has been nothing but a pain in my ass since she stepped into my town. But she makes it too easy, standing there naked and clutching her chest in the corner of my shower.

She thinks she's tough, but she'd be so easy to break.

I step back until she's barely visible. "I hope you cry yourself to sleep tonight, little sister. This is only the beginning."

I slip out of the bathroom, my skin on fire from her eyes and the fury she ignites in me. Our hate is so natural. Two people that shouldn't be around each other. But we're forced to be, and unfortunately, us mixing will only lead to death and destruction.

"Malik," my dad barks from down the hall. I can barely see him in the darkness, but he's there. I can sense him.

"What?" I give him my back, walking to my room. Not in the mood for him tonight. I don't care about whatever philosophy he wants to spew my way. Or whatever else he wants to hassle me about. Not tonight.

"Come here, Malik," he orders.

I sigh, my shoulders dropping. I turn around, scowling at him as I make my way into the shadows of his side of the house. He gives me a look, one that looks similar to the one he gives me after I've done a serious prank. The kind of pranks we can't come back from.

He nods his head, and walks across the hall from his room, into a smaller office he barely uses. I walk in, and he shuts the door behind me, turning on the light.

I can see the dust lingering in the air, floating around and making it look as foggy in here as it does outside. There's a desk on one end of the room, empty and unused. There's also a small bookshelf with reference books and types of boring as hell research information that he for some reason needs to have. Near the window sits one of those couches that you'd see in a therapist's office, with a white sheet covering it.

"I received a call from the school today, Malik. I have to say, I'm very disappointed in you."

I roll my eyes. "What did they say this time?"

"A knife in school? Really?"

I laugh. "I always have a knife on me."

He frowns. "What about the fact that you left without giving Vera a ride this morning, and someone from school dropped her off. Did you ditch her after school, too?"

I stare at him. "Yes."

He sighs, running his hand down his cheek and to the back of his neck. "This has got to stop."

I chuckle. "What's got to stop? I'm not doing anything."

He scowls at me, his face weathered and tired of my shit. I've always been tired of him, so he can fuck right off. "Exactly my point. Daphne is my wife now, and you have a little sister that goes to your school. You have to take care of her, maybe be friends with her a little. She doesn't know anyone, Malik!"

I point at him. "You're out of your fucking mind."

He steps closer to me, barely beating me by an inch in height. He's also broader than me, but at the end of the day, I'm stronger, and one move from me would lay him on his ass. "I think you're stepping out of line here, son."

I reach a hand up, grabbing his shirt and pulling him until his chest bumps up against mine. Me and my dad rarely fight. We don't like each other, and that much is obvious, but getting into an actual physical fight is rare. We mostly just ignore each other. "You bring a whore and her daughter into this house and expect me to be fine with it?" His face grows red, and I push him away from me, disgust tasting bitter against my tongue.

He shoves me, though it doesn't hold much substance. "Call her a whore again, Malik, and you can find somewhere else to park your ass." He breathes, and I can see the literal steam flowing from his ears. "You watch your mouth. And what the hell were you doing in the bathroom when she's taking a shower? You better not even think about getting her into bed and treating her like just another mindless girl you sleep with."

I bark out a laugh at this. I step toward him again, the toe of my boot pressing against the toe on his Armani leather shoe. "Don't step up to me again, Father, or you'll regret it." His face grows purple, and I take a step back. "If I want to take her to school, I'll take her to school." I walk toward the door, pressing on the handle and opening it a crack. "If I want to bury my dick in her, you better believe I'll do that just as easily."

I shut the door, keeping him inside. The son of a bitch can stay in there and fester with his thoughts. The thought of sticking my dick in Vera makes me nauseous. Her bad attitude doesn't make up for her killer body, even if she wishes it would.

I head down the hall, stopping at the bathroom door once again. The shower is off, but the light is still on, and I know she's still in there. I turn right, heading into her bedroom.

Flicking on the light, my shoe crunches as I step into her room. I glance down, pressing the toe of my boot onto a broken frame at my feet. Bending over, I pick up the dark wood, turning it over to see what it is she decided to destroy.

There she is.

Vera sits in the middle, with two equally as punkish-looking kids standing on either side of her. They all have their middle fingers in the air, like they're saying *fuck the world*. Their faces are even harsh, like they're pissed.

They're trying too hard.

I drop the frame, letting it shatter even more. I step over the glass pile, walking farther into her room and examining her things. She doesn't have much. Some other photos here and there. No art on the walls. A simple dresser and bed. One nightstand with a lamp on top. Two oversized brown boxes sit in the corner of her room. Shit the movers didn't unpack, I guess. Who knows if she'll ever unpack them, or maybe she just hopes they can stay that way and she'll find a way out of here.

I walk up to her dresser, pulling open the black drawer. Colorful panties and bras fill the space, messy and unorganized.

Like her. The messiness suits her.

Without a second thought, I grab a handful of lace, the scraps of fabric so small I can pull them all out with just one hand. I leave her bras in there, shutting the drawer and walking out, flicking the light off as I go.

15

VERA

Shit, it's cold outside this morning.

I groan as I walk to my closet, because as much as I wish I didn't have to go today, after my conversation with my mom yesterday, I know staying home is impossible. Not that I think she would've believed me. It's like these past few years have grown us into enemies. Our relationship we used to have has shattered, just like the picture frame from the night before. It feels like there's no trying to fix it at this point.

Like what we have is gone for good.

I drag my feet as I walk to my closet, grabbing another uniform off the hanger. The ugly plaid skirt is too long, and even after the nuns bickered about my dress today, I just can't dress like the other girls. It's not me, and if they want to whip me until each knuckle and bone in my body is bruised, well, I guess that's what it'll be.

I decide against fishnets today, and instead choose a pair of thigh high socks. Their warm, and it'll help against the bitter breeze that seems to be outside today. It feels like the coldness has seeped into the house, the floor against my toes so freezing that they feel numb.

Do they even have the heat on? I swear, it feels like it's below freezing temperatures in here.

I walk to my dresser, opening up my drawer to grab some underwear.

My jaw clenches when I see half of my drawer missing. Actually, *all of my panties are missing*. My bras still sit on the other side, completely untouched.

"That motherfucker…" I whisper.

I slam my drawer closed, making the entire dresser rock against the wall.

I walk back and forth at the foot of my bed, trying to figure out what to do.

I could go to his room and demand them back. I could go tell my mom and Samuel, or I can pretend like his childish games mean absolutely nothing to me. I can already tell it would piss him off to no end. It'd turn him rageful, a fucking beast to know he doesn't affect me like he wishes he could.

A smirk lifts my lips.

Bingo.

I button up my top, the button at my neck suffocating me, but I don't show off my cleavage. That's the only thing I ever keep concealed, because I hate the questions. My skirt slides on next, and I zip it on the side, clasping the top. It's thick and constraining, but the no panties leave no amount of protection between my legs. One gust of wind and everyone would see my bare sex.

I pull my black socks onto my feet, inching them up my calves until they roll over each knee, ending at my lower thighs. They're simple, black, with an edging of lace on the top. The guys back in Fargo loved my thigh-high socks, and I think even in Catholic school, I might turn some heads.

Maybe Malik's?

"Ugh," I grunt, shaking the thought from my head.

Why the hell would I even think about him? He's a piece of shit, for one. He has no sense of respect or boundaries. He doesn't care about anyone, except maybe for his friends.

But the way his hands lingered on my body last night in the shower. The way his eyes implored mine, searching for the answers to all his questions. Like I could be the one to fill his needs. The way he watched my body, like he wanted me and wanted to end me at the same time. I was drenched and suddenly so needy for so many things. So many impure, forbidden things.

I hate him, and he's my stepbrother.

Double no. Double gross.

I walk to my dresser, pulling the small box of makeup in front of me as I lean toward the mirror. I line my eyes with eyeliner, creating small wings at the ends. I brush dark eyeshadow along my lids and flick some mascara along my eyelashes. To top it off, I grab my shade of deep, dark purple and line my lips.

Rubbing them together, I make a kissy face in the mirror.

Perfect.

Lifting my backpack from the floor, I dig my hands inside and shift them around until they touch the smooth orange bottles. Popping open the tops, I take too many pills out and drop them into my mouth dry. A wince hits me as they get stuck in my throat, but I swallow through it as I sling my bag over my shoulder and head downstairs. I don't know if Samuel knows about me, if my mom told him. But on the off chance he doesn't, I don't want to deal with the questions. I don't like talking about myself in general, and talking about that part of me sounds excruciating, mostly if it's with my new stepdaddy.

The feel of the air brushing across my folds as I hop down the stairs is slightly exhilarating. The thought that I could just slip my fingers beneath my skirt and press a finger between them.

Fucking hell.

Just that thought alone makes me damp between the legs.

I walk into the kitchen, seeing my mom and Samuel already standing behind the island, coffee cups in hand as they whisper to each other.

I say nothing, slipping onto the bar stool and grabbing a banana from the bowl on the counter.

"Vera," my mom says, turning away from Samuel to look at me.

"Mom. Samuel." I peel my banana, not sparing them a glance as I eat. I'm not hungry, not in the slightest. I'd rather have a cup of coffee and smoke a cigarette, but I know I need to cut down. I'll be in serious trouble if I don't quit, but the stress of being here makes it unbearable to not take a hit.

That, and I need to eat or my pills are going to give me some serious cramps in about thirty minutes.

"Ready for your second day of school?" Samuel asks.

I barely raise my eyes, only passing him a glance before looking back down at the counter. "Nope. Not really."

"I know it's hard, but once you get past the old-school teachings, you'll find it's actually a great school to have on a transcript. It'll look good on your applications for college." He tries to be upbeat. Tries so hard.

I don't respond, chewing my mouthful of banana.

"Vera, do you think you can be a little more respectful today?" my mom whispers.

I lift my head, leveling her a look. "Sure." Sarcasm drips heavily from my voice.

She stands back, picking her coffee cup up and lifting it to her lips. "Good. I don't want any calls from the school today."

I nod, hating the eyes of her and Samuel on me. They judge me. They talk negatively about me in their thoughts. I hate it.

I hate them.

I pull my earbuds from my bag and slide them into my ears. I turn The Used on full blast, drowning out their voices. Breaking off the banana, I pop it piece by piece into my mouth, ignoring their condescending looks. I can feel them heating the crown of my head. I don't know if my mom is still trying to talk to me. I don't know if they're waiting for me to look at them.

Maybe they're just outright talking shit about me.

Nothing I have to say will make them happy. There's nothing that I can do that will change my mom's mind or convince her that the place she's sending me to is as corrupt as the son that lives in this house.

This entire place is swimming in evil and corruption, and I'm worried if I stay too long here, I'll no longer be the person I am, but the person this place will make me become.

My earbuds fly from my ears, and my head snaps up, my eyes widening when I come face to face with the dark eyes of Malik. A light dusting of facial hair lines his sharp jaw this morning. His hair is damp, like he just stepped out of the shower and couldn't find the time to run a comb through it. It's messy, the long, slightly wavy locks curling over his ears. His lashes even look damp, brushing against his cheekbones that look like they could cut glass.

"What?" I ask harshly, picking up the cords of my earphones.

"Let's go."

I frown at him. "What? No. Where are we going?"

He clenches his jaw. "To school. If you aren't outside in two minutes, you can walk. Or get a ride with my dad again, for all I care." With that, he spins around, stomping outside. His pants are trim on his waist, and his dark gray shirt molds to his body perfectly. He doesn't look like a boy at all.

He looks like a man.

I glance over at my mom and Samuel. Samuel has a glimmer in his eyes, one that breaks a chill down my spine. I slide from my chair as fast as I can, grabbing my bag off the ground and rushing outside.

Malik's Rover sits in the same position as yesterday, ready to pull off at any second. I scowl at the back of the SUV.

If he leaves me here again, I'll literally set this house on fire.

His hand lays on the horn, snapping me out of my thoughts. I rush to the passenger seat, opening the door and sliding onto the cool leather. My face turns toward the window, and I hold my breath, so I don't have to smell his intoxicating scent.

Pine. Smoke. Evil.

It bleeds from his pores and seeps to my side of the car. My fingers start shaking, and I can barely handle it.

Why is he making me feel this way? *I hate him.*

He doesn't say anything, but I can hear him shift in his seat as we drive through the dark woods and make our way to school.

Suddenly, The Smashing Pumpkins starts blasting through the speakers. I close my eyes and bite my lower lip, wanting to groan in frustration at his good taste in music.

Like, fucking seriously?

My toes tap inside of my combat boot as I sing the words in my head. My thighs rub together, and I remember that I have no panties on. Completely bare beneath my skirt, and the asshole next to me is the reason for it.

What did he even do with them? The thought of him hiding them in his room, bunching them into his hands on his bed in the middle of the night while he shoots his load onto my thin pieces of fabric makes my sex thump with need.

I squeeze my thighs together as Malik pulls into the parking lot at school. My stomach knots as I see the ominous-looking building in front of me. I knew it looked creepy yesterday, but now, knowing about the malevolence that lurks inside the bricks, the death that curls beneath the pews, and the sins that hide underneath the nuns' clothing, this place seems unbearable.

It's everywhere. It's like a virulent waste that burns in the air and leaks throughout the entire town.

"Get out of my car," Malik says as he pumps on the brakes. He parks in the back, away from the rest of the cars. Like he's worried about his baby getting scratched, even though everyone else at this place has equally as expensive vehicles.

I turn toward him for the first time since getting in the car. He stares at me, his jaw clenched and his fingers strangling the leather steering wheel.

"You know," I whisper, leaning into his bubble. His scent is so much stronger in his space, heavy and intoxicating as it swirls into my senses. "If you wanted to take a pair of my panties, all you had to do was ask." I smile at him, malice and fury in my eyes as I show him my teeth. He looks emotionless as he stares at me, like he can barely stand the sight of me. I open the door, stepping out of the Rover. Shielded by the door, I bend over, acting like I'm picking something up from the ground. My head bends to my shins and my fingers drift upward, curling around the edges of my skirt, and I lift it up, showing him everything he's missing out on.

Everything he'll never have.

My naked sex is shamelessly showing, probably half damp from his scent and my hate for him. My bare, pale thighs and ass on display, and my black socks, covering my knees and trailing down to my combat boots.

I stand up, fixing my skirt as I straighten my spine. Glancing over my shoulder at him, I give him a smile, and a small wink. "See you after school, big brother."

16

MALIK

Holy. Fucking. Shit.
My fingers should be going into formation as I pray to the Father, the Son, and the Holy Spirit, but all I can do is stare at her glistening cunt in the school parking lot.

Then she winks at me.

I can hear my teeth cracking as I clench my jaw. My hand even reaches forward, knowing it would take nothing to wrap my fingers around her neck, squeezing until the life leaves her body.

She walks away from me, her ass swaying beneath her skirt, and now I know her pussy is bare to the world, to the air. Anyone could see it if they really wanted to. It would take nothing. Only a slight flick of her skirt.

My nostrils flare, and I hop out of my truck, seeing the guys sitting inside Levi's black Mercedes. Smoke clouds up the car so much I can barely make out who is who. I walk up to the driver's window, tapping on it with the back of my knuckle.

Levi startles, and the window rolls down, a wave of smoke curling from the window. I reach my hand in, plucking the joint from his fingers and taking a hit. We usually smoke inside our cars while we're at school, because Sister Mary is an absolute bitch and will hound me for a week if she knows we're smoking on the property.

Not that she'd be able to do anything about it, but she still fucking tries.

"Dude, what's up? Was that your sissy in the car with you?" Levi chuckles, his eyes red-rimmed and glazed as hell.

My chest twitches with a cough, and I exhale through my nose, watching the front door. Vera makes it to the top of the steps, glancing over her shoulder. She brushes her fingers through her black hair, showing off the white underneath. Her nose piercing glistens in the morning sky.

Fuck. What is happening to me?

I pass the joint back off to Levi when she walks inside. "It was."

Atticus rolls down his window in the back seat, pressing his forearm on the frame. Another wave of smoke rolls out, and he shakes his hair from his eyes as he glances up at me. "How is baby sister doing this morning? Surprised she came back after yesterday."

I look to the empty steps, no Vera in sight. "She's got no choice. Mommy dearest forced her hand."

Atticus chuckles. "I figured she'd put up more of a fight than that."

I think back to last night, the scars on her back, the way she looked at me, with pure hate in her eyes. "She puts up a good fight," I say honestly, surprised at the words that come out of my mouth. Disgusted with them.

"What did you just say?" Felix asks, bending forward so he can look around Levi. "She puts up a good fight?" He laughs, confused.

I curl my fingers inside the car, gripping the door until my fingers turn white. "Game is still on, fuckers."

Felix leans back in his seat, grabbing the joint from Levi. "Good. Fucking scared me there for a second."

Not more than I scared myself.

The warning bell rings, and I slap the top of the car. "I'm going in."

Atticus leans out the window. "You're acting fucking weird, Mal."

I flip him off. "Because I've got a bitch of a sister and a slutty, gold-digging stepmother that hasn't even spoken a word to me." It's all true. My dad thinks this is what's good for the family, but he doesn't understand... there is no family.

There's him. And there's me. My dad fractured whatever was left of the family years ago. Now all that's left of our family is buried in the dirt, covered in pine needles from the nearby trees.

We're nothing.

And now my dad brought two more people into his poisonous life.

Who knows? Maybe he'll end up killing them, too.

17

VERA

"Are you feeling better?" Hazel asks from the desk beside mine. I glance over at her, not wanting to get hit again by Sister Marjorie. My hand still hurts from yesterday. Luckily, it's not my writing hand. I'm also worried that the next time she hits me, I'll snap.

And I really don't want to go back to The Room of Atonement.

I nod at her, looking back down at my paper, trying to finish our assignment for the day.

"Did you talk to Malik?"

I nod, thinking about how they brought me to the woods. How terrified I was and thought it was the end for me. Then there's the shower last night…

How he stared at my body. How he looked like he wanted to do things to me, things that a stepbrother and stepsister shouldn't be doing with each other.

Although, can we even be considered that?

I can barely consider us acquaintances. More like… enemies. Rivals.

"What did he say? Did he give you an explanation for dipping out on you like that yesterday?"

I shrug, pretending to write something down, but I'm just tracing my name, over and over again, until the lines are thick and black and cold. "He's an asshole. That's all there is to it. You know him better than I do."

She chuckles under her breath. "None of us know him. We all just assume the worst. I don't even know if the rumors are true."

This time, I do look over at her, interest piqued. "What rumors?"

Her skin pales a few shades, like she's said too much.

"Tell me," I urge.

She looks around and sees everyone engrossed in their work. At least, they're doing a good job of acting like they are.

"Malik and his friends... they prank people."

I clench the edge of my assignment in my fingers, hearing the crunch of paper in my fist. Of course, they do, I was a fucking animal to them last night as they prowled toward me in the woods. A sick game they play, and not one I plan to play again. "Sounds juvenile."

She shakes her head. "Not when people die. They're sadistic is what they are, Vera."

My eyes widen. "They've killed people?"

She nods, only slightly. "From what I've heard? Yes, they have. More than once. Like... a lot, actually."

I shiver, knowing his hands have been on my skin. On my naked body. That I trust myself alone with him. It makes so much sense, though. Like the final piece of the puzzle. His personality is so disassociated sometimes. Like a legitimate psychopath. He makes little comments to me, too.

I swallow, feeling like there's a lump in the back of my throat.

"I think he's playing his game... with me," I whisper.

Her fingers go around the edge of her desk, gripping it tightly. "How do you know?"

"I just do. I can feel it." I should tell her everything from last night. I should tell her how they shoved a sock in my mouth and brought me to the middle of the woods. I should tell her how absolutely frightened I was all alone.

Sister Marjorie clears her throat from up at the front, and I slap my palm against the crumpled paper, getting back to work.

"Come over tonight. I've got an idea," Hazel whispers.

I shake my head. I don't know if I should, or if I even could. I should go home, stay close to my mom. If Malik is planning something again, that means I'm not safe. That means none of us are safe.

"You have to. This isn't an option. If he's planning something, we have to act fast. I'll take you home after."

My eyes lift to the front of the room, and I see Sister Marjorie lifting her ruler from her desk. I nod at Hazel, ever so slightly. Then turning away from Hazel, I get back to work.

The old bell dongs loudly, echoing in my chest. I grab my things, slipping them under my arm as I stand up.

"I'll meet you outside for lunch, okay? Just wait for me out front."

I nod, watching as she rushes from the classroom.

Most of the other students are gone, and Sister Marjorie stands at the front of the room, watching my every move. Her veil makes her face nearly impossible to see. A chill breaks out along my spine, and I glance over my shoulder, expecting to see someone, although there's no one there.

But I felt… something.

I turn back around, and Sister Marjorie is standing only inches from me. I startle, jumping back, eyes wide. "Jesus!"

Her ruler slips from her sleeve, and she slaps the wood against my arm. "Language!"

"Ouch!" I step back from her, my hand going to the blooming red mark on my forearm. "Well, don't go sneaking up on people like that. You scared me half to death."

She smiles, her gray gums and thin teeth making an appearance. "Is that such a bad thing?"

My eyes widen. "What did you just say?"

She straightens, her fingers running down the wood of her ruler. "You seem to be causing trouble, Vera. Hazel is one of my better students, and you had her thoroughly distracted today."

Hazel hates everyone here just as much as I do.

But I don't say that. I don't rat her out and say she's the one that was talking to me. I won't throw her under the bus when her and her friends are the only people that've shown me any kindness since I got here.

"No more distractions, Vera. No more warnings either. Apparently, a few hours in The Room of Atonement wasn't enough for you."

My body tenses from head to toe, and I step back from her. I'll kill her and everyone else in this place before I let her bring me back to The Room of Atonement.

Her ruler extends down, and she uses it to brush against my bare thigh, scraping the edge along my skin. "The way you dress is an abomination. I don't want to see a skirt this short ever again. You will dress properly tomorrow, otherwise there will be consequences." She runs the ruler along the edge of my skirt, and I remember that I have no panties on.

I bat away her ruler, lifting my backpack from the ground and walking toward the door.

"Vera!" Sister Marjorie barks at me.

I flinch, stopping in the doorway and glancing over my shoulder. "Lose the piercing, too."

Fuck this bitch. Fuck her so hard.

After an uneventful lunch, I wave bye to the girls as I make my way to my locker. I'm over the day already. I don't want to deal with anyone, and I don't want to speak to a single soul the rest of the day. Making my way toward my locker, I don't pay attention, knocking into shoulders and walking between groups of people.

I don't care about anyone. None of them. They're meaningless.

This entire place is shit.

I slam my palm against the metal door of my locker, pissed and completely over this entire move. I'd much rather live in a homeless shelter, or go into foster care at this point, than deal with this shit.

And tonight, that's what I'm talking to my mom about.

I'm done with this. Emancipate me for all I care. I can't stay here another minute.

I open my locker, dropping my book to the bottom of it. It bangs and echoes against the thin metal walls, sounding so much noisier than it should.

I feel eyes heating the back of my head, and glancing over my shoulder, I come face to face with Barbie in the flesh. Blondish hair, a large set of tits, and enough makeup on her face that I'm almost positive if I pressed my palm against her skin, I could smear off at least five coats. And she'd still have too much makeup on.

"Um, can I help you?" I frown.

She looks at me like she hates me. She doesn't even know me, yet she already has the look that says she absolutely loathes me.

"You're the girl living with Malik?" She looks me up and down, like I'm the last person she'd assume was living with him. But, why? What did she expect? Some frail holy child?

She dresses like the rest of the girls here. Her shirt buttoned properly, her skirt brushing her pale knees. But I can see the whore beneath her clothes. A whore can't mask her dirtiness. And this girl screams filth from head to toe.

I turn around fully, letting my skirt inch up slightly. The toe of my boots bump against the toes of her flats. My boots are heavy, thick, and I imagine stepping on her toes, watching her scream in pain as I pin her to the ground.

She props her hand on her hip, sneering at me in disgust. "I didn't know he was housing prostitutes. Where'd you come from, anyway?"

She asked for it.

I lift my toe, pressing down on the tip of her shoe. "Be careful what you say, or your jaw may dislocate from the rest of your face."

Her eyes widen a moment before she scowls at me. "Are you threatening me?" She tears her shoe from beneath mine, taking a step back. "You fucking bitch. You're just asking for it, aren't you?"

I smile wide, showing all my teeth. "Of course not." I drop my smile, stepping forward until my shoulder slams against hers. "Now get the fuck out of my face."

She pushes against me. "Stay away from Malik and we won't have any problems."

I laugh. "Okay."

She frowns. "I'm serious. He's mine, and he's not going to want to go for someone like you, anyway. But don't get any ideas. Don't even fucking think about it. I'll know if you do. I'll know if you even talk to him. He doesn't exist in your world, got it?"

My hand raises, and I press it against her buttoned breasts, giving her a light shove. "Got it."

Her friends come up behind her, whispering in her ear. She narrows her eyes at me. "Stay away from me, slut."

I let out a laugh, giving her a salute with my two fingers. "Aye, aye, Captain." Dumbass. Watch me catch her out of here, I'll toss her flimsy ass into the water.

She walks away, shaking her hips like she owns the school.

"Hey," I bark out, forgetting one question.

She freezes, her body straightening up as she and her two friends look over their shoulder.

"What," she spits.

"I didn't catch your name." I smile. It's fake. She knows it, too. She can feel the hatred seeping from me. It's a slow leak, but only because we're in school.

The moment we're out, I'll turn it on full blast, and she knows this. She knows I'll demolish her, and that's probably why I see the inkling of fear in her eyes. She tries to hide it, but I see it.

Plain as day.

"Thea."

"If I ever see your ugly face out of this cement tomb, I'll rip the skin from your bones. I don't fuck around, and I don't take threats lightly. So, I hope you confront me in your shitty flats outside of this school so we can see who really wears the fucking *boots* in these halls."

Even with five pounds of makeup on her face I watch the color drain, leaving her a pale shade of ghostly white. I want to laugh at her fear, but instead I give her a small smirk. "See you around, *Thea*." I turn back to my locker, listening as the shoes squeak across the floors of everyone making their way to class. Sticking my head into the darkness of my locker, I breathe out my anger and breathe in the smell of old metal.

Once the hallway is silent, I grab my next book, shoving it under my arm. My hand goes to the door, ready to shut it, when a body pushes against me. If I could fit, I'd be shoved into my locker, but instead, I'm shoved up against it, as cold, hard muscle molds against my back.

"Tell me, baby sister, why can't I get the vision of your wet cunt out of my head?" His long fingers curl around my thigh, trailing up until they're around the side of my ass. My eyes widen, and I look over my shoulder, expecting to see a crowd of people staring at us.

Except there's no one.

Wait, what?

I attempt to wiggle out of his hold, but he's strong as he pins me up against the hollow doors.

"Get off of me," I growl.

"Make me," he whispers in my ear, his hand sliding between my legs, pressing against my wet heat. I grind my teeth together, hating and loving his aggressive fingers. I want to tilt my head back against his shoulder, moaning out my pleasure. I haven't touched myself since my mom told me we were moving, and I now realize how coiled tight my body is.

But I hate the man giving me the pleasure, and that only makes it worse.

Or... better?

"I hate you. Get away from me," I whisper, feeling my folds drench his strong fingers.

He does nothing besides move his fingers around, not any type of movement to actually get me off. And it's like he knows this, torturing me, turning me into a puppet that only he can control.

His breath fans against my neck, and I shiver, both hate and need warming my belly.

"I'd rather fuck my own hand, Malik. Get away from me," I moan, but my movements are pointless, because I'm turning into a boneless body in his arms.

"And I'd rather stick my hand in a snake pit than your pussy, so tell me, why can't I step away?"

My knees begin to shake, and I grip the metal door of my locker, doing my best to hold on.

"Or maybe, I just want to see you go crazy. Lose your shit enough that they tear you away and lock you in a loony bin. What do you say, baby sis? Would that be enough to get you out of my life?" His fingers withdraw from my folds, and with his free hand, he spins me around, slamming my back against the lockers. It booms loudly in the empty hall.

Malik presses against me again, and this time I can feel his erection, thick and straining against his pants.

He brings his hand up, and I can smell my arousal immediately. His free hand comes up and his fingers press into my cheeks until a hint of pain hits, and my jaw pops open. His wet fingers dive between my lips, gliding against every inch inside my mouth.

He lathers my tongue with my sweetness, rubbing against my cheeks and scraping the pads of his fingers along my upper teeth.

"I see the psycho in your eyes, Vera. Maybe, you were made for a place like this. Except, I don't want you here, baby. I want you out of this town. So, unless you want to play my game and lose, I suggest you pack your shit, and get out while you still can."

My hand reaches up, and I grip his wrist, squeezing until his fingers leave my mouth. "You act like I want to be here. *I fucking don't*. I don't want to play your game, and I honestly don't want to talk to you. So do me a favor, step away from me, and go take care of your problem." I nod to the bulge in his pants. "But don't think of me."

Sliding out from beneath him, I leave my locker open, rushing to my next class. The bell had to have already rang. How I didn't hear it, I don't know. Maybe it was from his fingers inside me. It was like he knew exactly where to touch, where to push, where to caress.

He knew exactly what he was doing, and that has to be the only reason my legs are weak, my sex is begging for relief, and my chest feels tight.

That has to be it.

I slip into class. Sister Mabel is one of the nicer teachers. Well, I shouldn't say *nice*. She's still a bitch, but she doesn't bother me as much as the other teachers do. She gives me the same disgusted look that everyone else does, but at least she doesn't say anything about it. She's younger than the other nuns, too. Sister Marjorie and Sister Mary look to be about five hundred years old. Sister Mabel looks to be in her forties, maybe. The youngest one I've seen here.

She gives me a look of disappointment as I walk into class late, and I give her a wince, slipping into the back of the room and ignoring everyone's heavy stares.

I frown as my ass aches once I sit down. These are not like the ones at home. With either the slot in the bottom to slide your books and pencils in, or the ones where the top opens and you can put all your things inside. No, this is just a square table set in front of you, a tiny black seat, and two bars underneath your chair where you put your belongings.

Nothing else.

I adjust myself in my tiny seat, trying to ignore the throbbing between my legs. My upper thighs feel sticky, like Malik wiped my need across my skin. He made a mess down there, and embarrassingly enough, if I were to inhale deep enough, I think I can still smell my arousal.

I shift from side to side, wishing the need would lessen, but it only grows stronger.

I can't get him out of my head.

My fingers curl around my seat, and I dig my nails into the hard surface, aggravated that he's at the center of my thoughts when I'm this needy.

His fingers, though.

They were so strong, so aggressive. His overpowering scent as he leaned over me. Towered over me, actually. He takes control in every move that he does. He doesn't care how I feel about it. It's what and when something suits him.

No one else.

His voice became raspy as he spoke to me. The utter hate still dripped from his tone, but it's like he enjoyed it. It sounded like there was a burning lust that he so badly tried to hide.

I heard it.

But how could he lust over me? He hates me. He's playing a game with me, and like Hazel says, people end up dying when they become part of his pranks.

Sister Mabel speaks in the front of the class, her black outfit covering her from head to toe. Her mouth moves, but I can't hear a word she says. The entire lesson for today might as well be burned to the ground because my mind is completely elsewhere.

The thumping in my ears matches the thumping between my legs.

It becomes unbearable, and soon enough, sweat starts to dot along my hairline. My hands squeeze my thighs, and my shifting becomes constant.

A sick thought comes to mind, and it finally stops my movements.

I couldn't... could I?

I swallow down a whimper, my fingers walking up my thigh and slipping beneath my skirt. I'm drenched, and I close my eyes when I feel a small puddle on the seat beneath me. I brush my fingers through my slit, and nearly jolt from my desk. My boots hook around the metal legs, planting myself down while my fingers press into my folds.

I move slowly, glancing around to make sure no one notices me. It would take nothing, only a fast glance in my direction to notice my fingers plunged beneath my skirt and the slow rocking of my arm.

The thought brings a shiver over my body.

Fucking hell, this feels amazing.

I haven't been this wet... well, *ever*. And I'm wondering if it's from doing it in public, or from Malik's dirty fingers beneath my skirt.

I lick my lips. I can still taste his finger and my juices on my tongue.

I stick a finger inside and bite my lip when a moan tries to work its way from my throat. I bring my fingers up to my bud, feeling a slight thump coming from it. It's swollen, needy, and so close to coming undone.

My mouth falls open, and a shaky breath leaves my mouth.

I can't take it.

My hand leaves my folds, and I stand up suddenly, the desk slightly squeaking on the floor from my movements. Sister Mabel looks over at me, and I open my mouth, not sure what I need, but it's something, and I need it *now*.

"Can I use the restroom?"

She frowns at me, severe disapproval in her eyes. She points to the wooden bathroom sign, the same one I used yesterday that led me to The Room of Atonement. I walk to the door, keeping my legs closed because every step makes me feel like my juices are about to drip down my legs.

I pull the door open, slipping into the empty hallway and making my way to the bathroom. I walk quickly and quietly, wanting to get the deed done and go back to class, no distractions this time. No smoking, no Malik, nothing.

I just… I feel pent-up, about to explode, and I don't know how much longer I can take without unraveling.

My shoulder pushes on the bathroom door, and I walk inside, my nose scrunching at the smell of public bathroom as I head into the first stall on the left. I can't even lock the door; I just kick it closed and set my boot up on the toilet seat. Yanking my skirt over my waist, my naked, dripping folds come into view. They're swollen and needy as they beg for release.

I finally give in, placing my pointer and middle finger against my clit, rubbing hard. Rubbing fast. My other hand snakes behind my thigh and into my folds. I dip a finger inside, instantly hearing the wetness against my fingers.

"Oh, shit," I groan, my voice loud, bouncing off each wall in the bathroom. I tilt my head back, my eyes burning with tears the feeling is so intense. The old, faded, white tiled ceilings make me feel dirty. Closing my eyes, I let the feelings overtake me. Overwhelm me. I've never felt this way. *Ever.*

My back leans up against the wall of the dark gray stall, and I whimper, feeling myself climb to the top. Every plunge of my finger pushes me further toward the edge. *Almost there.*

The bathroom door swings open, and I want to open my mouth and scream at the top of my lungs. But I don't. I leave my fingers where they are, controlling my breathing and making sure the stall door stays closed.

Boom.

The door kicks open, and there stands Malik, a wicked look on his face that screams mayhem.

"What have we got here? I expected to walk into another cigarette escapade, but fingers in your cunt? Now that, I didn't expect."

I scowl at him, not moving from my position, no matter how awkward it feels. He had his fingers in here less than an hour ago. He's seen me in the shower. He knows what's beneath the clothes.

"Why the fuck are you even in here? Are you stalking me? How do you keep knowing when I'm going to the bathroom?"

He presses his hands along the frame of the stall, keeping me trapped. "I know everything that happens in this school. In this town, for that matter. Nothing goes unnoticed to me."

I nod my head toward the door. "That's lovely. Get the fuck out."

He cocks his head to the side, pondering his answer. "I will. Once you come."

I shake my head viciously from side to side. He wants me to get myself off with his creepy ass watching me? *No thanks.* "No, not with you in here. Leave, *now*, so I can finish this shit and go back to class."

He leans against the side, crossing his legs at the ankles and getting comfortable. "If you want to wait until Sister Mary and Sister Maxine walk in here to catch us again. Go ahead, be my guest. But let me warn you, I walked away last time with no issues. I'll be able to walk away this time just as easily. You? Not so much."

He looks so cool, so damn confident in his words that I want to strangle him. Bury my wet fingers into his neck until he stops breathing.

Instead, I shift, giving him a full-on view. I prop my leg on the toilet paper holder, spreading my legs wide with my fingers still plunged knuckle-deep. "Fuck it. You want a show? I'll give one to you, but it's the most you'll ever get. So, watch fucking carefully, big brother, because this isn't happening again."

He looks bored, staring into my eyes instead of what's between my legs.

Fuck it.

I move my fingers, bringing my free hand back to my clit, I rub hard and fast, chasing the orgasm that's only slightly abated from yet another argument with him.

I close my eyes, tilting my head back and letting the heat take over me. Slowly, so fucking slowly, my orgasm starts climbing again. I can feel it in my knees as they start to tremble. I plant my foot, keeping the other secured on the toilet paper holder as I fuck my finger like it's the best sex in the world.

"Stop."

I growl, cracking my eyes open to find him staring at me. His hand digs into his pocket, pulling out his large blade. "Use this."

My eyes widen. "Are you sick? I'm not fucking myself with a knife."

He continues to hold it out. "You won't fucking die unless you want to open it and use the blade, but I don't feel like explaining your bloody corpse to anyone. So, keep it closed, and fuck yourself with the handle. Now."

I stare at it, unsure why he would prefer me to use a knife instead of letting me do what I want. But, of course, he needs to find some way to be in charge. Another thing to control.

Me. He wants to control me.

"Take it or I'll drag you out of here by your hair and tell Sister Mary I found

WICKED LITTLE SINS

you doing drugs and committing self-pleasure in God's house. She'd fucking love that."

I bite my tongue until the skin splits, warm blood spilling over my teeth. I don't doubt for a second that he would go tell someone about what he's seeing here.

With shaky fingers, I take his knife, feeling the weight in my palm. It's black and shiny, a heavy, cold metal that would feel so unnatural inside my body. I shiver just thinking about it.

"I don't have all day, Vera. Are you really that much of a pussy you can't fuck yourself in front of your brother?"

I scowl at him, fisting the top of the knife and bringing the handle to the crux of my thighs. I shiver when it touches my folds, the cool metal shocking my skin.

I press inside, the weight of the knife sinking in deep. It's smooth, not nearly as uncomfortable as I anticipated. It feels like the time I used my hairbrush, slightly uncomfortable, but still scratching the itch I so desperately craved.

It's foreign, but it feels so, so good.

I attempt to keep my eyes averted, cemented to the black silver that slides from my folds, glistening with each plunge. The wetness of my pussy against the metal is the only sound in the room besides my heavy breathing. Malik doesn't make a sound, doesn't even shift his feet, and for a moment, I'm wondering if he left me. Fled the bathroom.

Could he be that disgusted of me?

My eyes lift of their own accord, and they instantly clash against his brown ones. He orders me to fuck myself with his knife, but he won't watch?

"Why won't you watch me?" A tingling starts between my thighs, and my ankle on the toilet paper holder starts to shake, rattling the cheap plastic.

His jaw clenches, a slight twitch against the muscle. My eyes grow hazy, and I can't think of anything besides unraveling this tension that's been tied tight for so long. He doesn't say anything, doesn't answer my question. He only continues to stare into my eyes, as my body falls apart around him.

"Malik..." I whisper, feeling lost, confused, angry. So fucking angry. But I feel like I need something. I'm just unsure of what that is.

The tingling spreads through my limbs, a spark of a firework making its way down the wick. I'm not ready for the explosion. I've never felt this way. *So completely seen.*

"Please, Malik. Please," I beg, thrusting the metal faster inside me. I push harder, until it hits that spot. Over, and over, *and over.*

Malik's eyes darken, black orbs glaring down at me with so much malice burning in them.

I can't focus on his hate or his fury. My body crumbles, falling apart piece by piece. My hand lifts, pressing against the cool stall door as I hold myself up. My limbs tremble and my vision clouds, my orgasm pumping in my ears at the same pace my sex clenches in ecstasy.

It feels like hours, although I know it's only seconds, before my body pieces itself back together. I look up, feeling flushed, my skin damp and my face reddening, my consciousness finally hitting me.

What the hell did I just do?

Malik stands there, his face blank, emotionless, maybe slightly bored. His hand extends, palm up, as he watches me.

I'm confused for a second, unsure of what he wants. Then my eyes widen, and I glance down at the wet metal still plunged between my legs.

I slide it out, the cold metal now hot and wet. I think about wiping it off, maybe grabbing some toilet paper to clean the mess I made. But with clarity comes emotions, and I realize how much I hate him. My foot drops from the toilet paper holder, and I take a step forward, dropping his knife into his palm. I watch as it rolls slightly, leaving a wet streak along his skin.

He curls his fingers around the knife, closing his hand. His nostrils flare, as if the scent of my arousal finally hit him.

I stand before him, waiting for something. For him to speak to me, maybe, or yell at me like he always does. Put me down, degrade me. He's so good at all of it, yet all he does it watch me.

Suddenly, his eyes flash, and he spins around, stomping from the bathroom without another glance in my direction. The bathroom door slams, and I jump back, the feeling of ice dripping down my back cooling me to the bone.

What the fuck just happened?

My legs feel boneless, and the rest of my body feels electrocuted. My head feels like it is filled with helium, like I'm high.

I right my clothes, walking out of the stall just as the door bursts open again. Sister Mabel walks in. Her face screams apprehension, like she already assumed I'd be in here smoking or something. When she sees me only standing there, she halts in her step, confusion lacing her eyes.

"You've been quite a while. Is everything okay?"

I swallow. I just fucked myself in front of my stepbrother. "I'm fine.

Cramps." The lie flows from my lips freely.

A sympathetic look crosses her features. "Very well. Please hurry and get back to class, Vera."

I nod, spinning around and heading toward the sink. I turn it on, finally letting my shoulders drop once I hear the door close.

Holy shit.

18

MALIK

A rain drop hits my fingertip, followed by another. I look through my windshield, seeing the dark, swirling clouds moving through the sky. Rain begins to slap on the glass, big, heavy drops that pound quickly. I knew it was going to rain. Not even by the heavy clouds, but that humid, wet smell of an incoming storm.

I ash my cigarette, bringing my hand in from my window just as the heavy dong of the bell rings, alerting the end of school.

I've been sitting here for the last hour, watching the sky darken at the same rate as my thoughts.

I can't get her out of my head.

Scratch that. I can get her out of my head. She's meaningless. It's her cunt, dripping, peachy pink, and swollen as my knife plunged through her folds. I slip my hand in my pocket, grabbing my knife that's unfortunately now dried. I bring it up to my nose, inhaling her sweet scent.

She's unbelievable. A siren. A damn *witch*.

My blood screamed that I should have wrung her neck until her skin turned purple. My dick sat rock-hard as I listened to the sound of her plunging my metal knife inside her dripping cunt.

My head tilts back on my leather seat, and I close my eyes, wanting so badly for her to disappear from this earth so that I don't have to spare another moment of my life thinking about her. But I know that won't happen.

I tilt my head up when I hear the front door of the school open, and a flock of black uniforms rush out, their backpacks pushed over their heads to shield themselves from the rain. They sprint to their cars, not spending their usual after-school hour of chatting by their vehicles.

I watch as the guys walk out, slowly, unconcerned of getting drenched. It rains here. A lot. If it's not raining, it's snowing. It's never sunny, it's never bright. There's never the feeling of the sun beating down on your face, warming your skin and giving you a golden tan.

The guys notice me sitting in my car, and each one of their faces scrunch up in confusion. I roll down my driver-side window as they walk up to the car. "What the hell are you doing?" Levi shouts over the rain.

I take a drag, exhaling the smoke out of my nose. It trails toward my lap in two thick streams. "Waiting."

He frowns. "Waiting? Waiting for what?"

I point my cigarette at the girl running down the steps of the school. "Her."

The three of them turn their heads, watching as Vera and the weird chicks run toward a black Charger.

What the fuck? Where is she going?

"Why are you waiting for her? What the hell is going on?" Felix barks at me, shoving Levi out of the way. "Why weren't you in class? Were you with her?"

I open the door, shoving him out of the way. The water seeps into my clothes instantly, my hair flattening against my forehead. I push it out of the way, my cigarette fizzing out, the rain soaking into the paper and making it fall apart in my hands. I drop it on the ground and glare at my friends. "Quit being a pussy. We're still on. Actually, we'll get her tonight, okay? Just wait for my fucking word."

With that, I shove away from them, heading toward the enemy. What, does she expect I'll sit in my car like a damn puppy and wait to bring her home? She was just planning to leave with someone else, and not tell me?

More than that, where the hell is she going? Who is she going with? What the fuck does she plan on doing? She's not going to get comfortable here. I won't allow it.

I stomp through the parking lot, my boots viciously landing in puddles, making water fly in all directions. It's like she can tell when I'm near, because her hand freezes on the door handle of the car, her hair turning wet, her clothes sticking to every inch of her skin. She glances at me over her shoulder, the makeup around her eyes sliding down her cheeks.

"What do you want?" she screams as she opens the door.

"Where the fuck do you think you're going?" I bark at her.

She rolls her eyes, opening up the door. "To my friend's house."

My palm slaps the top of the door, shutting it so hard the entire car rocks. "You aren't going anywhere, and you don't have any friends here."

The window rolls down, and a redhead in the backseat shouts at me, "Actually, she is our friend. Now let her go and quit harassing her."

I pin Vera against the side of the door, curling my hand around the wet window and leaning down so I'm eye level with this random. "Who the fuck are you?" I know these girls; I'm just being an asshole. But I am being honest when I ask what her name is. She's clearly enough of a loser that she doesn't hang out with my crowd.

Weirdos.

"My name is Blaire, asshole. I've been going to school with you since forever." She rolls her eyes. "Let go of Vera and get out of here, you creep."

I laugh, shaking my hair out. It sprays against Vera's face, and she covers her eyes and wipes her cheeks. It's pointless and makes no sense, though, because her face is already drenched from the rain.

Or, maybe it's just me she's trying to rub off of her.

Doesn't she know? I'm already inside. Deeply, deeply inside of her.

My hand goes up, and I wrap my fingers around Vera's neck, cocking her face up to look me in the eyes. "Listen to me and listen good. Next time you feel like flitting off with your little sister whores, you let me know. If you ever, ever make me wait for you again, I'll make you fuck my knife again. But this time, it won't be your dirty cunt my knife will be inside," I whisper in her ear, my lips brushing the wet skin. Leaning back, I look her in the eyes, watching the large orbs stare up at me in shock.

She snaps out of it with a shiver. Standing on her toes, she presses her body against mine. "Promise?" she whispers.

I'm momentarily stunted by her raspy tone that I don't notice as she slips into the vehicle. I blink, glancing down at her hateful smile. The one I want to carve off her face and paste on my wall. I lift an eyebrow, knowing the moment she gets back to my house…

It's game on.

19

VERA

"What the fuck is wrong with him?" Blaire shouts as we drive away. The rain pounds against the windows, and I roll mine up, wiping the rain drops from my arm. The fast swipe of the wipers scraping across the windshield makes an obnoxious groan.

"He's a psychopath," I mumble, glancing his way through the window. Water drips from his arms and the back of his hair as he walks through the downpour.

It seems that whenever I'm around him, the worst of me makes its way to the surface. All the bad and dirty inside me seeps through my pores and I snap at him like the vicious snake he believes me to be.

I hate the fact that whenever he's around me, he turns my skin to fire. Even a slight touch is like static. We're oil and water, we shouldn't mix. Yet, we do. It's frightening, and I hate it, nearly as much as I hate him.

I hate him so much.

My fingers twitch to dig into his eyes, scrape my nails down his face until he has deep scores embedded within his skin. I'd love to see him, bleeding and in pain as he snarls at me, his teeth clamping together like a rabid animal.

But the other part of me… the other part enjoys the way he looks at me. I loved his dark eyes staring into mine while I touched myself. The seduction in his raspy tone as he whispers filthy, unimaginable things in my ear.

"He looks at you like he wants to fuck you. Are you sure you haven't done anything with him?" Hazel asks from the driver's seat.

I shake my head, lowering my face so my friends can't see my heated cheeks. "Nothing. I think he's just... possessive. He doesn't like me in this town."

She laughs. "Looks like he doesn't like anyone to be around you, Vera. Didn't seem like he gave a shit about anything else."

"Fuck no. We hate each other. Like, I'm surprised one of us isn't dead yet. I'm sure it's only a matter of time."

"That's why I have an idea," Hazel smirks, and I sit up straighter, my fingers curling around her headrest to get a better look at her. The scent of fresh leather hits my nose.

"What do you have in mind?"

She lets loose a full-blown smile at this point. "You'll see."

I stare at her a moment, wondering what the hell it is she has up her sleeve. But even from knowing her for such a short amount of time, I know she's not one to crack easily.

Leaning back in my seat, I tilt my head toward the window, glancing at the black trees that sway in the wind. It looks like it should be the middle of the night, yet the moon doesn't sit in the sky. It's an eerie feeling, one that has shivers breaking out along my damp arms.

Hazel's windshield wipers swing back and forth rapidly, but even going at the fastest speed, visibility is still nearly impossible through the glass.

We drive for what feels like forever, but eventually, Hazel flicks on her blinker, and we turn right, going up a gravel hill. The gravel has turned to a mud in the heavy rain, and more than once I'm afraid the tires are going to get stuck, sinking us into the ground and pushing us back down the hill.

"I'm fine. This happens all the time," she grunts, pressing on the gas as hard as she can. The engine whirs, and we shoot forward, jolting up the incline and ending in front of a small garage and a rambler type home. It's beautiful and black, more modern-looking than the rest of the houses I've seen in town. But still creepy and Gothic, with large columns in front of the house and a gargoyle-esque statue sitting at the entrance.

Hazel switches off her car, and we all open our doors, rushing toward the front door. It's dark, blood red in color, and rounded at the top. I can't help but feel like I'm constantly in some fucked-up story wherever I go.

Hazel presses down on the handle and steps inside. My brows furrow. "You don't keep your door locked?" That's weird, but I've always been on edge about people breaking in.

She shrugs, looking confused. "If someone wants to break in, they'll find a way in whether the door is locked or not."

Well, when she puts it that way...

She toes off her shoes, and we follow suit, padding through her house silently. I look around, noticing the old-school art placed throughout. She has tall candles on just about every table and cabinet, which must be the reason I'm having an overwhelming rush of fifty different scents. The house is large and extravagant, with dark wooden beams extending across the pointed ceiling. Yet, there's a feel about it that feels ancient, like I'm stepping back in time. Jars, blankets, and various plants decorate the house. Dried weeds and vines sit on the tables and hang from the ceilings.

My eyes widen at the abnormality of it all.

Large glass windows extend from the floor to the ceiling, showing off the forest around us, the dark, ominous trees in the distance.

"Vera, you coming?" Piper asks. I glance over at her and see her hand on a door handle to the basement. I nod and follow her as she heads downstairs.

The stairs are carpeted, plush against my feet as I silently walk behind her. My hand goes to the wooden banister once I get to the bottom of the stairs, and I turn around, my eyes widening when I see the open space in front of me. Large leather couches and movie theater style chairs sit in front of a screen that extends from the floor to the ceiling. It's beautiful, with a wooden bar on the side of the room, liquor bottles and a wine rack on the wall behind it.

Two completely different homes in one house. This shit did not look this big from outside.

"Wow," is all I can say.

Hazel goes behind the bar, ducking down and standing back up, holding a black box in her hand.

"I don't think it's going to work, Hazel," Piper sighs.

"Shit better not go south like last time." Blaire plops down on the couch, propping her feet up on the square coffee table in front of her.

"What's going on? What's the plan?" I ask, standing there, confused, unsure, a little leery. Even though my body doesn't get any bad vibes, I can't help the jaded part of me that wonders if these girls are trying to fuck with me.

Hazel walks to the couch, sitting down and setting the black box in front of Blaire's feet. "Girl, since you've been here, Malik has been nothing but hell for you. He's treated you like shit, belittled you, mentally fucked with you. Before he actually really fucking hurts you, it's time we put a stop to it."

I sit down on the opposite couch, the cushion curling around me like an oversized pillow. My interest is officially piqued. Excitement and relief start tingling in my fingers and toes.

There's a way to stop this nonsense? Yes, please.

"What do you have in mind?"

"Hazel is a witch," Piper says from behind me. She pulls a bag of chips and a Mountain Dew from behind the bar. "I don't like that Ouija board shit, Hazel. I'm not doing it again." Piper's entire body rolls with a tremor. Glancing at me, she says, "We did it last year and I had some creepy stuff happen to me for a while."

Hazel rolls her eyes. "It was all in your head. Nothing happened to either of us. And hey, I've been doing some digging, and there is a ton of shit we can do. Like repellant spells, or banishing spells…"

"Spells?" My eyes widen.

"She's serious," Blaire says.

"So, what do you say?" Hazel looks at me with an excitement in her eyes. I stare at her, blinking, unsure of what to say.

I mean, spells? Is this shit even real? The thought of banishing or repelling Malik from my life is extremely appealing. Maybe there's an ignoring spell, because that would be good enough for me. Anything to have him leave me the hell alone, then I can figure out how to get out of here on my own, without him breathing and threatening me over my shoulder the entire time.

But… *witches*? Hazel is a witch? I glance over at her, seeing her in a different light. But it doesn't surprise me completely. She seems different. And after seeing the upstairs of her house, it makes a lot of sense.

I've always loved the idea of the power of magic and something otherworldly. But have I ever thought I would be involved in something like this? I don't know. What is it, exactly? Black magic? Because that's an entirely different avenue.

"I say we do it." Piper sits down next to me, crunching on a chip. "I mean, as long as some creepy-ass spirit doesn't start harassing me like he did last time, I'm cool with it."

"There was no spirit last time," Hazel says, standing up. "I've got some shit that I put together. Hold on."

She stands up, stepping over Piper's feet and heading to a small door in the corner of the room.

"How do we even know this is going to work? What happens when you usually do spells? Do the lights flicker? Have you ever talked to ghosts before? What am I supposed to expect here?" My palms grow sweaty, and I rub them against my bare thighs.

Hazel's voice echoes as she laughs from inside the closet. "No, there are no flickering lights. At least none that I've ever experienced." She grunts, stepping out and shutting the door. "But, Piper is right. We did talk to some weirdo spirit when we did the Ouija board, and I'd rather that not happen again." Walking toward me, she has a large cardboard box in her hand. "It'll work, though. It'll work."

She walks over to us, dropping the box onto the couch. She grabs the corner of the table, pulling it toward the screen and giving us a big open area. Grabbing the blanket from the back of the couch, she lays it out. It's thin, almost like a sheet as it covers the carpet. There's a pentagram in the center, and suddenly this just got a lot more real to me.

I glance up at Hazel, suddenly unsure. I've seen scary movies. I know what happens when you don't know what you're doing. Pretending like this is just a game, like these objects are toys, or this is all in good fun? It never ends well. There's just so much that can go wrong.

Hazel goes to the box, pulling out black candles and placing them around the outer edge of the blanket. Walking back to the box, she grabs a bowl, placing it in the middle. She goes back and forth a few more times, silently grabbing things and placing them strategically around the blanket, like she knows exactly where they're supposed to go.

Okay, well, maybe I don't know what I'm doing, but hopefully she does.

When she stands back and walks to the box, I notice she's laid things out into a five-pointed star.

I swallow down my dry throat. *Yup, this is definitely black magic.*

She grabs some dried leaves, setting them next to the bowl in the center. Grabbing a few small vials, one with dark liquid and two with light liquid, she sits down, dropping them beside her thighs.

"Come on, sit down." She pats the spots in between the black candles. We all glance at each other, then stand up, sitting back down and creating a small circle.

"What are we supposed to do? Where the hell did you get all this stuff?" I ask, waving my hand around at all the creepy stuff in front of us.

Hazel reaches back, grabbing onto the corner of the box and pulling it off the couch. "I told you, I've been doing my homework." She reaches into the bottom of the box, pulling out a few more things. "There's also a small shop I found down in Duluth. It's, like, in the back of an abandoned street and looks broken down, but you'd never guess the type of shit I found in there."

My eyes widen when I watch her place a small square next to the bowl.

Picking up the tiny picture, I almost crack out a laugh, "Where did you get this?" My fingers brush over Malik's non-smiling face. He looks angry, but I guess he always does. It's black and white, like he's from a different time period. His hair is a bit shorter, and his eyes look a bit younger. It feels like he's looking at me. Directly into my soul. I can feel the hate in his stare.

Hazel rips it from my fingers. "I cut it out of the yearbook from last year. I figured you wouldn't have anything of his. A piece of hair, a pair of underwear?"

I scrunch my face up. "Gross, no."

"Exactly, which is why I needed this picture." She drops it into the bowl, sprinkling what looks to be black pepper and cinnamon on top of it.

"Why do you need all this stuff?" I ask.

She ignores my question. "Give me your finger."

I lift my hand, and she wraps her fingers around my wrist, pulling me toward her. She grabs a needle from the blanket, pressing the tip into my pointer finger.

"Hey, what the hell!" I try to pull my hand back, but she holds her grip tight as she pulls me forward, dropping my hand over the bowl and squeezes the skin on the tip of my finger until a dollop of blood falls directly on Malik's face.

"Maybe one more," she whispers, squeezing once more until a bigger drop than the first falls into the bowl. She releases my hand and grabs her phone, scrolling through while we all sit there silently.

"Okay. I've got it." She grabs a lighter from the blanket, going around and lighting each of the five black candles. For a second, I expect the flames to be black, too. But they aren't. The same gold ember lights from the flame.

Then we sit. The four of us in a circle, in dim lighting with lowly lit candles between us. We still have our uniforms on from school, and we look like some fucked-up horror movie about to go wrong.

"Everyone grab each other's hands," she states.

We do as she says.

"Okay, now repeat after me..."

__Viscous beast, with teeth like knives,__
__May you suffer like the most tortured lives.__
__For those that you rip in two,__
__May they finally come back to haunt you.__

Ripping flesh, bleed you dry,
May the entire world hear your cries.

We close our eyes, and I squeeze their hands tightly as the words leave my lips, praying for him to feel an ounce of the pain that he's inflicted on others. I want him to quit being the soulless human that he's made himself to be.

Once our chant is finished, I open my eyes, expecting the flames to grow or wind to blow through my hair. Nothing happens, and I look around, confused.

"Is that it?" I ask.

We all drop our hands.

"I guess only time will tell. But hey, there is something else I wanted to try." Hazel starts picking the things up from the floor, leaving the candles and blanket. She looks around at each of us, her hair falling into her face. "I've wanted to try it for a while, but we never had enough people."

Dropping the stuff into the box, she pops her hands on her hips and stares at me. "Vera, can I tell you something?"

My eyes widen, and I want to cringe, but I keep my face blank as I stare at her. "Uh, sure?"

An excitement grows in her eyes. "Ever since I met you, I've felt this… power within you. Have you ever tried any magic at your old house? Or has anything weird ever happened to you?"

I frown. "You feel a *power* in me? What does that even fucking mean?" I take a step back, not wanting any kind of *anything* to be in me.

I just want to be normal, dammit.

She sighs. "Have you? Ever felt anything?"

I shake my head.

She frowns at this, like that isn't the answer she expected. "Well, shit. I swear, even sitting with you during that chant, I just… I felt it. I think you're a witch, too."

"Too? What do you mean?"

Her eyes roll as she waves me off. "I come from a long ancestry of Wiccans."

My lips scrunch up and I nod my head. *Yeah, totally normal.*

"Okay, Hazel, what else did you have in mind?" Piper laughs.

"Have you guys heard of light as a feather, stiff as a board?" Hazel smiles at each of us.

This, I have heard of.

"Oh my God, I've always wanted to try that!" Blaire shrieks, helping pick up the rest of the things.

"How do we play?" I ask.

"Well, first things first. Who wants to levitate?" Piper asks.

They all look at me, and I widen my eyes. "Why am I the one that has to do it?"

Blaire pushes on my shoulder. "Because you're the newbie, so lay on your back. Oh, and I think you have to cross your arms over your chest or something."

Hazel nods, scrolling through her phone. "Yeah, she has to fold her arms. And then all we have to do is put our two fingers underneath her body. One person goes to her head or her shoulders, and then one person on each side of her body."

They crawl around, Hazel going to my head, Piper on my left, and Blaire on my right.

"Now what?" I whisper, sensing each of them hovering over me. I keep my eyes closed, feeling their fingers press against my skin.

"Now we chant," Hazel whispers.

Light as a feather, stiff as a board. Light as a feather, stiff as a board. Light as a feather, stiff as a board. Light as a feather, stiff as a board.

They repeat it so many times I start chanting it in my own head. Over and over again, I repeat it. Until my body feels weightless, and the air curls around me from every side of my body. My eyes fly open, and I'm not down by their waists, but up by their shoulders.

Their eyes are wide, shock and surprise on their faces as they continue to chant. My arms shake and my mouth drops open. I feel stable, like the air has a good hold on me, yet any breath of air might make me go crashing to the ground.

"Holy shit," Blaire whispers, disrupting the chant. That side of my body curves, and my arms jolt forward in shock as I crash to the ground. "Shit! Sorry!" she screams.

"Fuck," I groan, rolling onto my stomach. "That was scary as shit." I get up, looking at each of their shocked faces. *"But so fucking cool."*

They each crack a smile, awe pitched on their faces.

"I should probably get home." I stand up.

"Wait." Hazel stands up with me, going back to her black box on the table. "Now I'm all fucking excited. My body is humming right now, and I'm not ready for it to be over. We should try the Ouija board. Just once?" She shakes the box, and the board rattles around on the inside.

Piper and Blaire groan behind me.

Hazel scowls. "Come on, Piper. You were all for it last time. Wouldn't you like a chance to talk to Baylin again?"

My eyes widen, and I turn around, glancing at Piper. "Who's Baylin?"

She frowns. "My boyfriend, or, well, ex-boyfriend, I guess."

"He's... dead?" Why are there so many dead kids in this town?

"He died in The Room of Atonement," Blaire says.

My jaw goes slack, and the hair on the back of my neck raises. "He died in The Room of Atonement, too? How do all these kids die in this fucking room and no parents have done anything about it? Shouldn't there be some... school investigation or something? Figure out how these deaths keep happening at school?" I feel like a part of me is going crazy. What the hell is going on here, and why do I feel like the only normal person?

Piper's eyes are watery, but there's a darkness that glows beneath the irises, just like I see in everyone else in this town. Like the darkness is a poison and it's leaked into her pores. "Think of a curse. You can put a curse on a person, right? You don't curse their hand, or their face, although in a way, I guess you could. But usually, when you curse someone, you curse that entire person, and everything about them. That's this town. The moment you cross the border into this town, you step into the curse. North of us, when you step out of this town, you are out of the curse. South of town, you're out of the curse. But once you're here—*in here*—a part of it never leaves you. The curse extends to our homes, our food, the school we go to, and unfortunately, every person we speak with. The moment you came to live here, Vera, you became a part of that curse, too. Talking to people about the deaths won't do anything, because this place is nothing but death. All the way to six feet under with all the skeletons rotting away in their coffins."

My palm falls against my chest. "I'm... cursed?"

All three of them nod.

I laugh. "Well, how do I get un-cursed?"

Piper shakes her head. "You don't. If you ever happen to leave here, which happens to very few people, you'll always find your way back. The curse lives and dies here."

"What is the curse? Who put the curse on this place?" I fall back on the couch, feeling like the prologue of this town is finally being revealed. It's all been such a mystery. But now maybe I can finally get some answers.

"Folklore," Blaire groans, falling back onto the couch. "I fucking hate these stories."

"I guess I don't really know the full story. I've heard a ton of different half-assed theories that don't really make any sense, but there's one that I've heard many times, the most believable story," Piper says, grabbing the box from Hazel and sitting down on the floor.

It's an ancient thing. Not the Ouija board you'd buy at Target. This one is in a plain black box. It's thick, made out of some type of leathered material. There are scratches and indents across the surface, which makes me think it's not new, but weathered from years of use.

I lean forward, my elbows on my knees. Suddenly, going home is the last thing on my mind.

She opens the box, taking out the board and setting it on the blanket. "Scorned lover. Dead child. Same old, same old."

I shake my head. "No, I actually don't know what you're talking about. *Tell me*," I urge.

"Let me tell it." Hazel sits down next to me, grabbing the planchette from the Ouija box. "Apparently, like, one million years ago, there was a train track that went straight through the middle of this town. Some people say the tracks are buried deep beneath the ground, but I haven't found any truth to it. Anyway, a young couple had a small child, and one day, while the husband was at work, the wife had a man over. She was seemingly cheating on her husband. Well, while they were fucking like rabbits in the bedroom, the kid got outside and made his way to the train tracks.

"The husband ended up coming home from work early that day. He found them in bed together and stabbed the guy, who bled to death on the bed as he made the wife watch. It was only after the guy was dead that he realized his son was missing. He left her and her dead lover on the bed and went out, searching for him. But he never came home. Some people say he jumped off the cliff after he found his boy. Others say he got hit by a train, too. Others say he just left. But people say that sometimes at night, you can hear the train honking, warning away the boy and his father. You can see the glow of the lantern the dad was holding as he searched all night for his son.

"No one ever saw the son or the father ever again. Whether their bones lay in Castle Pointe or something supernatural happened to them, or if they just fled from the slutty mom, they're gone, and they were never seen again. Though, the most legitimate rumor is the dad saw the son being hit by a train and he lost his mind, killing himself, too."

I can barely breathe. "What did the mom do?"

"The mom went crazy after that. Never left her house. Apparently got into some dark shit, black magic and stuff. Some say she went schizophrenic. Others say she was just grieving. Either way, people say it's her that put the curse on this town. That she believed Castle Pointe held an evil, and she wanted to keep that evil contained. But at the end of the day, all she did was poison it with a spell that leaves us all trapped in this hell."

My eyes are watering, and my heart beats a mile a minute as I digest her words. I don't want to believe it. It just sounds like another horror story, something that I'd hear around a campfire or watch alone at home on Tubi. But I know there's a truth in her words. I can feel it, as they wash over me, the realization. The absolution in her words.

"What happened to the lady?" I whisper.

"She hung herself," Piper says.

Hazel scowls at her.

I blink. Then blink again. "What?"

They give each other a heavy look, and then Piper turns toward me. "She hung herself in The Room of Atonement. At school."

Ice-cold dread washes over me at her words. The room I was trapped in. The room that I heard voices, felt fingers on my skin, and got a wicked scrape on my back in. She hung herself in *that* room? *Get the fuck out of here.*

"No way," I whisper.

They all nod.

I shiver, feeling colder than I've ever felt in my entire life.

"So, what do you say?" Hazel asks after a few moments of silence.

I shiver, whiplashed from the entire story.

"Fine. Fine, let's do it," Piper sighs, walking over and sitting back down on the couch.

"Vera?" Hazel looks over at me, and I gnaw on the corner of my lip. I want to, but I've also heard enough shit about Ouija boards that I know this could be the stupidest thing I'll ever do. There's a mile-long list of things that could happen because of it. But should I do it? Do I really want to risk it?

The three of them sit on the floor, the old leather box between them, and my skin grows warm. I want to. The evil, doesn't care about anything, part of me wants to do something bad. See if I can talk to someone.

But not just anyone.

"Ah, fuck it. Let's do it." I walk over to the couch, sitting next to Piper, excitement and anticipation building in my belly.

Blaire walks over to the table, pushing it back in front of us. "I'm not asking the questions this time."

"I'll ask the questions," Hazel says, opening the box and setting the board on the table.

It's long, rectangular, and looks thick. This one definitely looks authentic, nearly decades old. The letters are painted with what looks like calligraphy or some Gothic script. She sets the planchette on the table, and I pick it up, feeling its weight between my fingers.

It's heavy. Heavier than I thought it would be. The rounded bottom curves around to the pointed top. The thick wood is cut out in the center and a foggy piece of glass covers the space. This piece looks old, too. Worn. Small carvings and details line the wood, swirls, and designs, and what looks like letters, although they aren't words I understand or know how to read.

Latin, maybe?

"Where did you get this thing?" I flip it back and forth between my hands. "This thing looks ancient."

Hazel shrugs. "It's been in my family for generations."

I set it down, feeling like it leaves a residue or some type of remnant on my fingers. I rub them together, not liking the feeling in the slightest.

"Ready?" Blaire asks, picking up the planchette and setting it in the middle of the board.

Piper and Hazel place their fingers on the planchette, and Blaire does the same.

"What do we do?" I ask, feeling the temperature in the room drop a few degrees.

"Just put your fingers on the edge," Blaire says, sliding her fingers over to give me some room.

I do as she asks, and it feels like the energy sucks from the room, filling the planchette against my fingertips.

"Is anyone here?" Blaire asks after a second.

I breathe through my nose, my fingers trembling as I wait.

"Is anyone in here with us?" she asks again.

"Are there any spirits present?" I choke out.

They look at me, and I glance down at the board. "I think you have to ask formally."

I watch the board, waiting for any kind of movement.

My fingers start being tugged, the wooden piece below me twitching against the board. Once it starts to move, my eyes widen. I look up at Piper. "Are you doing this?"

She shakes her head.

I look at Blaire and Hazel. "This isn't a fucking joke. Who's doing this?"

"I'm not," Hazel whispers, watching the wooden piece move up to the top of the board. It veers left, ending with the tip pointed at *yes*.

I let out a shaky breath, ready to lift my fingers. "I can't—"

"Don't!" Piper shouts. "Don't lift your fingers. We have to finish the game. It's the rules."

I settle my fingers down, one million questions building in me and my mouth not able to form even one.

We all stare at the wooden piece beneath our fingers, the pointed tip settling to a stop.

It's silent, not a word flows from our mouths and not a breath heaves from our chests. I can feel the planchette tremoring under our touch, each of our hands shaking with nerves.

"Are you a good spirit or a bad spirit?" Piper whispers.

Nothing. No movement. I can't even feel a pull of the wood against the board.

"How did you die?" Blaire asks, leaning forward as if she could hear the words lift from the letters.

The wood jerks, sliding across the board in a slow, almost lazy movement.

It feels wrong. My fingers on this wood. From the fear on all their faces, they aren't doing anything either. Whatever is speaking to us, it isn't a living being. It's something different. It feels heavy, thick. Like a sticky, black tar that cements itself to your skin and won't come off easily, no matter how hard you scrub.

"B-L-O-O-D."

We all say the letters out loud, each one punctuated with a heavy thump of fear that echoes in our bones.

"Blood? What does that mean?" I ask, my voice shaking the words from my throat.

"He drowned? Did he drown in blood?" Blaire asks.

"He? Maybe it's a she." Piper looks at us with wide eyes.

"Are you a man or a woman?" Hazel asks. Her fingertips are white against the pale wood. "Maybe he or she lost a lot of blood and died. Did you die from losing blood?"

The wood vibrates beneath my fingers but doesn't move.

"You're asking too many questions," Blaire sighs. "What is your name?"

It takes a moment, my heavy breaths shaky and hot as it blows across the skin on my hands. Slowly, it inches its way across the board.

"D," Blaire says.

"A," I whisper.

"D," we all say together.

"D-A-D. Dad? Whose dad?" Hazel frowns, confusion written all across her face.

My eyes widen, and my fingers fly off the wood. My heels press into the rug, and I shove my butt back, away from the board. "I-I don't want to play anymore."

They let go of the board, looking at me with hesitation and curiosity.

"What was that?" Blaire scooches over to me, wrapping her arm around my shoulders. "You look like you saw a ghost or something."

It's because I did.

Or at least, I felt something like one.

I shake my head.

"Tell me. I didn't see anyone. Did you see a figure? A shadow? Did you feel something?" Hazel's voice rings with excitement, but all I feel is a sick sense of dread.

All I can do is blink at the board.

"You look freaked out. Tell us, Vera. We're not going to say anything," Piper says softly.

I look up at each of them, seeing the sincerity in their eyes. I don't want to tell anyone my secrets, but I feel like I need to tell *someone*. I should tell them, since they seem to be my only friends here.

I shrug out of Blaire's hold, pressing my hands against the cushion beneath me and sitting on the edge of my seat. My fingers reach up, and I curl them around the top button on the collar of my shirt. I push the plastic through the hole, the front of my shirt loosening and opening. The girls are silent as they wait for my response, watching tentatively as I continue to undo button after button. Once I have enough room, I shove my shirt aside, revealing my black bra. Pulling the cups down slightly, I keep myself concealed but give them a glimpse of my biggest secret, biggest regret, worst nightmare, all rolled in one.

"Holy shit. What happened to you?" Blaire gasps, her hand reaching up to brush my skin. At the last moment, though, her fingers freeze, and she pulls her hand back, settling it back down into her lap.

I bring a hand up and press between my breasts, the large, ugly scar that runs from the top of my sternum to below my breasts. It's long, ugly, discolored, and the texture feels like burnt skin.

"I think… I think that was my dad," I say absentmindedly. "I think that was him through the Ouija board." I glance down at it, the wooden planchette still poised over the letter D.

"What happened?" Piper asks.

I blink, feeling like too much is happening too quickly. I want to grab the board and ask it more questions. See if it is my daddy talking to me. But I also want to run. I want to run from this town and never look back.

I look at each of them, their wide eyes, their pale faces all expectant and curious. They want to know, but the real question is, do I tell them? Do I trust them with a piece of myself that I've kept bottled up inside me for the past two years?

Sacha and Leena know at home, but even they didn't know about my deepest, darkest horrors and the feelings that drip through my body with blood as cold as ice.

"I have… or, well, had a heart condition. I was born with it, really. We all thought we had it under control. I took my medications, went to the doctor appointments, ate healthy. I did everything right, and my family thought I was fine."

"What happened?" Piper asks, stepping around the table and sitting next to me on the couch, opposite of Blaire.

I breathe, and for the first time since my surgery, it feels like my heart is in pain. I bring my hand up, rubbing it against my breast, attempting to lessen the ache. It doesn't do anything, though. If anything, the ache continues to grow with each passing moment.

"My dad and I were driving home one night, and it was raining super hard. He could barely see out of the windshield. The rain sounded like hail, like softball-sized hail pounding at the roof of the car as hard as it could. He was going to pull over because he couldn't see a thing. But before he could, he hit a road with standing water, and he hydroplaned." I swallow, my throat feeling dry, each inch of my mouth sticky and thick. "We went over the curb, straight down a hill and into a pond."

I look up at them, seeing their horrified faces of my tragic life. The nightmare that I relived while I was in a coma. The never-ending dream that I couldn't escape from. It played in my mind. For minutes, hours, days, weeks… I don't remember how many times I heard my dad scream in my ears until I woke up in the hospital room. "I blacked out. I don't remember what happened, not exactly. All I do remember is that I woke up, with a huge scar between my breasts and my dad's heart placed in my chest. The crash fucked him up pretty bad, and he was brain dead for a short while, but they knew he'd never get out of it. It was unnecessary to even leave him on life support because he would've been a vegetable forever. There was no *what-if* or anything like that. He was just a dead body. But me, I survived, I guess, even though I wish I hadn't." I rub my chest again, my dad's heart beating beneath my ribs. The steady, heavy rhythm thumping blood through my veins.

"I don't want his heart inside me. I don't want the reminder that he died, and I survived. It could have—*should have*—been me. I was the one with the broken body. My dad would have lived longer than everyone else. Except he didn't."

"So, what, your heart failed?" Hazel asks, scooching closer to me. Tears glisten in her eyes, her heavy black makeup smearing slightly.

I nod. "The problem that we all thought was under control was a roaring nightmare. My heart was halfway dead by the time I got into the car accident. I wouldn't have made it another year with my own pathetic heart in my chest. Unfortunately, or fortunately, as my mom says, my dad and I were a match. It took nothing, the doctors say. From one chest to another, our hospital beds only inches from each other. My dad lost a heart, and I gained his." I feel sick just thinking about it. Thinking about my lifeless father losing a part of himself when he never should have had to.

He was never supposed to die.

Blaire wipes her eyes, and Piper sniffles. Hazel looks lost, slightly depressed as heavy bags form beneath her eyes.

"I don't want anyone's pity. So don't look at me like that." I wipe my hand down my face, halfway wishing I didn't tell them in the first place so I wouldn't have to feel like I'm feeling now. But, at the end of the day, am I ever not feeling like this? Is there ever a time when I feel actually… content?

I don't think so.

"I think I'm going to head home." I stand up, buttoning my shirt.

"Are you sure? You can stay here, if you want," Blaire says softly, standing up beside me. Piper and Hazel follow suit, standing silently but watching me so, so damn loudly.

I think of what would happen if I stayed the night. How angry my mother would get if I didn't tell her where I was. If I worried her even slightly, she would freak out on me.

Then, there's Malik.

Malik, Malik, Malik.

He's a force. Something so much larger than anyone I've ever met. He's everything evil wrapped up into a hugely destructive man. Rock-hard, dark hair, dark eyes, creamy skin. He could be on the cover of a magazine. He should be. Hottest man of the year, or whatever. He's classically handsome, although there's a ruggedness, a piece of him that seems so unnatural. Like his nose has been broken a few times, or he's been built with scars. They may be invisible, but they make his imperfections all that more prominent.

He's controlling, too. And I have a feeling he's waiting for me, staring from the dark, dusted windows of his house, just waiting for the moment I step through the doors. Only so he can terrorize me. I seem to be his new toy in that regard.

I shake my head. "I better go home. I don't have service here." I look up at Hazel. "I don't have service anywhere in this town. Do you?"

She shakes her head. "There is a special phone provider for this town. If you look around outside, there are no cell phone towers. No towers at all, actually. This town is secluded from the rest of the world."

I wince. "I've gathered." I walk over to my backpack, slinging the black strap over my shoulder. "Can you bring me home?"

Hazel grabs her purse off the ground, digging around for her keys. "I can bring you guys home, if you want."

I nod, ready to get out of here. It feels like I'm being watched from every angle. Something feels wrong. Off. The air feels heavy.

"Do you really think that was your dad talking to you?" Piper whispers as we walk around the table and toward the stairs.

I glance over my shoulder, where the Ouija board sits on the table. I see the wooden planchette shake on the board, like it's trying to tell me something. My eyes widen only moments before the heavy, thick board lifts into the air, like it's weightless, even though I know the wood is heavy and dense.

"Guys..." I whisper.

They stop in their steps, following my line of sight.

"Do you see that?" My voice squeaks.

"Uh-huh." I can't tell who said that, the fear thickening the air in the room. I feel weighted down, like my legs could give out at any moment and knock against the ground. I steel my knees, locking them in place as I watch the Ouija board levitate across the room.

"What's happening?" Blaire whispers.

The board spins, then jerks, shooting in my direction at lightning speed. I duck at the last second, but the board still nicks my cheek, and I instantly feel the warm drip of blood trailing down my face.

The board and planchette crash into the wall behind me. So fast, so forcefully, that the board snaps in two. The noise is angry, the shards and splinters of wood crashing harshly against one another as they fall apart.

We all stare at the wood at our feet. My eyes are wide, burning and painful, as they watch the broken wood with unblinking eyes.

And suddenly, the realness of what just happened seems to hit us all at the same time. Our bodies twitch, and we don't say a word as we race up the stairs, taking two steps at a time.

We sprint from the house, bursting from the front door and running to Hazel's car. It started raining again outside, a light drizzle that hits our skin quickly. Even though the non-existent sun hasn't set yet, the cloud cover makes it feel like the middle of the night.

The many drops instantly turn my clothes into a damp fabric that weighs me down. Like it wants to keep me at the house, but I break through it, flinging myself into Hazel's car and slamming the door shut behind me.

Our heavy pants and the light rain are the only noises heard. It smells like wet pine and anxiety in the small box of the car.

"What the fuck just happened?" Piper shrieks.

I shake my head.

"What the hell are you going to do, Hazel? You can't go back to your house like that!" Blaire pants.

Hazel turns on her car, reversing out of her driveway before she can even turn her windshield wipers on.

"Hazel!" Blaire shouts.

Hazel blinks, turning to face Blaire in the passenger seat. "Oh, what?" Her teeth chatter lightly, the cold seeping into her skin.

"What are you going to do?" Blaire's voice sounds like she's near tears, and I don't blame her. That was absolutely terrifying. And I don't ever want to go near it again.

"I don't know. I'm not going back until my parents get home, though," she sighs, whimpers, and sighs again. "My family has never said anything bad about that Ouija board. It's never done shit like that to me." Her eyes tilt to the rearview mirror, and her eyes lock with mine. "I told you, Vera. You are very powerful. More powerful than I am."

My head whips back and forth. "I'm not a witch. That wasn't me. It was… whatever the hell that board was. It's cursed, just like you said Castle Pointe was. If it's been here for centuries, there has to be some creepy shit inside of it. Right? It wasn't fucking me."

Everyone is silent, and I can feel them inspecting me. They think I'm a witch. They think I have powers and have the ability to move the entire board or conjure up a spirit that can move the board across the room.

I'll admit, I felt… *something*. While we did the spell and once I was lifted in the air, my entire body hummed. A vibrancy ran through my veins, and it felt *so damn good*. But I did not, under any circumstances, move that board.

I blink, feeling a chill so deep in my bones, like my blood turns to ice.

Piper looks over at me. "Still feel like that was your dad?"

My blood shatters at that question, one million pieces of iced blood floating around in my numb body. I feel empty, but full. Full of terror and hatred. I knew whatever was talking to us in that room wasn't good. It was evil, everything my dad wasn't. He didn't have a bad bone in his body. But whatever breathed over my shoulder, whatever filled up the air in that basement, was filled with so much evil I could barely catch a breath without filling my own lungs with that same toxicity.

"It wasn't my dad," I whisper. "I know for a fact it wasn't him." I shake my head. "My dad is long gone. Whatever that was has been lingering on the surface, building and building hate and malice. Throwing a board across the wall felt like only an inkling of what it's capable of. It felt like only the beginning. Like… like a warning or something."

Piper's eyes fill with tears, with fear, flowing to the brim. I turn away from her, not able to take on anyone else's emotions when my own are out of whack. I glance out my window, seeing the blackened forest in front of me. The rain whips through the pines and makes the ground muddy and wet. Hazel finally turns on her windshield wipers, and they squeak as they whip from side to side, brushing the heavy drops off the glass as quickly as they possibly can.

I close my eyes, hating the feeling of driving in the rain. My body locks up from head to toe, and I rest my forehead against the cool glass, hoping to get back to my cursed mansion soon. For once, I think I'd rather deal with the evilness that is Malik, only so I can get out of the car.

My house comes into view, barely noticeable in the dark. The castle-like towers push up to the dark, heavy rainclouds that sit low in the sky tonight.

Barely any lights are on, the entire mansion encased in darkness, save for a low glow that comes from one of the upper-level rooms.

Malik's room.

"Are you going to be okay?"

I nod, grabbing my backpack and opening the door. The rain instantly hits my sock-covered knees, and I push off, giving them a small wave and shutting the door. I let the rain slap my face as I run to the house, not even bothering to wipe the drops away.

"Please be unlocked," I whisper. I don't have a key. I don't know any combinations to the garages or anything like that. If I'm locked out, I'll have to pound on the door until someone answers. But this place is so big, I doubt they'd even be able to hear me upstairs if I knocked. Especially in the rain.

My thumb presses on the lever, and I push down, the door easily gliding open. The stale air slaps me in the face, and just as I'm about to step inside, I feel the chilling sensation of someone watching me.

The sound of footsteps in puddles startle me, and I spin around, hoping to see one of my friends, but it's not them.

Four large, hulking figures stand in the darkness. So dark I can't make out who they are. Not exactly, anyway. But one stands out, and I don't need to see a hair on his head or the darkness in his eyes to tell me who it is.

Malik.

"What are you doing?" I shout over the rain, the drops turning thicker, dropping faster, the small drizzle turning into a light pour. "I'm not doing this shit again! Leave me alone!" I shout.

He steps forward, and the malice in his eyes make them seem possessed. Demonic.

My eyes widen, and I take that as my cue. I spin around, my foot lifting and stepping inside the house, when thick arms wrap around my stomach, lifting me off the ground.

"No. Stop!" I look over my shoulder, seeing the empty space where Hazel's car was only a minute ago. "Help!" I scream.

Malik's hand slaps over my lips, his skin wet and slippery against my face.

I can hear the door shut and see one of his friends still cloaked in the shadows of the night, his hand on the handle to the front door.

Malik starts walking, taking me down the steps and around the side of the house.

"Stop. Please, fucking stop, Malik! I'm sorry. I'm sorry for today. I'm sorry for whatever I've done. I'll leave you alone. I'll leave… I'll leave this fucking town. Just let me go!" I scream.

They don't speak as they walk, their footsteps heavy as they make their way around the house. I can barely make out the outline of Malik's car, but it sits there, beneath the overhang, staying fresh and dry. One of his friends opens the trunk, and Malik tosses me in like I'm a fucking inanimate object. *Again.* He turns me around silently, and I feel a coarseness around my wrists. My eyes widen.

He's tying me up.

"Stop! Please stop! *Someone help me!*"

"Shut the fucking bitch up," someone says.

I thrash from side to side, doing everything in my power to get out of the situation I'm in.

I can't. I can't handle their games tonight. Not after my day. Not after my fucking week. I refuse to run through the woods again. I refuse to be scared and terrified and fucking soaked in my sopping wet clothing.

But fighting is useless.

These guys are strong. Powerful. Menacing. There's no way I could ever get away from them. Not when there are four of them, and only one of me.

Suddenly, a body lingers over me, and I see Malik. Wicked, dark, and so, so commanding.

"Shut up, Vera. Save yourself some pain, because we won't be showing you any mercy." His face is blank and emotionless as he shuts the trunk, submerging me in complete darkness.

My eyes water with unshed sobs, but I swallow them back. My jaw feels like it's going to crack as I open my mouth as wide as I can and let out the most bellowing, screeching cry I've ever made.

"*Help!*" The words rip from my throat with such brutality my ears pop.

20

MALIK

"What's the plan?" Atticus asks, his eyes glowing with anticipation in the dark car.

I run my tongue along my teeth. "I was thinking the cemetery."

They're silent, surprise rolling through them as they come to terms with my plan. We usually have a theme of how we do our pranks. We start out easy, well, never *too* easy, but nothing that will kill them on the first go. Every prank becomes more intense each time.

The cemetery… it's *intense*.

There are voices and noises. You feel things that aren't there, you sense a presence that you don't want to be surrounded by. This cemetery, this isn't one where we put our loved ones when they die. This cemetery is centuries old and filled with broken, decrepit headstones that are so faded you can barely tell who is who. Spiderwebs and vines and unmaintained hedges overgrow the abandoned lot that lays smack-dab in the middle of the forest. You would never know it's there if you didn't know about it. It's about the size of a smaller home in diameter, with great big stones as tall as a child, chipped on the corners and weathered from the elements.

Behind the gravestones sits a mausoleum, which is where my mind has drifted toward tonight. I want her to be so scared she runs from this place, her feet refusing to stop until she wears her shoes down to nothing and blood runs from her bare feet.

People have gone missing in that cemetery. Some have gone mentally insane and had to be transferred to the hospital in the town over.

It was an easy decision to bring her to the cemetery. My stepsister is anything but innocent, and it was as simple as her showing me her dirty cunt for me to decide on my plan.

We drive around for a while, Vera's screams drowned out by the heavy metal music blaring through the speakers.

Eventually, I take the narrow turn that leads straight to the cemetery. Driving down the non-existent path, you'd never be able to tell there is even a road here, or any kind of indication of where it leads. It's hidden in between the trees, and the unpaved, gravel road makes it seem like more of a walkway than anything.

I turn down the music, only slightly. Vera's whimpers are terror-filled in the trunk, and it sounds like she's knocking around from one end to the other.

I chuckle.

I turn my brights on, and the cemetery lights up. Pressing lightly on my brakes, I switch off the stereo as everything goes silent.

We sit there a moment, and Felix shifts in his seat. "I fucking hate this place."

"Who doesn't? This shit needs to be on *Ghost Adventures* or something," Levi grumbles.

I shake my head. "I don't think anyone would willingly come to this place."

"Is somebody there? I've been fucking kidnapped by sadistic barbarians! Please, someone help me!" Vera screeches, her voice like nails on a chalkboard. The attitude in her tone doesn't go unnoticed either. The guys look at me because of her gall, and I smirk. Her words only reaffirm my decision.

The car starts rocking, and the sound of her kicking her feet against the door of the trunk makes my blood boil.

I open the door, my feet sinking into the wet ground as I walk around to the trunk. My finger presses on the release and the trunk glides open just as Vera's about to kick again. I grab her sock-covered ankle, just above her combat boots. They aren't socks like the other girls wear at school. No, these socks are for naughty girls who like to do naughty things.

And Vera has been nothing but naughty. Her creamy thighs rub together, not a hint of hair on them. The creamy skin looks like butter against my angry hand, pulsing and tensing with my veins ticking along my forearms.

I move out of her way, her legs writhing in an attempt to hit any body part it can connect with. I squeeze her ankle, hating that she affects me in any way. Even the sight of her pisses me off. How I can't make up my mind on whether I want to fuck her until she breaks, or spit in her face for stepping foot in my town. I can't decide.

"Quit fucking fighting," I growl, pulling her leg until she starts sliding from the trunk. Her skirt rides up, revealing her bare pussy and ass for everyone to see. When I hear the doors open and the guys step out of the car, I reach up and yank her skirt down, concealing her so the guys can't see.

Why? Why, Malik? Let them see. Let them have her.

I shake my head, disgusted with my indecision. It shouldn't be this hard to let her go, yet even the thought makes me feel like my bones are breaking.

I shouldn't care. Part of me wants to reach up and reveal her to everyone. Let them do what they want with her. She's not my problem. She never will be.

My nostrils flare and my body burns hot with irritation. I don't want anything to do with her. I don't even want to be pranking her. She's meaningless. A fucking pine needle that fell from a random tree.

Yet, there's something about her. The fierceness in her eyes. The hate in her voice as she lashes out at everyone around her. At me.

My cock twitches fiercely.

The way she plunged my raw knife into her dripping pussy. She was greedy and eager for anything to stop the ache. Even afterward, when she looked boneless, there was still a desperation in her eyes. She needed more.

I think she needed me, and part of me *wanted her* to want me, but I hate her. I hate her with a viciousness that is so brutal I think I'd rip her into pieces the moment I sink between her legs.

Vera looks up at me, her eyes wild and a little delusional. I don't know what it is about her, but I smirk at the madness in her gaze, the loathing in her eyes feeding my soul.

"How do you want to do this?" Levi asks.

I ignore him as I pick her up and stomp through the overgrown weeds, making sure not to step on anyone's cemetery plots.

"Dude, really?" Atticus laughs. "You want her dead that bad?"

I grunt, heading toward the mausoleum. I didn't expect her to be so bold today after taking away her underwear. I didn't imagine she'd turn it around and attempt to make me fall to my knees. I wasn't fucking going to, but the fact that she even tried.

Yeah, she needs to be put in her place.

I walk to the door, a massive stone fortress that seems impenetrable. Though, I've been here before, and I know that during the day it's locked tight with no way to open it from the inside or outside. But at night, the door lays opened just a hair. Why? I don't know. I've never had any desire to find out the reasons this town is as fucked up as it is.

The air is thick, a sliver of humidity lingering from the rainfall. The scent of pine is sharper than usual, as it always is after it rains.

The only light I have is from my headlights. I cinch my arms around Vera's waist, her body stronger than it should be as she tries to wiggle herself free.

"Quit fucking moving," I growl, sliding my hand between her thighs. Her movements make it easy to slide into her folds, and the moment my fingers touch the skin, her body freezes, and she bends back like a bow.

"Mal..." Felix's hesitancy doesn't go unnoticed. I can sense his unease about the situation. If it were any other situation, I'd stop and interrogate his ass. Tell him to turn his head on straight or get the fuck out of here.

But I don't have the time. Vera's body feels possessed, bending and contorting in ways it shouldn't as she tries to break free.

As expected, the door is opened, only a sliver. Atticus walks up, using both hands and curling his fingers around the door. He pulls, and the stone scrapes against the ground, loud and screaming with its protest.

The inside is pitch-black, though I know the gray brick is faded with water stains, and four crypts spread out along the walls. It's square, a small box with nothing else. I don't know who lives here, and maybe that's a good thing.

I walk in, chills breaking out along my spine as the dank air covers my skin. Dropping her to the ground, her knees knock together, and she scrambles to the door. I lift my foot, pressing it into her shoulder and shoving her back onto her ass.

"Wh-why are you doing this to me?" she cries, literal tears forming in her eyes. I didn't think she had any soft emotions, only anger and bitchiness.

I step forward, and her neck cranks back until it sits at an awkward angle. "Whatever you think you know about this place, wipe it out of that pretty little head of yours right now. That throne that you think your tight ass sits on, consider this me burning it from beneath you. You're sitting on a pile of ash right now, Vera, and that's where you'll stay. It's where you belong. Me, us," I stop to wave my hand behind me, knowing the guys are standing there. Formidable, unwavering, "We're the ones that call the shots. We don't follow your rules, because we made the fucking rules."

I step back, and fear fills her eyes in the form of big, unstable tears. "Consider this your warning. Bow down. We won't make you, but if you decide not to, well, you will die."

I can hear the guys' footsteps, and I take a step back. Vera instantly works to stand up, her hands still tied behind her back.

"Please. Please, I beg you. I'll do whatever you want," she pleads.

I stare at her, feeling the desperation rolling off her.

Too bad I don't care. Some people need to be taught a lesson, and the moment Vera stepped foot into my house, I knew she'd be one of the most conniving, vindictive people I'd ever meet.

I step out of the door, pushing it closed before she reaches it.

"No!" she screams. She cries so hard, but her voice is muffled by the thick stone. The rain has started up again, the heavy drips hitting my forehead.

A light fog has lifted from the ground, covering the gravestones and curling around our ankles.

"Dude, it's time to get out of here," Felix says, backing up toward the car.

We all hurry, wanting to get out of the cemetery before the fog overtakes us.

Before the dead come alive.

We all shut our doors quickly. I can't hear Vera's screams anymore, but I can guarantee her cries are ripping from her vocal cords.

I reverse out of the cemetery, the dirt and rocks flinging up on the sides of the car. I pull back onto the street, making my way back to my house.

"How long are you keeping her in there for?" Levi asks, staring out the window into the foggy night.

If we leave her in there until morning, we won't be able to get her until tomorrow night, when the door opens back up.

"I'll grab her before sunrise," I say.

It only takes a few minutes to pull into my driveway. I drove around town when Vera was in the car, making it seem like I was driving across town, maybe even out of town.

Little does she know, the cemetery she's in is only in our backyard.

21

VERA

"Help! Someone please help me!" I scream, pounding on the solid stone door, with my foot and my shoulders. Anything I can use to thrash harshly against the door as hard as I can.

At least, I think it's the door. There is no light, no windows, and from the feel of it, no door at all. My fingers trace around every inch of the room, and there's nothing. I walk with my back to the wall, tracing every surface with the little wiggle room my hands have with my fingers. No crack where the seal of the door should be. It's like it dissolved once the door closed.

"Please, someone. Please," I weep, my knees and the toes of my feet feeling sore. I can't pound with my hands being tied behind my back. The only things I can use are my knees, shoulders, and feet, but they're already sore. It feels like they're forming bruises.

"What did you do to me?" I cry.

What the hell is wrong with him? How could Malik put me, or anyone for that matter, in a place like this? He hauls me through a cemetery and throws me in, what? What the hell is this, a tomb? This shit is crazy! This entire place is absolutely batshit, and so is everyone that lives here.

I lean my head forward, pressing my forehead against the cool stone. It feels damp and rough against my skin.

It feels like everything stops once I hear a giggle behind me. My eyes widen, the hair on the back of my neck instantly standing on end. Spinning around, I lean my back against the wall, holding my breath. I glance around, expecting to see someone. Or no one. I don't know, honestly. All I see is darkness.

It's The Room of Atonement all over again. Although this time feels so much more sinister. The air in this place is ice-cold. Standing in a six-by-six cement cube in the middle of a cemetery leaves a chill on your skin. I can feel how alive this place is, which doesn't make sense when you're surrounded by death.

The giggle peeps out again, and I feel like every drop of blood drips from my veins. I can barely catch a breath as a shiver washes over me.

It's not the giggle of a child, like I'd expect.

It's the giggle of a grown woman. Not raspy, but throaty. Dark, like nothing is funny at all, but there's an evil in the atmosphere and she relishes in it.

"Who's there?" The most cliché question possible flows from my lips. But what else am I supposed to say? There's a fucking voice in this tiny, square cell, and I'm the only one Malik put in here.

"Me," the voice whispers against my ear, and I swear I can feel the lips against the shell of my lobe.

I scream, sprinting away from the sound. I slam into the wall, my shoulder taking the brunt of the force. It knocks me off balance, and I fall to my ass. Tears fill my eyes, because this place somehow feels so much more menacing than The Room of Atonement. That place, surrounded by God and so many people.

This place. This place is in the middle of nowhere, surrounded by death.

So much death.

I can feel it with each breath, as if every time I breathe in, I can taste the decay, the disease, and torture they endured before they died. It's bitter and rotten on my tongue, and it makes me want to gag.

Fingers wrap around my wrists, and I'm yanked onto my stomach. The fingers are cold and feel like bones, no warm flesh to cushion their grip as they wrap around my wrists. I let out a scream, pushing up on my knees to escape death, but it's no use.

It's everywhere.

Suddenly, the ties holding my arms together are loosened, as are the fingers around my wrists. I spin around, moving into a corner, my arms going in front of me as I feel the air, expecting to come into contact with a body, but I don't.

It's only air.

Without another thought, my lips crack open, and I start saying the Lord's Prayer.

"*Our Father, who art in heaven—*"

"God won't help you here, Vera," the voice utters, malice dripping from her tongue with each letter.

"Who are you? How do you know my name?" I sob, looking from left to right, but no one stands in front of me. I expect to see a woman. A nun from the school, even. The voices all sound similarly evil, but there's no one.

This ominous stirring slips into my stomach, and I feel like something bad is about to happen. Not the feeling from last night with the guys. Not the feeling from earlier when the Ouija board flung toward me in an attempt to hit me.

No, this is an entirely different type of evil.

It's filled with such wickedness that I can taste it on my tongue with each breath I take.

What's worse, is this terrible feeling. It's horrible, knowing that someone is staring at you when you don't have the ability to see them.

I reach forward, my hands going to the ground as I search for the rope, but it's nowhere.

It's gone.

"You will die here," she sighs, like she's disappointed in that fact. Like it's bound to happen.

I frown. "I won't. You don't fucking know anything."

I see a shadow appear in front of me. A thin arm, half decayed, bony and decrepit, slides in front of me. I press against the wall, my head cranking back, but there's nowhere to go.

I'm trapped.

The long nail, black and pointy, presses against my scar. "I know more than you think, Vera." The finger swipes up, the nail scratching along my cheek, and I wince, my hand going up to my face when I instantly smell the metallic scent of blood fill the room.

The finger disappears, and a glow lights up the corner of the room. A tall woman, her hair dark and matted, stands there. Her eyes are black, her mouth unhinged, and the corner is bone. She lifts her hand, and it's like she has an invisible string attached to my chest. I lift off the ground, floating in the air until I'm above her. Her hand is full of black veins, wrapping around her skin and traveling up her arm.

I let out a scream, terror clutching my insides and squeezing tight as my body arches. I can barely breathe, the feeling in my chest taking hold again, and my heart hurts.

It hurts so bad.

The light goes out, and I fall, my elbows hitting the ground with a zing of pain shooting up my arm.

The light flickers on again, like it's from an old lantern, though I can't see one anywhere.

My eyes widen when I see the same woman, with the rope from my wrists tied around her neck as she hangs from the ceiling.

Swinging, back and forth.

Her eyes are open, but she is so dead. Staring at me with horror in her eyes. They hook into me, and I can't look away even though I so badly want to.

I let out a scream, dread filling me from my toes to the threads of my hair. The air leaves my lungs, and my body turns cold as the woman's eyes stare into the pit of my soul.

I grow lightheaded, and everything feels hazy.

Then, everything turns black.

22

MALIK

The sharp, bare branches of the pine trees scrape along my window. I can't sleep, and I've tried. I've closed my eyes, turned on the music, turned off the music.

Nothing works.

Usually, the sound of the rain instantly puts me into a dead sleep. But not tonight.

I can't get her out of my head.

The pure terror on her face as she watched me close the door on her. The horror of what I was about to do to her. Leave her trapped, secluded, alone.

There are only a few hours left until sunrise. I should wait. I should wait until moments before the sun crests over the trees and grab her, but my body doesn't listen.

I slide out of bed, still clothed in my outfit from last night. I pass my dresser with my keys on it, grabbing the collar of my leather jacket by the door and walking out of my room. The lights are off throughout the house, leaving the hallway almost completely blackened, save for a few old-school lights on the walls in the hallway. They look like ancient lanterns, and their glow is just as dim, yellow, warm, but cold at the same time.

My feet pad silently down the stairs and slip into my black boots sitting in front of the door as I make my way outside.

The rain has stopped for good this time. Looking up, I can see the stars in the sky, seeming so much farther away than anywhere else in the world. I can't make out any constellations, only miniature dots in the sky. Too far away. So, so far away.

There's a chill in the air, and I slip my arms into my leather jacket, running my hands through my still damp hair as I walk through the backyard and into the woods. I can't imagine how cold it must be in the mausoleum.

She deserves it.

She's a siren. A witch for making something stir in me that's never been disturbed before. She makes my rage untamed. She turns my lust into a fiery ball, completely inextinguishable. No amount of rain in this place can drown the rage inside me.

Vera keeps the fire burning.

I snarl, stomping through the sticks and pine needles in the forest, the twigs snapping beneath my heavy leather boots. I ignore the other sounds, the whispers, the laughter, the glowing lights that flicker in the woods. I ignore it all, keeping my focus on the cemetery up ahead.

I don't let the dead scare me. They can try and intimidate me while I walk through the woods. I can feel the cool brush of wind graze across my skin. I know they walk next to me, even though I can't see them. I don't wish to see them. I know they're there. Having them appear before me wouldn't change my mind.

I know the dead walk through Castle Pointe. I don't know why, and I don't care to.

Maybe Castle Pointe is purgatory, and that's why there is always death surrounding me.

I shake my head clear once the mausoleum comes into view, and make a sharp left to the creepy, abandoned stone structure. It's silent, dark, but stands out in the eerie cemetery.

Slowing my steps, the rocks pop and roll beneath my boots as I come to a stop. I expect to hear her screams. I expect to hear painful pounding and pleas to escape. But I don't.

No sound. Nothing.

I walk up the stone steps, the gray cement decayed and crumbling to pieces from centuries of neglect. As expected, the door is opened a crack. Only a hair, and for a second, I wonder if Vera is inside. It wouldn't surprise me if she somehow found a way out.

My fingers clutch the cold stone, and I pull. It's heavy, and it takes all my strength to pry it open. The little light from the moon casts a glow inside the mausoleum.

And there she is.

My eyes widen, seeing her sprawled out on the ground. Her arms are splayed at her sides, the rope long gone. Nowhere to be seen.

Is she alive?

I step inside, hesitant to be in here at all during the night. I lean forward, pressing my fingers against her neck.

Thu-thump, thu-thump, thu-thump.

Still alive.

I use the toe of my boot and nudge her ribs. She lolls to the side, but she doesn't wake. Her body doesn't twitch.

What happened to you?

Getting the sense of someone watching me, I don't even glance over my shoulder. I bend down, curling my arms beneath her neck and legs, lifting her into my arms.

Walking out, I don't even close the door. It'll close itself.

I stomp through the forest, making my way back to the house. I use my elbow to push on the handle of the front door, kicking it closed behind me. I don't slide my shoes off, walking up the stairs and straight into her room. My shoes are noisy on the tiles, the only sound filling the quiet house.

She still hasn't woken up.

I lay her on the bed, more gently than she deserves. Her blonde-and-black hair fans out along her pillow, the strands messy and worn out. Whatever happened to her was rough. A slice, almost like a fingernail, or a knife, is cut straight into her cheek. A drip of dried blood coats her skin, like she never had the time to wipe it away.

My chest pulls, aches a bit in the center. With a scowl, I frown at her and walk out. I hate her, and I hate that she drags any sort of emotion from me. I don't even want to hate her. I want to feel nothing.

I want her to be as useless as the pine needles that fall from the trees.

But she isn't.

There's... something, and I refuse to give it a second thought.

I pull my boots off once I get to my room, shrugging my jacket off and leaving it at the foot of my bed. Falling onto my mattress, I lay my arm over my eyes.

And finally, *finally,* get some sleep.

"I'll just fucking meet you there," I growl into the phone.

"Why won't you pick me up?" Thea whines, and I grind my teeth together.

She doesn't know I saw her exchange yesterday at school with Vera. She's lucky I didn't see her after that, because I might have snapped her neck.

Vera isn't her toy to play with. She's mine.

"I've got shit to do." I pull my boots on, running my fingers through my hair for the millionth time.

I'm stressed today. I haven't seen Vera. Not once. I figured I'd wake up to her breathing over me as I slept, a knife clutched between her fingers, ready to plunge into my chest.

She never came.

I know she's awake, though, because I heard the bathroom door close.

All day. She's had all damn day and she hasn't once come to question me. Why? Doesn't she have any questions? Doesn't she want to cuss me out? Fucking maim me?

"But, Malik—" Thea snaps me out of my thoughts with her persistent whining.

"Thea. Shut the fuck up. I'm not picking you up. Walk for all I care. I guess I'll see you if I see you." I hang up my phone, shoving it into my pocket and walking out of my room.

I tell myself I'm not going to talk to Vera. I'm not going to go linger in her doorway, or even fucking think about her. But my feet have a mind of their own, and I turn left, walking straight into her room.

Her door is fucking open.

Her door is *never* open.

She lies in her bed, curled into a fetal position as she faces the window. I walk around the foot of the bed, standing at the edge.

She's not sleeping. She's not blinking.

She's just staring.

"What happened?" I question. Emotionless, bored. It's how I feel.

It's how I *should* feel.

She blinks, like she's coming out of a trance. She shifts her eyes to mine, just for a moment before looking back out the window.

"You don't care," she whispers.

I blink, staring at her tired face. Like she hasn't slept, even though she slept in my arms the entire walk back to the house. How long she slept before and after that, I don't know. But it looks like she hasn't slept in days, weeks.

I shrug. "Whatever."

Spinning around, I shove my hands into my pockets with the intent of getting the fuck out of there. Screw her.

I should torture her, play another prank on her until she cracks altogether. But I won't. I'll let her simmer in her fury until she snaps. And that's when I'll tear her to pieces.

Bit by bit.

Her voice cracks when I'm in her doorway, stopping me in my tracks.

"Do you believe in ghosts?"

My eyebrow lifts, and I look over my shoulder at her. She's rolled onto her back, her hands laced together on top of her stomach. She stares at the ceiling, a look of being lost and broken and a little scared reflecting in her eyes.

I debate on how to respond. I can tell her the truth, that the dead live here freely. There is no heaven or hell in Castle Pointe. There's the breathing, and the not breathing.

The evil, and the rotting.

There's no good here. There's nothing worth remembering. We're all beating hearts wandering aimlessly through life until we become heartless souls wandering aimlessly through death. There's no in-between.

There's no after.

"More than people," I utter, turning around before I can see how my response has affected her.

I don't care. I don't care. I don't care.

The orange glow from the fire illuminates everyone's faces. Their bottom halves disappear in the night, and their top halves are glowing, their teeth shining extra bright. Drunk and high, I'm surprised more of them don't drown in Superior.

The water laps at the edge of the fire pit, the large metal cage holding the old firewood, standing high enough off the ground that even if the water does rise enough, it won't extinguish the fire. It's a large pit, about five feet in diameter. About a dozen people stand around it, cans of beer in their hands while others linger in and out of their vehicles along the water.

We brought the party down to the water tonight. More people came than I thought would. This little section of the beach is filled with cars and people. Being fall, the crowd starts thinning out earlier than they usually would. Most don't like the cold, and when it's thirty degrees in Duluth, it'll be about twenty degrees here. It always runs colder. Doesn't matter the time of day or the season, Castle Pointe is just different.

I flick my cigarette into the fire, taking a step back. Thea showed up late, and her friends took her away somewhere. I'm going to take this as my chance to get the fuck out of here while I still can.

I slip out of the crowd, walking back to the Rover in the back near the hill.

"Dude, where the fuck you goin'?" Atticus stumbles through the sand, the beer in his hand sloshing over the top, spilling over his fingers and onto the ground.

"I'm goin' the fuck home." I pull the keys from my pocket, more irritated than I should be. I have no right, and I don't need to take it out on my boys. They follow my lead, so it's un-fucking-necessary for me to treat them like shit.

But I can't help it. Because the little witch at my house has turned everything I've ever known upside down. With just one glance.

Atticus frowns at me. "Thea pissing you off?"

I bark out a laugh. "When isn't she pissing me off?"

He lifts an eyebrow. "What's really going on?"

I shake my head, feeling like I shouldn't even be admitting this. Not to him. Not to myself. "Just not feeling shit tonight."

He takes a step forward, the tipsy snapping out of him in a second. A serious expression takes over his entire face, all our features so similar we could be brothers. "Is this about baby sis? Please don't tell me you're starting to dig her."

I sneer at him. "Fuck off. No. I just... she's fucking with my head, man."

He stares at me sideways, taking a step back. "I really hope not. One look at her and I can tell she ain't good. She's another Thea. Probably worse."

I grind my teeth together, knowing he's right. Involving myself with Vera would be like stepping into a pile of hot embers. She'd brand me for life, and I don't want it. I don't need it.

"I'm out of here," I mumble, and this time he lets me go.

"I'll talk to you tomorrow, man." He tips his drink back, swallowing the rest before crunching it in his fist and tossing it aside.

We'll have someone out to clean this place up tomorrow.

Hopping into my Rover, I pull off the beach, heading back toward my house. It's dark out now, even though it feels like I've only been here for minutes, when I've been here for over four hours.

The drive home is fast. Faster than I wish it was. I want more time to contemplate my next move. A part of me wants to start another prank on Vera. The other part of me wants to let her heal. But why? Why the fuck do I care? We've literally stripped the strongest men of all their dignity and continued stripping them until there was barely an inch of skin on their bones.

So, why do I care about a prissy little bitch?

Pulling into the driveway, I see all the lights are off. The castle is in the middle of the woods. I slip out of the car, walking into the house with only one destination in mind.

Her.

The bedroom door is opened, just as it was earlier. As I step into her room, though, I notice it's empty. The sheets she brought from home are barren, rumpled and used as they sit atop her bed. The pillow is wrinkled, with a heavy indent in the center. Like she's laid there for days, instead of just hours.

I walk up to the bed, my fingers pressing against the soft sheets. They're gray. A dark, heavy color that reminds me of the clouds. Vera isn't a light person. She comes with chips, but no cracks. A sturdy diamond that refuses to break.

But she seems lost. Like she's sat in the background for so long, she's about to be forgotten. Full of dust. Maybe that's what she wants. To be invisible.

I think about her piercing. Her hair. The way she dresses.

No.

She doesn't want to be invisible. She's too bold for that shit.

Her soft sheets crumple between my fingers as I squeeze them, the softness worn. Overused. Sheets that she's been sleeping on for a long time. I nearly bend down to take an inhale, but frown at them, not sure if I trust who she's been with.

That thought turns my stomach to stone and I step back, anger hitting my chest. I want to rage, to tear her into tiny shreds until there isn't anything left. Burn her at the stake. Remove her from my life so I never have to think about her again.

I notice her black bag that she carries around everywhere on the side of her bed, and my eyebrows furrow.

Where is she?

I walk up to her window, and my hand goes to the glass, coolness seeping into my palm. I exhale, a small circle of fog spreading across the glass from my breath.

I wipe my hand down, smearing the fog, then glance at the girl standing in the yard.

Vera.

She stares into the woods, unmoving. Looking toward the cemetery. Her arms rest at her sides, the light breeze blowing her hair over her shoulder.

Her body stands straight. Stiff. I almost wonder if she's sleepwalking.

Spinning around, I stomp down the steps, walking through the kitchen and out the back door. I walk up to her hesitantly, not wanting to startle her, even though I shouldn't really give a shit either way. The branches crunch with each step, and I watch her flinch as they snap.

I stay behind her, the light scent of cigarette smoke and Vera flowing toward me in the night breeze. She's in a light tank top and sleep shorts, not nearly enough clothes for this cool night.

"Vera," I bark at her.

She doesn't shudder at my voice, but it's like her shoulders drop. In relief? In resignation?

She turns around, and my eyes widen at her appearance. Her skin is pale, like every bit of life has been drained from her body. Beneath her eyes are rimmed in red, almost purple in color.

"It won't stop," she breathes.

My head cocks to the side. "What won't stop?"

"Th-the voices. The lights. The whispers. So many whispers. You don't hear them, do you?"

I chew on my bottom lip, wondering how far the noises go in her head. We all hear stuff in this town. We all experience the dead here. But it doesn't make people go crazy. At least, not like this.

"The dead don't sleep, Vera. Not here. Not in Castle Pointe."

She squeezes her eyes shut, frustration lining her forehead. "You don't get it. You don't…" She lets out a growl, her hands turning to fists at her sides, her knuckles turning as white as her face. "Why would you put me in that place? Why would you do that to me? You have no idea the shit I saw. The things I went through!" Her voice is loud as it echoes into the night.

I blink. "It was a lesson. You needed to be knocked off your throne, little sister. You have no crown here."

Angry tears flood her eyes, and she wipes them away with the heel of her palm before they can fall. "You had no right." Looking up at me, her eyes darken in fury. She brings her palms up and presses them against my chest, giving the strongest shove she can. I barely move, her small body not a threat to me, but her anger burns through my leather jacket and my shirt, imprinting on my skin.

"I hate you," she growls, swiping at my skin with her nails. They drag down my neck, and I whip my hand out, curling my fingers around her wrists and spinning her around, until her back hits my front. I pin her arms against her chest, so they lay trapped like she's in a straitjacket.

"I really hate you, too. My body boils when your body touches mine. My insides literally turn to flames the moment our skin touches. I can't stand your voice. I can't stand your face. I can't stand the way your pussy wept against my knife. I want nothing more than to bury you in that cemetery and never have to think of you again," I growl. Her body melts into mine with each word. By the end of my rant, she is boneless in my arms, and her back trembles along my front.

"Don't you see them?" Her head is tilted toward the ground, but her eyes stare into the forest. Haunted.

Hesitantly, I glance up, seeing black trees and heavy fog in between. No bodies. No dead. Nothing.

"Where?" I whisper.

"E-everywhere. There are h-hundreds, and they're all staring at m-me." She curls into me further, as if I can for once be her protector, instead of her punisher.

I spin her around, gripping her shoulders and squeezing tight. Glaring into her eyes, I say between clenched teeth. "Vera, there is no one there. No one."

Her hands reach up and grip my shirt, pulling, clenching, twisting as she shakes her head. "No. No. They are there. I promise you. I'm not going crazy." She begins twisting her head to look over her shoulder and back out into the forest. I grab her chin, keeping her staring at me.

"No one."

She pulls me closer, raising up on her tip toes. Her eyes are wild, light and dark. Burning and chilling. Glassy but foggy. "Help me," she whispers on a shaky breath, her lips brushing against my cheek. Her voice begs for help, pleads for safety within me.

My hand goes around her back, threading in her messy hair. Pulling my fingers tight, I crank her head back until she stares up at me, right in my eyes. Her watery, hopeless, blue eyes looking for any kind of salvation I may be able to give her.

I can't provide salvation. All I can give her is ruin.

I bend down, sinking my lips against hers. It feels like the wind whips up around me, curling around my ankles and blowing against our bodies. Sinking us together and pulling us apart at the same time. I'm useless, a mindless soul as I inhale Vera's every breath as my own. I want to bite down, sink my teeth into her skin until her flesh breaks. I want to drain her blood and leave her emptied on my lawn. Let the spirits do with her that they wish.

But I can't. All I can do is ravage her mouth. Take her tongue and taste the lingering tobacco. Scrape my teeth against her lips and swell them until there's a bite of pain.

I never want to stop. I want to stop. I don't know what I want.

Pulling back, I glare down at her. Hating her very existence.

"Go inside, Vera. You officially survived another day in Castle Pointe," I murmur, still tasting her flavor on my tongue.

She looks up at me in wonder, which quickly turns to distaste with my words. And oddly, she looks a bit hurt.

"I hate you," she whispers, stomping around me with her bare feet, walking into the house and slamming the door behind her.

I glance into the forest, seeing nothing but darkness.

I hate you, too.

23

VERA

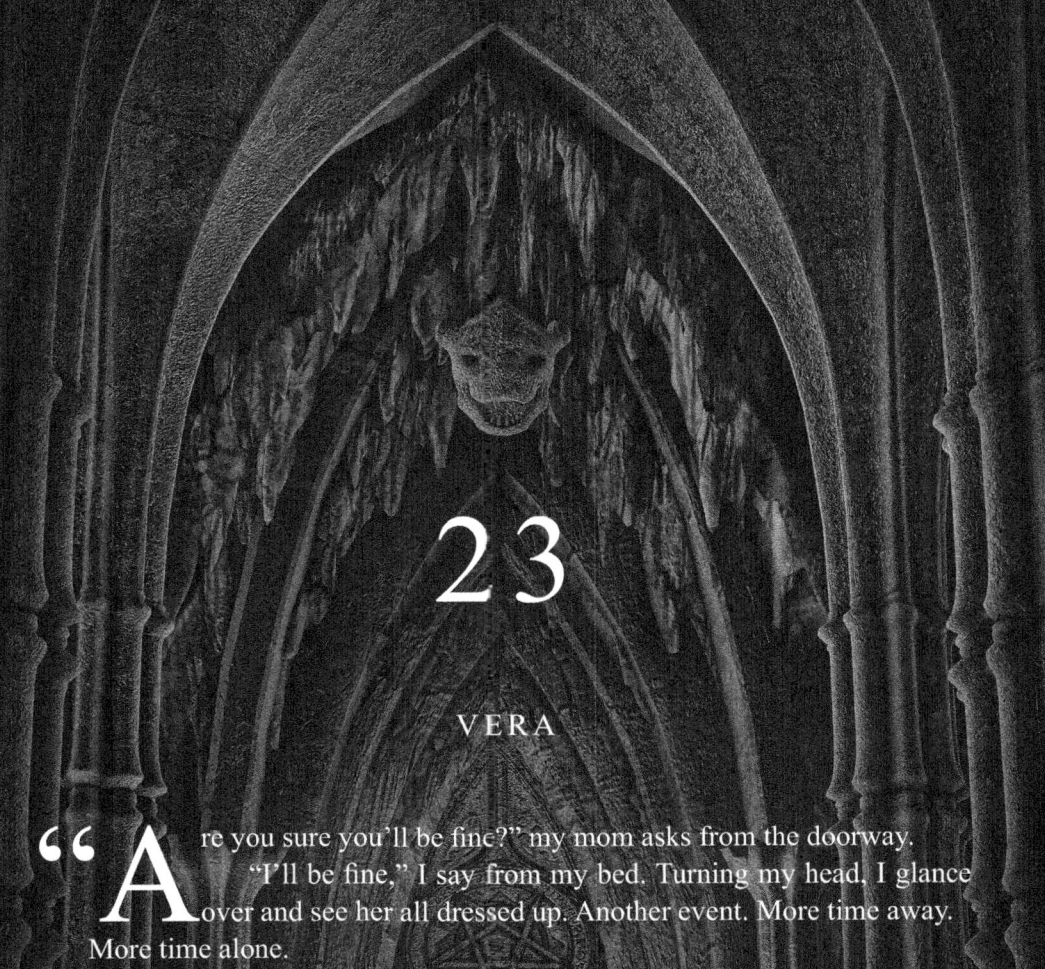

"Are you sure you'll be fine?" my mom asks from the doorway.

"I'll be fine," I say from my bed. Turning my head, I glance over and see her all dressed up. Another event. More time away. More time alone.

"Are you sure?" She steps into the room, walking up to the bed. Glancing down at me, she bends over, curling her fingers around my foot. "You haven't looked good lately. Has everything been okay?"

Now she asks? When she's about to leave for an entire week?

I curl my toes, inching away from her touch. "I don't like it here." A shadow moves in the corner of the room, and I close my eyes.

She frowns at me. "I thought you met a couple girlfriends from school?"

I shake my head. "It's not the people." Besides Malik and his friends. "It's this place."

Stepping back, she runs her hands down her skirt, ironing out the non-existent wrinkles. "Just give it a little more time. I know the environment is different from what you're used to. But I find it a bit… charming, or peaceful, out here."

I want to laugh and scream. It's neither of those things. If only she would open her eyes.

"Samuel is going with you?" My new stepdad keeps himself busy with work, and I've rarely seen him. He's just as dedicated to work as my mom is. Between the both of them, I have this mansion to myself most of the time. Malik has even been keeping himself away lately.

It's only me. And the dead.

"He will. But I'll have my phone if you need me, and I should be back next Sunday in the early afternoon. Maybe we can do something later in the day?"

I hear a creak above me, coming from the attic. I glance up, hearing footsteps. "Do you hear that?"

She glances up, frowning. "It's just a draft, Vera." She sighs, frowning at me. "Maybe if you wouldn't go to sleep watching horror movies all the time, you wouldn't be so freaked out about everything."

I roll over, giving her my back. "Have a good trip."

I can feel her staring at me, a mix between aggravation and sadness burning in the back of my skull. "I love you, Vera."

"Love you." My eyes burn, and I squeeze them shut.

If she loved me like she says she does, why isn't she listening to me? I think the only thing that matters to her these days are work and Samuel. Everything else she's just shoved on the back burner. Something she says to herself she'll deal with another day.

But that day never comes.

Her heels clack on the floor as she heads downstairs, and after a moment, the front door shuts.

It's just me.

I drop my hand to the ground, swiping my bag off the floor and pulling out my pack of cigarettes. Lighting one up, I don't even bother to go to the window. Everyone can fuck off at this point. If I'm going crazy, I might as well act like it.

I shouldn't smoke. It's terrible for my health. The doctors have warned against it over and over, but when life feels like it's closing in on me and there's no one around to help, what do I turn to?

My cigarettes are the only thing keeping me sane.

The cigarette burns, and I close my eyes as I take a drag. They pop open once the ceiling creaks, and I glance up when I notice the constant shadows flitting across my room. They make my heart race, and I drop my cigarette into my cup of water on my nightstand. I grab my phone and headphones from my bag and blare Scary Kids Scaring Kids. Sliding beneath my blanket, I curl it over my head, relishing in the dark and the silence from the dead.

I used to enjoy the weekend. Being away from school. Now I can't enjoy home or school. The teachers are hell, the school is hell, and this house is hell.

Squeezing my eyes shut, I let the music drown out my thoughts and my life, then I fall asleep.

I feel a hand on my shoulder, and my eyes startle open. I whip the covers over my head and sit up, ready to fight someone, anyone.

My shoulders drop.

"How'd you get in here?" I breathe, my hand going to my chest to slow my breathing.

"Uh, your door was unlocked?" Hazel says, sitting on the edge of my bed. Piper walks around my room, and Blaire stares me down from the other side of my bed.

They all look so different. I haven't seen any of them out of their school uniforms. They dress a lot like me. Black. Blaire is wearing leggings and a black hoodie. Piper has on a pair of black ripped jeans, huge holes shredded in the thighs with a black leather jacket on. Hazel is wearing a dark skirt, with fishnets and an oversized t-shirt.

Shit, she's got to be freezing.

"You've been distant. What's been going on?" Hazel asks, a hint of hurt in her tone.

"And where is everyone? This place is massive. I figured I'd be walking in to, like, a butler and a chef and shit."

I tear the sheets off, then pull them back on once I feel how cold it is outside the covers. "All by myself."

"Seriously, what the fuck is going on?" Hazel asks.

I debate whether or not to tell them what's been going on, but then realize they're the ones that got me into this shit in the first place. "Have you guys experienced anything... since that night?"

Blaire furrows her eyebrows, looking over at Hazel and Piper before her eyes land back on me. "No. Have you?" Her lips pinch as she stares at me heavily. "What happened to your cheek? Did someone cut you?"

I shake my head absently as my hand goes to the healing cut. It was only surface, not nearly as bad as the scratches on my back that are still healing, but it still hurt.

"It was just a scratch. But yeah, I have, actually."

"Like what?" Piper asks, concern etched on her forehead.

"Sounds, voices, shadows... everything. All the fucking time." I push my head into my hands, scrubbing my fingers down my face. "It won't stop." I lift my head, glaring at them. "You really haven't experienced anything?"

Blaire shakes her head. "Is this why you've been practically ignoring us?"

I sink lower into my bed. I haven't told them about Malik. Not about him throwing me in the cemetery or our kiss. Since then, he's been gone so much I almost wonder if I've been imagining the entire thing. Maybe our kiss never happened in the first place.

I've also been ignoring the girls. It hasn't been anything against them, but I can barely function with everything else that's been going on. I'm closing in on myself. My mind is building a wall that my heart has already had. I don't trust anyone in this place. Besides the girls, I guess. But even with them, there's this barrier that makes me feel like I'm losing my mind, and I just need to keep to myself.

Maybe I really am losing it.

"There's something else." I'm going to keep the kiss to myself, but I need to tell someone about the cemetery. I need to.

"What is it?" Blaire asks.

"After you dropped me off at home, Malik and his friends ambushed me. They threw me in the car and brought me to some creepy cemetery. Malik, he... he threw me in some crypt or something. A big stone block. He fucking left me there."

"What the fuck?" Hazel shrieks.

Piper's eyes go wide.

Blaire's face pales.

"Right?! I can't believe he left me in there. I couldn't get out! He left me in there, and I-I saw some things."

"What things?" Piper's eyes are wide, the rims of the whites turning red.

I take a deep breath. "There was a woman. She untied my hands and took the rope. She hung herself right in front of me."

"She was alive?!" Hazel shrieks.

I shake my head. "No. She was very much dead. Like, half of her body was bones, and the other half was old, like she was from a different century."

"Oh my God," Blaire whispers. She glances over her shoulder at Piper. "Do you think... do you think it's her?"

"Who?" I reach out, grabbing her wrist. "Who the fuck was that?"

She shakes her head. "I don't know. But maybe it's the woman who cursed this whole town. The witch."

I let go of her wrist, scooting back until my spine hits my wooden, black headboard. "Oh, shit. You think?"

Blaire shrugs. "I don't know. I don't even know where the cemetery is. There's the main one on the edge of town, but there's no crypt or mausoleum. Where the hell were you?"

I shake my head. "I don't know. It was so dark, and I couldn't see anything. It looked small, though. Like the gravestones looked hundreds of years old."

Hazel furrows her eyebrows. "I've never heard of that place. Are you sure it was in town?"

"Of course it was in town if some weird shit like that happened." Hazel rolls her eyes.

"Why didn't you tell us about this? It's been days and you haven't said a word." Blaire frowns.

I shrug. "I don't know. I just didn't want to bother anyone."

My ceiling creaks again, and I glare at my friends. "Did you hear that?"

"Uh-huh," they all say simultaneously.

"Girl…" Hazel looks at me, the color drained from her face. "I think you have a spirit attached to you."

"One?" I scoff. "I've been seeing spirits everywhere. It feels like this entire town is haunting me."

She stands up from the bed. "I need to go home. We need to get a protection spell on you before it's too late."

I slip out of bed with her. "Protection? Against what? Do you think they'll, like… hurt me?"

She winces. "Well, I want to avoid that. Come home with me. We can figure out what to do."

I shake my head, not wanting to do anything witchy. Not if it means possibly becoming more haunted than I already am. "I don't think so. What if it only gets worse? This is what started it all in the first place."

"We can protect you, you know. If we're all together, our energy is stronger than just one person alone." Piper walks up to me. "You should really come."

I think about leaving the house. About seeing and hearing things and having nowhere to go. As weird as it is, this place has become somewhat of a safe haven for me. My bed is my security, it's the only place that is comfortable.

I take a step back toward my bed. "I'm going to stay here."

"Not a good idea, Vera," Piper says with a frown.

I slide back into bed, laying the covers over my lap. Looking outside, I see it's already dark out, no stars in the sky tonight. It's filled with heavy clouds, which means it's going to rain soon.

"I'm not leaving. Not tonight. Just… figure out what to do and come back tomorrow." I slide down until my head hits the pillow, and the three of them stare at me.

"I'll pray for you," Hazel says. It only has chills breaking out down my spine, because I know she's absolutely serious about her words.

They walk to the door, and Blaire stops, turning around to stare at me. Her eyes are sad, a little concerned. "Is your mom home at least? Or Malik's dad?"

I shake my head, hating the fact that my evil mom and stepfather could give me safety of any kind. "They're gone for a whole week."

She cringes. "If you aren't at school tomorrow morning, we'll ditch and come over to make sure you're okay."

I nod, pulling my blankets up to my neck. "I'll see you tomorrow."

They walk out, leaving me alone once again. The moment I hear the front door close, the creaking in the ceiling starts up once more. I grab my earbuds, shoving them back into my ears, turning the music up to max volume. Pulling the covers over my head, I cloak myself in darkness as I fall back into a dreamless sleep.

My eyes shoot open, my unease strong enough to rouse me from a deep sleep. The stuffy air beneath my covers is unbearable. I have goosebumps along my arms, and my body stiffens as I pull the covers over my head. Pressing the button on my phone, I glance around as everything goes silent.

Nothing. No noise.

So, why do I feel so uneasy?

I exhale a shaky breath, the air in the room so cold, I can see it. I almost don't believe it's there. I let out another heavy breath just to see if it's true, and I once again see the puff of air in front of me.

Why the hell is it so cold in here?

I check my window to see if it's open, but it's not.

It's closed.

A soft sound hits my ears, and I glance at my nightstand, seeing the water in my glass shaking.

I stare at it.

It moves, ever so slightly. Like someone bumped the glass.

I shift away from the nightstand.

It moves toward the edge, just a hair.

It feels like I watch in slow motion as it lifts in the air, levitating for a moment before flinging across the room. The glass crashes against the wall, shards of sharp glass splitting into pieces, and my water, tainted brown from my cigarette, drips down the wall in slow rivers.

My entire chest, all the way down to my toes, shakes. I feel paralyzed, unable to move. Unable to run. Tremors take over my entire body, and a wicked burn shoots up my back. The only thing I'm able to do is open my mouth, and *scream*.

24

MALIK

An absolutely horrified shriek reaches my ears, and I shoot out of bed.
What the fuck?
I've barely just gotten home, avoiding this place and Vera like the fucking plague. Coming home late and leaving early. I'd only just gotten to sleep.

What the hell is happening?

I burst into the hall, running down the hallway and into Vera's room.

Her body lies ramrod straight on her bed, her face tensed in pain and her eyes frozen in terror.

"What the fuck is going on?" I roar.

Walking into her room, I see a glass in small shards scattered across the ground, water puddled against the wall.

Did she throw it herself? Is she having a fucking mental breakdown?

"Vera!" I bark at her, but she doesn't stop screaming. Her back arches, like there's a fire beneath her spine.

I walk up to her, whip the covers off her body, and place my hands on her shoulders, shaking the ever-loving shit out of her. "Vera! Shut the fuck up and tell me what's going on!"

Her eyes clear and they focus on mine, fear and horror glistening as tears trail down her temple. "Help. Me," she gasps.

"Help you with what?" I growl.

"It's so painful. It's so fucking painful," she sobs.

"Where?" I seethe.

"Everywhere!" she screams, her back arching off the bed. She contorts, and it looks so fucking disturbing. Her eyes roll in the back of her head and her neck stretches back, her pale, clammy skin growing taut with tension.

I whip her onto her stomach, yanking her shirt up to her neck. My eyes widen as I see three long, bloody scrapes extending from her shoulder down to her opposite hip. They're deep, wide, and jagged as hell. The ones from The Room of Atonement have only started to heal. These, though, these are much worse. Much deeper. Angrier. The first set felt like a warning.

These look like a threat. An omen of what's to come.

It looks awful. I run my finger along the edge of one of the scrapes, and Vera screeches and bends away from me, like I'm the cause of her pain.

"What the fuck happened?" I bark at her.

"I don't know. I woke up, and my cup flew across the room!"

"Flew across the room?" I narrow my eyes.

Her bed starts vibrating below me, and it feels like an earthquake is about to strike, even though we don't have them in Castle Pointe.

The foot of the bed lifts in the air before slamming to the ground, and the head of the bed lifts before it drops. It continues this game, this rodeo of movement that rocks the bed back and forth.

Holy fucking shit.

"Vera!" I slam her against the bed. "What the hell did you do?"

She starts crying hysterically. "I didn't do anything!"

The bed scrapes across the floor, moving to the middle of the room. I whip Vera off the bed, pinning her against the wall to protect her from whatever shit is toying with us.

The bed stops the moment I have her against the wall. Sitting in the middle of the room, I stare at it for a moment, the entire situation almost impossible to believe.

My heart feels like it's about to pound out of my chest, and I lean up against her, pressing my forehead against the wall. "What shit did you do, Vera?"

"Me?" she snaps. "Me?" She shoves my naked chest, but I barely move. I keep myself pinned against her, and I can feel her vibrating, seething into me. "You shoved me in that cemetery and left me to rot. Whatever was in that…

fucking tomb... was death. All I could see, and feel, and hear, was death. It surrounded me and filled me up. All I can fucking think about for the last week is the fucking hell you put me through! The Ouija board shit I did with Blaire wasn't nearly—*not even a fucking inch*—as terrifying as that cemetery. The cemetery *you* locked me in! So, fuck you, Malik. Fuck everything about you!"

My breathing stops, and I step away from her, just a beat, and glare down at her. "You played with a fucking Ouija board?" My voice is solemn, a deadly whisper that hints of the grave mistake she made.

Utter stupidity.

Her eyes shift to the window. "It has fucking nothing to do with that. *This* is all your fault. Shit wasn't happening until the cemetery."

I grind my teeth, and the pressure zings a painful headache to the front of my skull. "You're a fucking idiot." I step back, running my hand through my hair as I try and come up with a solution to why she would be so fucking thoughtless. "You played with a Ouija board? In Castle Pointe? Where the dead never sleep? You do realize the shit you did, right?"

Her neck burns red, lighting up the apples of her cheeks. Her eyes glow with emotion and burn me, as if they could light me on fire.

"I don't fucking know anything about this damn town. All everyone keeps saying is *the dead*. The dead. The dead are here. No one says shit. This place should come with a warning label. Or a fucking manual for all I care. I mean seriously, *fuck off*!" She shoves off the wall and goes to the foot of her bed. She attempts to push it back against the wall, but it barely moves. "Get out of here, Malik. Just go. Fuck off with your girlfriend and forget I existed. It's all you've done for the past week, anyway." She winces as the skin on her back moves, and I can't imagine how excruciating it must be for her.

I laugh, the jealousy and frustration in her voice not going unnoticed. So, she's hurt by me keeping my distance. Good. What did she expect, that I'd coddle her? That we'd talk it out after that night?

She's found the wrong guy.

I walk up to her, curling my fingers around the back of her neck. Her body shudders, hate and need making her press into me and pull away at the same time. "I hate you so fucking much. My bed just moved across the room on its own. You saw the shit it just did. Don't even try to fuck with me right now." She attempts to push her bed back to where it's supposed to be, but it's too heavy, and it doesn't even budge. "Get the fuck out of here or help me, would you?"

I sneer at her, pushing her out of the way and moving the bed back to where it's supposed to be before standing up straight to look at her. "You want to know what I think?" She scowls, crossing her arms across her chest. Her tits push up in her tiny wifebeater tank top, the lack of bra making her rosy nipples shove into the fabric. "I think you're a little bitch who needs to be put in her place."

I want to laugh at her when her face turns red. Her lips curl over, and the tiniest snarl appears on her lips. In the next second, she's in front of me, and her hand lashes out, her palm connecting with my cheek as a crack echoes throughout the room.

"Get the fuck out of my room," she growls at me.

I laugh in her face, the skin on my cheek burning. I feel so alive. Her *rage* gives me life.

"My, my, my, little sister. Is someone pouty?" I step forward, grabbing her around the waist and shoving her onto the bed. She arches her back, a cry bursting out of her from the painful cuts on her back. I spin her around, burying her face in the dark comforter. I rip her shirt up, tearing it over her neck and tossing it onto the floor. The white fabric is streaked with red, her back littered with dried blood. I brush my fingers over the cuts, the jagged marks that were in no way created by a human. "You're a foolish girl who's made a foolish mistake, and you'll pay for it."

She cocks her head back, glaring at me with spitting hate in her eyes. "If I'm going down, you better believe I'll be taking you with me. You're the one that shoved me in the tomb."

I bark out a laugh. "It's a mausoleum, dipshit."

"Whatever," she sneers.

Her waist is trim, the skin on her back creamy and white around the vicious cuts. Her hair is a mess, and I brush it over her shoulder, exposing the baby hairs and her slender neck.

My eyes widen, my fingers trailing up along the tiny scrawl on the nape of her neck. "A tattoo, baby sis? I didn't think you'd have it in you."

She moves to get out from under me, and I pin her harder into her mattress. "What does it say?" I run my fingers along the letters, a language that I'm unfamiliar with. Is it Latin? *Mors debet reddere vitam.*

"It says death must pay for life," she says in a moment of truth.

Death must pay for life.

"Whose death paid for whose life?"

"None of your business," she growls.

Creaking sounds in the attic, like someone is walking around upstairs.

Which is fucking odd, because no one ever goes in the attic, and we don't have any drafts in the house. I've never heard that before in my life.

I grab one of her boots off the ground, chucking it at the ceiling as hard as I can. Dust from the popcorn ceiling falls, scattering along our shoulders. "Get the fuck out of my house!" I roar, angry that any spirit or dead person has the audacity to walk in my house. I don't give a shit if they want to haunt Vera, but they can stay off my property.

The lights flicker, and I growl, my hand going to the mattress, trailing up her waist and along her breasts. I wrap my fingers around her throat, squeezing tight. "I should steal the breath from your lungs for bringing this shit into my home."

"I didn't mean to," she chokes out, her hand going up to mine. She curls her fingers around my wrist and pulls, attempting to get any air, any relief that she can. "I'm sorry," she wheezes.

I laugh, my other hand going down to her thigh, my fingers sliding between the smoothness of her soft skin. I hook my fingers around her shorts, feeling the heat from between her legs instantly.

So fucking warm.

"Don't. Touch. Me," she struggles to say as she chokes. I loosen my hold around her neck, and she gasps in a mouthful of air.

"I will touch you how I want. When I want. Wherever. The fuck. I want. You put my house, and my life, at risk, and now you owe me."

"I don't owe you shit."

I release her neck, bringing my hand to her back, placing my palm down on her cuts. "You owe me everything."

"I owe you nothing. You put me in that fucking cemetery!" she screeches.

My other fingers plunge between her folds. She arches in agony or pleasure. I'd prefer agony.

I dig deep, feeling every fold, crevice, and wall inside her. She wiggles and moves, grunting into the mattress as my fingers fuck her hard and fast. The back of her neck grows wet, sweat and desire dampening her skin.

"If I tell you to bow down, you will. No questions asked. Do you hear me?" I curl my fingers, and she moans. "You are not the boss here. You are not in charge. You do not have a say in anything. Do you hear me?"

She starts moving her body to my fingers, and I fuck her harder, my fingers taking and taking, her tight cunt barely able to take two of my fingers.

I'd almost think she's a virgin, but the way she moves, the way she fucked her own pussy with my knife.

No, she's not a fucking virgin.

I can feel her walls tensing, growing tighter with each thrust and pull. Her panting grows heavier, quicker, more erratic. I wait until she's on the brink, about to tip over the edge, and I pull my fingers out.

She whips over, sitting up and glaring at me. Rageful eyes and damp skin glisten in the dark room as she stares at me. "What the fuck are you doing?" she barks at me.

I glance down, seeing a wicked scar on her chest. My eyes widen, and I take a step forward, daring to touch it, but leery of it at the same time. "What?" I point between her naked breasts, the gnarly scar that looks old but fresh. Healed but still raw. "What the fuck happened to you?"

A rage builds in me, that someone gave her the scar intentionally. That's she's been through brutal pain in her life. That someone caused it. No one can cause her pain.

For a moment, it feels like I'm the only one that can decide when she is in pain and when she isn't.

She glances down, her arms going over her breasts, and covering the hideous scar from my sight. "None of your business," she repeats the same mantra from earlier.

"You're my business," I seethe.

She furrows her eyebrows. "I'm not. I'm definitely fucking not, and I never will be." The flush from her skin is gone, but the dampness remains. I can smell her scent in the air, even with her face void of emotion. The heat in her body has dissipated. "Now get out of my room."

I whip my head back and forth. "Not until you tell me what happened to you."

She stands up, dropping her hands until she's standing in front of me. Her breasts brush against my chest. I stare her down, my jaw tensing at the sudden bravado in her stance. In the way she breathes.

"Death must pay for life," she whispers. Walking around me, she heads to the door. "If you aren't going to leave, then I'll fucking leave."

With that, she walks out, slamming her door behind her, leaving me alone in her room.

For once, I don't follow after her. I don't bark orders or demand answers. I'm just… I'm fucking speechless.

25

VERA

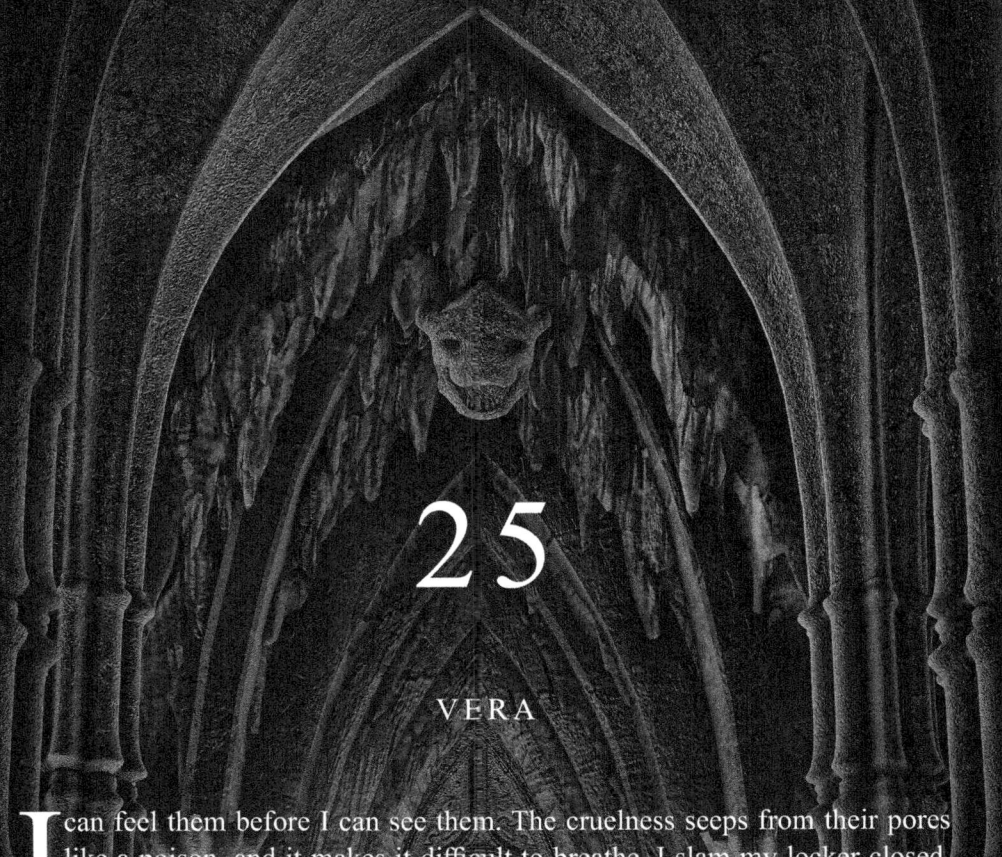

I can feel them before I can see them. The cruelness seeps from their pores like a poison, and it makes it difficult to breathe. I slam my locker closed, and there they are.

Malik, and his three friends. I don't even know their names. And to be honest, I've never seen them up close until now. I've never really had a good look at their features or have been able to tell what they look like. They're always lurking in the night and only come up to me when they torture me. Their faces are always obscured.

Until now.

It's almost painful to look at them all together like this.

They look so similar. Like they're all cut from the same cloth. Like somewhere along the bloodlines, their DNA mixed. Each of them have sharp but evasive features and creamy skin, with dark hair that's messy and slightly wavy.

Malik is clearly the head of the pack. He's the tallest, and he's slim, but toned in ways that could snap someone with a flick of his wrist. His eyes are a faded blue. Like a watercolor painting that's had too many drops of water in it.

The guy to his left has a smirk on his face, a cruelness swirling in his dark brown eyes. He's a bit shorter than Malik, but his hair is a bit longer, a bit more tamed.

On the other side of Malik is someone that's almost his same height. His eyes are nearly the same shade as Malik's. He's the one that looks the most similar to Malik, and the emotionless look on his face looks eerily similar, as well.

The last guy, standing beside Malik's twin, is shorter than Malik, with short, messy hair and wild, dark eyes. His mouth is twisted into an angry scowl, like he hates me. Like he wants me to leave.

"So, you survived the long night?" says the guy with a smirk on his face.

I blink at him. "Fuck off."

The angry one steps up to me. "Watch what you say in God's house, little lamb. I'm sure you wouldn't want to end up in The Room of Atonement again, would you?"

I sneer at him. "Like I told Malik last night, next time something happens to me, I'll be taking all of you down with me."

The bored one chuckles but doesn't say anything.

"If you'd get out of my fucking way, I'd like to get to class," I snap.

Malik stares at my breasts, like he can see straight through my white shirt and to my scar. Like just by looking at the jagged edges, he could read between the lines and figure out why I'm so fucked up in the first place.

I smoosh my books to my chest, stepping out of the little corner they've shoved me into. "Go away."

"She seems pretty bitchy still. Maybe she needs another lesson?" the one on the left says with a nasty grin on his face. My fingers twitch with the need to slap him.

I lean into him, smelling the intoxicating scent all of them have. Like cigarettes and marijuana and pine and fucking evil. "I've got my knife in my bag. Try me one more time and I'll shove the tip so far into your cock it splits in two."

His face grows serious for a second before a wide smile spreads across his face. His shiny white teeth glow at me. "Holy fuck. You are fucked up." He turns to Malik. "If you haven't fucked her yet…" His meaning is clear. He wants to fuck me.

I sneer at them. At all of them.

I watch as a dark shadow crosses Malik's face. He looks furious at his friend's words and furious at me.

I take this as my moment, and I slip around them, noticing Piper talking to a group of guys. A small smirk breaks free as an idea hits me, and I squeeze in between them, pressing my front to one of the guy's arms and lay my hand on his shoulder. "I don't think we've met. I'm Vera." I extend my hand, and he looks momentarily shocked before hesitantly placing his palm in mine.

"Penn." His eyes glance down to my torn tights, my skirt that I have folded too many times, my worn boots that have too many scuffs on them, and my shirt that is buttoned up to the top, contradicting the rest of my outfit. The naughty schoolgirl in the flesh. "You the new girl?"

"I am." My fingers go up to my septum ring, and I give it a slight pull, narrowing my eyes. "What grade are you in?"

The guy is cute. Slightly alternative, though it's hard to tell exactly when everyone wears the same outfits. But his hair is messy, and the way he looks at me screams approval. But, I guess, all guys look that way when they look at me, so that doesn't say much.

"I'm in twelfth. Y–" A large hand lands on his shoulder, and another on mine. Pine and smoke fill my senses, and I close my eyes before looking over my shoulder.

I knew he would come. I have to say, I'm almost a bit disappointed it took so long.

"I suggest you both stop talking to each other before I pull your tongues from your throats," Malik says quietly, but clearly.

Penn's face pales, and he immediately steps back from me. He doesn't say a word, to him or to me. He just walks off, a letdown yet terrified look on his face. He doesn't even spare me a backward glance.

Malik turns his glare toward me. "You are just begging to be fucked with, Vera. Have you not listened to a word I said?"

"Maybe I just don't give a fuck. Take your hand off me now, Malik. Your games are getting exhausting."

He leans in, his lips brushing the shell of my ear. "The moment you stepped foot into Castle Pointe, you started playing my game."

I shrug out of his hold, glaring up at him. I can see his friends in the background, waiting for the next move.

I bring my boot up, slamming it down on his expensive shoe. His face turns dark, a shadow covering everything besides his clenched jaw. His hand goes to my neck, and he takes a step forward, slamming me against the locker.

I can hear people scattering. Some gather closer, though most of them flee, everyone too scared to be around Malik and his friends.

I can feel them, gathering closer, surrounding me. Circling like vipers, just waiting for the right moment to strike. The metal of the locker digs into my spine, the painful scratches still too raw to hold back the wince that overtakes my face. Malik doesn't care as his fingers raise, pressing into my cheeks and keeping my face pointed at him.

My eyes move to his friends. "Let me get my knife and we'll see who wins the fight." I'd probably lose, to be honest. I'm no match when it comes to these four, but if I could get in one strike, I think I could lose happy.

"Mr. Myers… Miss Lowell!" A startled voice rings through the hall. "Mr. Myers, take your hands off her right now!"

Malik drops me, and I tumble to the floor, the phantom feeling of his fingers still pressing against my face. I bring my hands up, rubbing it away.

"What is the meaning of this?"

"It's just a sibling problem, Sister Marjorie." I wince, hating all the sisters, but Sister Marjorie is evil on a totally different level.

"Do we need to take this to the office, Mr. Myers?"

I shake my head, not even looking at Malik, but speaking up for him before he says something that'll get me sent to The Room of Atonement. "No. I just want to go to class." Picking up my books that must have fallen to the ground, I move past everyone, walking down the hall.

"Miss Lowell. Vera! Stop, right this second!"

I put my hand up. "I'm sorry, I have to go to class!" I pick up my speed, racing down the hall and ignoring Sister Marjorie's calls for me to stop.

I don't care if she comes after me.

All I want is to get away from Malik. I don't know what he's doing to me. His touch and his voice are controlling, like there's something in him that can bend me to his will. That isn't me. I've never been like that. But he is able to do it with such ease.

I hate him so much.

But this weird, small part of me, is starting to enjoy his touch, too.

And that cannot *ever* fucking happen.

"Girl, what the fuck happened to you?" Piper slams into me after class, her fingers clutching my wrist and pulling me away from the hallway, straight into the girls' bathroom.

"What are you talking about?" I frown at her.

"Uh, Malik? He fucking ambushed you and threw you against a locker?

People fled like someone had a bomb. What happened?"

Blaire and Hazel rush in at the next second, their eyes wide and concerned. "Dude, I heard Malik pinned you against a locker?" Hazel screams, looking at me from head to toe.

I shake my head. "It wasn't anything new."

"What kind of balls does he have to do that in school? You guys should have seen it. Felix, Atticus, and Levi were all there, looking happy as hell while Malik slammed her against a locker. It was fucked. Up." Piper shakes her head, shocked.

Don't they know Malik? This doesn't seem like anything out of the ordinary for him. He's hostile, violent. He and his friends are aggressive and being a bully to another student seems like something they'd do on the daily.

Blaire slices her hand through the air. "Okay, enough of Malik. He's a fucking dick, but that's not what's important. What happened yesterday after we left? Did you experience anything else?"

I nod. "Yeah."

I don't really want to talk about it. But I know they'll force it out of me.

"What happened?" Blaire asks, her eyes wide.

I close my eyes, thinking of the terror and paralysis rolling through my body as my bed rocked and shook like an earthquake was rolling beneath the earth. The way my back burned like flames were eating away at my skin.

I turn around, lifting the back of my shirt and showing them the lower half. The scratches still hurt as I walk, but they're healing. The shower this morning was epically painful, even a drop of water on the wounds was excruciating.

They all gasp, and I can feel the fear rolling off them.

"I-I've brought some shit in my car. I think we need to skip lunch and go take care of this," Hazel says.

I turn around, seeing the horror on her face. "Take care of *what*?" I ask.

She shakes her head. "Something has latched to you, Vera. You need a protection spell, stat."

I chill breaks out along my spine. "*Latched on to me?*"

She nods. "Yes. Let's go. Now."

Her hand snaps out, cinching around my wrist, and she pulls me out of the bathroom. Hazel and Piper follow behind me, sticking close. We walk through the halls, the girls creating some kind of barrier around me. I know they are trying to avoid another confrontation with Malik and his friends.

I don't see them anywhere, but that's difficult with the girls surrounding me. Their shoes pound into the ground simultaneously. Like the beat to a drum. Hazel's dark hair swishes from side to side in front of me, and I stare at it like a grandfather clock.

Her urgency makes my ears swoosh, and I feel uneasy at how intense this shit is becoming. Why does she think I'm in trouble? What could possibly happen to me? It feels like a dream. Like the moment I stepped into this town, I've been in a coma.

I just want to wake the hell up.

Be back in my house in Fargo, hang out and smoke. Watch the busy city in one direction or watch cows and the endless pastures in another direction.

I don't want to be here anymore.

Hazel's hand slams into the door, and it swings open, a blast of cold washing over us. The smell of the water from Superior reaches up the cliff and swirls in my nose. I can feel a rosiness instantly hit my cheeks from the cool wind.

I'm pulled to Hazel's car, and she releases me, popping her trunk and grabbing the familiar-looking black box from the back. Slamming the trunk closed, she adjusts the box in her arms and starts walking toward the woods.

"Where are we going?" I nearly dig my heels in. I don't like the woods here. They're eerie and creepy and there is so much unknown between the tall green pines jutting from the ground. They seem endless and extend in every direction I look.

The only times I've been in these woods, the guys have played me like a puppet. They've hunted me and left me for dead in an unknown cemetery.

I hate these woods.

"Can't have the sisters knowing what we're doing. We'd all be in The Room of Atonement for a week," Hazel huffs, hopping over an oversized branch laying on the ground.

She finds a small clearing, bending down and dropping her box to the ground. It feels like nighttime in the woods, and I can't see much of anything through the trees.

"I don't want to be weird, but you're kind of freaking me out." I laugh. But it feels off. Forced.

She looks up at me from unloading her box. "Do you know anything about possession, Vera?"

"Like *The Exorcist* shit?" My eyebrows furrow.

She smiles. "Exactly. Or *Paranormal Activity. The Exorcism of Emily Rose.* Any of those work. Do you know how it begins?"

I shake my head. "It's different in every case." Horror movies are my jam. I've been watching them since I knew what movies were. The feeling of being terrified is awesome when you're in the comfort of your own house.

But being scared as this shit actually happens to you is absolutely *not* awesome.

She nods, setting out what looks to be like a deer skull. The teeth are still intact, browned with age. "What's happening to you is how it begins. This is a scary fucking road."

"How do you know?"

She looks up at Piper and Blaire before glancing back at me. "One of my family members was possessed. A distant cousin or something. She lived on the edge of town and went to Castle Pointe Academy. It was like... eerily similar to what's happening to you. Small stuff here and there happened, then all the sudden, it latched."

My eyes widen. "Latched?"

She nods, her fingers tracing the outline of the skull. Small antlers extend from the top, sharp yet so smooth-looking. A chip sits in the left antler, giving away the age and death it must have succumbed to.

"Yeah. There are ghosts here, Vera, but what people don't know is there are also demons that walk the earth. One latched on to my cousin. She became violent and manic. People thought it was schizophrenia at first, but when a voice broke from her chest and she started speaking of a life she's never had, the priest was called in. It was a long road of trying to exorcise her." She shakes her head, a sadness filling her eyes. "The demon won."

"What happened?" I gnaw at my bottom lip, feeling the skin break away with each bite. I'm nervous. I don't really know how to feel, but the life her cousin endured is not one I want for myself.

"The demon broke her body. Cracked every bone until she was irreparable. The worst part is, she didn't die. The demon came forward and shattered her, then hit while my cousin screamed and cried in horror. There was no saving her, not with this demon." She takes a deep breath. "My uncle killed her. It was the only way."

Shaking her head clear, she lifts her fingers from the skull. "I'm going to do everything in my power to keep that from happening to you. And that starts with a protection spell."

I shake my head. "So, what you're telling me is that I'm about to be possessed by a demon?"

Hazel reaches her hand out and grabs my arm, pulling me down to sit next to her. "What I'm telling you is that the shit you're going through isn't good, and since you're our new friend, I feel the need to warn you, and protect you. I have that ability. So let me try, because you showing me those three scratches on your back and me not even trying to help you would be a fucking disservice to you."

I look at her, at the legitimate fear and worry in her eyes. My chest deflates, and a shiver racks my spine. "Okay." I exhale, all my hesitations blowing into the forest. "Okay, let's do this."

She nods, and Piper and Blaire sit down around us. It reminds me of her basement, but this is much more solemn. Before, they wanted to protect me from the evil that is Malik. Now, they want to protect me from the evil that is the unknown.

Which one is worse?

Hazel grabs her thin blanket from the box. Unfolding it, she lays it out between us. She grabs the skull, setting it next to her. Reaching into the box, she grabs her candles, herbs, some liquid jars, a knife, a matchbook, a container of salt, and a bowl and wooden spoon.

She gets to work, pouring things into the bowl, smashing the herbs and grinding it into the bottom of the wooden bowl.

"So, this Wiccan thing is pretty serious?"

She nods, glancing up at me with a smile while she continues pouring things into the bowl. "I suppose. My family are pretty serious Wiccans. Most of us have dabbled into the occult, but we mostly stay away from it. Nothing good has ever come from that side of our magic."

"What's with the five-pointed star, then? Isn't that black magic shit?"

She chuckles. "Sometimes it's better to keep a foot on the side of darkness to stay protected from it."

Setting the stones next to the bowl, one shiny and black, another light blue. She stands up, pouring the salt from the container around our small circle, cloaking us in safety.

She sits back down next to me, lifting the knife. "Give me your hand." She wiggles her fingers at me.

I shake my head. "Blood magic. That's not fucking good, Hazel. Let's do this without it."

She opens her palm, slapping the blade open and cutting down her own skin. "We all need to take part today. Whatever is clinging to you, it's powerful. Powerful enough to scratch you in this short amount of time. There's no time for fucking around."

Piper and Blaire open their palms, reaching toward Hazel. She cuts their pale skin, and they tip their hands, letting drips of red fall into the dark bowl.

"Your turn, Vera," Hazel says.

I lift my hand, and she doesn't waste any time. Bringing the bloody blade to my skin, she slices a small line down the middle. She pulls my fingers, bringing my hand over the bowl. I watch the blood drip down my palm, sliding off my wrist and falling and mixing with their blood.

"Your power is strong, Vera. Almost stronger then my own. It's not about lifting your hands and throwing people across rooms or lighting a flame while looking at it." She looks at me, a smile in her eyes. "Though, it is possible. It's more about the energy you create and what you do with it. You can choose to do good in the world, and you can choose to do bad. Your energy is good, whether or not you believe it. But whatever has a hold on you has you toeing into darkness. If you were to become possessed, you would be very, very dangerous."

Grabbing my hand, she folds her bloody one over mine and nods at Piper and Blaire. They bring their hands to ours, and we fold our fingers over each other's. "Blood sisters. Forever," Hazel says.

My body hums, and without wanting to believe it, I know she's telling the truth. Whatever power lies in a witch, also lies within me. I can feel it as our blood mixes and becomes one. Different DNA, different power, all within this small circle, uniting us into an unbreakable force.

Grabbing the matches, she strikes one, the yellow flame lighting up the dim forest. She drops it into the bowl, and it crackles and pops, a massive spark exploding from the bowl before lowering, small flames burning the blood and herbs.

Hazel reaches out, and we all connect our hands. Closing her eyes, she tips her head toward the sky and begins to mumble.

Evil spirits and dark forces,
Return to the place in which you came.
We do not fear you and refuse to keep you.
May our homes once again be safe.
For it is us you will never enslave.

She repeats the chant three times, each word distinct and punctuated with certainty. I can feel her words punching into my soul, and by the third time she says it, I'm mumbling the words along with her. We all are. With hope, with a pleading necessity.

Then, silence.

No wind. No crinkling of leaves or branches or any breath of the earth. Just us.

Suddenly, a gust of wind slams against our small circle. The salt enclosure is disconnected, a gap in the connection leaving us exposed to anything and everything.

The four of us are lifted off the ground, and we scream as we're suspended in the air, breaking our linked hands and leaving us vulnerable to the unknown. The force holding me is strong, and fear freezes me in place. Dread sinks into my body, as my arms fly out in front of me, my hair falling like an effortless sheet into the air. Then, with an angry whip, we're flung backward. My back slams into the stump of a tree, and I let out a scream as the cuts on my back scrape against the bark. I'm momentarily disoriented as my head pounds against the stump. I can hear everyone else get flung against trees.

Blaire's blanket and belongings are strewn about as we all fall to the ground. Then it's silence once again.

Fear reflects in each of our eyes as we stare at each other. Scratches line our legs and arms, and that's enough for me.

I stand up, wiping my skirt off. "I'm done. I'm fucking out of here. No more of this shit! I'm out of this town!" I screech. I grab my backpack, which has been thrown into the trees.

"This shit is too fucking scary. We need to tell one of the sisters!" Blaire stands up, tears in her eyes.

Hazel shakes her head. "I've never... I've never experienced anything like this. It's strong. It's *too* strong." She seems disoriented, staring off into the forest, her legs and arms shaking as she moves to stand.

"I'm about to freak the fuck out." Piper wipes blood from her leg, smearing it against her calf. "Maybe we should go tell the school."

A shiver racks my body. "You guys can go do what you want. I'm leaving." I slide my arms through the straps, preparing for a long walk.

"Want us to bring you home?" Hazel asks.

I shake my head, taking a step back. "I'm not going back to that house. I'm leaving this town. I'm leaving the school." I glance over my shoulder, in the direction of the creepy, cement castle through the woods. "Whatever the fuck is happening to me here is too much. I need to... get the hell out of here or something."

"You can't just leave," Blaire says.

I laugh. "I can, and I'm going to. Right now." I start walking. Away from the school. This town. Malik. My new friends. I walk away from it all, because I'm honestly afraid of what will happen if I stay.

"You don't get it! You can't just leave this town! It won't let you!"

I stop, turning around. "I have to try! I fucking have to!" Tears spring to my own eyes, and I feel so lost… "I don't want to leave you guys, but I can't fucking stay here anymore! I guess this is goodbye."

They look so sad. So forlorn, and a little disappointed. "We'll talk soon, Vera." Hazel turns around, grabbing her things and setting them back in the box. The girls stand there, watching me, so scared, absolutely terrified.

I know none of us expected this.

"Bye," I whisper, though I think the wind takes it away before it can reach them.

I turn around, walking away from the school and my only friends. I'm leaving this town, one way or another. Whatever evil spirit has ahold of me, or us, I refuse to let it. I fucking refuse.

It's time to go.

My legs ache. My heels, to my shins, to my thighs and back. Everything aches as I make my way to the edge of town. I know I've got to be getting somewhat close. I've been walking for what feels like days. I've passed the places I recognize, and I know I'm heading south, so I have to be hitting the Castle Pointe sign pretty soon. Right?

I sigh, digging in my cigarette pack and seeing it empty. I crumble the weak cardboard between my fingers, the chill of the evening making its way up my bare legs. The sun is setting over the tops of the trees.

I fold my arms over my chest, running my fingers up and down my arms to rid the goosebumps.

The forest is quiet, not that there are any animals that roam this forest anyway. I don't think I've seen an inch of wildlife since I entered this town. They stay far, far away from here.

They're damn smart.

The road seems endless, like I'll never make it to the edge of town. I look back, seeing the long road behind me and turning forward, seeing the long road ahead of me. The road shouldn't be this long. No, I know for a fucking fact that the road isn't this damn long.

Headlights glow from behind me, and I hop off the road, sliding down onto the shoulder and creeping along the edges of the trees. I don't want to go into the forest, not unless I absolutely have to.

I stop walking, not wanting to draw more attention to myself. But the vehicle slows, and soon enough, I can see the familiar-looking Range Rover roll to a stop ahead of me. The passenger-side window rolls down, and Malik stares at me, a bored expression on his face. "Get in the car."

I point to where the edge of town should be. "I left school early. I should've been at the edge of town hours ago! Where the fuck am I?"

He smiles. "You're in Castle Pointe, sister."

"What the fuck is this place? Why can't I leave?"

"Because you want to leave."

I frown at him. "What the hell does that mean?"

He sighs, like I'm putting him out, even though he's the one that drove here in the first place. "It means that you aren't fucking leaving, Vera. Now get in the damn car. It's late as hell, and I'm not going to sit here and explain the fucking physics of this place. Or stay out here for all I fucking care. Your choice."

He sits there, staring at me for a minute. I don't want to give into him. I don't want to give into the emotions he evokes in me. I glance over my shoulder, where I should be by now. Getting out of town. Hitching a ride home. To my real home. Instead, I'm standing here. With my monster. With my devil.

He sighs again, rolling up the window with a shake of his head. I can see the red glow of his headlights disappear, and he starts rolling forward.

"Wait. Wait!" I leap forward, running onto the street. He presses on his brakes, once again coming to a standstill.

I open the door, and the scent of cigarettes and Malik slap me in the face.

I sigh, settling into the seat and coming to terms with my fate. "Take me home, Malik."

26

MALIK

Take me home, Malik.

The words get me hard. So fucking hard I could bust through my uniform slacks. I want to tear her weak fishnets apart and fuck her until the insides of her thighs are raw. I want her screams to echo in the woods. I want her so fucking bad, but I hate her just as fiercely. And to me, that's a deadly combination.

I would never admit that a fraction of me was worried she'd find some way to weasel out of this town, and then I'd have the rest of the world to search for her in. She didn't get out, though. She'd be frustrated to know she walked only a few miles in over five hours. That this town plays tricks on you, and you might think you're nearing the edge, but you're only on a loop.

If you want to leave, you'll never leave.

If you have an intent of coming back, it'll let you go.

That's how it is. That's how it always has been.

Vera wants to leave so badly; I don't think this town will ever let her go. A part of me is excited at that thought, that I get to keep her for as long as I want her. And it only makes me want to strangle the shit out of my own thoughts.

I had to nearly throttle her friends to ask where she was. I knew when I saw them after school, fearful, scared, cut and bruised, without Vera, that something happened. It only took one stare and one step toward them for the witch to confess she was on her way out of town. Or her attempt to get out of town. They know the rules, too. Whether they told her how this town works or not, I'm not sure. Either way, they couldn't keep her.

And I'm the one that brought her back.

It doesn't take long, only minutes and we're pulling into the driveway. I sneak a glance over at Vera, watching as her eyes widen into saucers to know we were only a short distance from the house.

"I was this close to the fucking house? How is that possible?" she shrieks.

I ignore her, parking underneath the archway. She steals a cigarette from my pack, lighting it up as she exits the car. "This place is complete bullshit. Am I even fucking alive right now?"

I don't answer, walking in through the front door and leaving it open. She can stay in the car all night and contemplate the meaning of life if she wants, but it gets shit-ass cold at night, and I don't want to spend another minute outside.

I walk down the hall and into the kitchen, and I can instantly hear her boots stomping down the dark hallway. Stomping after me.

"This has got to be a joke. Is it a prank? Is that it? This is just another one of your pranks that you and your friends are playing on me?"

I grab a beer from the fridge, cracking the top open and tossing the top into the trash. "Shut the fuck up, Vera. This isn't a joke. I'm not playing a prank. Now quit bitching about it."

Her face screws up in pain. "You've wanted me out of here. How the hell would I have even left, if I *can't* fucking leave?" she screeches, her hands flying up in the air, her burning cigarette ashing on the ground.

I stare at it, and she stomps on the ash, smushing it into the dark tiles, growling as she takes a step toward me. "Answer me, you fucking asshole. You wanted me out of here so bad. Well, I want to go. Tell me how to get out of here."

I snap forward, my hand curling around her chin and squeezing tight. "Death, Vera. Death is the only way you can leave here," I mumble, my lips only a breath away from her.

She exhales, her shaky breath skimming across my lips. I lick them, tasting the tobacco.

I can feel the darkness chill her bones, and she steps back, gripping the counter with her shaky hand. "You want me dead? Is that it?" Her voice is cool, and I can feel the lash of anger she wants to whip at me.

I shrug, ignoring the dread thickening in the pit of my stomach. I don't care, is what I want to say. But I don't know how much truth that holds. Every day that goes by, she seems to burrow a little further beneath my skin. "I wanted you to die." I reach out, my hand grabbing onto the front of her shirt, right under her neck. I pull her close, hating her. Wanting her. Hating that I fucking want her. "I wanted to feel your heart stop. I wanted to feel your warm blood turn cold in my hands. I wanted to stare you in the eyes as you took your last breath."

She stares at me, her eyes going back and forth between mine, searching. "Wanted?"

I clench my jaw, my molars cracking from the force. I say nothing, because I don't know what to say. I'm fucking emotionless. I don't care about people, besides my boys. The most I've had that I could even consider a relationship is with Thea, and she could fall off a cliff tomorrow, for all I care.

My hand can't help but clutch Vera's shirt tighter at the thought of her jumping off a bridge.

I don't... I don't want it to happen.

I release her shirt, giving her a small shove away from me. "Want. Wanted. I really don't fucking care," I sneer, the lie flowing from my tongue with ease.

She frowns at me, and I swear I see a lick of disappointment in her eyes. "I really hate you, Malik, you know that?"

"Good. Go sleep in the backyard, then." I walk back to the fridge, opening it up and looking for anything to eat, even though I know there's not a damn thing in here. All my dad and Vera's mom do is eat out. They couldn't even stock up the fridge before they left. Sure, they gave us money. But who the hell do I look like, pushing a grocery cart around the store?

Her hands press against my back, and she shoves me. I don't move an inch.

"Why'd you even pick me up, then, huh? Why not just leave me out there to walk endlessly through the night? Why care, if you fucking hate me so much?" Her growls are pained, like a wounded animal.

I turn my head, staring at her over my shoulder. "Maybe I should have left you out there. Let the dead take you away."

Her face turns red, and she flicks the nearly burnt-out cigarette at my face. The barely lit cherry nicks my cheek before tumbling to the ground.

My nostrils flare, and I feel my restraint grow thin.

Vera can see it, too. Her jaw goes slack, and she shuffles back a bit.

My boot steps forward, and I smash the cigarette under my boot. "Vera?" I ask quietly.

She says nothing to me, her rapid blinking full of terror.

"Run," I mouth.

27

VERA

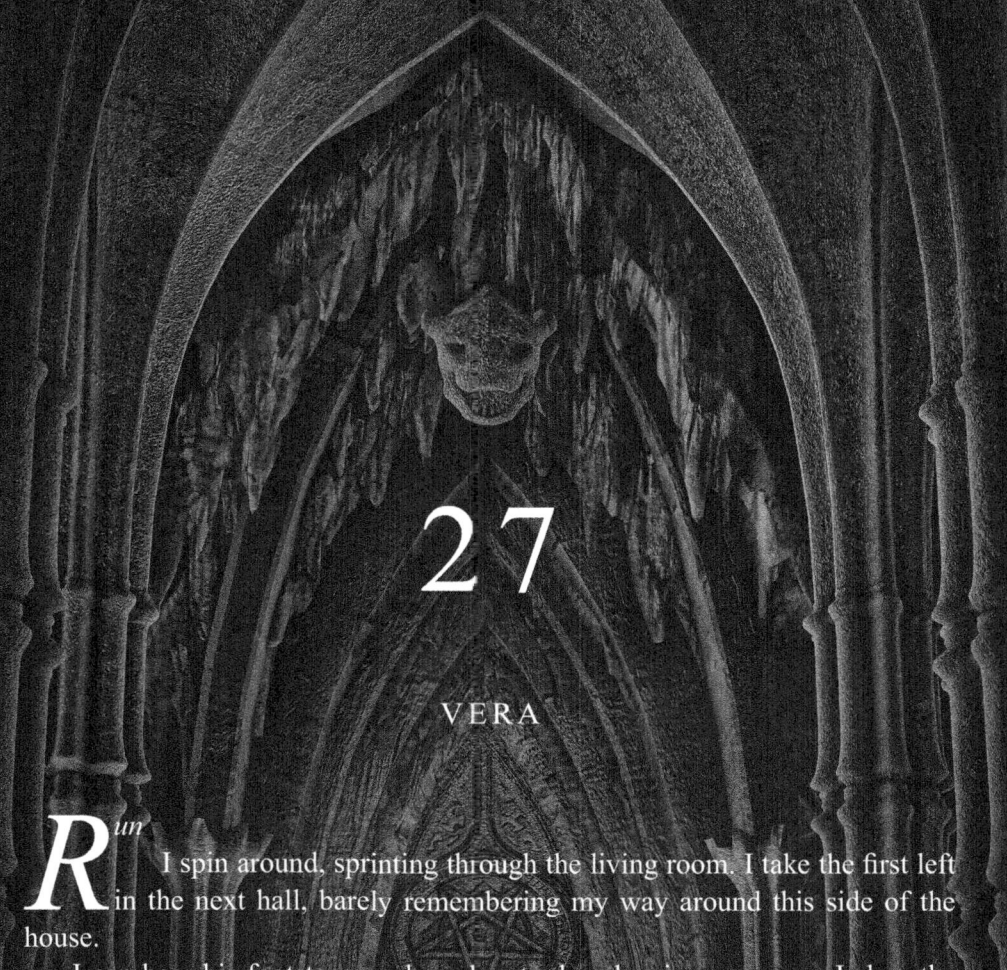

R^{un} I spin around, sprinting through the living room. I take the first left in the next hall, barely remembering my way around this side of the house.

I can hear his footsteps, and my heart whooshes in my ears as I slam the door, slapping on the light to the massive library. I lean my back against the door, breathing through my tremors. I press my hand on the handle behind me, flicking the lock closed.

I can't hear him anymore. His footsteps have dissipated, and so have his heavy, angry, growling breaths.

I turn around, pressing my palm and ear to the door to listen.

I crush my lips shut as I hold my breath, listening, waiting.

"Boo." His voice is muffled on the other side of the door, but it still startles me. I leap back, looking left to right. For any escape possible.

It sounded like his voice was right there. Right against my ear.

"There's no way out of the library, baby sister. You can search all you want. You're in the innermost part of our lovely castle. Now, you can open the door. Or I can break it down, but I don't think my father would be too happy to come home to that. Do you?"

I squeeze my hand into a fist, my fingers thumping against my palms. I'm nervous. I'm so fucking nervous.

What's going to happen if I open that door?

"Go away." My voice is shaky, barely audible as I speak the words.

He growls on the other side of the thick wood. It's massive, extending from the floor to the ceiling, the size of two doors put together. The wood is dark, with carvings in each panel.

It seems like nothing could break through that door. Though, I know it'll take Malik no effort to get to me.

"I'm giving you five seconds."

My mouth drops open, but no words come out. I walk backward, my feet moving of their own accord until my spine hits a bookshelf, novels surrounding me. The smell of books and old paper is inhaled with each breath. So many stories to be read, which feels like an omen, because this is maybe where my story ends.

"One." I hear a click, and the door slides open soundlessly. Malik stands there, a key in his hand. It's old, a skeleton key that's the size of his palm. He tsks. "I give you chance after chance, and you constantly fight me. Why?"

I whip my head back and forth. "You've given me no chances. All you've wanted is to hurt me. Since the moment I stepped into your home."

His head cocks to the side, a contemplative look on his hardened face. "Maybe. But fighting will only cause your situation to become worse. Take a wolf, for instance. The alpha. The head of the pack. What do you think happens if someone steps up to the alpha? The alpha puts you in your place, shows its dominance. Warns you, repeatedly. What do you think happens if the stupid wolf doesn't listen to the alpha, and attacks? Not once, but time and time again. How do you think it will end for that stupid, foolish wolf?"

I picture his vision in my head. The master alpha wolf. Black as the night, with shiny but rough hair. Wild and untamed. Teeth that snarl, sharp and tinged with blood. Making the pack bow down. I imagine the entire pack becoming submissive, lying down around the snarling alpha as he takes charge.

Except one.

A stupid, white wolf that fights back, time after time.

I imagine blood. And I imagine death.

I envision the black wolf standing over the white, torn-apart wolf. Blood dripping through his dark hair as he howls into the night air.

I shiver, staring up at Malik as he stands in front of me.

He smiles, his sharp teeth as jagged as the alpha wolf's would be. Stepping forward, he presses me further against the bookshelf. It grinds into my back, and I step onto my tiptoes for relief, but it doesn't help. Not one bit.

His hands go to the bookshelf on either side of me, trapping me. I lean my head against a thick spine, needing to get away from his scent, but even the smallest inhale has him surrounding me. It feels like he's inside me.

"What're you doing?" I whisper.

A hand drops to the collar of my shirt, his fingers hanging on the top button. "Are you a witch, Vera?"

My eyes widen. "No?"

His eyes lower a bit, like he doesn't believe me. His hand pulls, and I can feel the strain on my buttons. They are nice shirts, but they hold no power against Malik's strong hands.

The first button pops. "You look like a witch." He leans down, inhaling my scent. "You smell like a witch." His free hand drops to my bare thigh, squeezing my skin. "You feel like a witch. So, I don't really believe you, little sister. A regular fucking person doesn't have the ability to do whatever it is you're doing to me."

I look up. "What am I doing to you?"

He snarls and pulls, another button popping. My breasts heave, my scar poking through the top of my cleavage. I want to be self-conscious, cover myself so he doesn't have to see. But does it even matter? He's seen it already, and he's already verbalized his distaste for anything that is me.

"I can't stop thinking about my knife in your cunt." He pulls, and another button pops. Stepping closer to me, I can feel the hardness of his erection pressing up against my skirt. I close my eyes, because it's long. It's long and thick as hell. I'm not a virgin, but whatever hides behind Malik's slacks is not something I've ever experienced.

"I can't stop thinking about your filthy mouth, and how those pouty lips would look wrapped around my cock." I can feel a rush of heat flood between my thighs, and I bite my lower lip to stop the moan that tries to break free.

He pulls again, and the last button pops. The fabric separates, and cool air brushes against my stomach. My fishnets are high, rising above my skirt and wrapping tightly around my hips.

He hisses through his teeth, and I can feel the anger building inside of him. His other hand lowers, and his long fingers wrap around my neck, only barely cutting off my breathing. "And for some fucking reason, I can't stop thinking about your bad fucking attitude. Tell me, Vera, if you aren't a witch, how the fuck is this happening? Because I've had virgin cunts that felt like untouched velvet against my fucking cock. What is it that's so special about yours?"

I glare up at him, anger burning beneath my skin. I go to push him out of the way, but it only makes him pin me even harder against the books.

"This time, baby sister, you aren't going anywhere." His threat is final, certain.

"I don't want your cock that's dipped into a million different cups of whore. I'd rather fuck a sliver-ridden stick. Maybe the reason you can't take your eyes off me is because I'm an actual fucking human rather than the dumb whores you usually spend your time with. Now, get off me," I growl, reaching up and wrapping my fingers around his wrist, ready to pull him off and get away from him.

His hand tightens around my throat. "How easy it would be to snap your windpipe and let your bones disintegrate in my palm."

"Do it," I choke out. "You would be doing both of us a service."

His fingers loosen, his face turning red with rage at my words. His fingers go to the cups of my bra, and he pulls, the thick fabric holding them together snapping like a rubber band. No force needed. My breasts fall free, bouncing lightly in front of his gaze. He watches them, his eyes darkening into bottomless pits.

What the hell is it with this guy?

His fingers press into my ugly scar, and indignant tears immediately flood my eyes. "How did this happen?"

I whip my head to the side, staring at the wall. "It's none of your business."

He tweaks a nipple. Hard. My back arches and I whimper, pain and pleasure mixing in an unbearable combination. "You escaped death once. Why so eager to go back to that place?"

I bite my lip, blinking back the tears. He has no right. No right to break me as he seems to be doing. So effortlessly. I feel exposed and at his mercy. Completely.

He palms my breasts, and I let him, because a part of me wants the touch. But from him? I don't know what I want anymore.

"What happened to you?" he asks again.

My lips press together so tightly. I don't want him to know my past. I don't want him to know anything personal about me. He doesn't deserve it. Not an inch.

"Did you die?" he whispers, leaning into me. His lower lip brushes my nipple. Hardened, sensitive. He moves, his warm breath fanning across my scar. "Did you stop breathing?" His finger lifts, and it skims across the length, from top to bottom. "Did your heart stop beating?"

"My heart was rotten from the beginning."

His pauses on a breath, my skin turning from warm to cool. His eyes raise, his dark eyelashes fanning across his skin as his eyes spear into mine. "Is your bad heart the one beating in your chest at this very moment?"

His hand covers my left breast, feeling for the beat. As if he could tell, just from touch, that my heart is good or bad.

"My heart is in a wasteland, no longer beating." The words flow out of me, even though I don't want to say a word to him. I should ask if he's the witch, not me. How does he get me to speak to him so willingly, even when my brain tells me that's the last thing it should do?

His hand twitches. "Whose heart sits inside your rib cage?"

I look at him to see that he's already watching me. "My father's."

His hand drops, and he takes a step back from me. "You're serious."

"As my rotted heart."

He spins around, walking across the library. His back is stiff, tensed. He is coiled tight. It looks like he's about to leave the room. Leave me and my fake heart alone. Maybe for good, this time.

At the last moment, he spins around, his dark eyes hot and heavy as they land on mine. He takes quick steps, and somehow, within only a moment, he's back in front of me, pressing his dress shirt against my bare chest. Both hands cup my jaw, tilting my head back until I'm staring him in the eyes. "You are so fucked up, Vera." His head shakes, like he can't bear to be near me. "So, why can't I get enough of you?"

His mouth dives down, claiming mine. At first, I gasp, and he takes advantage, diving his tongue between my lips. I bring my hands up, sliding my fingers through his soft, messy hair. He slams me harder into the bookshelf, growling into my mouth. "You're a mess. A fucking disaster."

I pull on his hair, feeling the threads break between my fingers. "You're the worst person I've ever met in my entire life," I breathe.

His hands drop, and they fall to the bottom of my skirt. His hands lift, and my skirt bunches around my waist, my naked sex visible and feeling on fire as his eyes burn between my legs. I feel needy and so fucking dirty as my stepbrother engulfs my folds with his eyes. He leans back, staring between my legs. "Fucking witch."

My fingers drop from his hair, and I start working the buttons on his shirt. "Call me what you like. You'll forever be the devil in my book." I pull his shirt apart, and his hard stomach flexes and twitches from the exposed air. I run my fingers along his abs, wondering how someone can be so perfect and so flawed at the same time. He's essentially the perfect human, looks-wise. But he's evil, completely damaged on the inside.

His fingers curl around the holes of my fishnets, and he pulls easily, ripping my tights in the process.

My folds are drenched, and he doesn't waste any time as his fingers slide between the slickness, spreading the wetness around and diving in with two long fingers. "Fuck off," he groans.

I tilt my head back, riding the high of his touch. There's so much—*so fucking much feeling*—as the hard pads of his fingers grind against the walls. I whimper, wanting to tell him to fuck me. Wanting to beg him, for the first time in my life. But I can't. I *will not* beg him.

His free hand goes to his pants, and he rips his belt off and unbuttons, loosening them just enough to pull out his erection.

Holy shit.

It's massive, bigger than I've ever seen. It throbs in his hand as he grips it tightly, giving it a slow yank until a dribble of clear liquid drips from the tip.

My mouth waters.

He moves toward my cunt, and reality slaps me in the face. I raise a palm, slapping it against his chest. "Condom. Grab a condom."

He snarls at me, reaching into his back pocket and pulling out his wallet. He folds it open and pulls out—what looks to be like—a brand-new fucking condom.

Like the asshole needs to replenish every week or some shit.

I almost cover myself, but the throbbing between my legs is too much. I watch as he tears it open and slides it over his cock with ease, giving it another stroke once it's on.

He's settled. Relaxed. He knows how to work his body and he knows it's a fucking work of art.

While I'm over here feeling floppy, uncoordinated, and unattractive.

His hand snaps down and his fingers wrap around my thigh. The tips of his fingers dig into my skin. It's almost painful, and I whimper as he lines himself up and plunges in.

His head tilts back, his Adam's apple protruding from his neck as he swallows. I watch it bob up and down, and my knees nearly buckle.

He stays still, his cock twitching and growing even larger inside me. There's a pinch of pain, an ache deep in my belly where no one has ever been before.

I attempt to wiggle, but I can't even move with him pinning me against the bookshelf. "Move. Please. Do something. It's too much."

He slides out, until only the tip is stretching the walls, then plunges back in. So rough. So hard. My body snaps tight, pain and pleasure coiling through me like a snake, ready to strike. "Fucking shit."

"Consider this…" he says as he pulls out, only to plunge back in again, "as me knocking you off your throne."

My hand reaches out, and I grab onto his shoulder. I leap, and he has no option but to lift my other leg. Now I'm in his arms, and for a moment, this is where I want to stay. A weird part of me feels protected here. Safe in his wicked arms. He's strong, and I know he could battle whatever evil surrounds me.

But the other part of me wants to hurt him just as badly as he's hurt me. I rock to the side, throwing him off balance until he takes a step back, the heel of his foot catching on a nearby couch. He falls to the cushion, and my fingers thread through his hair. I pull him up, my lips sliding against his. "I hate you, big brother."

He growls, attempting to flip us over. I don't let him this time. Planting my boots on either side of the cushion. I keep my fingers in his hair and pull his head back, pinned against the back of the couch. It's more like a chaise, with only one armrest, the other side open and bare.

My skirt fans around my knees, and my shirt still lays ripped against my sides. I push myself up, riding him fast and hard, each thrust stretching my walls around his thick length. Using my own pace. There's still pain, but the pleasure overcomes that, and the heat in my belly grows with each thrust.

His eyes darken, and his mouth drops open, his tongue gliding against his sharp teeth. "You are playing a dangerous game, Vera."

"Maybe I want the danger," I breathe, my chest heaving from exertion. I can feel him growing harder inside of me. Longer. Thicker.

I keep hold of his hair while I ride him, taking the pleasure I want. Taking control. Watching him beneath me could make me orgasm all by itself. Watching him at my mercy.

A shiver rolls through me.

In the next moment, he lifts me off the couch and places my back against the cushion. Spreading my legs wide, until pain aches in my thighs, he presses in again. Fucking me fast. Rocking the entire couch with his movements.

My eyebrows furrow even as my jaw goes slack. He picked me up with ease. No hesitation.

"You didn't think you really had me pinned, did you?" He barks out a laugh. "Now that's fucking funny."

I bring my hand up to the back of his neck, digging my nails in and dragging them down his chest. Deep scores mark his skin, and I watch as his eyes squint in pain. I swear I even see pleasure within his dark irises.

His hand lowers, sliding beneath my skirt. The pad of his thumb presses against my clit, and he rubs roughly, but calculated. His fingers are experienced as they work me. I suddenly feel out of control, like his thumb pressed the button to make me crumble.

I'm finally as he wants me. Willing. Beneath him. Submissive.

"Come on my cock, Vera."

I do, like a lightning bolt shoots from the sky and cracks me wide open. I cry out, my back arching and my legs tensing, trembling, going numb around him.

"Fuck. Yes," he growls. I watch as his head tips back, the tendons in his neck going taut as he reaches his own orgasm. His thrusts become manic, punishing as he slams into me. Leaning down, he kisses me. Deeply, aggressively. Nipping at my lips. He catches my lower lip between his teeth, pulling on it and biting until the skin breaks.

Pain shoots through me, and as he releases my lip, I run my tongue along the ache, tasting blood.

"I hate you, too, baby sister," he mumbles against my lips.

I frown, bringing my hands to his hair and pulling. It's wild, unruly around his head. His eyes are the darkest I've ever seen. His face is a work of art, completely chiseled. I could stare at him all day.

As long as he doesn't speak.

I pull him down, until my lips rest against his ear. "Sometimes I wish everything bad in the world would happen to you," I whisper seductively, running my fingers along his sharp jaw. His head snaps to my finger, and he bites down, the sharp canine tooth digging into my skin.

"You too, baby." He shoves off me, pulls the condom off and tucks himself back into his jeans. Glancing at me once more, he steps back, his face once again cold and emotionless.

"That's it?" I ask, sitting up. I pull my shirt over my breasts and yank my skirt over my thighs to cover myself. "Just walking away?"

He frowns. "What, you want to fucking snuggle or something?"

My face screws up. "What? Fuck no." I mean, I don't know. I guess I just didn't expect him to be so cold. But, he is Malik, so maybe I shouldn't have had any high hopes in the first place.

He stares at me, his eyebrows raised as he waits for an answer.

I don't give him one.

He turns around, heading toward the door, when a book falls off the shelf.

He pauses in his step, and I turn around, spotting a book on the floor at the far end of the room. The spine sits bent against the ground, the pages fluttered up and blowing in the non-existent breeze.

"What the fuck?" he asks, taking a step toward the book.

I hear a scrape against wood and turn my head to the other end of the room, seeing a book fly from the shelf. Malik ducks, and it crashes against a mirror on the wall beside him. The book falls to the ground, and the mirror turns into a spiderweb of shattered glass.

My eyes widen as I stare at Malik. He stands up, glaring at me with a fierce scowl. "What the fuck is this?"

I shake my head, standing up. Terror racks my body, and I can barely get any words out. "I don't know," I whisper.

The scrape happens again, the sound of an old spine sliding out from between other books. I duck before I see it, and a red, thick, bound book flies across the room, knocking a figurine off the table.

"Move. Get the fuck out of here." He rushes toward me, and nothing else needs to be said. I'm already moving, sprinting toward the door before a book knocks one of us out. My hand goes to the handle, but it doesn't budge.

"It's locked."

"Move." He shoves me out of the way. A literal hand on my shoulder and he pushes. Hard. I scowl at him as I stumble. His hand goes to the brass knob, and he wiggles it, pulling on the door. All I can hear are the hinges working against one another.

"How is that possible? Doesn't it lock from this side?" I cry out.

He slaps his palm against the door, just as another book flies out.

"Duck!" I scream, falling to my knees.

Malik moves just in time. A black book flies out, crashing against the door before falling to his lap.

He turns toward me. "I should really fucking kill you for this."

My chest hiccups, and I stand up, slapping my palms against the wooden door. "Someone! Can anyone hear me? Help! Help us!"

He snarls at me. "No one's fucking here. Are you stupid?" He rushes away from the door, walking to a desk in the corner of the room. He opens a drawer, pulling out a thick black book with a cross on the front.

A Bible.

He opens another drawer, pulling out a small cross.

My jaw goes slack.

He looks like a conundrum. His shirt is undone, his glistening abs moving as he raises the cross into the air. His hair is a mess, completely disheveled from my hands. His pants are unbuttoned, barely hanging over his hips.

He's a god.

Or maybe he's just the devil.

Holding the Bible up with his other hand, he starts to mumble. *"Our Father, who art in heaven, hallowed be thy name. Thy kingdom come…"*

"Are you really reciting the Lord's Prayer?"

He glares at me a moment before glancing around the room, waving the holy objects like that can somehow protect us.

I don't think anything can protect us in this town.

A shiver racks my spine and goosebumps litter my skin as the temperature in the room drops by what feels to be twenty degrees.

Then I hear a growl. Low, evil, like a wild beast that's completely savage and full of pure, raging anger.

I close my eyes, not wanting to look behind me. Not wanting to see what I fear is there, but knowing I need to. I need to know what's been haunting me. Because I know, without a doubt, that this is it.

I spin, almost in slow motion. Another grunt sounds, and it sounds animalistic. Inhumane. Crazed.

All I can see is darkness. Like a shadow. Or cloud. It's not a solid figure, and it immediately makes me shiver.

Red eyes.

Antlers, sharp and decayed. Blackened.

Sharp, pointed teeth.

I let out a squeak. "Malik," I whisper, watching it stare at me. Breathe at me. I scream. "Malik! Help me!" I start backing up and can hear Malik curse behind me.

"Holy fucking shit. Move out of the way, Vera. Move out of the way!" He grabs my arm, pulling me across the ground. My back slides against the old carpet, my still healing scratches gnawing in pain as I'm pulled away from the menacing shadow. His eyes move as I do, following me every inch of the way.

Then the shadow moves, sliding up the wall as it watches me. Leers at me. My breathing stops. I feel like my lungs constrict. I can't breathe.

I can't fucking breathe.

Malik raises the Bible and the cross, restarting his chant of the Lord's Prayer.

The shadow figure continues to move, long fingers uncurling from the shadows. They're long, eight inches in length, at least. It's absolutely horrifying as the thin digits curl around the trim of the door.

"Leave! Leave my house!" Malik booms. "Get the fuck out of here!" he roars.

The shadow floats off the wall, growing larger and more ominous by the second as it fills up more space. It's a body, but it's not a body at all. I can see the stretching, thin limbs diluted by the fog. It's utterly terrifying, and I want to peel my eyes away, but I can't.

"It's not working," I whisper, my voice coming out as a cry.

"Shut the fuck up," he growls, his hands shaking as he stands only feet away from the shadow.

Its eyes land back on me, and I know—I know deep in my soul—that it wants me. It wants every bit of me, and dread makes me numb. I close my eyes, wondering if this is where my prayers are answered.

If this is finally the end.

"Fuck," Malik swears. I snap my eyes open, watching the shadow move toward me. Malik drops the Bible and the cross and reaches down, pulling me across the floor and out of the way. It speeds up, rushing me at lightning speed. Malik steps in front of me, covering me from its wrath. It plows into him. Like a bullet to his chest, the black shadow sweeps Malik off his feet as the shadow sinks into him. He stays levitated in the air while the massive shadow pierces his skin, like it's going through a tunnel. Except, it doesn't exit from the other side. It's like it fills Malik.

He doesn't scream. He doesn't shout.

His back is arched, his arms and legs dead at his side. His head tilted toward the ceiling as his shirt drapes on either side of him, his bare chest on display, showing a darkness, almost like a bruise forming where the shadow penetrates him. Until every inch of the shadow flows into him, and he stays levitated for another moment.

Then drops.

He falls to the ground in heavy limbs. Unconscious.

Where did it go? It didn't even come out the other side of him.

I look around, expecting it to be lurking in the corner, ready to take me.

But it's not. It's nowhere.

I don't waste another second. Scrambling to my feet, I rush to Malik's side, my knees knocking to the ground. "Malik," I cry, shaking his shoulders. He's unresponsive, his head lolling back and forth from my rocking. "Malik, please wake up!"

He doesn't wake up. He doesn't even stir. But pressing my fingers to his neck, his heart is beating. Heavy, steady.

He's alive.

"Please," I whimper, surprised at the tears that roll down my cheeks. I don't even wipe them away. I let them roll down my cheeks as I curl on my side, lying against Malik. I'm not strong enough to pull him upstairs, and I'm not going to leave him alone.

I'll stay here until I know he's okay.

I'll stay with him.

I'll stay with my monster. My stepbrother.

28

MALIK

My eyes fly open, and I shoot up, inhaling a gasping breath.
Holy fuck. What happened?
I glance around, seeing the dim library at home.
How did I get here?
Looking down, I see my shirt opened and wrinkled. I have scratches extending from my chest to waist. I bring a hand up, feeling the burning marks on my skin. In the center of my chest is a dark, massive bruise.
What?
My eyes widen when I see a body next to me, and I'm even more shocked to see it is Vera's. I stare at her sleeping form. Her own shirt is torn open. She curls in a ball on the floor, like she can be protected from whatever the fuck is going on if she burrows next to me.

Flits of my memory dance in the back of my mind. A broken video reel that tries to play a movie, but only bits and pieces come together in a mismatched story.

We fucked.
I fucked her.
I swallow down a groan, sliding away from her as gently as possible. It was never my intent to sleep with my new sister. Not only are we supposed to be

family, but she's a fucking wreck. She's a damn disaster.

She doesn't stir from my movements, so I stand up, wincing when it feels like I was hit by a truck.

What happened to me? Am I sick?

My body aches, and a splitting headache shoots between my eyes. I bring my fingers to my temples and rub, but it doesn't subside.

I step over strewn books laying on the floor. Did we fight? Did she throw a book at my head? That would clearly explain why I have such a killer headache right now.

Opening the door, I slip through, not even closing it behind me.

Why the fuck did Vera stay with me?

I stumble through the house, my eyesight fading in and out. My hand presses against a wall, and I right myself, shaking my head to clear the fog. I feel like I'm on a bad trip, or I have a wicked hangover or something. I don't know, maybe I am sick.

I head for the main floor bathroom, nearly falling to my knees. My fingers grip the granite sink in front of me as I take in my expression.

I look terrible.

My skin is sickly pale. Dark, purplish bags stretch underneath my eyes that look like I was socked in the face. My eyes are bloodshot, red spider-like lines splintering across the whites of my eyes.

I don't understand. What happened?

The light starts buzzing above me, and I glance up, squinting against the glow that seems to be growing brighter by the second. I lift my hand and shield my eyes, the humming and brightness becoming so much it's painful.

Pop.

The bulb shatters, the small pieces falling around my shoulders.

"Fuck." I brush off my shoulders and dig my hand into my pocket to grab my phone. Flipping on the flashlight, I point it toward the light and mirror.

"Holy fuck!" I dip out of the bathroom, whipping my shirt off my shoulders and feeling around my back as I fly down the hall.

An oversized black mass was curled around my shoulder, with red eyes glaring me in the face. Antlers you'd see on a deer extended from its head. It smiled at me, it's razor-sharp, elongated teeth only inches from my skin. They were brown and thin and looked fucking hideous.

I shiver, slapping at my shoulders.

But nothing's there.

I stop, looking behind me. It didn't follow me, whatever it was. Was I imagining it? Maybe Vera slipped me something when I wasn't looking. It wouldn't surprise me. She's such a damn menace, her trying to one-up me wouldn't be a shock. Turning back toward the bathroom, my feet are hesitant and light against the floor as I walk through the doorway.

"What the hell?" I let out a gasp, hesitantly stepping back into the bathroom. My heart pounds in my chest, and I lift the light to the mirror, expecting to see the shadow again.

Nothing.

"What was that noise?" Vera's soft voice comes from the kitchen.

I jump, growling under my breath as I step out of the bathroom. "What the fuck is going on? What did you do to me?"

She rears back, shock and anger lining her eyes. "What did I do?" She waves her hand down her shirt. "You're the one that ripped my shirt."

Her shirt covers her breasts, but the scar is clear between the gap of fabric. She notices where I'm staring and glances up at me, scowling as she folds the fabric over her skin to conceal herself. "What are you looking at?"

"I'm wondering how you ended up convincing me to fuck you. What'd you do? Did you fucking drug me?"

She frowns. "Are you fucking kidding? No, I didn't drug you, you bastard!" Her shouts are furious, her face red, and honestly, a bit hurt. "You don't remember what happened?"

I shrug, not sure how much I should be telling her.

She narrows her eyes. "You're the one that came onto me, asshole."

Really? "Unlikely." I chuckle.

I watch as red-hot rage fills her neck and reaches her ears. "Ugh! I hate you so fucking much, Malik! Why do you have to be such a damn dick all the time?" She spins around, stomping out of the kitchen and toward the stairs.

I take a step forward, reaching out and wrapping my fingers around her wrist. "Wait."

She doesn't look at me. "What do you want?"

"What happened last night?"

She glances at me over her shoulder, her makeup smeared from whatever debacle we went through. A lick of fear fills her eyes, and it immediately puts me on edge. "You really don't remember?"

I shake my head.

She turns around, her eyes sliding from my feet up to my messy hair. We both look wrecked. Fucking obliterated. "There was something... or someone, in the library with us."

I frown. "What?"

She pulls her hand out of my hold. "I don't know. We slept together." Her cheeks pinken, and it nearly makes me laugh. "And then there were books flying off the wall and the door was locked, and we couldn't get out."

"The door was unlocked when I woke up." I narrow my eyes at her.

"Well, it wasn't last night!"

"So, what? We couldn't get out, so we decided to snuggle on the floor?" I don't care what kind of shit I'm trippin' on, that's not me. I would've never—*never*—agreed to fall asleep on the floor with some chick next to me.

Most of all, my stepsister.

Her eyes fade out, like she's stuck in a dream. "There was some... figure, or something, in the room with us. It was coming after me, and you pulled me out of the way." She glances down at the ground, sadness and terror paling her skin. Her eyes lift, and they're glistening, filled with oversized tears. "It got you, Malik. Whatever it was, shot straight into your chest."

I blink. "What?"

She lifts her hands, hesitantly reaching out and grazing her fingers along the gnarly bruise on my skin, right between my pecs. "Right there. It... went inside of you, I guess. Right there." She takes a step forward. "You really don't remember any of that?"

I stare at her. She sounds like she believes the words coming out of her mouth. The look in her eyes is full of horror, like whatever happened traumatized her. But her story? Unbelievable.

Castle Pointe may be filled with some creepy shit. But a black figure sliding into my chest?

I step back, and her hand drops, falling to her side.

"Next time you want to fuck your brother, you'll need to come up with a better story than that, baby. Just a heads-up for next time, I don't snuggle." I slip around her, her trembling body barely contained as I head toward the stairs.

"I'm going to take a shower. Better get ready for school if we want to make it on time," I shout from the stairs.

The sound of glass shattering reaches the top of the stairs, and I smile, knowing we're back to being enemies again.

29

VERA

There's something wrong with him.

He looks sick.

I glance down, the decorative plate laying at my feet in large shards. I'm sure I'll get chewed out by either Samuel or my mom, but I don't care. Malik is a douche.

I kick a shard of glass when I hear the shower turn on upstairs. The asshole is so careless that he can sleep with me, treat me like shit, and go about his day like nothing ever happened?

I don't want anything out of him either. I don't want to date him. I don't even care if I ever sleep with him again, no matter how earth-shattering it was. But even as I think the words, the lie burns in my gut.

Malik *consumed* me.

The way he held my body and took what he wanted. He is such a man, not at all like the guys from Fargo. The guys back home, their bodies were slim, their muscles undefined, their facial hair soft, childish.

Malik is a different species. He and his friends are brutally attractive, their faces sharp, their jawlines rough with scruff. Everything about them screams trouble.

Malik, though, he screams something on a completely different level. One look at him and my alarm bells ring.

Danger.

Malik is danger.

I step on the broken glass, my boots crunching the pieces into dust on the darkened floor.

Hopefully it doesn't leave a scratch, I think as I head toward the stairs.

Malik's nonchalance is irritating. More than I thought it'd be. His ability to brush me off is offensive.

Maybe it's time I play a prank of my own.

I race up the stairs, my fingertips gliding across the iron railing as I make my way to the second level. The shower is still on, with the door only opened a crack. I pause, leaning on my toes as I peek inside.

I feel like a damn creep.

The deep shower makes it impossible to see much. But then he shifts, his head tilting back as his fingers run through his dark tresses. His arms flex with the movements. I watch as the water glides from his hair, down his toned back, and over the rounded globes of his ass.

Holy hell.

I feel a thump between my legs, and swallow through my suddenly parched mouth.

He is so fucking perfect.

Why does he have to be my brother? Why does he have to be such a terrible person?

I blink, shaking my thoughts from my head at his last words.

I don't cuddle.

His mocking voice in my head makes me snarl. What a fucking dick. My nostrils flare as I stomp off to his bedroom, not even caring about my torn shirt at this point. It floats against my sides as I walk to his door. It's shut, as it always is. I've never been in here. Never had the guts. I don't even know what it looks like, actually. I just know that this dark, tall door looks ominous.

Frightening.

A chill breaks out along my spine as I press my hand on the cold knob. My fingers shake as I turn the knob, and a gust of Malik hits me in the face. I can't help but inhale, breathing in the scent of pine and water and smoke and so, so much Malik.

My mouth fills with water.

Not only that, but his room is shockingly clean. Like, not an article of clothing on the floor. Not a slightly opened drawer in his dresser. No dishes on his nightstand. His bed is made.

Like, what? How is a teenage guy cleaner than I am?

I walk up to his bed, running my fingers along his black comforter, the king mattress oversized and tall, sitting on a huge wooden frame. The Gothic-looking headboard is tall, a nearly midnight dark wood as it sits against the wall. The entire bed looks overwhelming and gigantic. I walk up to the nightstand, jumping up so I'm able to sit on the edge of the bed. The heel of my boot balances on the edge of the frame as I lean forward, pulling on the handle of the nightstand.

A box of condoms. A knife. A Bible.

Wow, good combo.

A smirk lifts my lips as I grab the handle of the knife. It's not the one he keeps on him. This one is more like a dagger, old and heavy. The handle looks brass, small, with deep carvings making it look like a historical object more than anything else.

I press my finger on the tip, watching the pad whiten a moment before the blade pierces the skin. Blood drips down my knuckle, and I press my finger against his comforter, watching as it seeps into the fabric.

Lifting the blade to his headboard, I run it across the wood. It's thick. Not a hollow, cheap wood that you find at IKEA.

I sigh. Poor Malik and his bad attitude.

My hand shoots forward, and the blade plunges into the wood. I drag down, watching the dark wood turn to light as it starts shredding beneath the blade. I start carving into the headboard, a smile on my lips as I listen to the water continue to run in the shower.

I shift on the mattress, getting comfortable as I make my art on Malik's bed.

Once I'm done, I lean down and drop the knife into the drawer, pushing it closed with the tip of my boot.

A small giggle escapes as I admire my work.

Well done. I deserve a fucking pat on the back.

Vera's bitch is written in sharp, jagged letters across the dark wood.

I kick my feet out, swinging them back and forth as my blood hums through my veins. What else can I do? After everything Malik has done to me, it feels like child's play to draw on his headboard.

One glance at his dresser and I know exactly what I'm going to do.

The son of a bitch took my underwear and made me go to school commando.

Maybe it's time he figured out who the hell he was fucking with.

It doesn't matter that the morning after the mausoleum when I went to change out of my damp clothes, I found them back in my drawer. Like it was some sort of peace treaty or something. The asshole took them in the first place, and because of that, he deserves payback.

I open the top drawer, seeing neatly folded underwear and socks all laying in the same direction.

I frown. *Does this guy have OCD or something?*

The groan of the pipes as the shower turns off makes my eyes widen. I grab a handful, looking back and forth as I think of what to do.

I could go to my room, but I wouldn't get too far with his things. I glance at the window and rush over to it, dropping his things to the ground. I push up the wooden frame, opening the window wide and glancing out the front of the house.

It groans and creaks, the old wood heavy as I push the window opened, but about halfway up, it releases, gliding easily to the top of the frame.

Perfect.

I grab his things and chuck them out the window. Running as quick as I can back to his dresser, I shove the drawer closed and open the next drawer, pulling out his shirts and racing to the window, throwing them into the air as well. I feel like I should stop, but I rush and do one last drawer, grabbing a handful of his dress pants for school and rushing to the window, throwing them over the edge.

I don't even close his bottom drawers, leaving them hanging open as I run from his room and back into mine. I slam my door closed, instantly hearing the creak of the bathroom door opening and Malik's footsteps walking down the hallway.

A chill of instant terror hits me.

Oh my God, what did I just do?

I think about running. Running out of the house and as far and fast as I can go. But instead, I walk into my closet, shutting the door behind me as quietly as possible and squatting into the corner. I shove my suitcase in front of me, curling behind it. I hold my breath. And I wait.

It doesn't take long. Less than a minute for Malik's feet to sound in the hallway again. He doesn't knock. I can only listen as the door flies open, the knob banging against the wall, and he storms inside. I can hear his angry breaths from across the room.

Is he... is he growling?

My palm goes to my mouth, and I hold my breath.

Please. Please go.

Fuck, why do I have to be so damn stupid?

Because he's an asshole.

I should stand up, walk out of here like nothing happened. I should act as nonchalant as he acts, pretending like I don't have a care in the world.

My closet door opens, like he can sense where I am. My suitcase flies from my closet, and there he stands. His damp body, heaving with fury. His hair wet as it falls across his face. The towel, cinched around his waist. Water dripping to the floor from the dark hair on his legs.

His eyes. White. No pupils, no irises. Only white as he glares down at me.

My eyes widen, and I crab walk backward, as far as I can into my closet.

"M-Malik?"

He growls, and it sounds horrifying. Unnatural. Unhuman.

"Malik? Malik!" I scream as he walks toward me. "Malik, stop!" I shout.

He doesn't stare at me, or maybe he does. I can't tell when the entirety of his eyes is a milky white.

I scream at the top of my lungs as he grabs my hair, his long fingers tangling beneath the tresses. He pulls me up, and I cry out from the pain as he drags me across the room. I curl my fingers around the frame of the door, but his strength is too much, and they pop off effortlessly.

My palms slap against the dark floors and make an obnoxious squeak as they drag across the tiles.

"Please! Please! Malik! I'm sorry."

He doesn't say a word, just another low growl emitting from deep in his chest. It's manly, deep, and sounds like a vicious animal buried beneath his ribs.

He suddenly bends down, wrapping his hands around my waist and hauling me over his shoulder. My stomach drops on his muscles like a fucking bag of potatoes, and I let out an *oomph* of pain. He steps into his room, another growl breaking from his chest as he faces his bed.

With a quick pivot, he makes his way to his window. I grab onto his arms. "Please. I'm so sorry, Malik. I'll go get your clothes right now. Just, please, put me down!"

His fingers dig into my hips painfully. He lifts me off him like I'm nothing, suspending me in the air above him. He looks absolutely terrifying. The bags underneath his eyes are pronounced around the whites of his eyes.

He looks like hell. He looks like death.

A shiver rolls through me, and a tear leaks out, sliding down my face. "Please," I whisper.

"You fucked with the wrong person," he growls, and the hair on the back of my neck stands on end.

It's Malik's voice… but it's not.

Malik's voice came from his throat, but there was a second voice laced with his. Something raspy, gritty. Like his throat has been overworked for thousands of years.

It didn't sound human. Not at all.

Before I have a chance to respond, I'm suspended from the window, Malik's fingers around my waist the only thing holding me up. I close my eyes, not wanting to look down. This place, it's bigger than a house. It's a castle. The second story is more like the fourth story of a regular house. I wouldn't survive the drop

He spins me around, and I move to grab the window, but he grabs my wrist, letting my other dangle in the air.

I swing to grab the window again, but he pushes me out further, too far. Too fucking far.

I glance up at him, and he smiles, his canines sharp against his upper lips, the whites of his eyes so desperately terrifying that it takes my breath. I can't do a thing besides scream.

"Only death can hear your screams." His voice comes again, the two-toned voice that sounds half like him, and half animal.

"M-Malik, if you're in there, please stop this. I k-know you wouldn't do this to me. I know you wouldn't," I cry, tears streaming full force down my cheeks at this point.

"Say hello to death, Vera." The voice, not at all Malik's this time, growls at me, and then he releases me.

I let out a scream as my hand flies forward, my fingers curling around the windowsill. I can barely catch my grip, and my fingers instantly begin to slide.

"Help me! Somebody, help me!" I scream.

Malik—or what was Malik at one point—stares at me, a smile on his face that doesn't at all look like Malik's.

My fingers grow weak, and I let out a choked sob. "Malik! Please help me!"

I watch as he blinks, once, twice, three times. The white fades from his eyes and his dark orbs come into view just as my fingers slip. The evil smile falters, his lips furrowing into a confused frown.

I let out a cry as I fall, closing my eyes as the inevitable hits.

Thick fingers wrap around my wrist, and I glance up, opening my eyes and seeing Malik leaning halfway from the window, his dark eyes alight with worry and terror. He extends his other hand down. "Grab my hand." I do as he asks, swinging my arm and wrapping my fingers into his palm.

He pulls me up, grabbing me by the waist and lifting me into the room. He tumbles to the ground, and I fall on top of him, our bodies a mass of limbs.

He grabs my shoulders, pushing me back to look me in the face. "What the fuck just happened?"

Another sob breaks from my chest, and pure, hateful anger lights me up. My hand cocks back, and I crack him in the eye. My fingers instantly scream in agony at the force. "You fucking bastard! I almost died!" Tears flood my eyes, rolling down my cheeks and falling onto his bare chest. He looks shocked, pissed as hell, and a little worried.

I spit in his face.

It lands on his cheek, sliding down to his tense jaw.

"I fucking hate you."

Standing up, I fold my shirt to cover myself, and go to run out of here. Away from him. Out of this room. I never should have come in here. I never should have slept with him.

His fingers latch around my ankle, and he pulls me to the ground. My elbows slam into the floor, and I let out a cry in pain. "Ow! Fucking hell!"

He whips me around, my spit still dripping down his cheek as he drags his body over mine. "I don't—I don't fucking know what happened." He grinds his jaw. Is he angry at me? Or angry at the unknown? "I keep… missing fucking pieces. I'm here one second, then in the next blink I'm somewhere else. I'm taking a fucking shower, and then you're falling from a window. I don't understand." His nostrils flare, and his eyes narrow. "But I could cut off your fucking tit, and I don't give a shit how pissed you are, punch me in the face again, spit in my face again, and I'll toss you from the window next time." His tongue rolls around his mouth, and he spits, a giant, hot glob of Malik slapping against my forehead. "There you go, baby."

My fingernails dig into the floor, and I press hard, feeling them crack. Needing the tension and the pain so I don't lose my damn shit.

He lifts himself off me, and I slide out, hopping to my feet running from the room as quickly as I can.

"Get fucking ready! We're leaving in fifteen minutes!"

I wipe the spit from my forehead and slam my door closed, walking to my closet and laying my fist into it as hard as I can. The wood splinters around my skin, and my knuckles immediately start bleeding from the shards of wood.

I stomp to my bed, falling face first onto my pillow and screaming so loud my vocal cords crack.

I hate him so damn much.

With my coffee in hand, I walk to Malik's car. My stomach turning from my meds, but unable to eat even a bite of food after the day—shit, week—I've had. He already sits inside, the engine running as he waits for me. I avoided him while I got ready, and I'm not afraid to admit I stretched out my time getting ready just to piss him off.

He says fifteen minutes?

He can wait twenty.

Son of a bitch almost killed me this morning.

I open the door, avoiding eye contact as I slip my backpack between my feet. Closing the door, I stare out the window as he starts driving down the driveway.

That's fine. We don't have to talk. Perfect.

The drive is silent, and I watch the morning fog rise from the trees, the darkness in the forest clearing. I crack my window, pulling out a cigarette and lighting it. The smoke trails through the crack, disappearing as it escapes the car.

His hand snaps out, and he lowers his window, tossing the cigarette from the car. "You aren't supposed to smoke after a heart transplant. Are you a fucking idiot?" His words lash out at me, but he refuses to look at me.

My mouth pops open in outrage, and I go to pull another cigarette from the pack when he rips the entire package from my fingers, throwing them from the car as well. He slides the window up like it's just another morning. "You aren't smoking anymore."

My nostrils flare. "The gall. Are you fucking serious? You have no say."

He laughs, saying nothing else.

"I hate you. You know that? Like, honest to God despise you."

Malik doesn't say a word, but I can feel the thick tension in the car. We both have so many things to say. Our laundry is dirty, and it desperately needs to be aired. But both of us are stubborn, and I don't think either one of us wants to be the first one to crack and talk about what the real problem is.

We are.

The tension is thick enough to slice with a blade. Even with my hate toward him, the chemistry I feel pumps like a perfect heart, steady and fucking heavy. I deny it in my brain, but it doesn't stop the fact that I'm attracted to him. It doesn't matter how my body heats when he's around, it doesn't matter how deep my hate runs for him, my body aches. It aches heavily for him, and I don't think I can stop it, no matter how badly I want it to.

I would never confront him about this, because I'm sure he'd just laugh in my face and call me pathetic, but now I certainly can't. Whatever happened to him inside the house… with the white eyes, the voice that wasn't at all his. What was that? Whatever it was, it wasn't Malik.

The thought brings a shiver through my spine.

My eyes shift to Malik's as we pull into the parking lot. His uniform slacks are perfectly tailored to his trim body. His gray shirt molds to his form. He's a fucking enigma. He goes against the grain.

I thought when I came here that I'd be walking into a school with a ton of goody two-shoes. Catholic pupils that care of nothing except doing right by God.

I had it all backward.

This school—this entire town—is so incredibly corrupt. These people do not worship a god. If anything, I would think that this town bows down to the devil.

I look away from Malik as he starts to turn his gaze toward mine.

I think Malik may be the devil.

Pounding on the window startles me from my thoughts. I glance up, seeing Malik's friends at his window, their eyes shifting from Malik and back to me. Malik turns off the car, stepping out and opening the back door to grab his backpack. "Get the fuck out of my car," he utters, slamming the door shut so hard the car rocks.

I flip him off, but his back is already turned as he walks off with his friends. "Fucking dick," I mumble, lifting my backpack and sliding from the car. Shutting the door, I look up at the school. The creepy-ass cross sitting on top of the monstrosity of a castle. It sits on the edge of a cliff, like a lighthouse should be. But instead, it's a Catholic church.

It's just… weird.

"Vera." Hazel's voice makes my eyes snap across the parking lot. Piper and Blaire stand next to her as they all lean up against Hazel's car.

A light drizzle starts, and I hop over a puddle as I walk across the parking lot. "Hey," I say once I reach them.

They stare at me, sympathy and understanding in their faces.

They told me I wouldn't be able to leave. I should have listened to them instead of wasting the entire day walking through the forest.

"Well, I didn't get out." I shrug my shoulders, not sure what else to say.

Hazel winces. "I'm sorry. I know you don't want to be here."

I step toward them. "It's not that I don't like you guys. You guys are awesome. Seriously. You're, like, the only people that've talked to me nicely in this fucking place. It's just... it's not home, you know? It's weird here."

Hazel laughs. "It's funny. Because this place is weird, but I have lived here my entire life. I don't know anything else."

I frown. "I'm sorry. Have you ever been out of here?"

She looks into the distance, over the water of the dark Superior. It's a miniature ocean. Only water as far as the eye can see. "Yeah. We've been to Wisconsin for vacation and stuff. It's... bright. Other places are just so sunny and bright. This is just what I'm used to."

I nod, understanding, even if I don't completely. This might be home for her, just as Fargo is for me. But to only be used to a place as dark and depressing as this place is, it's just odd.

The dong of the bell rings, but it's different than it usually is. My face wrinkles, and I look over at the girls. "What the hell is that?"

"Mass today. Come on," Blaire says. They lift their bags from the hood of the car, and we start walking toward the entrance.

"Mass? Like church?"

They nod.

"What if I don't want to go?" After yesterday, I really just need some normalcy. As un-normal as this place is, I just wanted to sit in the back of a classroom and wait for the day to be over.

Piper looks back at me. "The Room of Atonement."

I blink, my insides jumping at the thought of going back in there. I'll do almost anything to avoid going back in there. I refuse.

The scent of aged pews and old paper is extra strong today as we enter the school. The hallway is mostly empty, the remaining students walking toward the prayer room, or the nave, as I've heard some of the sisters call it.

"I have to put my stuff in my locker. Save me a seat," Hazel says, stopping in front of her locker.

"Yeah. Me too. Sit in the back, though, if you can." I wince, thinking of being front and center during this thing. What a fucking nightmare.

Blaire laughs. "Sure thing."

I speed to my locker, tossing my bag inside and slamming it shut. Turning around, I don't even hear the squeaky shoes of students at this point. It's just… complete silence.

The temperature in the room drops, and the hairs on my arm raise.

"Fuck this," I whisper, rushing off toward Mass. I hear a cackle in my ear, an old, nasty-sounding woman rasping. I jump, looking over my shoulder and seeing nothing.

"Get away from me," I growl.

It feels like someone grabs my ankle, cold, rough fingers wrapping completely around my skin and pulling.

My hands go out in front of me, and I can feel it happening, but nothing can prepare me for falling flat on my face. My eyebrow slams against the ground, and my palms make a loud clap against the tiles.

I groan, rolling over and staring up at the ceiling.

Lying above me, directly horizontal from my own form, is the woman from the mausoleum. Her face stares down at me, one dark eye and one boney eye socket. Her face transforms halfway across from decayed skin to bones, tinged brown from age and dirt. Her dress is white, it looks like it could be a wedding dress. Or maybe a nightgown. It's ripped, torn, dirty, and in shreds.

I press myself into the floor as much as I can, for once wishing a sister would come and find me. A student, anyone. Even Malik would be a blessing as this woman levitates above me. I feel like I can't breathe. I can't blink. I can't do anything besides stare at her and hope this is all just a dream. Just like everything else.

She opens her mouth, a dark pit of absolutely nothing. It opens wider than it should, like there are no jaw bones or hinges as her mouth engulfs her entire face.

And she screams.

I let out a blood-curdling scream and roll over, getting up and running as fast as I can to my friends. I refuse to look over my shoulder as I sprint to the door. I reach out before I'm even close enough to the door, and breathe out a sigh of relief as my fingers touch the handle. Yanking open the double door, I stumble inside.

To complete silence.

I bend over, my hands on my knees as I stare at the ground. My breaths come out in heaving pants. The sound of people shifting hits my ears, and I can suddenly feel the burning of eyes—so many damn eyes—on the back of my head.

I cringe as I go to stand. Everyone, and I mean everyone, is staring at me. Every single student, all the sisters, and the priest, who I've never met, stands at the alter in the front, with a Bible in his hands as he frowns at me.

I glance to my left, seeing Blaire, Hazel, and Piper watching me in shock from the back row.

I shift to the side. "I'm sorry, I-I… I'm sorry," I mumble, ducking my head and sliding onto the bench, sitting down next to Piper.

Everyone continues staring at me for a few moments, though it feels like hours, and then the priest clears his throat at the front of the room and continues on with his prayer.

Piper nudges me. "What happened?" she whispers.

I shake my head, not sure if what I saw was even real. Maybe I'm just losing my mind. That has to be it, right? I couldn't possibly be seeing all this… death around me, all the time. Right?

Fucking right?

Everyone moves to their knees, a small table on the back of the bench in front of them where they rest their elbows as they get into a prayer stance. I swallow down the lump in my throat as I follow suit, watching everyone.

Some hold their Bibles, others clutch their crucifixes around their necks.

All I can do is gawk.

Is this really happening right now?

Suddenly, the priest quiets down again once shuffling starts up, only this time it's in the front of the room. My eyes widen as I see Malik stand in the aisle.

My jaw drops when I see how pale he looks. He looks sick. Like he has the flu or something. His face is damp, his dark shirt splotched with sweat as he stumbles back and forth down the aisle, walking toward the exit.

One of his friends stands up, and I immediately clutch the cushioned seat behind me, so I don't run after him.

His hands slam on the door handle, and the double doors fly open.

And then he's gone.

It's silent for a moment before the priest begins for a second time with his Mass. I shift back and forth, feeling out of sorts. Feeling wrong for sitting here like this.

It feels like there are spiders crawling all across my skin.

Fuck. *Fine.*

I stand up, not even glancing at my friends as I walk out. I hear movement up front, but I don't look. "Vera, stop right now!"

I can't. Whatever is wrong with Malik, I need to help him. He *needs* my help.

"Vera! You stop this instant!" It sounds like Sister Mary, and a shiver breaks out across my spine. She's the very last sister I want on my bad side.

I shove the door open, ignoring Sister Mary, ignoring everyone as I step back into the hallway.

Once again, by myself.

"Malik?" I ask softly, stupid to think he'd ever answer me anyway, let alone in the condition he's in.

I look left and right, hoping for any kind of clue to which direction he walked in. There's nothing. It's silent. Everywhere.

I hear the doors open, and I glance over my shoulder, expecting Sister Mary to either drag me back in there or into that room.

But it's not.

Piper, Hazel, and Blaire stand there, and a moment later, the door opens again, and Malik's friends step out.

"What the fuck did you do?" growls one of them. He steps toward me, his hand reaching out and grabbing onto my shirt. He yanks me toward him, and another one steps forward, pulling his friend back.

"Cut it out, Levi. Can't you fucking tell she's worried, too? Just look at her." He waves his hand in my direction. My friends step up, walking behind me.

"Put your hands on her again and I'll make you fucking pay for it," Hazel snaps at Levi.

He narrows his eyes at her. "Hazel, is it?" She nods. He nods. "Fuck off."

The only guy who seems to be on my side steps forward, pushing his friend back. He turns his gaze toward me, a seriousness in his face that echoes to my core. "Do you know where he went?" He looks so much like Malik that I blink a few times. Are they brothers? My eyes flit to the other two. They look like him, too. All three of them look just like Malik.

What the hell is wrong with this place?

Fingers snap in my face, and I scowl, glancing up at him. "No. Obviously. If I did, I wouldn't be standing here dealing with your bullshit."

The shortest one laughs behind Levi. "Maybe we should quit fucking bickering and just go find him?"

"Thank you, Atticus!" Hazel sighs, just as the doors to the front of the school clank, echoing down the hall.

All our eyes widen simultaneously, and in one silent decision, we make a run for it. Through the halls and out the door, rain instantly starts pelting against our faces.

"Why the fuck does it always rain here?" I growl, swiping away the wetness from my forehead.

"There!" Atticus shouts. I look over at the cliff, where I ate lunch with the girls my first day. Malik stands there, on the very edge.

"Oh, shit." I start running, sprinting across the lawn. I can hear the pounding footsteps behind me of everyone else following behind. Rain pelts my face, splashing in my eyes and drenching my outfit. My legs freeze in the cool breeze. There's no sun. It's only clouds and rain and darkness.

"Malik!" I scream. His back tenses and I slow to a stop when I'm only feet behind him. "Malik?"

"Dude! What the fuck is going on?" Atticus asks, shoving past me as he walks up to Malik. "Mal, you okay?" He presses his hand on Malik's arm, spinning him around.

White eyes.

"Holy shit! What's wrong with him?" Blaire screams.

"Dude!" Atticus releases his arm, stepping back in shock. "What the fuck?"

Malik blinks, and the white fades, his dark eyes clearing as they go back to normal.

"Malik?" The one who hasn't spoken to me at all steps up to him. "Mal, it's me, Felix."

Malik stares at him, looking confused. "Felix? What the fuck?" He looks around, his eyes widening when he sees how close he is to the edge. He shuffles away toward us, running his hands through his wet hair. "I don't... I don't know how the hell I got here." He looks around, his eyes growing confused when he sees Blaire, Piper, and Hazel.

Then they land on me. "You," he growls, stepping toward me. "Every time this happens to me, you're here." He stomps toward me, and his wet fingers wrap around my neck, lifting me off the ground like I weigh nothing at all. "What the fuck are you doing to me!" he roars through the rain.

I choke, grappling at his fingers for any kind of relief, but he gives me none.

"Malik!" Blaire screams, running up to me. She pulls at his arm, and Piper and Hazel rush to his other side, yanking on his clothes and any inch of body they can grab onto.

"Bro, calm down." Felix grabs the back of Malik's neck and gives it a squeeze, just as my sight starts to grow hazy.

He drops me.

I fall to the wet grass, gasping for breath. My hands go to my neck and I rub the ache where I'm sure fingerprints will be bruising soon enough.

Malik steps back, lifting his hands in the air. "I need to get the fuck out of here."

"Let us—" Felix starts.

"No," Malik snaps, interrupting Felix. "I just need to… go."

He walks past me, not even sparing me a glance as he rushes toward the parking lot. "And nobody fucking follow me!" he shouts, fading off into the rain.

Felix walks over to me and extends his hand. I blink up at him, feeling like this is some kind of joke, but the impatient look on his face makes me place my fingers into his palm. He pulls me to a stand. After picking a twig from the back of my shirt, he looks me in the eye. "I think it's time we finally talk."

"What is this place?" Hazel asks, echoing my thoughts.

We're… somewhere. Somewhere, meaning a decrepit old house that's barely standing. The house is slanted on one side, and rain leaks from the roof and broken windows. It looks like people have been staying here, or maybe some homeless people have been squatting at night. Either way, it's a pit. Abandoned, empty liquor bottles, litter strewn across the ground, broken windows, and trash make this place a disaster.

"A hangout," Levi says, plopping down on the couch. The feet are gone on the right side, so he leans to the left, nearly falling on his side.

"Hangout? This is where you hang out, Levi?" Piper laughs.

He lifts an eyebrow. "I can show you where I get my dick sucked if you're interested."

She sneers, "You're fucking vile."

"Enough," Felix barks, walking up to me until the toes of his shoes touch my boots. "Tell me. Tell me everything."

I glance at Hazel, and she winces, suddenly looking uncomfortable.

His fingers go up to my chin, and he turns my face back toward him. "I'm not talking to Hazel, and you don't need to get any information from her. I know what kind of girl she is." He turns toward her, spitting on the ground. "Witch."

"Shut the hell up!" she screams.

"You know I'm not lying. You dabble in the arts; you've got some dark shit swirling around you." He turns back toward me. "What the fuck did you do that made him end up like that? I've never seen him like that, *ever*. Not to mention, since you came around, he's been all fucked up." He taps his head with his pointer and middle fingers. "Something's up, and we're not leaving here until I know how to help my boy."

He releases my chin, and I gasp. "I don't know." Tears flood my eyes, and my usual hard exterior melts as fear consumes me. "I don't know what happened."

"Start from the beginning," Levi barks from the couch. He folds his arms behind his head, spreading his legs as he gets comfortable.

I shiver. There's absolutely no insulation in this house. We're all exposed to the elements in here, and I have nothing on besides my button-up shirt, my skirt, my fishnets, and my boots. I didn't even have time to grab my backpack before we left the school.

"We did a... a spell."

Felix narrows his eyes. "What kind of spell?"

Hazel steps up to me, glaring at Felix. "It was nothing. It was a stupid protection spell on Vera, because Malik was treating her like shit. All we did was banish Malik's evil away from her."

Levi barks out a laugh, staring out the window into the forest. I glance at him and watch as his shoulders shake, but he doesn't turn around to look at us.

"Then what?"

I cast a side-eye at Hazel. "We played the Ouija board."

Felix blinks at us, then tips his head back, closing his eyes. I watch as his neck tenses, anger rolling through his body.

These guys are so damn hot.

But as similar as their appearances are, none of them compare to Malik, at the end of the day. Malik is his own species. He's his own universe. No one has or will ever compare to him.

I hope he's okay, wherever he left to. And I hate that I care. I hate myself for having even an inkling of remorse for him. He doesn't deserve it. He doesn't deserve it after how cruel he's been to me.

I hate saying it. I hate even thinking it. But I know a part of me is starting to grow feelings for him. It doesn't take away my hate for him, because it's still as fierce as ever, but a shard of my emotions is melting, and becoming mixed with another emotion I didn't realize I could ever feel. Especially for Malik.

Then there's the whole thing of him being my stepbrother. No one would ever understand. Most of all, here. My mom would probably beat me to death.

No, I need to keep it to myself. Nothing good would ever come from speaking my feelings. I'll just suffocate them until they can't breathe, and eventually die.

"You what?" Felix snaps me out of my thoughts, his angry eyes glaring down at me. "You played with a fucking Ouija board? Are you guys fucking idiots?"

"Save it. I've already had the speech from Malik."

"Well, he's right!" Levi shoots off the couch, coming to stand next to me. "Playing with a Ouija board is dumb shit here. It's like a death wish. I can believe you doing something so stupid." He glares at Hazel. "But, you?" He points at Piper and Blaire. "You were okay with playing a Ouija board in this town? You know the consequences."

Hazel's eyes water. "We've done it before. Nothing like this ever happened after it."

"Jesus Christ," Atticus mumbles from the door.

I can feel the animosity toward my friends, and I know they aren't the ones to blame. They only tried to help me. Keep me safe. Yeah, maybe the Ouija board was a stupid idea, but it wouldn't be such a big deal if we weren't in Castle Pointe.

"You want to know when shit started going sideways?" I frown at Felix, and his face goes blank. "When you guys threw me in the cemetery, in that fucking mausoleum at night. When I was trapped with no way out, and I saw and heard shit I never want to witness again." My eyes water, and I blink them away before they can notice. "Everything was fine up until that moment, and I blame all you fuckers for putting me in that situation. Is this a game? Look where the fuck it got you. Your friend is fucked up!"

Atticus turns around, a sneer on his face as he stomps up to me. "If you're the one that was locked in the cemetery that night, why isn't it you that's fucked up, instead of him?"

I breathe, feeling it in my gut that what happened last night was supposed to flow into me. Malik… he helped me. He pulled me away at the last minute, and whatever entered him, whatever that black mass was that flew into his chest, was meant to enter me.

"Last night… last night we were in the library in his house, and books started flying from the shelves all by themselves. We tried to get out, but the door was locked. Malik grabbed the Bible and a crucifix and started praying just as this huge, black smoke appeared behind me. Malik, h-he pulled me out of the way. It shot into him. He flew off the ground and was suspended in the air for so long. The black thing went inside him. It's like his body swallowed it…" I swallow through my dry throat, the tears not easily blinked away this time. "Then this morning, his eyes were white. He almost killed me," I whisper the last part, my fingers going to my aching throat, Malik's fingerprints already forming bruises. "Then he comes to, and he doesn't remember a thing."

"Holy shit," Hazel whispers. "He's possessed."

Felix stares at me, shock covering his face. He lifts his hand, digging his fingers into his forehead before dragging his hand down his face. "Yeah. Fucking sounds like it."

The sound of crashing startles us all. I look over at Levi, whose heaving breaths are full of aggression. Splintered wood lays on the ground where he must have chucked what looks to be like a small table. "This is your fucking fault." He points his finger at me and Hazel. "You fucked up." He glares at Felix. "You know what Malik would do if it was one of us, right? You fucking know." He slips a knife from his pocket, opening the blade. "He'd fucking get rid of them right now."

Felix lifts his hand, glaring heavily at him. "We're not going to fucking kill them, Levi. Put that shit away." He swings his gaze back to mine. "You fucked him, didn't you?"

My eyes widen. "Where the hell did that come from?"

He smirks, though I'm not sure if it's really friendly or not. "Because if this shit would've happened a few days ago, you wouldn't be cryin' like you care about him. Now your eyes keep filling, like you're emotional about Malik. You wouldn't be emotional about him if you didn't care about him, and you care about him because you fucked him, right?"

I grapple for any words, any kind of excuse or anything I can say to deny his words.

Hazel touches my arm, her eyes wide. "Is it true? You slept with him?"

My mouth opens, but all that comes out is a squeak.

Felix shakes his head. "Well, maybe I can at least trust that you want to help him now, instead of fucking with him anymore."

Oh, I'll always want to fuck with him. But do any more harm to him than he's already experiencing? Definitely not.

"So, what're we going to do?" Atticus asks.

Felix rubs at his chin. "I mean, I don't know. What do you think, witch? What kind of potion do you have for this shit?" He directs his question at Hazel, and she scowls at him.

"Quit calling me that, and… I don't know. I don't think there's a spell… or a potion that can fix this. I think we have to go to the church." She winces.

Everyone winces.

"Malik even *not* possessed wouldn't like that shit," Levi grumbles, sitting back down onto the couch.

"Honestly, whatever we do, I just want to do it soon." I look out the window, feeling like it's darker outside than it should be. "I want to go home and see if he's there. Can someone drop me off?"

"Do you really want to go alone?" Hazel asks.

"I probably should." I think about him being normal and everyone storming into his house, asking one million questions and demanding answers. If he wasn't already on edge, that'd definitely tip him over.

They all look at me, and Felix nods. "Let me give you my number and let me know how he is. He hasn't been responding to my texts." He slips his phone from his pocket, and the screen lights up.

Blank.

He shakes his head.

"I don't have a phone."

He frowns, and I clarify. "I mean, I have a phone, but it doesn't work here. So, actually, I don't have a phone."

He sighs. "I'll pick you up a burner and drop it at Hazel's house. She can get it to you."

"Don't come over," Hazel growls.

"Why? Because you know I'll end up in your bed again?"

Her eyes widen, and her face pales. She spins around, stomping out the door and into the rain. "Come on, Vera! I'll bring you home."

I stare at Felix, wondering if there's any truth to his words.

Felix and Hazel?

That, I didn't expect.

I feel a hand on my arm and see Piper nodding her head toward the door. With one scowl at Felix, she pulls me from the abandoned house and into the rain.

"Let me know how he is, Vera!" Felix shouts through the sound of the rain slapping against the ground.

I lift my hand in a wave, and then we're off.

30

MALIK

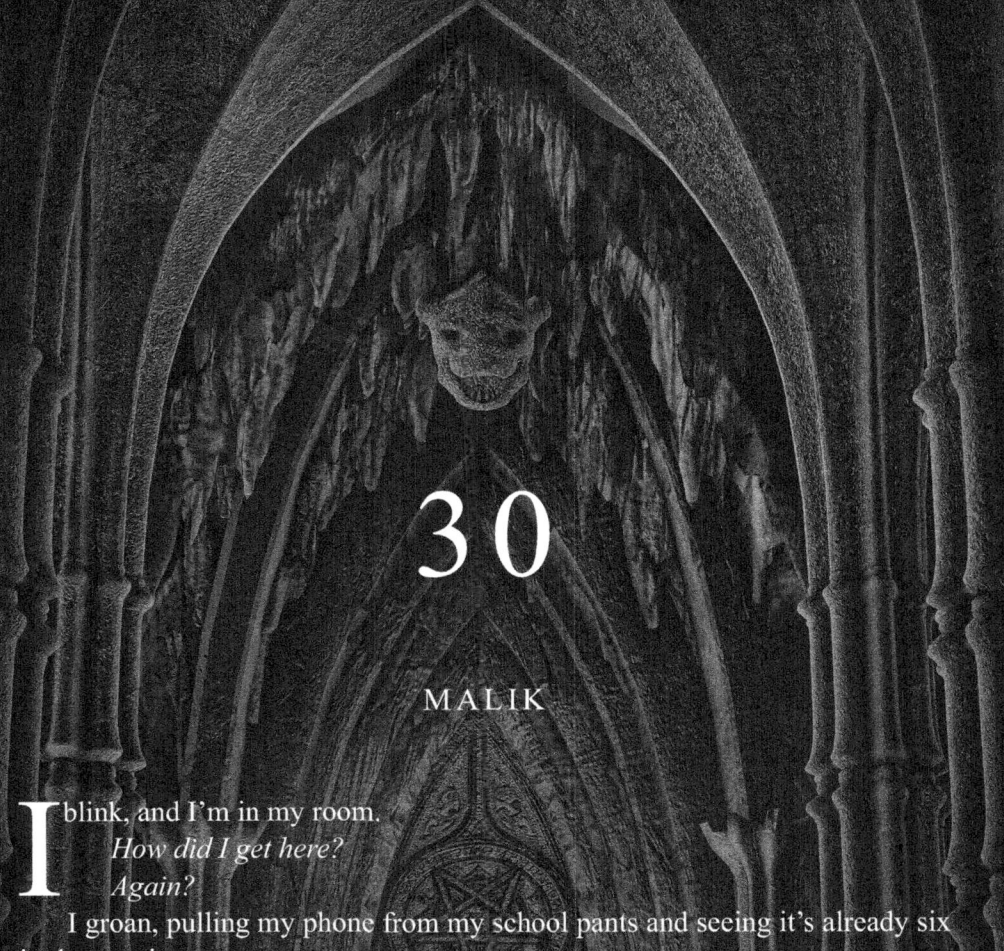

I blink, and I'm in my room.
How did I get here?
Again?

I groan, pulling my phone from my school pants and seeing it's already six in the evening.

Where did the day go? What have I done?

The last thing I remember is getting to school. It was Mass today. And then I was outside, and everyone was staring at me. My friends, Vera, and her friends. Like they were terrified of me.

But... how? Why?

What happened to me?

I feel sick, like I'm depleted of energy. Like my energy has darkened, and I need sleep to feed it. My body feels cold, which is odd, because I'm warm-blooded as fuck and thrive in this cold town. But now, everywhere is freezing, like walking into a fire wouldn't warm me up.

Everything went dark after I left my friends at school, and now I'm here. But how can that be? An entire day has passed. Where have I gone? What have I done?

It's raining out, the heavy drops banging against the gutters. I should be hungry, but I'm not. All I feel is exhausted, like I could lie down and sleep for a fucking year. It doesn't make sense.

What's happening to me?

I unlock my phone, seeing all the texts from the guys.

They're fucking worried.

I scroll through their threats and pleading for me to answer, tossing my phone onto my bed.

Fuck this shit.

I slip into the bathroom and lean over the sink, staring at the dark bags beneath my eyes. My skin is pale, and I look feverish, my skin damp and shining in the bright light.

My fist rocks forward, and my knuckles slam into the glass, splintering the mirror. My fist crunches the glass into tiny pieces, and the rest of the mirror crackles into web-like cracks.

Knock, knock.

I growl as I stare at the shadow beneath the door. I'm not in the mood to talk to anyone. I don't want to answer anyone's questions. Whatever the fuck is happening to me is my problem. No one else's.

"Malik?" Vera's soft voice filters into the room. It turns my freezing skin into fire. The door creaks as it pushes open, and my toe shoves up to the corner, stopping her entrance.

"Go away, Vera."

She sniffles. Is she crying? I scowl, yanking the door open. "Who the fuck hurt you?"

She startles, leaping back. Her clothes are dripping. She looks like a soggy dog, with her wet hair flattened to her face, her runny makeup flowing down her cheeks.

"I'm just... we're worried about you."

I can feel my face twist. *"We?"*

"Me. Felix, Atticus, and Levi. Your friends are worried about you."

A laugh falls from my lips, and I step up to her. Fear fills her eyes. Every step I take forward makes her step back. We continue this dance until she's pressed against a wall, her back flush against the dark paint.

"Stay the fuck away from my friends."

Her face screws up with irritation. "I can do whatever I want."

My hand slams up, my fingers curling around her slender neck. They tighten, her skin flexing between my fingers as I squeeze lightly. "No the fuck you can't.

Not today. Not any day."

Her fingers reach up and she presses them against my cheeks, scraping down the skin. It burns, but it's a delicious burn. One I revel in and enjoy. For some reason, when Vera causes the pain, it's full of sexual tension. It makes me want to tear her to pieces.

I loosen my fingers around her neck, and she gasps in a breath. "Why not?"

"Because you're mine." Her nostrils flare and I smile, my canines shining in full force. "And I don't fucking care if you like it or not." My free hand slides beneath her skirt, cupping my fingers between the crux of her thighs. "I've fucked you. I've claimed you. As long as you're in my town, in my house, sliding on top of my cock, you're mine."

I listen as a growl rolls through her chest and rips from her throat. "And if I leave this house? What about what I want? Maybe I don't want to be with you."

I clench my fingers, and she presses on her toes, simultaneously wanting more and to escape my rough grip. "You want me. Your pupils dilate every time I come into view. A shiver rolls through your spine whenever I step within touching distance. Your lips part every time I speak." My fingers around her neck release and I bring them up, sliding them between her supple lips. She clenches them closed when the pad of my finger glides across her tongue, biting down on my knuckle. I graze it out, my skin scraping against her sharp teeth. "You hate me with everything in you, and that hate is fueled by a desire you can't contain. You don't even want to, if you were honest with yourself. You're mine, whether you want to believe it or not." I release her, removing my hand from beneath her skirt and taking a step back. "And if you fuck with my friends, I'll toss you into Superior and let the water wash you away."

Her eyes, glazing over from my words, sharpen into dark orbs of fury. "You always have to go and say cruel things that make me want to fucking stab you."

I leave her in the darkened hallway, standing between black-and-white photographs and an emptiness that curls around her tiny form. Her face is fierce, strong, angry, aggressive. But her body contradicts that, curling over in defeat, want, hesitation.

I abandon her and allow the darkness to engulf her, just as I know it's beginning to engulf me.

31

VERA

I stretch out on my bed, my textbook abandoned at my feet as I scratch the lead tip of my pencil up and down my leg.

God, this place can be so damn boring sometimes.

The house has been quiet, and these last few days have been utterly dull. My days are filled with nothing but school and this empty castle. Luckily, I've been able to keep myself out of The Room of Atonement. Not that it's been easy. Every time one of the sisters calls upon me, I turn the other way. I avoid them at all costs. It's like they seek me out. Like they want me to fail, to crumble beneath them. They want to watch me falter, but I refuse. I'll do everything in my power to survive this wicked place, no matter the cost.

Felix did get me the cellphone. Hazel handed it to me with a scowl on her face, grumbling about how much of a piece of shit he is. It's something that I'll dig into at some point, but as of right now, keeping my head down is what's most important.

And figuring out what's going on with Malik.

He's been distant since that moment in the hallway last week. He's barely shown his face at school, and according to his friends, he's been MIA around them, too. He rarely goes to school, and when he does, he's never around long enough for any of us to talk to him.

He's never home.

No one is, actually. After coming home from a week away at work, my mom was quickly immersed into her new job. She and Samuel are never home. It's almost like they do it on purpose, though I know they have busy jobs. They're gone more than they're here.

I'm left alone here most of the time, listening to the creaks and groans. Feeling the draft of the night air brush across my skin. Feeling death curl around my limbs like an oil that refuses to be washed away.

I feel lost. I feel alone.

My phone buzzes, and I slide it from beneath my skirt, unlocking the screen and seeing a message from Felix.

Felix: He at home yet?
Me: Nope.

Dropping my phone onto my nightstand and my pencil onto the mattress, I roll onto my side, tucking my hands beneath my cheek and closing my eyes. I'm hungry, not having eaten since lunch, but I refuse to walk around this house by myself. I hate exploring the empty, echoing rooms. Mostly by myself, where every breath bounces off one wall to the next.

Not even the library, where the books entice me, and the smell of old paper flutters against my heart. So many demons, so much bad energy filled that room, and I can't even bear to look at the beautiful walls.

Every other room in this house is filled with such a hideous beauty, something I hate but am slowly growing familiar with. The black-and-white photos are taken with the oldest camera, the sculptures and figurines that fill the rooms are ancient and expensive, yet abandoned over time. They only serve to fill a space, no sentimental meaning to them in the slightest.

I fade into a dreamless sleep, filled with an endless pit of darkness that I can only imagine is Castle Pointe. It consumes me, chilling me to the bone and prickling my sensitive skin.

Until my eyes pop open at the sound of a train, rolling through the house so loudly it feels like the walls are shaking.

I shoot up in bed, my eyes wide as I take in my bedroom. As I would expect, the walls aren't shaking. There is no train barreling through my room or outside the house. My window stays shut, but the noise is so loud it echoes, almost like the window is shoved all the way open. All I can see is darkness.

Yet, the train still echoes on.

I slide over the edge of my bed, my bare feet pressing onto the cool floor as I make my way to the window. The trees are dark, a heavy fog lingering in the air. I can barely see beyond the tree line, the gray mist so thick it looks like a movie.

Closing my eyes, the train continues to echo into the distance.

There is no train in Castle Pointe. I think back to the story Hazel told me about—the evil woman who cheated on her husband. About the death by train, and how Castle Pointe was built on top of the tracks.

There are no tracks anymore, but I can certainly hear a train.

A chill runs through me, and I shake out my arms as I walk back to my bed, grabbing my boots from the floor and sliding them onto my feet. I'm fucking terrified… but I have to know.

Zipping them to my ankles, I leave my room, heading toward the other end of the second level and to my mom and Samuel's room. I know they won't be here, but it doesn't stop my hope that maybe they slipped into the house without my knowledge.

Knocking on the oversized wooden door, I shout, "Mom?" I pound harder, an urgency filling me, making my legs tremble. I'm scared and tired of dealing with the unease of this town. I wish it would stop, be normal in a sense so I could go back to living an ordinary life. I could maybe even find peace here, if it weren't for all the fucked-up shit that happens on a daily basis.

I grasp the handle, pressing down and opening the door. Only darkness surrounds me, no bodies in the bed, no lights in the room, no noises, no people. Nothing.

I sigh, closing the door and walking back to my side of the house. I pass my room and walk to Malik's. His door is closed, as always. I don't give him the benefit of knocking. I turn the knob, entering his dark room and stopping.

Empty.

"Where the fuck is everyone?" I groan.

His bed is empty, made, unslept in. I am weak enough to admit this isn't the first time I've been in here during the last week. I find myself continuously wandering into his room, hoping to catch a glimpse. Wishing I could find him, just so that I could know he's okay. I need to know he's alright, that his eyes aren't white and his soul isn't destroyed. I need to know.

The sound of the train running through the yard sounds again, this time even louder. I wince, tempted to cover my ears as they start ringing. I rush out of Malik's room, slamming his door shut as I make my way to the stairs. I bounce down them two at a time, my boots echoing against the marbled tile. My hand curls around the banister, my hand sliding around the carved wood at the base of the stairs as I spin around, making my way toward the kitchen.

I race past the dining area and out the back door, into the backyard. The instant chill covers my skin, and I wish I would've brought a sweater, or changed out of my skirt and into a pair of pants. But there's no time.

The sound of the train rumbles through me, and my chest feels tight as my entire rib cage rattles. Wide-eyed, I look around, searching for anything, something that can make this true. I can't be imagining it when I feel it in my bones, right?

How the hell is this happening?

There're no lights, only darkness from here into the distance. Only the smell of damp pine swirls into my nose, and I only feel a hint of mist dotting my skin as it falls from the black sky.

I blink, stepping off the patio and into the grass. It crunches beneath my feet, and the muddy ground wets my boots.

A shaky light bobs in the distance, and I blink, wondering for a moment if I could be imagining it. Who would walk in the night? Not only that, but I believe this is part of our property. Is it Malik? Is someone lost?

"Hello?" I ask, a little too quietly, slightly leery of who may be lingering in the woods at night. But curiosity itches at my skin, and I can't help as my legs pull me into the woods. I keep my feet light, my knee-high socks protecting my legs against the sticks, though my thighs are exposed and damp from the misty rain. My arms prickle with goosebumps, but I don't pay attention to them as I pull branches aside, slipping into the blackness of the night and into the darkness.

The light bobs, further and further away. I pick up my pace, and rush through the trees, following the light at a silent but fast pace. It leads me farther into the forest, and a part of me feels in a trance. I shouldn't be doing this, and my conscience knows this, screaming at me in the back of my mind.

But my mischievous side knows no bounds when it comes to curiosity, and I need to know where the sound of the train and the light are coming from. They have to be connected, and if in any way I can find my way to Malik, I'll suffer those consequences.

Somehow, at some moment in time, the lines blurred between hate and a softer emotion, and what I feel for Malik has become somewhat messy. A child's drawing that isn't quite right, not at all perfect. It's illegible, and that's what my feelings are like when it comes to Malik.

It only becomes messier when the knowledge that we're stepsiblings comes into play. In Fargo, it's unheard of. It's incest, really. We might not be bound by blood, but we are bound by marriage, and that means something.

Even if life turns into some kind of normalcy, what Malik and I have will never be normal. Our relationship is cruel, and we are unconventional. There will never be an us, no matter how bad that sliver of emotion beating in my chest that aches for Malik begs me for that possibility, it just can't happen.

It won't.

The trees begin to thin out, and soon I reach a clearing. I pause at the tree line, glancing around with wide eyes.

How am I here?

The cemetery where Malik trapped me surrounds me. The large, ominous stones lay slanted on the aged ground. The orb bobs in the distance, and it soon sways right, directly into the opened door of the mausoleum.

Opened.

I take a step back, a twig crunching beneath my boot.

Oh, no. Fuck no.

I spin around, ready to forget the entire thing—the train, the light, everything—when my face slams into a cold, wet stone.

No, not a stone. A body.

I shriek, falling back over a tombstone and flat onto my back.

Mist falls atop my face, dripping mascara down my temples. I blink through the drops of water, staring up at the dark figure on top of me.

"Malik?" I whisper. "What're you doing here?"

"I should be asking you the same question," he murmurs, like it's not the middle of the night in the rain and fog, in the middle of a cemetery.

I roll over, my fingers digging into the wet dirt beneath my hands and shoving myself to a stand. I brush my dirty hands on my skirt. "Didn't you hear the train? Or see the light?"

He shrugs. "Yes."

I rub the dirt and water from my bare thighs and step toward him. "Yes? What—" My eyes widen. "What the hell?" His eyes, white as a thick, milky cloud. He is possessed, I realize. Whatever darkness hovered on the edges has swallowed him completely. This is not Malik, it cannot be Malik.

Though, the face is the same, save for the eyes.

His voice is the same.

So much is the same, but I can feel it from here. This man, standing in front of me, is not the same man that I've known over these past few months.

No, he is so, so much different.

"Hello, Vera." His voice changes, his own voice graveling out, but a darker, more sinister voice rolling beneath his, and my jaw drops.

"Malik?" I take a step forward, getting directly in his face. I can feel his hot breath brush across my cheeks, heating the coolness on my skin.

"It's me, little sister. Whether you'd believe it or not, it's me." This time his voice is predominately his own, and I can't help the heat that floods my belly.

"Where have you been?" An intimacy curls in my voice, and I bite my lip to cover my wince. I hate him, and his words are almost always cruel. He doesn't deserve my worry, yet I can't help the concern that fills me.

"Living."

I blink at him, my fingers brushing his drenched shirt. "Outside?"

He shrugs again. Blinks. The whites of his eyes remain, eerie and so damn uncomfortable.

I take a step back, remembering where I am. I shouldn't be here. Malik shouldn't be here. "You should come home. It's cold outside."

"I'm fine."

I take another step back, and he curls his fingers into my skirt, pulling me toward him. I grab his hand, attempting to push him away, but his grip is too firm, and I can't get him to release me. "Let go of me. If you don't want to come home, fine, but I don't want to stay in the cemetery."

"You came all this way just to leave? Don't you want to hang out? Visit?"

"Come home and we can talk. We don't have to talk here."

His free hand comes up to the back of my head, and he curls his fingers into the base of my skull. "Maybe here is the best place to be."

"Please, Malik," I whisper. "Just come back with me. I don't like it here."

"What about me?" He leans in, his lips only a breath away from mine. "Do you like me?"

"I hate you." I frown.

"But you like me, too?"

I lean back, but he doesn't let me, keeping me against him, every inch of my body aligning with his cold, wet one.

"Why are you asking me this?" I whimper, not wanting to be put on the spot, most of all here, in the cemetery. "Why are your eyes like that? If I couldn't see your face, I wouldn't even think you were Malik. Your voice, your eyes, something is fucking wrong, and I'm telling you to let me go," I growl, stuck between falling for his soft words and his hard body and wanting to flee from the unknown, from his toxicity that I know lies buried only beneath the surface of him.

"I know you have a freckle on your cunt, and your juices smell like sweet peaches. I know you moan the moment I touch your clit. I know you have an ugly scar that separates your breasts that should disgust me, but it only turns me on. I know you should be dead, and that somehow turns me on even more. I am your brother, Vera." He pulls me toward him. "And I hate you so fucking much, but a part of me wants to eat you alive, and I always get my way."

"That's a shame." I smile at him, showing off my sharp teeth shining in a vicious smile. "Because I always get my way, too."

He bends me back, and my spine arches along the oversized stone. My body curves easily from his strength. I want to fight against it, but there's this weakness in me that won't allow me to. A slight push of his fingers against my body, and I melt.

He's my weakness. Maybe my only weakness. I hate that about him. I hate that he causes me ruin. I hate that so little effort from him can shatter me into pieces.

"Who do you think would win? Would you fight till the death? Or would I win without even breaking a sweat?" He pulls my skirt to my waist, and my thighs quiver against the cold, wet, gray stone.

I can feel a shake roll through my entire body, desire and hate burning in my eyes. "You might be stronger than I am, but believe me, Malik, I could tear you apart with my eyes closed."

He chuckles, his fingers curling around my inner thighs and as he cranks my legs apart. The scrap of black fabric between my legs is so thin and sheer I'm sure he can see the slit reflecting in the moonlight. I can feel as small drops of rain fall atop my sex, and my legs instinctively rub together, gathering the wetness and spreading it. They feel slippery, and I'm not sure if it's need or rainwater covering my skin.

"You could try, but you'd never win." His fingers curl beneath the sheer fabric, and he pulls, the thin strings snapping like a twig in the forest. It falls from his fingers atop a grave, letting it get lost with the rest of the souls and ghosts of the world.

"Whatever lives inside you, I don't think I stand a chance against him. But you, Malik, you I'm not afraid of."

His hand goes to my throat so quickly I can barely intake a breath, and he presses down, causing my spine to arch further until my head lies upside down, staring up at the starless sky. "You should always be afraid, baby sister."

His free hand goes to my sex, pressing between my folds. He hisses out a breath, like he loves my desire and hates it at the same time. All we know is love and hate with each other. It's a sick game. But this game we play, it turns me on. I'm ashamed to say it, but I'm also not. Malik is a wet dream. He's a fucking glorious, terrifying monster that I get lost in.

He's my nightmare, and at the moment, I don't want to wake up.

I thrive off his vicious hate just as much as he thrives on my terror.

My body strains in the uncomfortable position, and he takes his time, spreading the lips of my pussy and sliding the wetness across my thighs. My clit hums, aching. It's torturous. Malik brushes his thumb against it, once, twice, three times, my body twitching each and every time his thumb passes the swollen bud.

"Please, Malik."

"What do you need?" he grumbles.

I snap my head up, staring at him with malice in my eyes and heat burning between my legs. "I need you to fuck me, or I need you to get the hell away from me," I snarl. I shouldn't poke the demon. Mostly the demon with white eyes. I don't know what he's capable of. I don't know what Malik is capable of, really. But this demon? Whatever lies beneath his surface? I fear it may break me, completely beyond repair.

He laughs without humor, snapping his fingers into my messy hair. He pulls me off the tombstone, tossing me onto the ground. It's wet, sticks and pebbles painfully digging into my palms. I glare at him over my shoulder. "Dick. Fucking forget it."

He pounces on me, his freezing body covering mine, yet somehow, I turn into fire beneath him, melting into the ground. He knows what he does to me, and he enjoys it. His hand goes to my jaw, turning my face toward his. His sharp teeth sink into my cheek, the skin screaming in agony at his pursuit. "How easy it would be to snap this pretty little neck. Listening to your bones break might make me harder than your wet cunt."

I swing my head back, trying to knock him in his face. He grabs the back of my head, pushing my face into the dirt. "You can't hurt me. Nothing can hurt me, little sister. Least of all you."

Rage burns in the pit of my stomach, mixing with lust over his growly voice rasping in my ear. I should hate him with every beat of my pretend heart, yet I can't stop the hurt over his absence, the lust over his possessive hands, the need to have his eyes on mine.

What is happening to me?

He pushes my skirt back up, his hands palming the meat of my ass. He squeezes hard, and I yelp, squirming out of his hold, but he pins me against the ground, making me completely immovable.

"Hate me more, baby. Give me that rage. I promise you, I'll swallow it whole."

I press my thighs together, so close to already orgasming, and he's barely even touched me.

In this dark, depressing, haunted cemetery, how can I even think about sex?

Because Malik is here, and anything that has to do with him turns me on. So aggressively.

I press back, my butt rolling against his straining erection in his pants. His hand goes to my shoulder, and he flips me onto my back, his hands going to his pants as he undoes them quickly, hurriedly.

His erection springs free, angry, with a bead of precum glistening on the top. He slaps it against my mound, and I arch my back, needing more, but wanting nothing at all.

Maybe I should stop fighting. Maybe I should just give into him, give into this town, and accept my destiny to be here, with him, in this place, with the horrors and soulless entities filling the air around me.

"Spread your legs," he growls, pressing forward on his knees and lining up between my thighs.

I do as he asks, placing my ankles on his shoulders, giving him a straight view to my drenched folds.

A rumble echoes in the depths of his chest. Rabid. Raw. He is untamed.

His hips piston forward, and he sinks into me, stretching my walls. I wince, adjusting to his length, the thickness of his hardened cock that is so much bigger than anything I've ever had in my life. He is such a man, when all I've been used to are boys, young kids who don't know how to use their cocks or know their way around a woman in any form. They never knew how to pleasure me, and I always ended up in the bathroom afterward, rubbing at my clit as I searched for the orgasm that seemed so unattainable.

Yet, with Malik, one plunge and I'm already cresting the edge of euphoria.

I stare up at Malik, and he blinks, his eyes clearing, the whites fading and his dark eyes coming into view.

"Malik?" I whimper, feeling the pumping of blood flooding between my thighs.

"What's on your mind, Vera?" he spits through clenched teeth.

"You're the best I've ever had," I whisper on a vulnerable breath, feeling the words spill out of me before I can swallow them.

His hand goes to my hair, and he pulls back, my head arched up, my eyes staring directly into his. "I'm the only you've ever had. I'm the only you'll ever have."

I lick my lips, wanting to deny his claims, his possessive snarls. He doesn't like my hesitations, and he squeezes my hair. I can feel the threads popping from my scalp.

"My cock is the only one that's been in this pussy, little sister. Tell me. It's the only one that will ever be in this pussy."

"It's yours," I cry out, my eyes squeezing shut on emotion, on pleasure. "My pussy is yours."

His fingers release my hair, and my eyes pop open, staring into his dark eyes as they spear me like burning flames. "I'm yours," I whisper.

His jaw drops open, and his lips curl back, his teeth gleaming in the night. He picks up his pace, ramming into me, pistoning me into the wet ground.

Rain splashes on us, wetting our skin and making us slip against one another. I can't grasp him. I couldn't even try if I wanted to. Malik rams against me so aggressively, all I can do is bury my fingers in the dirt and grab onto any root I can grasp.

"You are mine, Vera. You've been mine since the moment you stepped into Castle Pointe, and you'll be mine until the moment you take your last breath. So, breathe now, little sister, because I'll consume every inch of air from your lungs before it's over."

My vision fades, and my entire body starts trembling as the most powerful orgasm swallows me. My spine arches above the ground, and I scream into the forest as Malik pummels into me like he's searching for his own air. He grasps it, bruising my thighs and my hips as he grips me so harshly, so violently, I know his fingerprints will be left for many days afterward.

My body melts back down into the dirt, and Malik stays suspended over me, his breath fanning across my face. I glance up at him, watching him stare down at me heatedly, and maybe a little bit of softness inches around the edges.

He sits back on his knees, slipping out of me and tucking himself back into his pants. He buries his face in his hands, digging his knuckles into his eyes like he has a horrible migraine coming on.

"Malik?" I whisper, sitting up and sliding my skirt back down my thighs.

When he looks up at me, his dark eyes slowly turn cloudy, like he's losing himself by the second. He looks pained, tortured, and so full of fury I can barely catch my breath.

"Run," he growls, his tone edging on two voices, one his own and one that I've come to know as his second self.

"Run!" he roars at the top of his lungs, his eyes blinking once more, turning fully white. His lips curl back, a sneer covering his face that looks so lethal, a wicked chill breaks through my entire being.

I don't spend another second in the cemetery. Pushing to my feet, I race through the forest, ignoring the sharp branches that scrape along my bare thighs. I run as fast as I can, ignoring the laughs, the sounds of footsteps, and the sound of the train picking up behind me.

It doesn't make sense. None of it does, but it doesn't stop me this time. I run all the way back to the mansion, barely having enough sense to lock the back door behind me and run up to my room. I shut my door, flying into bed and pulling the sheets over my neck.

Sleep doesn't come easily. It takes long hours of listening to the creaking in the attic, and the feeling of cool air brushing across my skin, almost like a fingertip sliding down my cheek.

In the moments between consciousness and dreams, I realize I'm starting to fall for my stepbrother. But the biggest question is, am I falling for him, or am I falling for the demon inside him?

32

MALIK

I blink, my eyes coming into focus as I stare down at the desk in front of me, my papers a mess and sprawled out across the dark wood. I glance up, looking around at the class. Sister Mora stands in front of the classroom, lecturing on about who the hell knows what. No one looks at me, but it doesn't stop the feeling of being watched in just about every direction.

I curl lower into the desk, feeling a sickness fill me from head to toe.

How did I get here?

I'm losing track of time.

I'm losing track of myself.

I know whatever is inside of me, it's consuming me. I figure I don't have much longer until I lose myself completely.

I spent days trying to figure out a solution. Trying to fix the mess Vera made.

But was it even her?

Or was it me, trapping her in the mausoleum with so much death it probably clung to every inch of clothing and slithered its way into my house.

I don't know what happened, and I don't know how it happened, but I need to figure out how to stop it. And fast.

My research got me nowhere. I even went down to Duluth, searching historic libraries in hopes of finding a method to rid the disease inside of me. There is nothing, only myths and fabrications of demonism and exorcisms.

Every time I feel like I'm about to get somewhere, I blink, and when I open my eyes, I'm somewhere else, and every inch of research I feel like I learned is wiped from my memory.

I know I only have one option at this point. I need to go to the church. I need to ask the priest, or one of the sisters if they can help me. But I can't do it. I tried, and then I lose track of time. What I should do is stand up now, demand Sister Mora listen to my problems and fix every single one of them.

But the thought puts a disturbing nausea in my gut, like the thought of speaking to anyone holy or godly will only send me into illness.

I squeeze the pen in my hand, having no idea how it got there in the first place.

Vera.

Is she here, at school? Is she sitting in class, wondering where I am? How long has passed since I ravaged her in the cemetery, her eyes a mixture of awe and horror?

The feel of her soft body beneath mine is unlike anything I've ever experienced. The hate in her eyes lights a fire in me. I want to wash it away and make it burn brighter.

Being with Thea was never like this. There was never any excitement, or savage need to be with her again. It was more of a chore, some inevitable task that felt good, but left nothing inside afterward.

With Vera, everything is different.

I detest her. I can't stand her naive thoughts and actions. Sometimes she acts so fucking stupid I want to wring her neck. And the way she treats me makes me want tape her mouth closed so I don't have to listen to her whining.

But it's also exciting. A breath of fresh air in the wasteland of Castle Pointe. Something that makes my black heart beat quicker in my chest.

Maybe Vera isn't supposed to be alive, but she is. She's alive, and she's here. She's in my town, she's in my home, and she's wiggling her way into my thoughts.

The problem is, I don't think I even want to be rid of her anymore.

I wanted her pain. I wanted to see her suffer. And maybe, on some level, I still want those things. But I want so much more at this point.

I want so much more from Vera.

I grab a piece of paper from my desk, scribbling down some notes as Sister Mora discusses her lessons for the day. I write as quickly as I can, my small, illegible scrawl scratching across the lined white paper. Hopefully by the time I get through all this, I won't be so far behind in school.

Narrowing my eyes, I watch the pen move, words I can't read being written instead of what's in my thoughts.

Omnes interficere. Et illorum sanguinem super animabus suis effundet festum.

My vision starts to darken, and I drop my pen, gripping the edge of the desk as realization hits me of what's about to happen.

No. I refuse to lose myself for another length of time. I can't keep fading into the darkness and letting this thing take me.

I won't let it.

Shoving up from my desk, I gain the attention of everyone in the room. Most of them look at me with hesitation. I glare at each of them, a sneer covering my face.

"Malik, is something the matter?" Sister Mora asks worriedly from the front of the room.

I don't answer her, whatever sits inside me makes it impossible to form the words on my tongue. I even open my mouth, tasting the bitterness of the words, but nothing comes out.

With a growl, I grab everything from my desk and stomp out of the room, ignoring the pleas and complaints of Sister Mora barking my way.

I drop everything in a waste bin and stomp down the hall, only one destination in mind.

I need to talk to Vera.

I walk to the other end of the hall, seeing her sitting in Sister Marjorie's class through the small window attached to the door. I don't knock, and it's like she can sense me watching her. Her eyes lift from her textbook and lock with mine, widening for a moment before turning leery.

Opening the door, I listen to the aged wood creak. Stomping through the aisle, an entire set of students glance up, laying their eyes on me. I don't pay attention to them, my only focus is Vera, and Vera alone.

"Get up," I growl.

Her eyes widen. "Malik, what're you doing here? Is everything okay?"

No, everything is not okay. I can feel the darkness seeping into me, and I know I have barely any time left before I lose myself again.

"Vera, move," I bark at her.

She looks at Sister Marjorie, who stares at me with trepidation.

Vera doesn't say anything, just stares at me with her wide, glistening eyes.

The darkness settles into my skin, and I can feel myself turn cold. Reaching out, I secure my fingers on the back of Vera's neck and lift her from her desk, sliding her across the aisle and out of the classroom.

"Malik! Mr. Myers!"

I ignore her, kicking the door shut behind me. It slams so hard the glass shakes. I walk across the hall and slam Vera against the lockers. It echoes in the large, empty hallway, and the sound of Vera whimpering slithers into my gut.

"I need you to fix this. Fix whatever the hell you did to me."

"I didn't do anything," she whimpers. My palm presses against her chest, right between her breasts. I can feel her fake heart beating a million miles a minute against my hand.

My palm slaps against the gray locker, the metal ricocheting against the hinges. "Fix this. Fix. Me!" I roar, slapping at the locker again.

"I don't know how!" she cries out, tears springing to her eyes and flooding down her cheeks. "I want to help you so much, but I don't fucking know how!"

A flash of brown slips through my vision, and Vera cries out, bringing her hand to her chest and cupping it with her other hand. "Ow!"

I glance over, seeing Sister Marjorie standing to the side with a wooden ruler in her hand. "Vera! I've had enough of your foul language." Settling her ruler down at her side, she lifts her other hand toward us. "We've all given you too much leniency. Apparently, The Room of Atonement didn't do as we'd hoped the first time around. Maybe a longer stay would do you good."

Vera is ripped from my arms, and Sister Marjorie drags her down the hall. Just before she turns the corner, she opens the black door and shoves Vera inside. "If you make it out of this, well, I hope you've learned a valuable lesson." Her words echo as she slams the door closed, leaving Vera in the unknown. In The Room of Atonement.

Clutching her ruler in hand, she walks back toward me, the whites of her knuckles wrinkled and weathered. She looks to be about three hundred years old just now, and I wonder how easy it would be to shatter her bones.

She glares at me. "Mr. Myers, your behavior is quite uncalled for. I have every right to call your father and speak with him about this. I don't believe he would be quite happy."

The hair on the back of my neck stands on end, and the whooshing in my ears tells me I only have moments before I lose myself.

A growl starts deep in my chest, rolling its way through my rib cage and growling out of me. "Et conteram in vobis pulvis et ossa tua defecto corpore dissipate peribunt, tu vestus nitida femina."

Her eyes go wide, taking a step back. She stands in black, cloaked from head to toe in the color of death, yet she pretends to represent life. "What is the matter with your eyes? They are turning white." Her voice shakes with the words, barely held together with her fear.

My hand raises, and she slams against the locker. She lets out a yelp, the ruler falling from her hand and clattering to the ground. "What's happening?"

Raising my hand, Sister Marjorie lifts with me, her back sliding against the lockers until her head nearly hits the ceiling.

"Tibi anima eorum quasi favilla erit in terra hac. Et non invenietis pacem, Sister." The words flow from my lips and the control I have over myself is dwindling by the second. I don't know who I am anymore.

Her face turns a ghostly white, sickly and pale and her skin sits wrinkled and puckered in the most disgusting way. Her hand goes to her neck, and she pulls out a crucifix. Lifting it in the air toward me, she stays suspended as she starts mumbling verses from the Bible.

"Nec deus nisi tu. Haec ecclesia, et non liberabit te. Non stupri crucis manus tuas. Non est salutaris, Sister. Et non morieris." The words slip from me, yet I don't know a word of what I'm saying. I want to break free from the cage I'm locked in. The cage of my own body. But I have no power anymore, and I'm trapped inside myself with no way out.

She speaks louder, tears flooding her eyes as she screams words of prayer at me. She doesn't realize, it's too late. I'm already gone.

My wrist cranks to the side, and her neck bends awkwardly, the part of her spine connecting to her skull snapping in half.

My hand drops, and she falls to the floor in a pile of black.

And my soul? Well, that goes black, too.

33

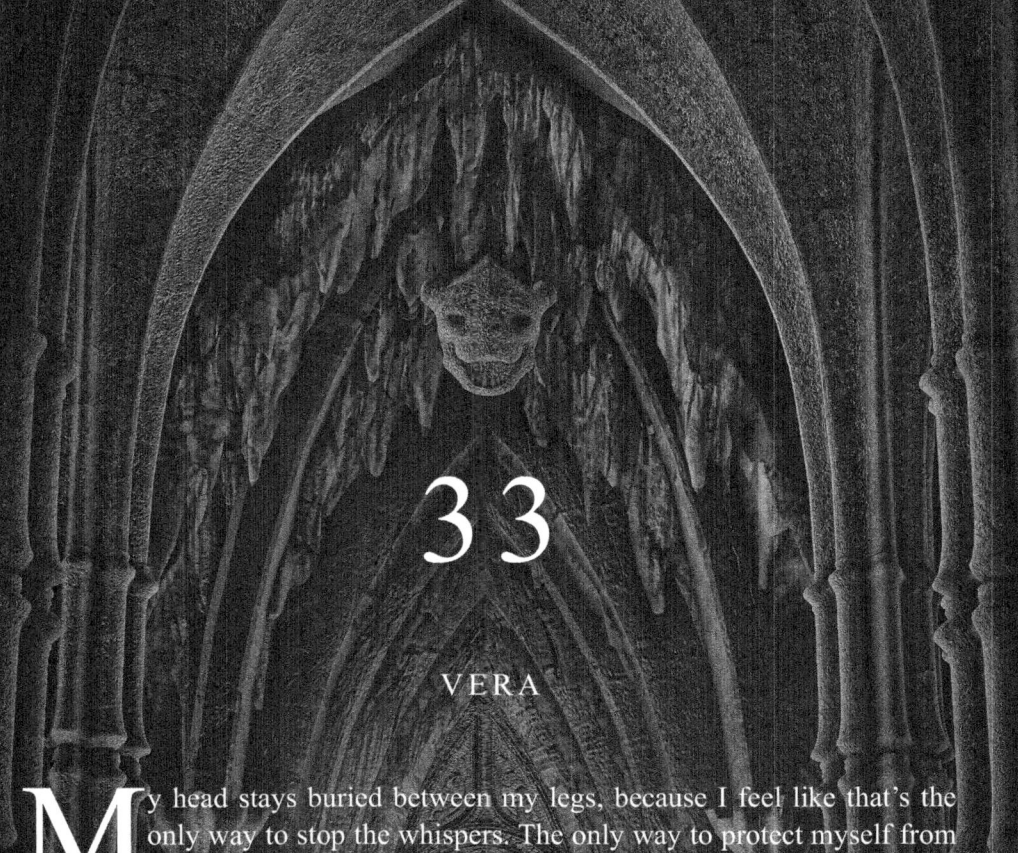

VERA

My head stays buried between my legs, because I feel like that's the only way to stop the whispers. The only way to protect myself from whatever lingers in this place.

"She's dead," whispers a feminine, raspy voice. "Dead." The voice comes straight into my ear, and I wave my hand around, rolling away from the sound.

"Stop!" I scream. "Leave me alone!" It feels like my throat is about to bleed from the force of my voice.

I can't see a thing. But I can feel, and I can hear, and there is so much in this room that I feel like there's no way to escape it.

I am trapped.

I swing my arms into the darkness, connecting with nothing. But the giggles don't stop.

And then I'm shoved. My bare knees scrape against the aged carpet, an instant burn tearing apart my skin.

Something grabs onto my hair and pulls. I'm swung backward until my back lay flush against the floor. My arms are pinned at my sides, and I try to move, but it feels like I'm tied down, even though I'm not.

"Leave me alone," I grit through my teeth. "Leave me the hell alone!"

I can feel breath on my skin, brushing against my cheek and neck. I squeeze my eyes shut, wishing this was all a dream.

This has been going on forever.

I feel like I'm going crazy. I've been here for so much longer than I was last time. Weeks. It feels like I've been here for weeks. I'm so hungry it feels like my stomach is eating away at itself.

I couldn't hold my bladder, and I had to squat in the corner to relieve myself. *Will I ever be released from this hell?*

I can't take it anymore, but my relentless pounding on the door has gotten me nowhere. Maybe it wasn't the door at all. Maybe it was the back wall, where nothing sits on the other side. I can't tell which way is which in here.

"Go to fucking hell!" I scream.

Sharp pain hits me in the side of the neck, like someone put a match against my skin and let it burn until the wick burns out. A shriek falls from my lips.

Whatever pinned me against the ground falls away, and I curl into a ball, my hand going to my neck. I instantly feel blood.

"Ow," I cry. I'm strong. I know I'm strong, but this place, it will make anyone shatter. It'll tear you apart piece by piece until you can barely remember who you are.

"Just kill me," I whine, shuffling to a corner and curling into a ball. Blood wets my hands, and I rub my fingers together, curling them underneath my cheek as I lay against the wall. Maybe death will take me if I sleep.

No one will remember me, anyway.

At the end of the day, all we leave in the world are our bones. No reminders of ourselves, because what are we leaving? Nothing. My mom will forget about me.

Samuel doesn't care.

Malik… Malik will be happy. Whatever is left of him, at least.

I drift in and out of sleep. I'm not sure how much time passes, but the urge to go to the bathroom again stopped long ago. My mouth is parched, my tongue sticking to the roof of my mouth. My eyes have dried up, whatever fluids left in my body must be conserving itself.

The voices are gone. The frosty air has returned to the cool dankness of the school.

My eyes fly open at the sound of pounding. Sitting up, I inch toward the voices.

Familiar voices.

"Vera! Are you in here?" Hazel screams.

"Yes! Yes, I'm in here! Help me! Please, help me!" I cry, feeling like this may not be the end of me, after all.

"Shit! She's in there. Get something! Get something to open the door!" Blaire's voice barks out, and tears flood my eyes. I bat them away, the ache against my neck thumping so heavily a headache is forming between my eyes.

"Vera." My name is whispered from over my shoulder, and my shoulders hitch up to my ears. Closing my eyes, I take a deep breath and turn my head to glance behind me.

A face glares at me, illuminated in a low light, all bones and decayed skin. Burnt and aged with a thick, long worm crawling out of its eye socket. Its jaw sits unhinged, the old teeth rotted away and blackened. There is one eye in the other socket, and it glares at me, black and bloodshot, and so, so fucking evil.

I scream at the top of my lungs, and the bony hands reach out and grab me, pulling me back until I fall to the ground. It reaches for my bare ankles, right above my boots, and starts pulling me toward the back of the room.

My fingers dig into the frayed, rough carpet, but it's so worn I can't get a grip. It doesn't stop me trying, though, and I squeeze so hard as the thing pulls me backward that my nail snaps in half.

"*FUCKING HELP ME!*" I scream at the top of my lungs.

"Someone help her!" Hazel's voice screams from the other side.

I hear thumping as I'm pulled into the pitch darkness, every inch I'm pulled backward, more and more hands grab at my body. I can feel old and new hands, grappling at my skin. Boney fingers, thick fingers, thin fingers. Sharp nails and fingertips that feel like they're wet with blood. They pull me away from the door.

Away from my only salvation.

One more boom sounds, and the door swings open, my three friends standing there with Malik's friends standing behind them. Their eyes are wide and horrified as they stare at me. I glance over my shoulder and see so many bodies, partly transparent and all equally frightening and decrepit, pulling me into the wall.

Their mouths drop open and their teeth chomp at me, like they're hungry for me. Hungry for my soul. They so desperately try to grab for me and pull me into the depths of their hell. Their dirty, browned fingers reaching for my bared skin.

"Get the fuck away from her!" Levi shouts, opening a vial and splashing water across my body. The fingers drop, and my limbs fall to the floor in exhaustion.

"Dude. Look at this." I can hear Atticus's voice and can barely lift my head to look at what he sees.

My eyes widen.

The cross on the wall sits upside down, cemented in place. I knew it. From the last time I was in here, I knew there was an upside down cross on the wall. But seeing it in person, in the light of day, makes it entirely more frightening then feeling it in the pitch blackness.

All around the back wall are claw marks. Is that…?

That's a fingernail.

I roll over, my stomach heaving, though nothing comes out.

"Shit. Get her out of here." Felix pulls me by the arms, sliding me across the floor until my back hits the tiled floor of the hallway.

Blaire kicks the door closed; her eyes traumatized by the sight of the room.

I stare up at the ceiling, my heart racing and pounding in my ears.

"You okay?" Hazel kneels down beside me, her hand going to my shoulder, then flinching away as she gasps. "What the hell is that on your neck?"

I bring my hand up, wincing when my fingers touch the skin. "I don't know. It felt like I was burned."

Levi snatches my hand away, crouching down beside Hazel. "You weren't burned. You were bitten. Who the hell did this to you? Was it Malik?"

I shake my head, the headache growing fiercer by the second.

Wait, Malik.

"Where's Malik?" I sit up, my eyesight growing hazy for a moment. "Is he okay?"

"Did he do that to you, Vera?" Blaire points her finger at my neck, anger screwing up her lips.

"No." I shake my head, rolling over to stand. "He was… scared, I think. Really freaked out."

Levi stares at Felix. "It had to have been him."

The way they look at each other puts me on edge. "What do you mean, it had to have been him? What are you talking about?"

"You don't know? How long have you been in there?" Piper asks.

I shrug. "It feels like I've been in there for weeks."

"Vera, that's impossible. We were with you earlier today." Blaire frowns at me, and I frown back. Confused.

"Wait, what? How is that possible? I literally feel like I've been in there forever. Days have passed. No, weeks."

Piper shakes her head. "No, it wasn't."

I let out a shaky breath. It's impossible, but more important things need to be dealt with. "Where's Malik? He needed my help when I was thrown in The Room of Atonement."

Atticus shakes his head. "You really don't know what happened?"

I shake my head, sensing the seriousness in his tone. Then worry hits me, terror that something happened to Malik. That he's hurt, or worse...

"Where is he? Is he okay?" My voice edges on hysteria. I take off, heading toward the front door when Levi wraps his fingers around my wrist.

"No. I don't know where he is. I haven't seen him since earlier, and I wasn't even able to talk to him."

"Then what?" I lash out, anger and worry hitting me. Severely.

"It's Sister Marjorie."

My eyes widen, and anger hits me. "Sister Marjorie was the one that put me in The Room of Atonement."

Blaire shakes her head. "She's dead, Ver. They found her dead."

I take a step back, and Levi drops his hand. "Wh-what?"

"They found her dead in the hallway. Her neck was snapped in half."

"What? How?" I think back, but the only thing that comes to mind, I don't even want to think about.

Did Malik do something to her?

It's like they can all read my thoughts.

"Was Malik with you earlier? When Sister Marjorie put you in The Room of Atonement?" Levi asks.

I take a shaky breath, not wanting to give him up, but if it'll help me find him, I have to tell them everything.

I nod. "He was. But only before I was put in The Room of Atonement, I don't know what happened after that. But Sister Marjorie was fine, and Malik was freaking out, so I doubt he would've done anything! I don't think it was him!" My heart starts racing, and panic fills my bones. I want to protect the man who hurts me, who verbally lashes out at me at every turn.

But I also want to protect him, because whatever good lingers between us, I don't want to lose that. Not for a second.

"Just admit it, Vera. We all know it had to have been him," Blaire says.

I shake my head. "I won't. I won't admit it, because I don't know a fucking thing. I have to go look for him. Can someone... can someone bring me home?"

They all stare at me, leeriness in their gazes.

Hazel nods. "I'll bring you home."

"Fucking text me if you find him. We need to figure this out. Now." Levi shakes his phone at me, and then the three of them stomp off through the dark hallway, and out into the night.

The four of us follow after them, and I look into the sky as we walk down the steps. "How did you know to find me? How are you even here at night?"

Piper glances at me. "We looked everywhere. We even checked your house. Your mom is freaking out, by the way. She got a call from the school."

I roll my eyes. Now she's worried about me?

"We searched all over town. The only other place to look was at school, and there you were."

I sigh, feeling like so much time has passed. How only a handful of hours have gone by seems impossible, yet I know it's the truth.

It's weird, but it's not something I can think about right now.

Right now, my focus has to be on finding Malik.

He needed my help, and I'll do anything I can to give it to him.

"Text me in a bit," Hazel says from the driver's seat.

I nod, giving the girls a wave and shutting the door.

The mansion sits in front of me, tall walls that expand to the clouds. It looks ominous, the gray brick with dark vines crawling up the sides. The lights are on, which is unusual. Samuel and my mom's car sit outside.

I don't know if they came home because they got a call from school, or what. But something's up.

With a sigh, I step forward, walking up the steps to the front door. Before I can even put my hand on the knob, the door swings open, and my mom's tear-stained face greets me.

"Vera! Oh my God, where have you been?" my mom cries out, grabbing my hand and pulling me into her arms. "I was so worried about you! We called the police, but they wouldn't do anything!"

"I'm fine, Mom."

"You aren't fine. Samuel! Vera's here!" She pulls me inside and shuts the door. "Where were you? We've been out looking for you for hours."

"I was... at school."

She frowns at me. "At school? What were you doing at school this late?"

Do I tell her the truth? Or do I lie to her?

I decide to evade it altogether.

"Have you seen Malik?"

My question comes just as Samuel walks down the hall, his steps hurried in his navy suit. He looks like Malik, and for a moment, I want to fall to my knees. A little older, a little softer around the edges. Where Samuel has a little more weight on him, though he's still muscular, Malik is trim, no ounce of fat to be seen. No bit of rounded face. No gray hairs.

Malik is dark, sharp, and brutal. He's filled with a darkness inside and out, and it makes him seem unattainable, untouchable.

Yet, I've been with him. I think I've reached inside that darkness, and I've found peace mixed with malice. I like it.

I shouldn't, but I do. So fucking much.

"Have you seen my son?" Samuel looks livid, worried, and frazzled all at once. He looks like he's barely hanging on, with the lines on his face deepened, and his phone clutched so tightly in his hand I'm surprised it hasn't shattered in his palm.

I shake my head. "Not for hours."

"Do you know where he could be? I've been looking for him everywhere."

I shake my head.

My mom wraps her arm around my shoulder, ushering me into the kitchen. "Vera, what happened today at school? We received a call from Sister Mary, who said you and Malik were both missing, and one of the sisters was found dead in the school." She settles me onto the stool at the island, leveling me a look. "Did you have anything to do with it?"

I rear back. "Are you asking me if I fucking killed a nun?" I laugh. I can't help it. My head tilts back and a cackle breaks from my throat. "Honestly, I know I'm not the best kid, but killing someone? Killing a nun? Fucking hell."

She frowns, anger and embarrassment tinging her cheeks. "Cut it out. I have a right to ask. I haven't seen much of you lately, and you were the last person to see her. I'm not the only one that's curious. The teachers want to know and the police came by. This is serious, Vera. Someone died."

I look down at my hands wringing together in my lap. "I'm more worried about Malik. He didn't look good earlier."

"What do you mean?" Samuel steps toward me, curiosity in his tone.

My mouth opens, ready to speak, when my mom's hand snaps out, pressing into the bite marks on my neck. "Vera! What the hell happened to you?"

I wince, shoving her hands away. "Ow! Stop!" My neck curls into my shoulder as the pounding starts near the wound. "I was bitten, obviously."

"By who? Malik?"

"Daphne!" Samuel snaps. "Really?"

She looks at him with wide eyes. "I had to ask!"

"No!" I shout. "It wasn't Malik! It was…" I trail off, my teeth gnawing at my lower lip. "You don't understand what goes on in this town!" I shout at my mom. I turn to Samuel, and his eyes are forlorn. He knows where this is going. "This town is filled with so much fucking evil, and most of all, that school. I've been tortured, abused, scared shitless. This town is overflowing with death, and both Malik and I are being fucking haunted at every turn!"

His eyes widen. "Malik's in trouble?"

I give him a dead stare. "Yes! He is!" My palms slap on the table, and they both jump. "Something has happened to us. To Malik, mostly. There's something wrong with him. Like, seriously wrong."

"What is it?" Samuel grinds out between his teeth.

I shrug, not really sure how to put it into words. "He's being… haunted? He's possessed? I don't know the right term for it." I snap my finger. "*The Exorcist*. You know that movie?"

Samuel takes a step back, fear in his eyes. "What about it?"

"Malik is that little girl. His eyes turn white, his voice changes, he grows superhuman strength. There is a demon in him." My eyes water as I think about his face earlier. Hate and fear commingling into one terrifying emotion. "He's scared. Like, really scared. Whatever is taking him over is taking over everything. Malik is losing himself."

I can hear the phone crack in Samuel's hand.

"I need to call the priest." He stomps off, heading down the hall. A moment later, the door to his office slams shut.

I stare at the front door, willing Malik to walk through with his dark eyes. I don't want the white ones. I want the real Malik to walk through the door. Even if for just a moment.

It's almost as if I conjure him home. I can sense him before I hear him or see him. My chest quakes and my body trembles. Need and fear heat between my legs. I swallow down the whimper in my throat as the door swings open, the heavy wood slamming against the wall. I stand off my stool, wanting to run from him and run to him at the same time.

He stands in the doorway, his dark uniform shirt rumpled and wet. His chest heaves beneath his shirt, with his hands clenched into fists at his sides. I can barely see his eyes, with his hair curled in front of his face.

The smell of wet pine slides down the hall and into my senses, along with the strong scent of cigarette smoke, and my fake heart thumps in my chest. *He's home.*

But one step in the door and I immediately know it's not Malik.

I can sense it.

He storms in, leaving the door opened in its wake. His leather boots stomp through the hall, leaving wet marks on the dark floors. His gaze is on me, not that I can see it, but I can feel the combined heat and ice in his gaze spearing me. I'm suctioned in place. I can barely move.

"Malik," I gasp. "What happened? Where have you been?"

He steps into my space, and my back lay flush against the rigid island. "Malik?"

His hair brushes away from his eyes. One eye stays black, and the other is white. Paper white and pitch-black glaring down at me, and I swallow the lump in my throat, so lost and alone, but also found. It doesn't make sense. I'm starting to feel so at home when it comes to him, yet I want to tear him into pieces for how cruel he is.

"You," he growls. "You were locked away."

"I got out." I stare up at him, my neck cranked back in an uncomfortable position. My spine aches, my healing scratches stretched into discomfort, the scabs screaming in pain.

But right now, it doesn't matter. He's here. It's just us, here, together again.

What's happening to me? To us? To him?

He pushes against me, his finger sliding beneath my chin. He tilts my head up until I can't tilt it anymore. His eyes clash into mine, and a chill runs through my body at the two different colors. The two different souls living in one body.

"Vera, what is going on?" My mom's heels clack on the floor as she grows closer, and I know her tone is one of disgust. Of our closeness. Of our intimacy.

I hear a door open, and the heavy footsteps of Samuel walking down the hall echo into my ears.

"Malik? Malik! Where have you been? I've been looking all over town! Why weren't you answering your phone?"

He doesn't flinch, doesn't look away from me. Doesn't remove his hand. He keeps his eyes on me, and I stay pinned in his gaze, in the trance we're lost in.

Our own dark world.

"Malik! Answer me, goddammit! And get your hands off your sister."

He smiles, his sharp teeth glistening at me. "She didn't seem to mind the other night when I was buried between her thighs."

My eyes widen, and I can hear my mom gasp.

Malik is ripped away from me as his dad spins him around by his shoulder. He grips his arms, shaking him a bit with his reddened face and furious expression. "You what? What the fuck did you do?" he roars. His hand goes back, and he backhands Malik across the face.

Malik doesn't move. Isn't fazed in the slightest.

His hand goes up, his palm slamming against his father's chest. It doesn't look powerful, but the move shoots Samuel down the hall. He tumbles to his back, sliding on his suit pants against the tiled floor.

And that's where he stays, dazed and confused as he stares at his son who isn't really his son at all.

"You," he points at him, his fingers shaking. "You aren't Malik. Get out of him, demon! Get out of him!" Samuel roars from the ground.

Malik laughs, and the menacing voice croaks out beneath Malik's.

"Non usquam ego vado, vos maluit frumenta," Malik says, the Latin flowing from his lips fluently.

Samuel stands up, horror and fear in his eyes. "A priest is on his way over. He'll fix this. He'll get you the fuck out of my son!"

A hand brushes on my bicep, and I glance at my mom who stares at me with fear and concern. She starts pulling me away, and even the slightest movement has Malik's gaze whipping toward mine.

"No." He turns around, his hand snapping out, his fingers extended in my direction. "You are mine, Vera."

"She's not yours! Stay away from her!" my mom cries, her fingers clutching my arm. Her fingers shake, and her manicured nails dig into my skin.

I'm caught between what I've always known and what I've grown to know.

The old and the new.

The bad and the worse.

My hand goes up, and I peel my mom's fingers from my skin. Tears spring to her eyes as she stares at me, shocked and hurt. "Vera?" she whispers.

"You've been gone since long before we moved to Castle Pointe. I've been alone, fighting whether I wanted to live or die." I glance up at Malik, and the white eye fades, only slightly, his dark brown iris shining through the cloudiness. His fingers twitch. "But I've found myself, and I've found comfort in Malik. I've found someone to not pull me from the dark, but walk through it with me. Malik sees me for me, and he doesn't want to change me."

"I don't want to change you!" she cries.

I shake my head. "You do, though. You've wanted to change me for a long time. That's why you brought me here, right? It's why you threw me in a Catholic school that is worse than anything you could've ever put me in. This town is so fucking evil, and you dropped me in it like a damn parachute and hoped that I'd find my way." I swallow, emotion building that I didn't know was there. "I found my way, and oddly, I found it with Malik."

"But he's your stepbrother!"

"Step! He's not blood, and even if he was, it's my fucking choice whether I wanted to be with him or not. It's not your choice to make, it's mine. And I. Want. Him."

"Hello?"

We all turn at the sound of a knock at the door. The priest from the school stands there, a briefcase in hand with a dark coat draped to his ankles.

"Thank you for coming on such short notice, Father Moran." Samuel stands and walks to him, grabbing his hand and giving it a heavy shake. "My son, Malik, he's ill, and I have reason to believe he's being possessed. I mean, look at his eyes!" Samuel is growing manic, his face pale and his mouth pulled back in distress.

The temperature in the room chills beyond belief. It feels like we've all stepped into a walk-in freezer. With a shuddering breath, I can see the steam puff from between my lips.

Malik's entire body locks up, still as stone as he stands there, glaring at Father Moran.

"I'd much prefer we do this at the church, but I understand the circumstances we're in." I think that's code for Samuel and his family have a shitload of money and the priest will do anything requested of him. "Is there somewhere we can go that's more appropriate than the kitchen?"

"I'm leaving," Malik utters, his hand snapping around my arm as he pulls me down the hallway.

I dig my heels in, the rubber of my boots squeaking along the marble. "No."

He stops, his lip curling back over his teeth as he sneers at me, "No?"

I shake my head, stepping up to him. I press my hand against his chest, feeling the erratic beat of his heart. "No. Whatever this is between us, it's real. But whatever is inside you, it's not you. It's toxic."

"We're toxic," he growls. "And that's why we belong together."

I narrow my eyes at him. "Love shouldn't be toxic."

He makes me have second thoughts, and that only puts a bitter taste in my mouth.

"Our toxicity is what makes us perfect. You couldn't handle boring. You like my rage, and I like your chaos." The whites from his eyes have faded, and the true Malik stares at me now, though I can feel the true evil lingering just below the surface, ready to break through at any moment.

"I want *you*, Malik. I don't want him," I whisper, my eyes beginning to burn. I just want a normal life, and if that's here, in Castle Pointe, I don't want it to be with whatever it is that lives inside Malik.

"Malik, you aren't going anywhere!" Samuel barks at him. "Everyone, move to the library, we can do it there."

"Vera," Malik barks, pulling on my arm. "Come with me."

I look between everyone, my eyes ending on Malik. I feel pulled in so many directions, but at the end of the day, I know which one is the right one. "No, Malik. You come with me. Let me help you get better." I say the words softly, hopeful he'll break down his walls, if only for a moment.

It does the opposite.

The darkness fades in his eyes, and the whites shine full force.

"Malik—" His dad steps toward him, and Malik raises his hand, his dad once again flying into the air and across the room. This time, my mom screams, and he raises his other hand, my mom flying into the stools next to the island. They knock over, and my mom crashes into the middle of them.

Oh, fuck no.

"Malik!" I bark. "What the fuck!"

He glares at me, his eyes white and somehow more menacing than they've ever been before. Whiter. Deadlier.

My breath becomes stuck in my throat, and I watch as the priest pulls a cross from his pocket, holding it out in front of him.

Malik doesn't even turn to him. His hand raises, and the cross flings straight into the air, and becomes lodged into the ceiling.

Upside down.

"A fucking cross does nothing for me, you fucking shit." He whips his gaze toward the priest. "If I go to hell, I will take you with me. Delectamentum vita tua erunt."

His fingers curl, and the front door swings open. He flicks his wrist, and the priest swings around, flying backward and out the door.

The door slams shut.

"Look at me, Vera," Malik orders. I glance up at him, watching as his teeth bare, his eyes growing venomous, and his body becoming taut with rage. "Come with me, Vera. *Now.*"

I can barely breathe. I want him. I want him so badly I could fall to the ground and weep. I want to be with him every day and every night. I want him to consume me like he always does, and I want to fall deep into the darkness that is Malik.

But I don't want him to be my ruin. And how he is exactly that at the moment; he will completely obliterate me.

"I'm sorry," I gasp. "I can't."

He snarls at me, complete hatred spitting from between his teeth. "I hope you rot in this town with all the spirits in this place. I hope they drag you down and rip your pretend heart from your fucking chest."

A tear leaks from my eyes, and I don't wipe it away.

"I hate you," I whisper. A lie. A terrible lie, but one I feel, if only for the moment.

He doesn't respond. He barely spares me a glance. He pushes by me, the scent of smoke and forest slapping me in the face as he storms through the back door. He leaves it opened, and the cool breeze flows in, washing goosebumps over my skin.

"Vera," my mom whimpers.

I snap out of my trance, glancing over and seeing her still on her back, her limbs tied between the wooden legs of the stools. I rush over to her, helping her off the ground. Her arms shake—no—her entire body trembles like she's having a seizure.

"What happened? What's… what's wrong with him?"

I shake my head. "It's so complicated, Mom."

"I think we need to leave. Get out of town until this can get sorted. You aren't safe here."

The word *yes* plays on the tip of my tongue. I should leave. I should leave now and never come back.

But my mom doesn't know the horror of this place. If we want to leave, we'll never be able to. A part of me wants her to know. Know how terrible this place is. Maybe that'll get her to move us out of here for good, if only she could find a way.

But this soft part of me doesn't want to hurt my mom. Even after everything she's done to me—everything we've been through—she doesn't deserve to be tortured like I am.

I can't do that to her.

I shake my head. "We have to help him, Mom. We have to help Malik."

Her eyes widen. "Did you see the condition he's in? There's *no helping him*."

"We have to try!" I urge.

I glance over, seeing Samuel starting to stir from being knocked out. My mom glances over at him, indecisiveness in her gaze.

"We can't leave them now. Aren't we supposed to be a family?"

She bites at her lip, worry breaking at the skin. "I know… I know. You're right." She shakes her head, rushing past me and kneeling by Samuel.

She checks on him, and I turn my back to them, looking out the back door. The nightly fog has started, and I can barely see beyond the tree line.

I can't see him anywhere, but I can feel him.

I know he's watching me.

I have to save him.

I pull my phone from my pocket, unlocking it and punching a text into our group chat.

Me: SOS. Come over now.

34

MALIK

*E*go dominus occidere eos.

35

VERA

Samuel, my mom, and me sit around the kitchen table when the front door bursts open. The girls rush in first. Blaire, Piper, and Hazel all dressed in black from head to toe. They look like they're about to go on a mission.

And I guess, in a way, they are.

The guys walk in after them. A little more leisurely, but Levi's eyes glance up at the cross plunged into the ceiling. Felix stares at the stools knocked over. Atticus watches me, the bite marks on my neck, and my mom and stepdad with the horrified looks on their faces.

"I'm going to take a guess and say Malik was here," Levi sighs, like he's becoming a nuisance.

I just want to help him.

I nod. "He was. A priest was here too."

Samuel stands up. "I spoke with Father Moran. He said he refuses to do an exorcism in any place besides the church. Whatever hides inside Malik is stronger than anything he's ever seen."

"It's not hiding." I glance over my shoulder and look at him. "He isn't scared of us. Not me, or you, or the fucking priest. He wants people to know he's here. He wants to rove over everyone that stands in his way."

Samuel swallows, apprehension widening his eyes. His suit is now rumpled, not the pressed, perfect suit he usually wears. It looks worn. Actually, Samuel himself looks like he's aged twenty years in the last few hours.

"So, what's the plan?" Atticus asks. "We going to just sit here and shoot the shit or actually go fix this?"

I lift my hands up in a shrug and drop them at my sides. They slap against my thighs. I'm still in my uniform, and a permanent chill has made its way across my body. "He left. I don't even know where he is. He's not going to just come to the church. He knows what we're trying to do. Whatever is in him is smart as hell."

"So, we don't just ask him to come to the church, then. We make a diversion," Levi says. I can see the wheels churning in his head.

He snaps his fingers. "Remember how earlier, when we opened the door, and I threw holy water on those things that were all over you?"

"What?!" my mom shrieks.

I wave my hand at her, ignoring her hysteria. "Yeah? What about it?" I ask Levi.

"So, let's say we get him somewhere. Close to the church, right? We'll sneak up on him and douse him in holy water. That should knock him down for at least a second, right? Maybe for enough time to get him into the church?"

"He should be weaker there." Felix nods, lost in thought.

"How would we get him even close to the church? He'd probably ignore my texts."

Samuel steps toward me. "He wants you to go with him, right? What if you said you wanted to leave with him? Convinced him that you guys can be together?"

"Samuel! I'm not putting my daughter up as bait," my mom snaps.

I shake my head. "I'll do it." I'll do anything for him at this point. "I'll do it."

"Vera, no." My mom's order is certain. She refuses to put me in danger. Too bad the moment we stepped into Castle Pointe, she dropped me into the pit of hell.

I snap my head toward her. "I'm doing it. You aren't going to convince me otherwise."

She opens her mouth to object, but from the look in her eyes, she knows I won't back down. She exhales loudly, closing her mouth and glaring at me. "I don't like this."

I lift my eyebrows. "Me neither, but we don't have another choice." Turning toward the guys, I ask, "So, what do we do?"

I push the hoodie over my head, still not able to stop the chill from taking over my body. Even changing into leggings and one of Malik's sweatshirts, the night is extra crisp. It's brutal, actually, and the fog is extra thick too.

I hope this works.

My fleeting text of, *please come meet me, I changed my mind*, had gone unanswered. I told him to meet me in the woods near the school. That I ran away from my mom after she tried to get me to leave, which to me makes it obvious that I want to meet by the school. The real Malik would know instantly that I'm not stupid. I know we can't leave town, and my mom's threats would be comical. But Levi seemed to think whatever is inside of him would be too manic to know otherwise.

I don't know if I really believe that. This thing inside him seems to be more intelligent than anyone knows, but I had to give it a shot.

Everyone is silent around me, hiding in the woods, save for my mom who both Samuel and I made stay back at the house. She's pretty useless when it comes to anything physical or dangerous. She's a high-heeled, manicured businesswoman who doesn't know how to throw a punch. She said she'd get ahold of us if she saw any sign of Malik.

So far, she hasn't. Which I hope means he's on his way here. But I've been standing out here for fifteen minutes with no sign of him.

Levi stands in the darkness, hidden behind some thick trees with a half-gallon jug of holy water he received from Father Moran. If we want this to go as planned, Levi will have to act fast.

The crack of a branch has my entire body stiffening. I wrap my arms around my midsection and stare into the distance, hoping for any sign of life.

There is none.

"Malik?" I ask, my voice echoing in the trees. The hair on my arms raises, and a feeling of being watched falls over me. Everyone has been staring at me, but this sensation is familiar. Hateful and possessive. Toxic but full of a need that I understand way too deeply.

Malik.

Another crack of a branch, and he appears, leaning up against a thick, aged tree. He looks nonchalant, like he doesn't have a care in the world. Like he didn't just toss a priest out of his house, knock his dad out, and tell me he hopes

I rot in hell.

"What made you change your mind?" he mumbles.

I can't tell from the distance whether his eyes are dark or white. I don't know who speaks to me. The voice is Malik's, but I guess that doesn't mean too much.

"Do you really have to ask?" I take a step forward.

He shakes his head, standing up straight. "I knew you'd come eventually."

My eyebrows lift. "Is that right?"

"Yeah." He moves closer to me, and I can see his eyes.

Dark.

I breathe out a sigh of relief, stepping the rest of the way toward him until we're toe to toe. His dark boots pressed against mine.

"I just want you to be okay," I whisper.

"I'm better than ever." His eyes rove over mine lazily.

I bite at my lip, holding back the tears at his words. He's not better than ever. He's tainted.

He's poisoned by hell.

"Let's go, then. Let's get out of here," I whisper, leaning toward him and pressing my palm against his chest. It's rock-hard, solid as he moves up to me, pressing his firm body against my soft one.

He leans into me, his hand going to my jaw. He combs my hair back, pushing it behind my ear. Bending down, his lips brush the shell of my ear. "I don't believe you." He yanks on my hair, and my head cocks back, spearing my gaze straight up into his burning eyes.

Then, he *demolishes* me.

His mouth comes down on mine, his tongue slipping inside, his teeth scraping against my lips. The rough pads of his fingers squeeze at my jaw until pain ricochets through me. I whimper, and he easily swallows my cries.

The way in which he kisses me makes me weak in the knees. It's like he wants to tear me to shreds and protect me in the same moment. He's fighting with his inner demons, both literally and figuratively.

The sound of a boot crunching into the ground makes Malik freeze. His lips stay frozen against mine. I keep my eyes closed, but I can tell his are opened, glaring at me heavily.

My fingers go up, and I grip his arms.

He whips me around, holding me in front of him as he spins. His arms go above my chest, pinning me against him tightly. My breathing cuts off, and panic seizes me as I feel his body freeze.

He's angry.

Levi stands there, a milk jug in his arm as it hangs at his side, the cap gripped in the other. I watch as the holy water sloshes around inside the plastic.

"Malik, let her go," Levi growls.

Malik's grip tightens until I can barely take a breath. "I told you to stay away from him," he growls in my ear.

"There's nothing going on," I whimper. "He's your friend. He just wants to help you."

He squeezes me even tighter, and my breathing cuts off. Levi can tell, his jaw clenching in the night as he glares at his friend.

"Let her go, Mal. You're hurting her. You don't want to fucking hurt her."

"You know nothing," Malik sneers.

"I know you care for her. I know you started changing since she came around. I know whatever's inside of you is turning you into a fucking beast. Someone you don't want to be. I'm your friend, bro, not your enemy. Let. Her. Go."

I can feel him twitch against me.

Terror seizes me. It doesn't feel like he's understanding Levi's words.

It sounds like they're provoking him.

I stare at Levi, pleading with him for help. My lungs cry in agony, scream for relief.

Malik moves, his hands going to my head and my jaw, and I scream, knowing he's about to snap my neck.

Levi thinks fast, leaping forward and tossing water from the jug all over mine and Malik's face. I choke as I get doused, my sight momentarily washed away. I can't see, and it makes me panic. Completely seize in fear.

The sound of burning sizzles in my ears, and Malik's arms release me as he falls to the ground.

Everything happens so fast.

I run away, slamming into the arms of Hazel as Levi, Atticus, Felix, and Samuel rush to Malik. Levi pours the entire jug on Malik, and he roars, his screams echoing so loud in the night they vibrate in my chest.

He sounds like he's in pain. In absolute agony. I can't bear it, and I press my hands over my ears to drown out the sound.

"It's okay. They're bringing him inside." Hazel rubs her hand down my back.

I shudder, the torment echoing in my chest long after they fade from the trees. After a few moments, my sight comes back, and I peel my hands from my ears. Glancing behind me, I see the guys gone. They must have already made their way inside.

"Are you ready?" Piper asks, walking up to me. She links her arm through mine, and it helps me stand a bit taller.

"I don't know. What if it doesn't work?"

"It'll work," Hazel says. "I don't like the church, but I believe in it." She lets out a sigh, defeat and worry in her eyes. "All I know is that I'm throwing away the Ouija and all the other shit after this. I'm done reaching out to spirits. This town is already fucked up enough as it is. I'll stick to the good shit after this."

I nod my head. That's a really fucking good idea.

In agreement, we all walk toward the front door of our school. Whatever waits on the other side of that door, I'm ready.

I have to be.

The door slams shut behind us, and we're immediately basked in darkness. It feels dreary in here. Dark and depressing. The lights aren't on, and the usual bustle of the students doesn't rush down the halls. I glance at the floor, where Malik left me as I was dragged to The Room of Atonement.

Sister Marjorie died in this hall.

A shiver runs through me, and I squeeze my wet sweatshirt tighter around my chest as our shoes squeak on the tile.

"They'd be in the sanctuary," Blaire says, leading the way.

I can hear the echo of voices as we grow closer, and the obvious voice of Malik roaring in pain.

I stop. "I don't think I can do it. Maybe I should just stay out here until you guys are done. Can someone keep me updated?" I unlink my arm from Piper's, but she grabs hold of my wrist.

"No. You're going in there. He needs you, Vera. Don't back down now."

I gnaw at my lip. I don't want to go in there, even though I know I should. I should be in there with him, but it feels like a knife in the gut to see him like this.

It's brutal.

But I know I have to. If what we have is or could be real, I have to be there for him.

"I'll go," I sigh, the words like acid on my tongue.

They nod, and Piper once again links her arm through mine. Blaire opens the door, and we step through, my eyes widening once I see the events unfolding before me.

"Oh my God," I whisper, then wince. I'm surprised I'm not struck down at this very moment for saying God's name in vain. In his own fucking house.

The priest stands in his robe, a white belt cinched tightly around his waist. He has a Bible in hand, and a cross in the other—he must have replaced his other one. He holds it toward Malik, spitting prayers and the Lord's talk at a rapid pace.

Malik is on a table of sorts. It's gray, stone, and looks heavy and solid as it sits in front of the pews. His wrists and ankles are tied to the legs of the table, stretched so tight it looks painful. His back arches, his neck straining as the holy words penetrate his entire being.

"Et non flectere. Non ego conteram. Tu bitumen, sordes terræ. Vigilate et inebriabo te trahet statim ab inferno ardes impium." Malik mumbles the words quietly, almost to himself.

"Banish, you demon, I banish you to hell!" the priest shouts, his voice booming off the walls.

Malik's body arches unnaturally, his arms twisting in a way that should break them into a million pieces. His elbows bend awkwardly, his wrists contort backward, tendons nearly pop through the skin of every limb.

My hand goes to my mouth as I gasp, horror and disgust at the sight in front of me.

"Leave my son! Leave my son, demon!" Samuel commands.

"What is your name?" the priest asks.

"I have no name." The voice is not Malik's. It's wicked and unearthly. It sounds like a monster who has been through gravel and a grinder. It's terrifying.

"I demand you to tell me your name!" Father Moran booms.

"Leave!" Samuel shouts, stepping closer to Malik. Too close.

Malik's hand twitches, and Samuel shoots into the sky on his back. He shouts, horror and terror making his screams crack in the air.

Malik clenches his fist.

Snap.

We all gasp in horror as Samuel's head connects with his ankles as he bends backward, his entire body snapping at the waist.

"Lord have mercy," Father Moran whispers, his prayers stopping as he falls to his knees.

Samuel collapses, his body broken beyond repair.

"Father, you must not stop now. Malik needs you." Sister Mary lays her hand on the weeping priest.

We all weep.

We're all *broken*.

"Please, Father," Sister Mary cries out. "We need to finish this."

We all watch as Father Moran pushes himself to stand, a newfound determination in his eyes.

Malik laughs, the cackle evil and full of malice. "Spineless scum. He was nothing but a leach to the world. A manipulator." Another round of cackles sound, and it breaks goosebumps across my skin.

"It is only the Lord's will to decide when to give and take a life. Not yours. Now tell me. *What is your name?*" he orders, taking a glass vial from Sister Mary.

Malik's arms twist again, bending behind his back as he writhes in an attempt to get free.

Twisting the cap from the vial, he flicks water across Malik's face. "What is your name, demon?"

Malik screams, his voice and the voice of the demon clashing over one another. I can barely differentiate one from the other. They are both tortured. They are both immensely pained.

"My name... is... *Asmodeus*!" he seethes between clenched teeth.

With a deep breath, the priest hands the vial back to Sister Mary. He grabs his Bible and cross, pointing the crucifix at Malik as he starts praying.

"In the name of Jesus Christ, our Lord and Savior. In the name of Jesus Christ, our God and Lord, strengthened by the intercession of the Virgin Mary of the Immaculate Conception, Mother of God, of Blessed Michael the Archangel, of the Blessed Apostles Peter and Paul and all the Saints. And powerful in the holy authority of our ministry, we confidently undertake to repulse the attacks and deceits of the devil. God arises, His enemies are scattered, and those who hate Him flee before Him."

Malik's spine arches, his body bowing back as he howls. His mouth cocks open, and a black cloud starts shooting from his mouth.

The walls shake.

It feels like the world is about to come down. It feels like the church and entire school are about to crumble around us. We grab onto each other, and the guys in the front pews take a step closer to each other as well.

The podium at the front of the room glows, with a gold cross about eight feet in height, standing tall and ominous, glaring down and creating a brightness around Malik.

The black cloud—the same black cloud that entered Malik that day in the library—pours from his mouth like a flame.

Father Moran continues his prayer, shouting at the top of his lungs so loud that even I can't hear over the roaring in the room. Sister Mary presses her palms together, bowing her head as she begins to pray.

"I command you to hell!" Father shouts at the smoke in the air.

It swoops down, flying toward us so fast that we drop to the ground. Then it shoots to the window, breaking the stained glass into tiny pieces as it disappears into the night.

And then, there's only silence.

We sit there for so long, only our heaving breaths filling the space of the church.

"Is it over?" Atticus asks from the front of the room. His voice shakes, clear terror in his words.

"It is done," Father Moran says. We all get to our feet, and the father walks to Malik, praying over him silently. He presses his hands to his chest, and Sister Mary quietly walks over, handing him the glass vial.

We all watch silently as Father Moran continues to pray upon Malik's unconscious body.

"He'll never be the same after this. Not after what he did to his dad," Levi says.

"It wasn't him," Felix snaps.

"Not like his dad was a good person, anyway. Whether that was Malik or the demon, whatever the fuck his name was, he was right. Samuel was a piece of shit through and through," Atticus grumbles.

I ignore the guys, my gaze focused on Malik. "Is he okay? Why isn't he waking up?"

Father Moran picks up Malik's wrist, feeling for a pulse.

"His heart is strong. After what he's been through, he might be out for a while. We can let him rest here, where he's safe," Father Moran says.

My phone buzzes in my pocket, and I pull it out, seeing my mom's name light up the screen.

I silence it, wincing.

"I don't know what I'm going to tell my mom." My eyes start filling with tears. Samuel wasn't my dad, and he might not have been the best man, but my mom obviously cared for him. I don't want to see her go through another round of heartbreak.

"Do you want me go to your house with you?" Hazel asks, walking up to me with tears in her eyes. She squeezes my shoulder, her voice cracking and shaking with her words.

I glance over at Malik, seeing his pale skin damp with perspiration. I turn to look at Samuel, but Hazel grabs my chin, steering me away from that general direction.

A tear falls from my eye, trailing down my cheek. "I don't know what to do."

She brushes the tear from my face. "You go home. You take care of yourself and your mom. We will take care of everything else."

My chest hiccups. "But what about him? What about Malik?" I cry out.

"We'll take care of it, Vera. Get the hell out of here. Go home," Levi says, his face completely distraught.

I nod, sadness dripping into each bone and limb of my body. It feels like my legs weigh one thousand pounds, or they're filled with sand and water. I can barely move as I trudge from the church, making my way to my mom's car that's hidden in the trees.

How will we ever survive this?

36

MALIK

My eyes crack open, and I'm instantly confused, lying on a cot in the back room of the church. Father Moran sits on a chair on the other side of the room, clutching a cross as his other palm rests against the pages of the Bible.

He startles at my rustling, and his eyes widen, then soften at my opened eyes.

"Malik. How are you feeling, son?"

I stretch out my limbs, confused about how I came to be here.

"What happened?" I ask as I sit up. "Where's Vera?" Thoughts of her skip through my mind, pieces of a puzzle that don't add up. Her face sits at the forefront of my memories, afraid, terrified, alone. "Did I fucking hurt Vera?"

He shakes his head. "Vera is okay."

"Where is she?" I demand.

"She is at home with her mother," he says cautiously.

My friends. Vera's friends.

"Where is Felix? Levi? Atticus? Where is everyone?"

He turns around in his chair, crossing one leg over the other. He settles the crucifix inside the Bible, closing the pages and settling his hand on the black leather. "Tell me what you remember."

I run my fingers through my hair, thinking back. I don't remember much of anything, to be honest. I don't know how long has passed, but I can only remember bits and pieces of the past few weeks. Like I've been here, then I'm gone. When I wake up, I'm somewhere completely different.

I'm so confused.

"I-I don't know."

"You were sick, Malik." My brows furrow at his words, and he reaches out, patting the top of my hand. "But you don't need to worry. You're fine now."

"What do you mean sick?" I stand up, unease gripping at my chest. "Like cancer or something?"

His eyes widen. "Oh, heavens no. The sickness of a spirit lived inside you. A demon, and a nasty one at that."

A demon.

Memories come back like a video reel. Flashes of time where I'm hanging Vera out my bedroom window, where I'm throwing Father Moran from my home.

Sister Marjorie. I wince.

My father.

My jaw goes slack. "Where's my dad?"

He sighs, leaning forward and grabbing onto my fingers. With his free hand, he reaches into the pocket of the robe and pulls out another crucifix. He drops the beads and cross in my hand, closing my fingers over it. "Some of the sisters brought him to the morgue. We'll help you arrange everything and ensure everyone is notified of his passing."

I lean back, squeezing my palm so hard the sharp edges break the skin. Blood runs over the cross, dropping onto the toe of my boot.

"I-I killed him? I killed my dad?"

He tsks. "No, of course you didn't. It wasn't you, Malik. And we will make sure everyone knows the... tragic accident he was involved in."

I narrow my eyes, gritting my teeth together until pain spreads across my jaw.

I killed my dad.

He wasn't a good man. He wasn't even a kind man. But he was my father, and I killed him.

Memories and flits of memories come back to me. Things I've learned over the last few weeks that somehow were planted in my brain. Things I wish I would've never learned, but they're memories that I'll never be able to forget.

What am I supposed to do now?

It's like I spoke my thoughts out loud. "You will finish school and decide whether or not you want to take over his empire. He built it for you, you know."

I shake my head, too many things piling on too quickly. Information overload, and I don't know how to handle it.

"I don't..." I growl, gripping and pulling at my hair, my palm still wet and dripping with blood over the crucifix. "I don't know how this fucking happened. I've been here, then I haven't. I couldn't... how could I kill him? My own father?" My voice cracks on the end, and I feel such a loss and desperation. It's like a part of me has emptied out and now I'm left grasping for the threads. Though, there's nothing to hold on to.

It's gone.

"Malik," Father Moran says, stepping in front of me and halting my steps. He presses a comforting, warm hand on my shoulder. "No one will ever know what happened here tonight. It's just between us, and it will stay that way."

He doesn't get it. I don't care if people know what happened. I've done worse. I am worse.

It's the fact that it's my father, and I didn't... I didn't even get to say anything to him.

Not even *goodbye.*

His hand squeezes. "God works in mysterious ways. When the devil comes into play, only God can be the judge of our path. Don't fret about the little things. If this is our life, then we must live it."

I swallow down the boulder-sized lump in my throat, wanting to believe his words, but not knowing how high I can hold them.

I'm bitter, I've always been. I don't believe in much besides the shadows and being a deceptive character. I'm cruel, and I hate, and I don't do much else.

But if this is supposed to be my life, well, then I must live it.

Unfortunately, I know what that means.

37

VERA

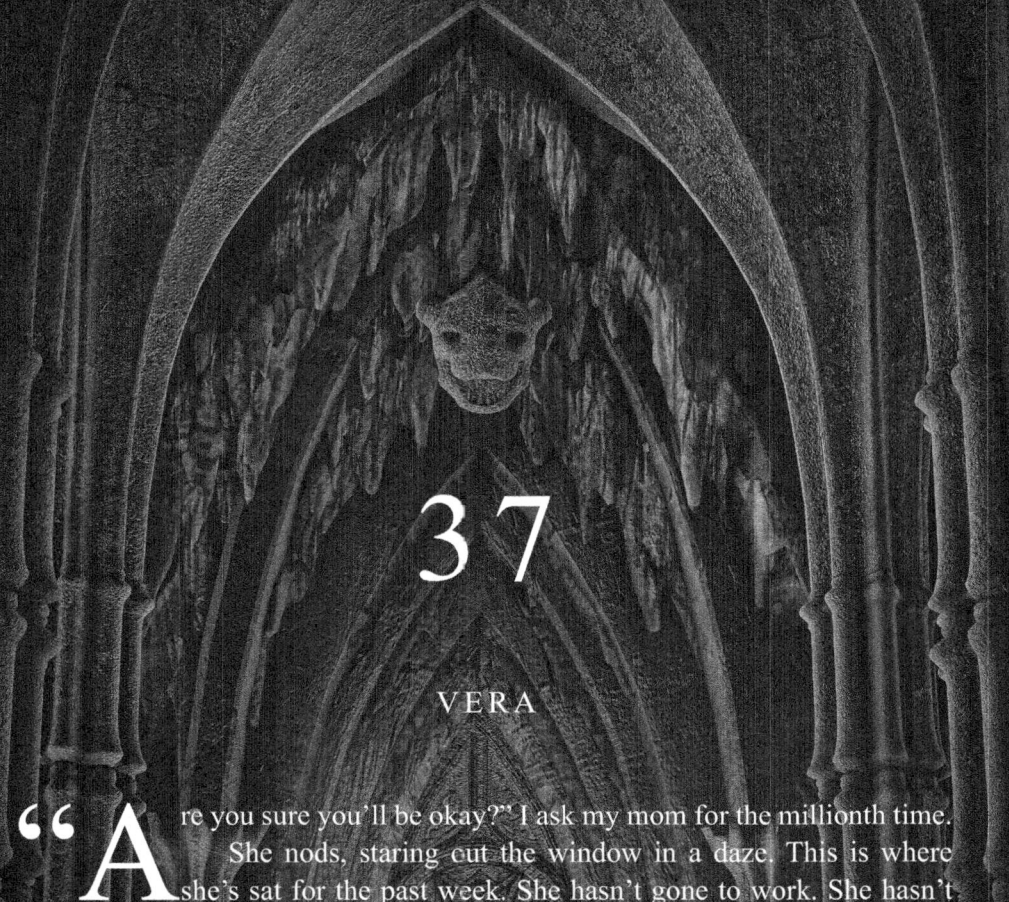

"Are you sure you'll be okay?" I ask my mom for the millionth time. She nods, staring out the window in a daze. This is where she's sat for the past week. She hasn't gone to work. She hasn't even gotten out of bed. The only time she's left is to attend Samuel's funeral yesterday. He was buried in the town's cemetery. Not the creepy one sitting in the backyard. I don't know how many people even know about that one. The one we went to was maintained, beautiful, actually.

So many people went to the funeral. School staff members, some of which I've never met, kids and parents, employees from his company. I even met some of Malik's family members.

Though, there was no Malik.

I haven't seen him since that day.

School called the day after the exorcism and told me I could take this time off and that my schoolwork would be arranged so I could do it from home. I'm not sure what that meant, assuming Sister Mary would drop everything off.

Instead, I found my three friends at the door with sympathetic looks on their faces and a pile of textbooks. They wanted to come inside and visit, but with the state my mom has been in, I didn't think it would be good to have visitors.

I've barely spoken to them since. A few texts here and there, but I'm so worried about my mom and Malik that I barely have an ounce of time to think about anything else.

"Please, just go, Vera," my mom whispers, snapping me from my thoughts.

I lean over, pulling the covers up to her shoulders. "I'm not going anywhere."

She shakes her head, her usual perfectly brushed and pinned hair a tangled mess. Her eyes have been without makeup for days, and the bags have started a permanent pit beneath her eyes. Her nails are chipped, worn, and the paint has faded.

She doesn't look like my mom, and that worries me.

The room has been permanently dim, with only the minimal light from outside shining through the window. It makes the room more Gothic than it should be, with their tall bed and dark floors, everything is so mysterious in here. It still has a hint of Samuel's strong cologne, and I wonder if that makes it worse for my mom, or better.

She turns her head, looking me in the eyes for the first time in days. "I need you to go be a kid, Vera. Quit fussing on me. I'll be fine."

I almost laugh at that. Like, literally cackle. "Mom, I don't mean to be rude, but you aren't fine."

Her eyes shift back to the window. "I just want to be left alone right now. It's hard for me to feel better when I have you leaning over my shoulder all the time asking me how I'm feeling."

I wince. I have been hovering, but she can't blame me. If she was in my shoes, she would do the same.

She has done the same.

"I'll just come check on you later," I say, sliding off the side of the bed. She doesn't say anything, only closes her eyes as the barely-there sun fades behind the trees. I walk out, keeping the door open so I can hear if she needs me or if she starts having a mental breakdown.

She had those the first few nights. Hysteria filling her until she mumbled incoherent words. I admit I gave her enough drinks that she passed out. Those were rough nights.

I leave her bedroom, walking down the hall silently and toward my wing of the house. I hear the click of a door close and stop in my tracks, the lack of light in the house slightly freaking me out.

Who was that?

There hasn't been anyone here. I haven't even noticed any ghosts or spirits. No more creaks above my room. I've listened, I've even snooped the halls at night.

Nothing.

Malik also hasn't stopped home, not that I know of at least. I've checked. Nightly, actually. I've walked through each room to the point of memorizing where every piece of furniture and knickknack sits in this entire castle.

Malik hasn't been here. He hasn't even stepped foot in the house.

I tiptoe down the hall, ending in front of his door.

He's here. I can feel him.

I breathe out a sigh of relief. My messages to his friends have mostly gone unanswered. At first, Levi would message me back and let me know everything is fine and I needed to take care of my mom. But soon enough, those messages went dark.

Pressing my palm against the door, I swear I can feel the heat of him emanating from the other side.

Is he mad at me?

Does he still want me?

I haven't been able to talk to him at all. I've had no way to contact him. I've been so desperate to hear his voice, to see his brown eyes swimming with the darkness only he possesses. I've wanted to touch him, even for the sake of touching him. I just want to make sure he's okay, but I haven't been able to do that.

Can we still be something? What is something?

What do I want? Would my mom even approve of it? Now that Samuel's gone, is it even taboo? Even in just the short amount of time we've known each other, I feel like we've grown so much.

There is *so much* between us.

Does he still feel the way he did before?

Pressing my hand against the knob, I turn it, cracking the door open.

There he is.

The strong scent of marijuana hits my senses as I stare at him. He lies on the bed, his head cast toward the ceiling with a joint sitting between his plump lips.

I know that he notices me because his body stiffens slightly. Yet, he won't look at me. Not even a glance.

"Malik," I breathe.

He pulls the joint from his lips, his eyes shifting to mine, even as his head remains pointed toward the ceiling.

He doesn't respond.

"Where have you been?"

He shrugs.

I inhale, his strong, manly scent giving me butterflies. Like it's my first day meeting him all over again. Although this time, there isn't as much hate burning as there was then.

Stepping toward the bed, I walk until my thighs hit the mattress. "I haven't heard from you all week. Where have you been staying?"

"With friends."

With friends?

"Why haven't you come home?"

No answer.

"Do you... do you remember what happened?"

His lips pinch around the white joint as he takes a hit. Exhaling, his chest hiccups with a cough as the hit burns his lungs. Stubbing the joint into the ashtray on his nightstand, he utters, "You mean, do I remember that I killed my father? Yes, actually, in great detail."

I bite my lip, not sure how to respond.

He glances back up at the ceiling. "I remember everything. Took me a while, but I remember every moment of it."

I want to get on the bed, snuggle up next to him and help him get back whatever piece of himself he's clearly lost. He seems so... disconnected. Like he's lost himself in this battle and hasn't fully recovered.

I don't know how to help him.

"Do you remember... us?"

"Vividly," he tells the ceiling. Completely emotionless.

I blink. What?

"I don't... I don't know what to say." I take a breath, feeling guilty for wishing he could go back to being manic. Possessed. For just a moment, because at least then he showed me he wanted me.

Now he acts like I'm a stranger.

"Then say nothing," he says.

I frown, growing angry. "So, what? Now that you're back to normal, you want to go back to, what... hating each other?"

He swings his legs over the bed, giving me his back. "I want to go back to not knowing you, Vera."

My nose burns, and I can feel the sting of tears starting. "*What?*"

His back stiffens, his entire spine going rigid.

My knee presses against the bed, and I give his back a shove. "Talk to me, Malik! You go from acting like you want me, acting like you care, to not even wanting to know me? What the fuck?"

I expect a reaction. I want one. I crave the fight between us. I'm a fiend for his anger. I thrive on the madness. I want every inch of him.

He gives me nothing.

Standing up, he walks to the window, keeping his back to me. "I think you should leave."

My brows furrow. "Leave?"

"Yeah. Go home."

I crawl across the bed, climbing off the other side. One step closer to him. "I am home."

"No." He whips around, his eyes on mine for the first time. They're back to being brown. He's completely himself again, except he's not. His eyes are empty. Not even hateful. Not vicious. Just empty. Like everything has drained from him. The only thing left is his shell of a body. One that I've never known. "Leave my house. Leave Castle Pointe."

My mouth falls open, my jaw unhinged. Leave?

"I can't leave. You know I can't," I whine. I can't help it. He wants me to leave? After everything? It feels like he reaches into my chest and squeezes my heart with all his strength. It feels like my blood stops pumping through my body, and everything grows cold.

"Yes, you can."

"How?" I shout. "How can I leave? You know I can't! This place is cursed, Malik! I'll be here forever. What kind of sick fucking game are you playing with me?"

He shakes his head, boredom dripping into his eyes. "You can leave."

My breath leaves me. "How?" I whisper. And more than anything, why am I in pain? Why do I suddenly not want to leave? Why does it hurt when he tells me to?

"This... demon that was in me. *Asmodeus*. He was the demon that possessed the witch of Castle Pointe. The woman that you saw in the mausoleum?" My eyes widen. "Yeah, that was her. She was possessed by Asmodeus. The witch was evil, studying black magic and opening a massive portal in Castle Pointe for demons and spirits to come and go as they please. Asmodeus was one of the most sadistic demons to roam Castle Pointe. When Father Moran cast him from my body, the witch was also cast. It's like... they were connected in some way.

I don't completely know how, but it's like they've stayed tethered to each other after all these years. Once Asmodeus was sent back to hell, the witch was cast with him."

My eyes are wide as I take in the immense amount of information.

"How did she come back after all this time?" I ask, my voice barely a whisper.

His eyes shutter, his lips tightening around his teeth. "The mausoleum."

My eyes close in sadness. This could have all been avoided if he never wanted to play his sick pranks. But would it have been, really? Or maybe it was inevitable all along. Maybe this was the path we were meant to take.

Maybe we were always supposed to be standing here right now.

In shambles.

"How do you know all this?" I whisper. I can't imagine he would understand everything that's happened. How could he? It's almost like he took a portal to the past. "Does this mean Castle Pointe is no longer haunted?"

He laughs at this. "Castle Pointe will always be haunted, Vera. The number of spirits roaming around the living is not something that can be stopped. It will never be stopped. But the curse... being stuck in this town, that's done." He takes a deep breath, turning around to give me his stiff back. I can't see his face, but his body screams unease. "And now I think it's time you go home. Go back to where you belong, and don't come back here."

Tears flood my eyes this time, and I can't wipe them away fast enough. My chest fills and my body aches. "Malik... what? I don't... I can't..."

He whips around, his fists clenched at his sides. "Do you know what else I learned, Vera? I learned how fucking sick this place is. Did you ever hear the evil of Castle Pointe? The curse?"

"Yes," I whisper.

"I found out something interesting the last couple weeks. Did you ever hear the part of the curse where the couple not only had the son who was hit by train tracks, but also a baby girl? Only an infant."

My eyes widen, and I let out a gasp. "Oh my God."

He stares at me blankly, not a lick of emotion on his face. No sadness, or shock. No happiness or sadness. It's like he's reading from a transcript. Straight to the point. "That baby was my grandmother. That grandmother gave birth to four sons. Samuel Myers, Oliver Port, Michael Berlin, and Jack Sloan."

I feel like everything I've known has been ripped from beneath me. "How... how is that possible? How did you not know any of this?"

This time he cracks a smile, though it's not at all full of humor. It's full of malice. "Maybe because my grandmother was the daughter of a horrible witch that cast a curse on this entire town. My grandmother ended up being a whore and a witch, too, and I'm glad she fell into an early grave. People always comment on me and the boys' similarities in looks, but I've never even blinked about it. Never even felt like drawing the connection. This town is fucked up, so why even look into it? But come to find out she gave birth to four different sons with four different men, each taking their own last names. Why my father and my uncles never knew or never talked about their relationship is unbeknownst to me. I don't fucking care, really. My dad is dead, and the shit him and his friends did over the years is fucked up."

"What did they do?"

His eyes darken to black pools, and goosebumps break out along my arms. "They preyed on the weak. Weak businesses, weak women, weak men. Anyone who was below them succumbed in one way or another. Corrupt, powerful men who tortured and killed their victims just for fun."

Tears spring to my eyes. "What?"

He glances away, like he can't bear the sight of me. "The blood that runs through my veins is sick. The boys, our fathers, our entire bloodline is tainted with evil. My mother knew this, tried to escape it. What did my dad do? He killed her. He and his best friends tore her body apart piece by piece and buried her in my *fucking backyard*!" he roars, his voice echoing off the walls. I jump back, my heart hammering in my chest as I stare at him.

"How do you know all this?"

He laughs, and it feels sick. Distorted. "I learned everything about this town, my history, my father's history. Whatever lived inside me gave me each page in the history of Castle Pointe. There is nothing I don't know. They preyed on the weak, Vera. Don't you see fucking history repeating itself? My father and his friends, they prey on the weak. Me and my friends—cousins—we fucking prey on the weak."

He shakes his head in disgust. "I'm a carbon copy of my dad's filthy blood. We're all replicas of their toxic genes. Get the fuck out of here, Vera. Get out of here before I fill you with the same toxic air my father filled my mother with."

My heart pounds in my chest. I am speechless. I have no idea what to even say.

Malik is a descendant of the witch who put the curse on this entire town? What the hell?

I can barely breathe, my throat closing up more by the second. My hand lifts, my fingers wrapping around my neck as I gasp for air. I want him. Even now, I want him. But I'm also terrified of him. Of the things he's capable of. "I don't… Malik…"

"Leave, Vera. I don't fucking want you here. This is my house now, and you aren't welcome in it any longer. Get your fucking mother and get out of here." He stomps to his nightstand, swiping his keys from the dark wood. "I'll be back in a few days, and I want you gone. Take your shit and go." He walks out, giving me a large berth.

My entire body screams. Hollers. Begs.

"Malik! Wait!" I step toward him, and he freezes in the doorway. I melt, hopeful that he'll turn around.

But he doesn't.

He grabs the knob, slamming the door shut. With him in the hallway, and me in his bedroom.

His footsteps pound down the hallway, and I faintly hear the front door slam. A moment later, his headlights fly down the driveway and onto the street.

And he's gone.

38

VERA

Malik was right.
We had to leave.
Telling my mom Malik ordered us to leave was downright painful. Helping her pack up her things that she hoped she could share with Samuel broke my already damaged heart. She could barely do it; she could barely function through the motions of taping boxes and shoving her clothes inside. It was horrible, absolute agony.

My mom fought it at first. She called a local lawyer and came to find out that Samuel never had time to change his trust. Everything in his estate was rolled over to Malik.

My mom owns nothing of Samuel's. It was excruciating to watch her heart break all over again. It doesn't matter that they were married for such a short time, what they had was real, I realize. My mom really cared for him. They connected on the loss of their loved ones and found a unique bond. With each other. I didn't spend enough time with them to even notice.

I didn't have it in me to tell her how corrupt and evil Samuel really was. I think it'd shatter her completely.

She did end up taking some things. Small belongings that Malik would never even notice were missing. Things they bought together or items she bought for him, or he bought for her. Those went into the brown boxes and are now stuffed into the back of a truck.

Back to square one.

I've been holding my breath all day, worrying that we'll never make it to the border. That we'll be stuck here forever, and what Malik said was wrong. But as the back door of the truck closes and latches, we hop into my mom's car and make our way out of town.

I haven't seen Malik. Not once. After he walked out of his house, leaving me in his room that smelt so much like him I wanted to cry, he's been absent. Avoiding me. I've tried texting him. I've even gone out, looking for him. I went to the small, run-down shack, walking through a light drizzle and heavy fog. Freezing by the time I got there, I was so hopeful he'd be inside, drunk or high or even passed out on the couch with Thea. I didn't care. I just wanted to see him.

He wasn't there.

All my messages to his friends have been ignored. The little *Seen* message pops up, so I know they're receiving them, but they don't respond. Not once.

I've texted my friends, but they refuse to get into it. They're glad everything that happened is over, and they all just want to forget about it and go back to normal. They want to hang out with me and show me how life should be in Castle Pointe.

They want me to stay.

I just want Malik.

I let out a shuddering sigh as the sign *Leaving Castle Pointe* comes into view. A left would take us to Canada, and a right would take us to Duluth, toward home.

My mom turns on her blinker, pressing on the brakes.

"You ready to go home? I'm sorry we have to rent a place for a little while. I couldn't coordinate a closing in time. But I've already found a few homes I think we'll like. I'll schedule a few showings for us next week."

"Anything is fine, Mom." I can barely get any words out as she starts pulling forward. This is the closest I've been to the border.

"Are you sad to go? Sad to leave your friends?" I nearly choke on air as she pulls forward, and I grip the leather seat beneath me as we cross over.

And we're gone.

Castle Pointe sits behind us, and suddenly, it's bright outside. Sun shines through the window, and I wince, feeling like I haven't seen daylight in ages.

"Vera?"

"What?" I snap, then wince. "Sorry." I feel sick and sad and happy and so fucking angry at the same time. More than anything, I'm mad at myself. Why am I sad to leave Castle Pointe behind? Why does a part of myself beg to go back to the mansion in the woods, return to the place I fought against for so long, but now where I feel the most at home?

Because it honestly feels like I've left my pretend heart behind, and there's nothing but an empty cage sitting beneath my skin.

"I asked you if you're sad to leave your friends behind. Maybe you can come back and visit sometime? Or they can come visit you in Fargo?"

I nearly laugh. Malik will never let me back in Castle Pointe, and I can't see any of my friends coming all the way to Fargo. Maybe they will, but I'm not holding out hope.

"Maybe." I settle into my seat, watching the sky continue to brighten with every mile we go. By the time we get to Duluth, the air is clear and free of fog and the sun shines. Birds and wildlife run about in the woods as we pass, and it's like everything that we came from was actually nothing at all.

Does Castle Pointe even exist? Did I dream it all up? Was it even real?

But even as I say those things, I know none of it is true. Castle Pointe is real. *He* is real. My fingers brush to my neck, skimming the fading bite marks in my skin, and I squeeze my thighs together, feeling the ache that's never fully passed. I know who's been between my legs. I know that everything I've been through has been real.

So damn real.

Leaning back against the headrest, I close my eyes, letting the vibration of the car flying down the road lull me to sleep.

Whatever I've been through in Castle Pointe doesn't matter anymore. Malik doesn't want to be with me. He doesn't care. I'm as good as dead to him.

His feelings were a lie.

Our entire *everything* was only a lie.

39

MALIK

ONE YEAR LATER

"Yes, sounds good." A knock on my door has me looking up, seeing exactly the man I've been waiting for. "I have to go. I'll get back to you later." I hang up the phone, business so fucking busy I can barely see straight.

Inheriting a real estate empire at the age of eighteen was more than I anticipated. I knew how busy I'd be. Shit, I lived with my father my entire life. I barely saw the man, and I knew it wasn't because he was a complete piece of shit.

He had a business to run.

I guess I didn't realize what running a business meant in all aspects, not just selling, investing, and purchasing real estate. There's a lot more to it, and it's taken me months, nearly the entire year, to get my bearings.

And now that I know what the fuck I'm doing, I'm only that much busier.

"Is now a good time?"

I nod, sliding my chair back and standing up. I adjust the coat of my suit and give him a nod. "How was your trip?"

"Good, sir." He steps forward, setting a Manila folder down in front of me.

I lean forward, grabbing onto the corner and sliding it off the desk. "Any updates for me?"

He shakes his head. "Not much to tell. She keeps to herself. Has a few friends she hangs out with, but otherwise, it's mainly just school, work, home. Wash, rinse, repeat."

I open the folder, seeing a summary, pictures, and every other piece of information I'd expect. I slap the folder shut. "Anyone I need to be concerned about?"

He cracks a smile. "There was one, but I did as you asked."

That makes my lip curl back into a smile. "What's his name?"

"Trevor Hamilton."

"Tell me." I set the folder back on my desk and grip the back of my chair.

"He went to her work, asked her out on a date." He rubs a hand down his sharp jaw, caught between angry for me and laughing at the situation. "I roughed him up a bit. He won't be messing with her again."

I grunt, sitting back down in my chair. "I hope that was enough."

He huffs. "Trust me, the kid was barely able to walk back to his car."

I nod, appeased at my PI's report. "Thanks, Jordan. That's all."

He nods, slipping his hands into his jeans. "I'll check in again with her next month and be back with another report."

"Sounds good." I give him another nod, and he's off.

With a sigh, I slide my phone from my pocket, unlocking it and pulling up her Instagram.

Fuck, she's beautiful.

Exactly as she left. But not. She's beautiful with a slight tan, her skin lightly bronzed from the sun. But when the darkness fills her as winter hits, and her skin is a light creamy white, she's fucking stunning. The darkness suits her. It doesn't for everyone, but with Vera, this was her element. It took her a while to realize it. Shit, it took *me* a while to realize it.

I didn't want her. I didn't even like her. But before I could even breathe, she slithered her way beneath my skin and sunk her fucking soul into my chest. The worst time in my life was also the best time. Time that I can't get back. Moments where I lost myself to a fucking manic demon, and it was a time where I became a different person.

And it wasn't because of the demon.

No, it was all *her.*

I scroll through the photos of her and her friends. Her by herself, taking selfies. Her with her friends, Leena and Sacha. I know those friends more than Vera does. I've done the most in-depth searches on everyone who has the slightest contact with Vera. I've done heavy research on the movie theater she works at, getting the pervert, who was a little too fucking friendly around the kids, fired.

Anyone who gave me a bad feeling that was associated with Vera was removed from her life, instantly.

Her life this last year hasn't been easy. She went from Castle Pointe to Fargo. From a small apartment to a house that was much similar to her old one. She went back to her old friends, and to an outsider, it almost looks like she slipped right back into her old life. Like she was never here to begin with.

I swipe down, going through her photos of herself. My thumb hovers over her eyes, that have grown dark as days and months have passed.

She's sad.

She's lost.

She's so fucking empty.

I'd hoped she'd forget about me, and I'd wished that she'd be in pain at the same time. I fought with myself over what I really wanted, but at the end of the day, I realized that I knew the endgame. I've always fucking known.

She'll be back.

I know she will.

I wanted her out of Castle Pointe because I assumed it was best for her. I thought she was only here because she had to be, and that it was the shit going on around her that made her want me. I didn't think she really wanted me.

Who the fuck would? Especially after I killed my father with so much ease all it took was a flick of my wrist.

I'm a damn bastard, and I don't deserve her.

But if she ever comes back to Castle Pointe, it won't be the ghosts that don't let her leave, it'll be me. Because if she walks back into my life, she'll never be walking out of it.

But it's not my decision to make. It's completely hers. She needs to want me so much she'll give up a part of herself. She needs to be desperate for me.

Only time will tell.

I press the home button on my phone, and her face disappears, creating an ache I wish I could rub away, but I know a simple palm against my chest can't cure it.

Only Vera can make the pain disappear.

Until that time comes, I'll be sitting here. I'll work, I'll continue to build the empire my dad set up for me. The place that slowly Felix, Levi, and Atticus have been integrated in. They work alongside me, and the founding fathers have been peeling their feet out one toe at a time. It's now our business.

Women don't matter to me. I keep to myself if I'm not working or with my boys. Even Thea, who so desperately wanted to slither herself into my life, be set for life on the arm of a millionaire. It took one fuck with her after Vera left to realize Thea would never do it for me. No girl ever would.

None besides *her*.

My boys and I, we essentially own Castle Pointe. But we own so much more than that. Most of the northern arrowhead of Minnesota is owned by us. We'll continue to expand, too, and grow our empire until we own everything we want.

I'll build the wealth, but it's not what fuels me.

I'm only biding my time. I'm sitting on my hands and waiting for my girl to come back.

Because whether or not she believes it, I believe it enough for her.

She'll be back.

And I'll be waiting.

40

VERA

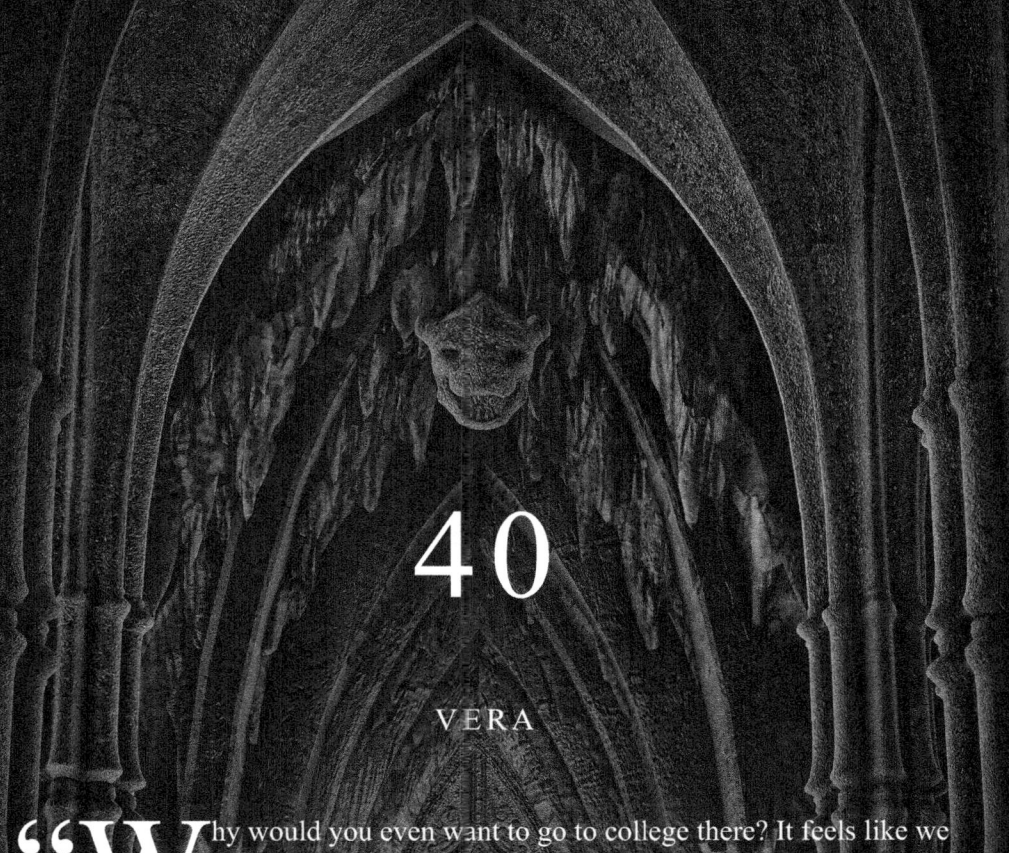

"Why would you even want to go to college there? It feels like we just got you back, and you're already fucking leaving again," Sacha whines through the phone. I roll my eyes, grabbing my suitcase from the conveyor belt and lugging it through the airport. I press my phone against my shoulder, pinning it with my ear as I walk through the heavy throng of people.

"It's actually pretty cool here. You should come and visit. Or better, come to school here with me."

Sacha groans, and I can hear Leena behind her, whining about me leaving them.

"Tell Leena I'll be back by next week. I had to come for college weekend. You know I couldn't get out of it."

"I know that, but it's annoying that you feel like going to school all the way across the state. You knew our plan was to all go to Moorehead. Why change the plan? The plan was fucking good, Vera. *Stick to the plan*," she growls at me.

I laugh, stepping outside and instantly feeling the crisp Superior air hitting my skin.

"Moorehead isn't nearly as good of a school as Duluth. I couldn't pass up the opportunity. You know that. Just because I'm going to Duluth doesn't mean we aren't going to see each other. You can come here any time, and vice versa."

"You're only going to Duluth so you can be closer to *him!*" Leena shouts in the background.

I sigh, rolling my eyes as I walk to the rental car place across the street. "He has nothing to do with it at all. I haven't seen him in over a year. He doesn't even live in Duluth."

Sacha snorts. "Whatever you want to tell yourself, Ver." Sacha's tone is snarky and sarcastic.

It doesn't matter what I say. I can fight and deny it all day, they won't stop thinking that I came here for Malik.

Going home over a year ago was painful. It should've been easy, folding back into my life with my friends, in the only town I've ever known. But it wasn't. It was the hardest thing I've ever done.

I didn't feel like me anymore.

I didn't want to do the same things I used to do. I didn't want to go to parties or hook up with guys. Sacha and Leena thought I was a different person, bitching and fighting against me every step of the way. They thought it was culture shock and that I just needed to go full force back into my old way of living.

It didn't work.

Nothing worked.

It didn't matter how many parties they dragged me to, or whatever they tried to get me to do. I changed.

He changed me.

I knew the moment school started talking about colleges that Moorehead was no longer on my radar.

I no longer loved the brightness of the world. I no longer loved the smell of cornfields. I no longer wanted to experience the life of a college party girl.

I wanted the darkness.

I wanted the tall green trees and the smell of the blue Superior flowing through my senses and every house in Castle Pointe.

In only a short time, Castle Pointe became home.

I knew this, even though I pretended it wasn't true.

Everyone around me knew it. Even my mom.

She struggled, for quite a while. She went through a whirlwind depression that swept through me as well. It was hard for her to get up and work. It was hard for her to provide for us. It ended in me getting a job, so that I could help with adult things that I wasn't even slightly versed on.

Paying bills? Getting groceries?

I didn't know a fucking thing about it.

But I learned, and slowly, I was able to pull my mom out of the pit she was living in. Once she was able to scrape herself off her bed and get herself back to work, she realized how different I was.

How much I have changed after Castle Pointe.

She asked me if I loved him. She asked me if I wanted to go back.

No, I said. *No,* I consistently said.

Every. Single. Day.

It worked, eventually.

Then she just disappeared.

Off to work my mom went, once again. Becoming less and less of a mother as time went on. I barely see her now. She lives to work. She doesn't work to live. I don't know if she even cares about me at this point. She stays in hotels more than she sees her own bed.

She talks to her co-workers significantly more than she talks to me.

Does she even know I'm in Duluth? Probably not.

I didn't even bother to call and let her know. I left a note on the kitchen island. If she sees it, she'll know. She probably won't call. She'll just repack her suitcase and be on her way out the door again.

I don't blame her, not completely. The woman found love twice in her life, and both times they died. I think she's just emotionally disconnected to her heart at this point. I'll let her do what she wants. I've been a shit kid, rude as hell and fighting her at every turn. She doesn't know I'm different. She doesn't know I'm a fucking grown-up now.

She doesn't really care, to be honest.

"Vera, are you even listening to me?" My eyes widen. I look up and see I'm standing on the sidewalk in front of the rental car store. I'd completely forgotten about even being on the phone.

I shake my thoughts free. "Look, I have to go. I'm picking up my car and have to be on campus in less than an hour. I'll call you tonight?"

Sacha whines. "Why does this feel like the end of us? For good this time? Like, last time it didn't feel like you were really leaving, and you actually were. This time you say you aren't leaving, and it feels like you are."

I sigh. "I'm not going anywhere. I'll be home in two days, and you guys can hang out in the movie theater for the next week all you damn want."

"You let us do that anyway!" Leena shouts through the phone.

I laugh. "I have to go. I'll call you later!" I hang up to the both of them shouting over one another.

I pocket my phone, heading inside to pick up my rental.

On my way.

The text makes me smile as I curl my sweatshirt further around my shoulders. The breeze is cool this evening, the brisk air from the water strong as it whips my hair around my shoulders.

The day was long, filled with orientations and getting to know people and walking around the entire campus. My legs ache, my brain is overflowing with information, and I'm literally so exhausted I could fall asleep in this chair outside Caribou Coffee.

But I'm excited, because ever since I planned on coming to Duluth, I knew I had to tell someone. Someone who I knew would be as excited as I was.

My fingers tap along my blue-and-white cup, the coffee not doing enough to warm my body. Even in the spring, the chill in the air still gives way to the lingering winter. Small snow piles remain in the corners of the street, barely dripping away under the dim sunlight.

It feels like I sit here for hours, but soon enough three sets of footsteps pound down the sidewalk, and glancing over my shoulder, a wide smile breaks out across my face.

"I still can't fucking believe you're here!" Hazel shrieks, wrapping her arms around the back of my shoulders. I lean into her, smelling the familiar woodsy scent that's lingered on her from Castle Pointe.

Ugh. It smells like home.

"I missed you guys." My eyes water as I hug Piper and Blaire. They pull out their chairs, the metal feet dragging obnoxiously along the pavement.

"Why aren't you sitting inside? I'm going to freeze my tits off in this weather."

"I like the smell of Superior." I smile, inhaling and watching the water in the distance.

They stop in place, smiling at me in understanding.

"Didn't hear much from you over the past year. How's everything been?" Piper asks.

I shrug. "It is what it is. My mom had a hard time. I got a job. It's been…

different."

"Different good or different bad?" Hazel asks.

I chew on my lower lip, the skin breaking beneath my teeth. "Just different."

"You miss it, don't you? Castle Pointe?" Blaire has a knowing look on her face, and a part of me wants to slap it off. But then I just want to cry.

"Why do I miss it, guys? It's crazy to me, but I just can't stop missing it. I miss the trees and the houses and Superior. I miss you guys so damn much." I shake my head. "I don't miss the school. But everything else, I really fucking miss."

Blaire chuckles. "You miss it because it's home, girl."

I let out a groan. "Why would I miss something that holds so many bad memories for me?"

They stare at me.

"Do I really have to spell it out?" Blaire lifts her brows like I'm being dense.

"What?" My face scrunches, confused.

They say nothing.

"Are you going to ask about him?" Hazel asks. "Like, at all?"

I frown, leaning back in my chair. "No, I'm not. This has nothing to do with him. I don't miss him; I just miss the place."

They blink.

"I'm being fucking serious!" I scream and shrink down in my seat when a couple glare at me from the next table. I bend down, lowering my voice. "I'm serious. I don't care about him. I've barely even thought about him. I just... I didn't realize how much I loved the place I tried so hard to get away from."

Piper winces. "It's Castle Pointe, babe. You don't realize it's a part of you until it's all of you."

I nod.

"Do you want to come back with us? You don't need to stay in a hotel," Blaire asks.

I shake my head before she's even finished her sentence. No, that's the absolute last thing I need. If there's a chance I may see him, I don't want to go anywhere near Castle Pointe. No matter how badly my heart aches to go back there. *I can't.*

I won't survive if I see him.

"No, thanks. I actually have a busy day on campus, and I'll probably crash tomorrow night and then I have an early flight the next morning. Otherwise, I would." The lie flows easily off my tongue.

They see right through it.

"Okay. Well, if you have time tomorrow night, we can come have a party at your hotel," Blaire says.

Piper smiles at this. Her grin is pure evil. "Let's get super drunk."

I laugh. "Okay, that I would be okay with."

I toss and turn all night.

By all night, I literally mean *all* fucking night.

After hanging out with the girls for hours, eventually moving inside the coffee shop to warm up by the fire, we stayed until it closed, talking about life and what we hoped for the future.

Overall, I don't think any of us really know.

We all want to do something, but none of us really know what that is.

I left them with a hug and a promise to see them the next day as I stumbled across the street and into my hotel, my body exhausted and my mind complete mush. But the moment I fell into bed, I couldn't switch off.

I couldn't for the life of me fall asleep.

It got to the point that I turned on YouTube with some mediation music. I even started counting. Nothing worked. I don't know what it was, but my mind was wired.

No, I know exactly what it was.

Him.

At three in the morning, I knew I wouldn't be getting sleep. Not tonight, anyway.

Throwing on a hoodie and my black boots, I swipe my keys off the table and head down to my rental car.

I stayed near campus, and a heavy sigh leaves me as I move away from the crowds. I had the same overwhelming feeling earlier. It felt like I was trapped between waves of people, each one higher than the next. It was hard to breathe or even think with all the people laughing and talking around me.

Don't get me wrong, the school itself seemed great. It was modern yet had a historical touch. The classes looked nice, and I think I'd really enjoy it here.

It's the people. The people with partying and sex in their eyes. The perfume and the clothes that are too small. Everyone was vibrating with energy, and I only wanted to get away from it. I don't care about the parties or hooking up or connecting with other girls my age.

That was high school. I'm past all of that. I no longer have even the slightest bit of interest to do those things.

Now my only desire is to study and keep to myself.

I pull the straps of my bag around my shoulders as I head down the street to where I left my car. The girls walked me to my hotel, and I ended up leaving the rental next to Caribou. It's only a short walk down the block, and we weren't quite ready for our night to end. But now that I'm walking in the middle of the night, unease hits me.

I don't know this place. I'm unfamiliar with these people. I've always been leery of people in general, but this last year has brought out a whole new level of apprehension with the unknown.

I turn down an alley, taking a shortcut. The tall buildings also block the wind, which is extra chilly this evening. But maybe my shiver is more from my anxiety than anything else.

My legs move quickly, the thin leggings barely enough fabric to protect the cool breeze from chilling my skin.

Turning down a second alley, I pause, seeing two men standing at the end, talking to each other in a hushed whisper.

They can't see me, and I back up, turning and walking behind a large dumpster sitting against the wall. The lid is propped open, and it gives me a thin opening to watch them.

"Where are they headed?" the tattooed one asks. He sounds harsh. I can only get a side profile of his face, but it's sharp, angry. He looks fucking dangerous. He listens as someone barks into the phone, his head giving a barely-there nod every few seconds. "We won't make it in time. Fucking stall them."

"What is he saying?" the taller one asks. He looks just as brutal, though maybe a little less pissed. More emotionless. He reminds me of Felix in that regard.

I blink, completely enthralled and terrified at the sight in front of me. It feels like I'm watching something I absolutely shouldn't. Like there's a secret happening in front of me that I shouldn't be privy to.

What—are they the FBI?

"I'll see you in a few hours." He hangs up, pocketing his phone and letting out a string of curses that makes me smirk.

"What did he say?"

He shakes his head. "Z and West are in Winnipeg right now. Z is fucking pissed because West is all sidetracked and shit. They got into it last night."

The tall one grunts. "I don't care about their petty shit. What's going on with the Russians?"

"They were in Winnipeg. They aren't now." His voice is defeated.

"Motherfuckers. I'm going to kill West!"

I jump, his voice startling me. My boot rolls over an empty glass bottle, and I wince as it clinks and rolls against the dumpster, and a loud, echoing bang rattles through the empty alley. I crouch to the ground, shuffling back against the dingy wall of an old building. It smells like old beer and urine, and I hold my breath as the sound of footsteps echo down toward me.

Please don't find me. Please don't find me. Please don't find me.

A shadow falls over my form, and I close my eyes, for the first time in what feels like forever wishing I could be back in Fargo. In my empty house and far, far away from these men.

"Well, well, well. Look what we have here."

I keep my eyes closed. Maybe if they think I'm some passed out junkie, they'll leave me alone.

"Get up, girl. I can see you trembling. Don't piss yourself now."

I crack an eye open, seeing the ripped guy with tattoos look so vicious as he stares down at me. Not a friendly feature on his face.

My shaky hands press against the ground, pebbles and rocks pressing into my palms as I push myself to stand. My spine aligns with the wall, wishing there was space—so much more space—between me and them.

It feels like one wrong move from me, and they'll snap my neck.

"I think she's a junkie," the tall one mumbles.

The mean one lifts his brows. "Why do you think that?"

"Look at how she's trembling like that."

They're talking about me. In front of me. And they don't even know me.

Rage starts in my toes, working its way up my legs and into my belly, burning fiercely as it fills me.

"I'm not a fucking junkie," I snap.

Their faces blank out, and they watch me with a dangerous curiosity.

The tall one grunts but says nothing.

"I'm leaving," I say after a moment of silence. I don't want to be trapped with these guys anymore, and they seem more dangerous than a group of homeless people.

I shuffle around them, ready to sprint out of there and back into the world. Why is it so quiet here? Like no one ever comes back here unless they're looking to get into trouble.

Of fucking course, Vera. It's a damn alleyway. What was I thinking?

They both move toward me, keeping me pinned against the wall.

The angry one reaches behind him, pulling out a shiny black Glock and pointing it right at my face. He looks uninterested, like he's sticking his thumb up for a taxi instead of pointing a deadly weapon in my face.

"What are you doing back here?" he asks calmly, though impatiently. Like he's in a hurry.

"I-I'm just a fucking student. I'm going to Caribou to get my car. Just let me go, and you guys can go to Winnipeg or whatever, and we can forget this ever—"

He cocks the gun, and I swear I can feel the bullet lodged inside preparing to enter my skull.

"You stupid kid." The tall one chuckles emotionlessly.

My eyes widen, and I don't know what to do. I could scream, but they'd probably snap my neck before I opened my mouth. I could run, but their long legs are no doubt faster than mine.

I stare at them. Their fucking breathtaking faces. People shouldn't look like this, though I know one person who surpasses it.

Malik.

He's so fucking stunning. His harsh, unmarred features could cut glass. He's the only beauty in the rough. He belongs in Castle Pointe, because the world wouldn't be able to handle his features, his entire body. He's ripped, hardened, absolute stone from head to toe. The perfect mane, the sharp jaw, the slender yet ripped body, the brown eyes that hold so much depth.

I'm ashamed as I subconsciously press my thighs together, thankful they don't notice. How can I even think about something like that right now? How could I even think about *him* right now? How would he react to seeing a gun pointed at my face? Would he even care? Would he laugh and take the gun, point it at my face himself and get it over with for me? Or would he kill the both of them without a second thought?

I don't know, and that leaves a lonely clink in my soul.

"Please, just let me go," I whisper.

The angry one shakes his head. "Can't. You know too much."

"I know nothing at all." My voice is firm. Because I don't. I know nothing about what they're doing. They could be meeting extended family for all I know.

I mean, I know they aren't, but they don't need to know that.

I watch as his finger curls around the trigger, and without a second thought, the Lord's Prayer starts falling from my lips. The words are bitter on my tongue, but they still flow smoothly, the words clear and meaningful as they spill from me.

It's funny how such a short amount of time at Castle Pointe Academy had such a drastic effect on my life.

"Jesus Christ, dude. She's a fucking religious freak." The angry one drops his gun, groaning as he looks at his friend.

"I can fucking do it if you want. Fucking hell, you're such a pussy since you got married." The tall one wiggles his eyebrows at his friend, ready to end my life without a care in the world.

A whimper works its way through my throat, squeezed between the holy words.

The angry one pulls his gun back, glaring at him with a burning rage. "Fuck off." He tucks his gun back into his pocket, and within an instant, his fingers are around my throat. He slams me against the wall, his grip tight and aggressive. It's not like Malik, where there's a tenderness and sexual heat between us.

This guy doesn't like me. This guy doesn't even want me alive.

"You open your mouth about this little encounter, and you can guarantee I'll skin you, your friends, and your family alive. I'll use you as a dishrag to wipe the blood from my hands. Your friends will be the rug I wipe my dirty-ass shoes on, and your family can decorate my walls like a piece of abstract art."

I say nothing, my chest seizing as the thought of him using my skin to wipe his hands on makes my back break out in chills.

"You should answer him before he pulls his gun back out and paints the brick with your brains."

"I won't say a word," I choke out.

His fingers release my neck, and I drop to the ground. They don't step back, crowding me against the wall, but I don't take another second. I scramble to a stand, slipping around their legs and sprinting down the alley.

I don't look behind me.

I just keep moving.

⛤

It takes me a while to stop the panic from my encounter with the creeps in the alleyway. But, maybe I don't panic as long as I should've, because my mind instantly strayed from them and onto someone else.

Malik.

I just have to know.

What do I have to know, though?

I don't know whether I want to see if Castle Pointe is real, or maybe if my house is still standing.

Or maybe I just want to see him.

Look at him from afar and make sure he's still living and breathing.

That he wasn't a figment of my imagination.

I crank up the heat, placing my hand over the vent as I fly down the highway toward Castle Pointe, my fingers slowly thawing from the warm air.

I don't even turn on the radio, my eyes focused on the trees as they become denser with each mile that passes.

The road feels endless, like I'm lost in a loop as the road extends for miles. It feels like forever. Though, time eventually comes where the air turns heavy and wet with dew. The cliffs of Superior grow sharp and jagged, the dark waters in the distance violent as they slam against the rocks.

When the aged stone of Castle Pointe comes into view, my breathing stops entirely.

I press on the brakes, slowing to a stop as my fingers shake against the steering wheel.

I don't move, don't take another breath as I stare at the sight in front of me.

Parked beside the Castle Pointe sign is a familiar car. Black and sleek, exactly the same Rover as I remember from over a year ago.

He sits on his hood, facing me. His eyes dark, his limbs long and lean as they curl over the hood of the truck. He looks relaxed as he stares at me. Like he's... waiting for me.

Is he waiting for me?

How would he even know that I'm here?

We sit like this for minutes, maybe an hour. Me sitting in my car with my foot against the brake. Him sitting on top of his truck, staring at me in the night. We both just... watch each other.

"You can do this," I whisper, shifting into park and turning off the rental.

I have no idea how he even knew I'd be here.

I don't know if I planned on making it past this point. Maybe getting to the sign would've been enough for me, and I'd turn around and finally be able to fall asleep.

I'll never know now, though.

Because as Malik sits there on top of his car, I know I'll never be able to walk away. Not without speaking to him first.

I step into the fog, breathing in the fresh, woodsy air for the first time in so long. A chill breaks along my skin, and I'd smile in bliss if I weren't in complete shock right now.

His eyes flare as I step toward him, with me standing on one side of the Castle Pointe sign, and him on the other.

We stare at each other, the wind blowing my hair over my shoulder. Longer than he remembers. I'm thinner, too. I know he notices this, as he glances up and down my slender body, a sneer taking over his features.

I fold my arms across my chest, thinking of what to say. I've envisioned it so many times. Imagined myself talking to him again after all this time. Telling him how much he broke me. Admitting how much he means to me. Taking my anger out on him.

Now the moment comes, and I stand here, silent. Unable to speak. Unable to breathe.

"What took you so long?" he asks, his voice deep, aged like a fine wine. Raspy and edgy. So much the same, but so incredibly different. Painfully so.

What took me so long?

It's almost like he's been waiting for me. *Waiting for me.*

My mouth drops open, my tongue gliding along the top edges of my teeth. I want to speak, the words form in my mind, but trying to get them to flow from my lips is a completely different type of struggle.

"What?" I squeak, and my cheeks flame. I clear my throat. "What're you... what're you doing here?"

"Waiting for you," he says it so simply, like it's the most obvious thing in the world. It makes no sense to me, and I don't understand.

He slides from the car, leaning his back against the grill as he stares at me. *Waits for me.*

I take a step toward him, nerves making my knees week. One gust of wind would blow me to the ground. His words will make me falter.

I'm weak in his presence, and yet he's the only thing that makes me strong.

"How'd you know I'd be here? How did you know…" I trail off, so confused. So many questions fill my head, and I can't make sense of any of them.

He lifts an eyebrow, like my questions are foolish.

"How did you know I was coming here?"

His head tips to the side. "Why wouldn't I? This is my town." His head lowers, his hair falling to the side, and I watch as his eyes burn into mine. "And you are mine."

My chest hollows out, and I can feel his words slip down my throat and into my soul. They warm me, and the chilly air is no longer prickling against my skin. I turn hot, my body heating from his raspy tone.

"You—you told me to go. You didn't want me here," I whisper, hurting as the feelings return. How cruel he was. The hate in his tone and the malice in his eyes. I felt broken for so long. I still feel broken. And then he claims me. "You told me to leave Castle Pointe."

He shoves off the front of his truck, stepping toward me with purpose. He doesn't sway, he doesn't hesitate. I'm his only focus, the only one in his sight.

He stops directly in front of me, his heavy, controlled breaths fanning across my cheek. "Yet, you came back."

"I didn't come back for you. I came back for me," I lie. It makes me nauseous. I can't fall back into the hole of wanting him with the most desperate need; he's the only thing on my mind. I can't do that again. I won't survive it.

His hand flexes at his side, like he's holding himself back from grabbing me and pulling me to him.

"Did you get what you came for?" he asks.

I nod, not able to say the words.

"You're a liar," he growls. "I can see the lie in your eyes, Vera. Don't forget, you were my sister at one time."

"You never wanted me to be your sister," I whisper, my lips pulling down in sadness.

He must have reached his peak, because he reaches forward, his fingers threading through my hair. He squeezes his hand into a fist, my hair tangling through his fingers and pulling tight. "It doesn't matter whether you were my sister or not. I always knew where you'd end up."

I tip my head back, the heat from his hand burning my skin alive. "And where is that?"

"With me."

His other hand goes to my hip, and he pulls me forward, straight into Castle Pointe. The town pulls me in, and my heart settles, whether it's this place or this person in front of me, I don't know. But every worry, every stress, every bit of heartbreak fades.

Completely.

"What happens now?" I whisper against his lips. "I have to go home."

He pulls me closer against him, my body becoming flush against his. "You are home."

I step back, frowning. He can't do this to me. I don't want to be his puppy. The one he can drag back and forth however he pleases. "My home is in Fargo. Castle Pointe stopped being my home the moment you dropped me and my mom on our asses. With nowhere to go and no one to turn to." Anger flushes through my body, remembering the weeks after we left and how hard it was for the both of us to find some semblance of life.

I take a deep breath. "I may never get over you, Malik, but that doesn't mean I'll ever forgive you for what you did."

His eyes narrow. "You blame me for killing my father?"

My eyes widen. "No. Not at all. You aren't to blame for that. *Not at all.* It's the fact that you treated me like such a piece of shit. Like me... like *we* were nothing. Like we meant nothing. Did I mean nothing to you?"

He says nothing.

I shake my head. "This was a mistake." I spin around, ready to leave Malik behind once and for all. I don't need him. I don't know why I ever thought I did.

He swoops me off my feet, spinning me around until I'm pinned against his car. My back arches on the hood, and he leans over me, seething teeth and bared lips. "Know this, Vera. I let you go once. Not because I wanted you to, but because I needed you to. I needed to pick up the pieces that were left of my town, and I had to do it by myself. You were always going to come back to me. You can deny it and say you never planned to, but I knew. I knew you'd walk back into Castle Pointe one day, and when that day came, I'd never let you go." He leans down, his lips brushing against mine. "And that day is today."

41

MALIK

I tear down the road, my eyes pinned in my rearview mirror as Vera's car drives slowly behind me. I fear that I'll blink, and she'll disappear. This fear, this worry, is a new emotion in my chest. Not one I knew I even know how to produce.

But it's here, and it's thick. I can't get rid of it no matter how hard I try.

I pull through the gate, rolling up to the house that finally feels like home again. Not for anything I've done, but for the girl who pulls into the driveway behind me.

She didn't want to come.

She told me she wanted to go back to her hotel and meet up tomorrow. But I know her. She'll get cold feet and she'll flee back to Fargo before sunrise. She'll be lost to me again, and possibly forever.

I couldn't risk that.

I pull to the side, allowing her to pull closest to the front door. Switching off my car, I slide out, heading to the front door and opening it, stepping inside.

My chest settles as the sound of her feet step through the door.

I watch her from the corner of my eye as she looks around the house, looking for subtle differences. There isn't much that's changed, I've left most of the house the same. But I've taken down a few things here and there, a few pictures, a few ancient knickknacks that held no purpose to me.

"It feels… weird. Like I never left, but it also feels like it's been so long since the last time I was here. Like centuries. It's just a surreal feeling."

"Get used to it, because you aren't leaving again." I don't look at her face as I slip off my shoes, walking into the kitchen and pulling a bottle of scotch from the counter, pouring two fingers into an already awaiting glass.

I knew I'd need it.

When my PI called me last week and told me her plans, I haven't been able to peel myself out of this daze. I've been shit at work and shit at home. I'm supposed to run a company, and the back-to-back conference calls and meetings have been me half-assing shit because I can't focus on anything besides my stepsister.

He's been watching her closely. I know how her day at college went. I know she met with her friends from Castle Pointe.

I know about the fuckers in the alley.

I sat in my car with a loaded gun in my lap. My PI could've taken them down. He could've put a bullet in their heads and let her run free. But she wouldn't want that. Vera is stronger than that. She can hold her own, and she did.

I knew she was on her way to see me. I knew I had to wait, because with even a slight possibility that she may turn around at the entrance to Castle Pointe and go, I couldn't chance it.

It was time.

I flew down the street and waited at the entrance. It felt like hours as I sat on top of my car. The eventual glow of headlights made my dead heart stop. I woke up for the first time in over a year and there she fucking was. Just as beautiful, maybe even more so, than the last time I saw her. Pictures and updates don't do her justice.

This girl is a literal fucking diamond.

"Can I have a drink?" she asks, snapping me from my thoughts.

I tip it back, swallowing the murky liquid in one go. I chuckle as I settle my glass on the table. "No."

She frowns. "Why not?"

"Because you aren't old enough to drink." I walk out of the kitchen, heading toward the living room. Unused, untouched. Perfectly expensive furniture that never gets sat on.

I sit on it now; the cushions a bit stiff, but I'm never home. I got rid of my dad's old couch and got an extravagantly overpriced one, only because I wanted it.

"Come over here," I order, leaning my arm along the back of the couch.

I listen as she huffs, her small feet slapping against the floor as she makes her way across the room. She steps in front of me, dressed in black like a fucking misfit.

I reach forward, my fingers latching on to the pocket of her hoodie, and I pull. She stumbles forward and into my lap. Her arms grip the back of my neck, and her fresh floral scent turns me ravenous.

"I'm still mad," she sighs, not sounding angry in the slightest.

"You can hate me all you want, but that doesn't mean I'm letting you go." I nip at her neck, and she bends her head to the side, exposing her pale, flawless skin for the taking.

I do. I bite and suck until she's moaning and writhing in my lap.

My hands slide over her back, down to her ass and to the backs of her thighs. I spin around, lifting her from my lap and settling her back on the seat of the couch. I crouch to the ground, her thighs wrapping around my shoulders.

Her head lifts, and she stares at me curiously.

"It's been a long time, and I'm fucking famished for you." My fingers curl around the waistband of her leggings, and I pull. Her hips lift willingly, even with the slight hesitancy and irritation still lingering in her eyes. She wants to fight me, but she wants me more than the fight.

Honestly, we're terrible for each other. But we're dangerously perfect at the same time. We're a toxic mix, and it's fucking phenomenal.

I toss her leggings and panties behind me, forgetting them completely as her milky skin presses against my shoulders.

Her arousal is intoxicating. I can smell her scent already, her desire for me obvious. It always has been. Since the first moment we met each other, I could see the want in her eyes. We're undeniable.

I bend down, my lips pressing against her naked mound. She quivers, her stomach shaking as my lips press against her sensitive flesh.

I dive in.

I pull her thighs apart, my fingers digging into her inner thighs as I spread her lips with my tongue, heading straight for her clit. It's throbbing already, pulsing against my tongue with uncontainable need. I suck and flick it with my tongue until her spine is arching off the edge of the couch. She wants to get away. She wants to get closer. She can't decide and ends up riding against my mouth, her juices spreading across my lips and cheeks and chin.

"Ride me like you hate me, baby sister. Show me how horrible you think I am."

She moans, her neck tilting back as she screams toward the ceiling. "I'm not your sister anymore."

My finger glides down, sliding into her dripping cunt. It tenses around my fingers, so fucking needy and wanting. "You'll always be my sister, Vera. You'll always be mine."

She groans again, hate and some other emotion commingling and crackling through the air.

She sits up suddenly, her eyes as foggy as the night sky. I think something's wrong until she pushes me against the ground.

"What the fuck are you doing?" I growl, grabbing at her thighs. "I wasn't finished."

She pushes my hands away. "I want you, too." She pulls at my pants, her hands shaking as she takes off my bottoms. I lean back on the ground, and her fingers wrap around my straining erection, already hard as a rock from just one glance at her needy pussy.

Our pent-up tension has been building for over a year and combusted the moment we touched each other.

She hauls a leg over my head, her ass in my face and her head near my cock. I get the perfect sight of her ass, round and fucking perfectly plump as it sits in my face. My hands reach up, and I grip both cheeks in my hands, spreading them and wetting my lips as both holes come into view.

My finger presses against the puckered hole, and I feel her tense. "Someday, Vera, but not tonight."

I slide my fingers down to her drenched cunt, and she relaxes, her head going down.

Down.

Down.

She swallows me, almost completely. I can feel the back of her throat flex around my length. I'm too big for her. Too big for her tiny mouth. But it's warm and wet and so perfect as her tongue slaps along the edge and she sucks.

So fucking hard.

My head lifts, and I bury my face between her thighs, licking and sucking and biting every single inch and fold and crevice. She moans around my cock, the vibrations making me unable to stay still. My hips lift, and I begin fucking her mouth while I ravage her pussy. It's cohesive how we go at each other, starved for one another. The air crackles. It heats. It dampens. It's hard to breathe. I swallow down an aggressive groan as she tenses around my fingers.

I know she's close.

I fuck her harder.

My fingers go to work, her ass shaking and slapping against my fist as my fingers plunge into her over and over again, until she tenses.

My eyes drift to the back of my head.

She tenses, and I slurp—*fucking slurp*—the juices as they drip out of her. Her pleasure is at a fucking peak and her mouth drops to the base of my cock, her throat vibrating against the tip.

I can't. I just fucking can't.

I rip her off me, my face drenched in her need as I flip her around and slam her down onto my cock. She's still pulsing, still vibrating through her climax as I fuck her. She bends down, our lips connecting in a sloppy kiss.

I plunge into her so damn hard, a growl rips from my throat, my hands going to her hips as I dig my fingers into her creamy skin, leaving deep bruises that I know will be there later.

"Fucking starving for you, baby. Couldn't wait another fucking second," I growl, bringing her mouth back down to mine. Her juices slide across my face, and she isn't the least bit deterred. She laps at it, kissing me with everything she has in her.

"You're too much. Too big. It hurts so fucking good," she moans, the walls of her cunt fluttering against me. I know she's close, yet again, to another orgasm.

"It's good because you're mine, Vera. And you're never leaving again."

She moans, her body tensing again as a new orgasm starts to roll through her.

"I want you to come all over my cock, Vera. *Drench. Me*," I grit between my teeth, my own orgasm roaring at the surface, ready to break free.

Tremors begin rumbling through her, and I squeeze my eyes shut and grip her hips so tightly as I empty myself inside her, claiming every single wall in her body.

She screams, her voice echoing throughout the entire house.

Fuck. Yes.

She falls against me, and I release her hips, pulling the hair back from her face as I slow down my thrusts, dragging out the orgasm for as long as I can.

The slippery sound of our juices echo through the room, and I grit my teeth together, so I don't start fucking her all over again.

She loses all muscle in her body, her limbs dead weight as they lay against me.

She's done.

I pull her from me and lift her into my arms. Pushing myself to a stand, I walk upstairs and silently pad to my room. She keeps her head rested against my shoulder; her eyes fluttering as sleep begins dragging her further into dreamland.

I pull the covers back with one hand, laying her on the mattress and tugging them up around her. She looks at me curiously, and I walk around to the other side of the bed, slipping underneath the covers and pulling her against me.

She snuggles deep, burrowing herself against my body as closely as possible.

I bury my nose in her hair, inhaling her scent. Becoming familiar with it again after over a year. But it doesn't matter, really. Because she's here to stay, for good.

"Welcome home, Vera. This time, you're here to stay."

Malik and Vera's story isn't finished. Want to read more in a secret bonus scene?
Sign up for the newsletter here for more of their story.

ACKNOWLEDGEMENT

There isn't enough words in the world to write about how grateful I am. Not to specific people, but to everyone around me. Every single person has had an impact in my life which has gotten me to where I am today. Each of you are so damn special and if you've been with me through my entire writing journey, you will know what an impact and the growth I've encountered over the last few years.

I want to thank my husband and kids for loving me and being with me through my busy nights and endless weekends of sticking my head in the computer. To find a passion that is a part of you is one thing but having people around you who want you to thrive in your passion means that much more. Thank you, guys.

Savannah, my PA, you are always a godsend. I couldn't be where I am today if it weren't for you. Thank you for helping me grow and teaching me endless knowledge.

Hailey, my cover designer and longest friend. I miss you across the country now, but the art you create is magnificent, and the hours upon hours of stress I put on you is out of love. I promise. I can't wait to see you again.

Rachel, my bestie. I can't wait to meet you. I vent and I complain to you and the number of times you've talked me off the ledge of insanity is endless. I couldn't do any of this without you. Thank you for reading my words and standing next to me through everything. I love you.

Thank you Kenzi for taking the plunge on me. You are such an amazing editor and literally click with me so much. Thanks for being such an amazing editor, but more than that, a wonderful friend. Love you.

Rumi. My Rumi. You are my lifesaver. Thank you for being there for me always. You are an amazing person and such an amazing friend. Your excitement over my stories makes me that much more excited to write them. You're never leaving me, just FYI.

To all my readers, ARC readers, bloggers, and followers, thank you! I write for you. You guys motivate me and inspire me to write dark, deep stories from deep in my soul. Every story has a part of me in it, and for you guys to take the plunge on me means everything.

Thank you, I love you.

BOOKS BY A.R. BRECK

Grove High Series
Reapers and Roses
Thorn in the Dark

The Grove Series
The Mute and the Menace
Lost in the Silence

The Seven MC Series
Chaotic Wrath
Reckless Envy

Standalones
BLISS
Where the Mountains Meet the Sea

ABOUT THE AUTHOR

A.R. Breck lives in Minnesota with her husband, two children and two dogs. She enjoys reading, writing and sharing her stories with the world. When she isn't working, A.R. Breck loves to watch horror movies, road trip around the country and read forbidden romance novels.

Follow me
[Instagram](#)
[Facebook](#)
[Goodreads](#)
[TikTok](#)
[Newsletter](#)
[Pinterest](#)
[Twitter](#)
[Spotify](#)
[ar.breck@yahoo.com](#)

Printed in Great Britain
by Amazon